Nicotine Dreams

Dan Ehl

Published by Rogue Phoenix Press
Copyright © 2015

ISBN: **978-1-62420-179-0**

Credits
Cover Artist: Designs by Ms G
Editor: Kitty Carlisle

Dedication

To Barb Ehl
"How time flies."

Chapter One

"And the bear raised back, stretching his paws high above his head until he could place the moon back in the heavens." John Waterrock ended his monologue.

The sudden absence of the ancient Apache's low, guttural voice brought Trent's attention back to the dim room. Waterrock's imagery had kept everyone entranced for fifteen minutes. Trent Rowen shifted weight and crossed his legs. He wasn't used to sitting on a stone floor and one side of his butt was asleep. Trent was also slightly chilly in just his Hawaiian boxer shorts and a Hunter Thompson T-shirt reading, "He who makes a beast of himself gets rid of the pain of being a man."

The silence was tribute to the old man's skill in retelling a recent dream, where clarity and richness of description counted as much as content. Trent again looked about in wonder, having a hard time believing he was actually here.

The "here" was a small, smoky room off an adobe home somewhere near the Mexico border in West Texas. Oil lamps contributed a dim, yellow light and a tantalizing, familiar fragrance that Trent couldn't pin down. The Midwesterner's sojourn had taken him to a Talking Circle, where warriors passed a talking stick from person to person and recounted visions. The tribal spiritual leaders were according Trent one of the highest honors by allowing him to participate. Next week, they promised, he could accompany them to a mountain cave to join in a ceremony revolving around the ingestion of peyote buttons.

The talking stick was handed to him. It was a slender piece of wood, varnished through the years with the oil from countless hands. It was capped on both ends with leather. Hawk feathers, strings of beaded leather, and small satchels of sage, cedar, sweet grass, and tobacco dangled from the ends.

Trent gripped the stick and looked at the expectant faces of those now focusing entirely upon him. He wasn't a born storyteller like Waterrock, but he knew the fine line between keeping a tale too sparse as to lose its flavor, or too involved as to lose the audience. Trent also knew that one's own dreams are always so much more interesting than those of someone else's. He cleared his throat and nervously spoke.

"I've been wearing these nicotine patches to help me keep from smoking," Trent began, "and they've been giving me the weirdest dreams. The other night I dreamed I was driving down this dusty, gravel road. It was your basic, archetypical Iowa country road. There were fields, stands of woods, occasional cows, and now and then farmhouses with old barns and sheds.

"I pulled into a farm lane lined with pickups. There was a sale going on. An auctioneer and his helper were standing on a hay wagon loaded with an assortment of rusty tools and equipment. They were castaways on an island surrounded by a shifting sea of farmers. Instead of white caps, there were eddies of brightly colored baseball caps—all bearing brand names of seed corns, tractors, fertilizers and herbicides.

"Off to the side was a small Airstream trailer converted into a food stand that was selling sandwiches and coffee. Near it was a pasty-white man in a blue, double-breasted suit—slightly overweight and looking out of place among the sunburned farmers in their frayed work clothes. He was selling what looked like wind-up toys from a shallow cardboard box. As I got closer, I could see they were yellow and black ducklings, hardly two or three days old. They were dressed in bird costumes. Some looked like penguins in black and white felt material. Others were in suits to look like chickens, turkeys, pheasants, pelicans and parrots. I remember being impressed by the ones dressed in silk peacock outfits with long, rainbow tail feathers."

Trent paused to see the effect his recounting was having on the others. Their faces remained as blank as the plaster walls, while the flickering lamplights cast long, dancing shadows behind them. He continued, though suddenly his dream didn't seem as meaningful as Waterrock's tale of how the bear saved the moon after the trickster coyote kidnapped her.

"One of the baby ducks kept flopping around and I saw that it was costumed in bright pink to look like a flamingo. The man in the suit was constantly standing it back on these little stilts with plastic flamingo feet. The duck would take about a half dozen steps before the others would bump into it and send the poor thing crashing. I felt sorry for it, so I bought the duckling and took it back to my car where I peeled off the costume.

"I somehow knew the tight suit had kept the duck from having a bowel movement. I rubbed its stomach as it screwed up its tiny face and tried to take a crap. The duckling looked like it was in pain, but finally, out popped this shiny, metallic blue object the size of a sparrow egg. Then I woke up."

There was a hush similar to the sound-devouring quietness that prowled the room after Waterrock's recital, but Trent detected a tense difference. Someone coughed and looked at the others. Though their faces remained empty of expression, Trent was sure some sort of communication was taking place. He didn't like it.

Trent didn't see the hurled rock until after the explosion rattled his head and the stone dropped into his lap. Before Trent could raise a hand to touch the painful point of impact, an adobe brick fragment caught him in the ribs. He lifted both hands to protect his face and screamed.

~ * ~

"For God's sake, what's going on?" Al asked, a blend of worry and exasperation coloring his voice. "Are you having another one of those dreams?"

Trent sat up in bed and gingerly massaged a lump the size of a quarter. "Hell, one of the bastards nailed me."

"What are you talking about?" his friend groggily asked while feeling around for the light switch. "Your nightmares are driving me nuts too. I could hear you screaming from my room. I thought some burglar was beating you to death with a baseball bat."

Trent squinted when the lamp clicked on. Al Chives was standing at the edge of the bed looking tired and irritated in a faded, red rayon bathrobe that sported a flamboyant dragon on the back. His mussed hair stood up on one side like a rooster's comb on one side of his head where he had been sleeping on it.

"Some old Apaches didn't like a dream I was relating and they began throwing junk. One caught me in the head. Here, feel."

"Everyone's a critic," Al sighed and let his hand be guided to his friend's scalp.

"See, feel that? He hit me with a rock."

"There's a bump, all right. Big surprise after the way you were thrashing around. Probably hit yourself on the edge of the bed."

Trent winced as he pressed the sore spot too firmly and eyed Al irritably.

"There's no way I could smash the top of my head on the edge of the bed," he protested. "And I also have an ache in my ribs where I took a brick."

"Listen to yourself, dummy. What happens in a dream can't hurt you. You're still half asleep or you'd know how goofy you sound. I almost wish you'd go back to smoking. I knew nicotine patches could cause weird dreams, but I've never heard of anyone reacting to them as you have."

Both worked for Lunar Limited, making gaskets for Bear River's only real factory. Most were shipped to a Mexican Volkswagen plant. Al, an old friend, moved in with Trent two years ago after his painful divorce. Trent had

4

lived for ten years in the rambling old house after buying it from his grandparent's estate.

Trent lifted the blankets and rolled out of bed in his T-shirt and Hawaiian shorts.

"Now what are you doing?"

"I'm going to get some ice for my imaginary bump," he answered.

Trent couldn't blame Al for being annoyed. For the past four nights he'd awakened his friend with shouts about killer pygmies, heathen idols adorned with rubies and pissed-off, giant, prehistoric cave poodles.

"There," Al had said to Trent's insistence that scratches across his leg were from the claws of an ice age poodle, "that proves these are just dreams. There is no such thing as a direpoodle."

"How do you know?"

"Have they ever found the bones of a giant poodle?" Al asked curtly. "Are there any cave drawings of poodles attacking mastodons?"

Each morning in the cold light of day, Trent would feel sheepish about his nocturnal outbursts. But the dreams seemed so real right after waking that he often had a hard time telling if he was yet awake.

Trent returned with a bowl containing three ice cubes wrapped in a washcloth and eased himself into bed, pressing the soothing coldness against his head. After five minutes, he rolled over to return the wet cloth to the bowl and felt something hard. Trent explored under his ribs and retrieved what appeared to be a piece of adobe brick.

Trent stared at the chip in surprise, rubbing its course texture with his thumb and turning it in the faint light. He was tempted to wake up Al and show him the stone but knew his friend would just get upset and refuse to look at it.

Trent laid back and tried to sleep. The dull throbbing from the bump on his head distracted him for several minutes before he finally drifted away.

~ * ~

"It's simple. Quit wearing the patch if you're getting so wacky," advised Al as he drew in a deep lung full of Marlboro. "Sounds like some primordial poodle is going to do you in before lung cancer. Or start drinking more. You know I don't drink, but I'll split a pitcher with you."

Trent was sitting with four of his friends in the New Yorker Lounge and Supper Club, located in the center of the four-block downtown area of Bear River, Iowa. Al, a militant smoker's rights advocate, felt betrayed each time one of his friends tried breaking the nicotine habit.

"I'd just like to know what these dreams mean," Trent said. "What the hell does a direpoodle or Dorga, the Fish-Headed God of Death symbolize?"

"Though Henry David Thoreau said dreams are the touchstones of our character, Jung said it is a mistake to give preconceived archetypes to dream symbols; that each should be interpreted in regard to the patient's psychological state at the moment," related Lorenzo Spasm, who had remained quiet until now. "He warned that if the practitioner operates too much with fixed symbols, there is danger of falling into mere routine and pernicious dogmatism, and thus failing his patient."

Al and Rich Stuart looked at each other, rolled their eyes and smiled—they knew the signs. It sounded like the preamble to another lengthy discourse. Lorenzo was in his mid forties; about a dozen years older than the other three. Trent often wondered if he'd start rattling off volumes of trivia in another decade.

"Jung also believed the deepest layers of dreams were part of the collective unconsciousness that all humans share. They are from mankind's earliest memories and experiences, much like our genes still carry traces of our earliest physical makeup. These primal dreams are expressed in cultures as myths and even children's fairy tales."

"This doesn't mean I'm advising you ignore these dreams,' cautioned Lorenzo. "As the Hebrew Talmud reads, 'A dream not interpreted is like a letter to the self unread.'"

"Are you making this stuff up?" asked Al. "You always seem so much more knowledgeable after you've had a few beers."

The tall, lean Lorenzo eyed his shorter friend like an Elvis fan accused of farting while touring Graceland. "I usually drink to make you seem more witty."

"You can't fool us," said Rich, "we know that's a W.C. Fields' quote."

"I know one thing about dreams," volunteered Rich as he lifted his empty glass to catch the bartender's attention. "If you have to take a whiz but suspect it's a dream and you don't want to wake up in a wet bed, try reading something."

The other three paused and eyed their short, broad-shouldered friend with curiosity. A self-employed woodworker, Rich was usually brimming with folk remedies and sayings learned at the knee of his Scottish great-grandmother.

"And why, pray tell, is that?" Al asked when it became apparent Rich was waiting for a bit of prompting.

"Because you can't read in dreams," he answered. "It's impossible. You might make out a newspaper headline or large sign, but that would be it."

Rich turned to Trent. "So the next time you're at a urinal and wondering if you're dreaming, pick up a newspaper."

"I don't know if that will help since I've only been aware I was dreaming once, and there wasn't anything to read in the temple of Dorga. And besides, what would it matter when I can get just as injured in a dream as when I'm awake?"

"You don't actually believe you got that knot on your head from a dream, do you?" asked Al. He looked with worry at Trent and glanced at the others for their reaction.

7

Trent wiggled his glass and solemnly studied the tiny bubbles zipping to the surface.

"No, I guess not. At least not now, but they seem so real when I first wake."

"Actually, Rich's idea isn't too far off. The shamans and priests of many religions practiced dream control," Lorenzo interjected. Even Rich looked surprise as Lorenzo gave one of his offerings some credibility.

"There are exercises they practiced that allowed them to master their night travels. The Yaqui medicine men of Sonora, Mexico, believe that harnessing dreams allows them to become men of power."

"Western scientists, on the other hand," continued Lorenzo, "look at it in a less romantic light. Sleep researchers call these 'lucid dreams' and have developed techniques to let the dreamer be aware that he or she is dreaming while it is occurring."

"I guess I never paid much attention to dreams before," Trent admitted.

"Dreams have puzzled humans since man first climbed out of the trees. There are a series of 'Dream Books' written by the Assyrians on clay tablets in the fifth or sixth millennium B.C. They deal with dreams about death, the loss of teeth, and even about finding oneself naked in public."

"I wonder if they dreamed about showing up to a class and realizing that they hadn't done the homework or knew a thing about what the test was to be about," Al asked. "I used to dream that while going to college."

"And do these dream books deal with waking up with a goose egg?" Trent wanted to know.

"My grandmother used to say if you dreamed you were falling and actually hit the ground, you'd wake up dead," volunteered Rich.

"How do you wake up dead?" Trent wondered out loud.

"I think dreams are just the mind spinning in neutral while you sleep," opined Al. "They usually don't mean anything, other than you're worried about flunking statistics."

"What about Friedrich Kekule von Stradonitz's discovery of the molecular architecture of benzene?"

Al groaned at Lorenzo's latest contribution to the conversation.

"The nineteenth century German chemist had been doggedly trying to find the structure of the molecule until one night he dreamed of atoms dancing in long chains, turning in snake-like motion until one of the serpents caught its own tail and a ring was formed. Later experiments proved his vision correct. The benzene molecule is a loop or ring of carbon atoms. This breakthrough greatly speeded the development of organic chemistry."

"Just where did you come up with all this?" asked Al.

"I used to have plenty of spare time to read while I was in the Merchant Marines. I researched the topic extensively after the Captain asked me to cure the first mate of habitually dreaming he was a chicken."

There was a moment of silence while Lorenzo's friends attempted to digest this latest morsel. Al was the first to break down and prod their friend to continue.

"Why would the Captain ask you to cure someone of dreaming he was a chicken?"

"It was interfering with his duties. The poor guy was a wreck. He'd wake up perched on the dresser in a nest of shredded sheets and blankets. It got so he was afraid to fall asleep."

"Did you cure him?"

"I could have—the answer was in a twelfth century Arabic tome I discovered in a small Algerian-port junk shop."

"And you didn't?" Al continued the expected prompting.

"No," Lorenzo answered solemnly, "the captain changed his mind and ordered me to stop."

"Huh, how come?"

"He said we needed the eggs."

Everyone groaned at being caught by such an old joke and Trent banged his head on the bar.

"Do you believe dreams can be more than just …eh, just dreams?" Trent asked Lorenzo after he steered the conversation back to his night visions. "That maybe they have a reality of their own?"

"Chuang Chou, a fourth century B.C. Chinese philosopher, once dreamed he was a butterfly idly fluttering around flowers," Lorenzo spoke. "When he woke up a man, he wondered if he was Chuang Chou who dreamed he was a butterfly or a butterfly dreaming he was a man."

Trent cocked his eyebrows in puzzlement.

"It means people have always been captivated by the distinction between dreams and reality. Many people have believed dreams were real," Lorenzo began hitting high gear in his lecturing mode. "Li Yuan Chou, a twelfth century Chinese professor, argued that since the states of dreaming and being awake coexist in each person, there must be a point where the two touch. And because a person dreaming is not aware of the waking state, the dream is taken to be real. On the other hand, while awake, a person does not know about the dream state, so it also should not be regarded as true."

"I think I've seen that point where the two touch," Trent sighed, rubbing his bump.

"Jung once said that it could be we continually dream, but that the consciousness makes such a noise that we can't hear it," Lorenzo added. "Then, again, the Hindus say all creation is just a dream of the god, Vishnu."

Trent looked longingly at a woman with a cigarette heading to the back door and alley for a smoke. A cigarette would sure taste good now, he thought.

"Maybe my dreams are where I touch other worlds, real worlds, or they could even be worlds I created like Vishnu."

Lorenzo didn't like the strange tone of his friend's voice.

"Then again, it could be just some high powered REM caused by the nicotine patch," he tried cheering Trent. "Blood pressure, pulse rate, and brain waves increase to those comparable with an awake, alert mind. Except for the rapid eye movement and small twitches of the toes and fingers, the rest of the body is temporarily paralyzed. Some people awakened from REM are unable to move for a few seconds."

"That couldn't be me, since I must thrash around quite a bit."

As they were walking to the door, Lorenzo again advised Trent to become the master of his dreams.

"Use the dreams to your benefit," he said.

"Yeah, dream you're on the beach and wake up with a tan," laughed Rich.

"Remember the poet Coleridge and his most famous poem, 'Kubla Khan.' He was smoking opium and reading about the Khan in 1797 in a lonely farmhouse when he fell asleep. In a dream, he composed a poem some two hundred to three hundred lines long. Coleridge awoke and immediately began writing it down until he was interrupted at line fifty-four by a bill collector. But by the time he got rid of the fellow, he'd forgotten the rest of the poem.

"The same thing almost happened to Otto Loewi, the German Pharmacologist, while investigating the transmission of nerve impulses in frog muscles. He was stuck at one point until he woke from a dream in which both the theory and experiment to test it were revealed to him. He jotted down some notes and went happily back to sleep. But in the morning he couldn't read his writing or remember the dream."

His three companions paused by the door while waiting for Lorenzo to finish. They all kidded Lorenzo about his stories, thought Trent, yet he never failed to hold their attention.

"All right, I'll bite," Al urged his friend. "What is 'the rest of the story'?"

"The next night, the same dream came to Otto and this time he leaped out of bed, rushed to his laboratory, and by daybreak had discovered the chemical transmission of nerve impulses, which later won him the 1936 Nobel Prize in medicine."

"That's great, Lorenzo," Trent admitted, squinting in the bright sun as the group exited the bar, "but how is that going to save me from giant cave poodles?"

The group broke up and Trent and Al turned to the right.

"It's hard to believe people were dreaming about finding themselves naked 7,000 years ago," Trent said as they walked to their autos.

"That sounds like something a man with a tarantula tattooed on his head would say," Al replied. He tended to take much of what Lorenzo said with a grain of salt.

Lorenzo left Bear River for college twent-five years ago, was kicked out for yet unknown reasons, and then skipped about the globe before finally returning to his hometown. He told his friends the tattoo was a memento of a drunken shore leave in Hong Kong.

"His hairline must be receding; I think I can see some of it."

"I can just make out a pair of hairy legs starting to crawl out," Al agreed then turned serious. "You hang around the house too much. You should get out more, meet other people; then maybe you wouldn't be having these weird dreams."

"You mean meet women, don't you?"

"Well, maybe that. It's been a long time since Melissa died…"

"We don't know that she's dead," Trent interrupted.

Al took his friend by the arm and stopped in the middle of the sidewalk. "Don't you think she would have come back, have called her parents, let someone know? Why would she run away? She was happy, she loved you. I didn't want to believe the worst either, but it's been almost eight years. I think the police are right. She's dead."

Trent didn't want to meet Al's gaze. "I know she is. I've known it for a long time. I just don't like saying it out loud. It feels disloyal or something, like she'll die for sure if I say it."

Neither of the two men spoke. Al became flustered and patted his friend on the shoulder. "So get out more."

"I date now and then."

"I don't mean those cheap, meaningless relations you get into so you won't have to be serious," he said, obviously trying to make it sound like light banter.

"I don't see you getting out that much since your divorce."

"I don't sit around and mope like you do, either."

"It's not intentional," replied Trent. "I just can't imagine spending the rest of my life with any of the women I've dated. There's nothing wrong with them except they're not Melissa. It's something I can't turn off; that I have no control over."

Al walked with his eyes on the sidewalk and hands shoved deep into his pockets. He was clearly uncomfortable with what was such a painful subject for Trent. "Still, it has been over eight years."

"It's like trying to quit smoking," Trent continued. "I can go for hours without thinking about a cigarette. Then I'll see a pack laying on a table and bam, there's this rush. For a split second the cigarette pack is the only thing in focus. Then I'll shrug it off and be okay for another couple hours.

"That's how it is with Melissa. I can go days without thinking of her then something will set me off—a smell, a phrase, the mention of her name. It's instantaneous, like an explosion. I feel it before I even know what it is. An invisible hand reaches into my chest and squeezes. I only wish there were patches for things like that.

"At first it was the feeling of helplessness that made it so bad. I would have done anything to get her back—but what was there to do? I'd go crazy at night in bed when there wasn't anything to distract me.

"I'm getting better," Trent continued as he stopped next to his pickup. "I was angry for a long time. I guess I still get mad if I think about it too much—we got along so well. I am getting better at not thinking about it. Still, I know I'm not over her when I still dream about her or wake up calling her name."

Trent forced himself to shut up. For a long time after Melissa's disappearance, he'd gone on talking jags, usually while drinking, until no one wanted to be around him. Friends felt sorry for Trent, they told him later, but they could only stand so much depression.

"Al, how do you think that brick got in my room?" Trent said, purposely switching the subject back to his dream.

"I don't know, but you probably saw it out of the corner of your eye before you went to sleep. Your subconscious noted it and incorporated it into the dream."

"Yeah, that's probably it," Trent admitted, not sounding too convinced.

They had to be just dreams, he decided while driving his pickup home. The one about the Fish-Headed God of Death was too weird to be anything else. What made it odder was that he had been aware that it was a dream while it was transpiring. What did Lorenzo call that, Trent thought to himself, a lucid dream? He had taken for granted that he could enter and exit the sleep worlds, as well as make off with dream objects like the ruby.

Trent recalled the dream with a smile. It had been rather amusing, beginning with him in a large temple hiding behind a pillar...

Chapter Two

Trent eyed the distance very carefully. It was twenty yards at the most. He could silently cover the ground and return to his hiding place without being spotted if he were quick. Trent did wish he was wearing something more appropriate than Hawaiian boxer shorts and a Grateful Dead T-shirt.

He took a deep breath and left the shadows, flitting from pillar to pillar until he was at the side of the monstrous brass statue of Dorga, the Fish-Headed God of Death. Its face was that of a gulping carp attached to the upper body of a very obese woman, which in turn was connected to the bottom half of a very well-endowed male.

This dude belongs on The Jerry Springer Show, Trent decided. The entire statue was about twenty feet tall. Embedded in the palm of one downward-extended hand was a cupcake-size ruby.

At the bottom of a steep flight of stairs, a squad of black-robed priests prepared to disembowel a young slave woman in front of a crowd of warrior nobles. She lay naked upon a marble slab altar—her long brown hair spilling over the edge. Trent guessed the slave was heavily drugged by the vacant expression on her face. He gazed up at the ruby and back down to the girl.

They had to sacrifice her at just the right moment. That was when the equinox sun sent a sword of light stabbing down through a hole in the domed roof to strike a polished silver bowl positioned to catch the slave's blood. Tradition had it that she would go free if they waited too long. The timing had been perfect for the past two hundred years. Trent didn't question his knowledge of this world. It was a dream and one just knew these kinds of things.

Trent tiptoed to the hand and hurriedly pried at the stone with a small dagger while all eyes were on the unclothed girl. He was surprised at how easily the gem came free and scooted back to behind the pillar without being seen. The giant gem felt almost hot and seemed to pulsate with power in his hand. He put the gem in his pocket and took a quick peek around the column.

The rest should be easy, he thought. Just a quick dash to the side door. It led straight to the walkway atop the garden walls. From there, a leap to one of the trees provided escape into the jungle. He would hide until waking with the ruby still held firmly in his hand.

Trent couldn't help looking back down at the girl. The top priest held a wicked dagger above his head, waiting for the signal that would plunge the blade deep into the slave's stomach. It wasn't a particularly quick or painless death and Trent had planned to be out of the temple before the sacrifice occurred. Yet doubts kept tugging at his conscience—if the ruby proved to be real, did that mean the inhabitants of his dream worlds were also real, no matter how strange or bizarre? Were these all alternate universes and the slave a real woman at the bottom of the massive granite stairway?

Trent looked longingly at the escape door then back to the slave. There was no way the priests or warriors could scale the steep steps before he was out the door and over the wall. He could see the tension rise in the crowd far below. There wasn't much time left.

Next to the statue were five or six pikes crossed like the poles of a tepee. He pulled one away, sending the rest clattering across the floor. Several startled warriors glanced up and spotted Trent. The high priest remained frozen over the slave girl.

Not sure if he had any mental influence over his dream worlds, Trent tried willing the spear to its target. There was the chance that he might miss and hit the girl, but he figured she wasn't going to complain about the risk.

Whether it was a lucky shot or mind-over-matter, the weapon flew straight and true, catching the priest squarely in the back. He dropped like an ox under a sacrificial axe. The jerking body fell over the girl just as a bright ray of sun shot down to the bowl, which at that same moment was catching the first drops of the priest's flowing blood.

"Yes," Trent screamed like a basketball player sinking the winning shot, jitterbugging in front of Dorga until he noticed the warriors running to the foot of the stairs. They appeared very upset. Trent turned to make his escape only to find the exit blocked by a half dozen angry priests flying at him with knives as wicked looking as the one wielded by their former boss.

"Ya-a-a-ah," was the most intelligible thing Trent could yell as he turned to make his exit out the opposite door.

"Ya-a-a-ah." It, too, was blocked.

The hunted instinctively seek higher ground. Trent began frantically climbing up the lap of Dorga. Offended cries at the sacrilege escaped from the priests' mouths. Trent knew it was death to even touch the god, let alone crawl up its massive belly.

Trent wormed his way up through the ponderous breasts and reached above his head to grab the lower fish lip with both hands. He hoisted himself up and swung a leg into the carp maw. This brought further cries of outrage. The climb up the slippery brass belly and breasts had been difficult and it gave the warriors time to reach the base of their god. Trent feared he would have been a pincushion if they hadn't appeared afraid of upsetting Dorga with a rain of arrows and spears.

Trent peeked out from the carp lips. The warriors and priests milled below in confusion. Further down, he could see the slave girl being helped to her feet. She appeared dazed and confused as she was covered with a robe. The woman glanced up at Dorga, and for just an instant she locked eyes with Trent. He smiled and waved before she was jerked around and led away.

This is all right, thought Trent. He'd just stay swallowed until he woke. A warrior angrily shook his fist at Trent, who responded by placing his thumbs in his ears and wiggling his fingers while sticking out his tongue. The warrior howled in anger and pulled long clumps of oily hair from his head. Trent mused that he'd heard of pulling one's hair in frustration, but this was the first time he'd seen someone actually do it.

Trent decided he didn't like the looks of a group of priests holding a time-out. Heads bowed together, they whispered excitedly among themselves. One turned and grinned evilly at Trent while the others scattered. Now that they were closer, Trent could see that the lead priest's hands were tattooed with fish scales—a look not for everyone, he decided, but it worked for the beady-eyed fellow below.

"It's really you," Trent yelled down, "but I think you'd look good with a tarantula tattooed across your head."

The priest screamed even louder this time. Trent caught part of what the man said, surprising Trent because he hadn't considered these barbaric people would be speaking English. Part of the message contained good old Anglo-Saxon cuss words.

The other priests returned carrying wood. They heaped it in the giant bowl resting on Dorga's lap that would have been for incense on a small Buddha statue. Trent didn't need it spelled out for him. It appeared they were preparing for a bonfire party, and he was the guest of honor. He guessed that a blazing fire would soon heat up his haven. The dreamscape explorer hoped to be awake by then but decided that it wouldn't hurt to see if there was a back entrance.

It was quite dark by the tonsil area, as well as a tight squeeze. He stopped wiggling when his outstretched hand told him the tongue abruptly dropped away. No escape here, he thought, and attempted backing up. He couldn't. The combination of the small passage, gentle slope and slippery metal prevented the maneuver. Trent wasn't claustrophobic, but being caught in the throat of Dorga, the Fish-Headed God of Death, was not a pleasant experience. Was it his imagination or was the metal beginning to warm?

Struggling didn't help. In fact, he felt himself slipping further into the god's gullet. The slipping soon became a slide. Try as he might, Trent couldn't find any handholds or traction.

"Ya-a-a-ah."

The drop wasn't far, but the sudden stop knocked the wind out of him. Not that he was complaining. Trent had expected to break his neck on the bottom of a brass belly instead of landing on a musty smelling bundle of rags and straw.

Thin beams of light were visible as they cut through the clouds of dust raised by his impact. The sunrays were coming through several slits in the statue's back. Trent could just see out by standing on his toes. The holes continued through the temple wall and opened about thirty feet above a garden. He decided that it was unfortunate the openings were too narrow for escape.

Trent began an investigation of the cell. In one corner was the crumpled skeleton of what once must have been a priest. It was partially draped in rotting, black cloth. The area of the cell near the outside fire was radiating heat. Off to the side were three oddly shaped pipes. Upon closer inspection, he discovered that one was a simple periscope. He could see the priests throwing on even more wood on the fire as he squinted through the end of the brass tube.

The second tube funneled in noise from the outside. Trent wasn't sure about the purpose of the third pipe. He couldn't see anything through it. Trent blew into the pipe and the muffled babble of the crowd became softer. He peered again though the periscope. To his amazement, the warriors and priests were all kneeling. He could hear one voice moaning, "Dorga, speaks, Dorga speaks..."

This time he whistled in the third tube and quickly placed his ear to the middle pipe—"Dorga whistles, Dorga whistles..."

Trent smiled.

"I am the great and wonderful Dorga," he shouted in the tube, ' God of Death."

"Ya-a-a-ah."

This time the familiar scream was coming from someone else. Trent recognized his friend with the fish scale tattoos, who was busy groveling across the floor and wailing lamentations.

"I am very unhappy with my priests. They shall no longer be allowed to serve me but must be driven into the jungle—now. And put out the damn fire."

It doesn't get any better than this, Trent thought, and watched the warriors turn on the black robed priests and send them scurrying with the flat of their swords.

"From now on, you will no longer sacrifice living creatures," he commanded with as deep a voice as possible. "That includes today's slave."

For the next ten minutes, Trent chanted commands through the tube.

"Do unto others as you would have them do unto you," he thundered and watched as a clutch of clerics quickly scribbled down the latest commandment.

Some appeared to puzzle the audience—"Don't hit your children; use positive reinforcement."

It didn't take too long before he started having trouble thinking of additional pearls of wisdom

"Don't stick anything in your ear sharper than your elbow."

Several warriors looked with puzzlement at their elbows, shrugging when they gazed at each other. Gods often don't make sense, they seemed to say.

Trent took a breather. He was surprised he hadn't yet awoken and felt his pocket to make sure the gem was still there. The bag of bones caught his attention. By the look of the skeleton, Trent thought, it had been some time since Dorga spoke to his people. He went back to the megaphone after pacing the small cell a few more times.

"Don't judge a book by its cover."

"Be nice to old people."

"Don't open a new jug of milk until you've finished the old one—and don't drink from it, get a mug."

"Don't butt into a line."

He looked in the periscope when he heard a commotion sounding from the middle tube. The tattooed priest was madly pushing his way through the crowd. He managed to shove his way to the statue before he could be stopped. Like a monkey, he shinnied up the penis of Dorga. A hush fell upon the crowd and they watched with open mouths as yet another fool threw himself into Dorga's gullet.

Trent nervously wondered why the hell he hadn't woken yet. He did the only thing he could think of—and pulled the pile of rags and straw away from the middle of the cell. "Let the little bastard bust his head," Trent mumbled as he leaned against the wall and crossed his arms and legs.

It didn't take long before the black form of the priest came hurtling down. The sound of the body hitting the floor wasn't that of a watermelon bursting. It was the slap of leather sandals. The priest came down feet first.

Trent tripped as he pushed himself away from the wall while untangling his arms and legs. The priest's blade flashed as it sliced through the dusty sunbeams and clanged noisily against the inside of Dorga's brass belly. Trent barely had time to duck the whistling blade. The priest pulled the long knife back for another sweep as Trent rolled to the other side of the cell.

The priest smiled wickedly and, keeping an eye on his unarmed opponent, leaned over to the megaphone and shouted, "Do not believe a word that was just spoken. A false god has been speaking, but Dorga has won the battle. Bring the slave girl back for another...umph."

The priest became distracted just long enough for a flying shinbone to catch him alongside the head. Trent rushed him with the second shinbone and delivered another blow before the priest could recover.

"Pay no attention to that other voice," Trent commanded in a gasping voice. "I am the great and powerful Dorga. Dodah, the god of deceit and cheap beer attempted to delude my followers, but he is defeated. Let the girl go, brush your teeth twice a day, look both ways before crossing..."

Trent ducked. The priest was staggering around, half blinded by the blood from a nasty gash. He also appeared dazed and confused. The blade whistled wildly about and several times whisked by just a little too close for Trent's comfort. He waited for an opening as the priest spun about and then landed a solid blow. The impact seemed to spin the figure even faster and the priest whirled across the cell to crash into the wall. He slid to the floor and disappeared.

Trent walked to a hole that had magically appeared in the floor.

The priest must have bumped into a hidden latch that opened a trap door, he decided. It figured—there had to be way for the priests to have gotten out. Trent squinted into the dark hole. He could just make out the sprawled form of his adversary at the bottom of a ladder.

Trent pulled the trap door up and it locked. He sat back on his heels to catch his breath. His right shoulder was sore from the fall down Dorga's throat and he massaged it. Trent was about to stand up again when...he woke up still massaging a sore shoulder.

~ * ~

Now that's a dream, Trent thought as he parked the truck. If only I'd brought back the ruby instead of an old adobe brick, then I'd have something to show the boys.

He stopped at the mailbox and retrieved an electric bill, a notice of an overdue library book, and a flyer for an adult toy store called World of Whips.

"Mr. Balton," he yelled next door to a balding man in his seventies who was trimming a row of rose bushes. "I think I got some of your mail again."

That night, Trent shifted restlessly around in his bed. He was tired, but the thought of sleep did not relax him. Several times he almost drifted off, but a sudden nervous twitch or shudder would jerk him wide awake again. After what seemed like several hours, he found himself swept before an irresistible urge to smoke.

To hell with this, Trent mumbled to himself. He sat up and peeled the nicotine patch off his arm then swung his feet to the floor to feel for his slippers. Guided by just the faint streetlight beams filtering through the curtains, he moved quietly around the bedroom as he dressed.

It was a brisk evening and Trent zipped up his light jacket. He decided to walk the five blocks to the convenience store rather than risk waking Al by the sound of his old beater starting in the driveway. His friend seemed overly worried about his mental state.

The bugs were still active, though it was a cool night. He could hear the chirping of crickets and see faint clouds of flying insects swarming about the streetlamps. He paused in mid step for just a second when one of the bugs careened from the swarm and bounced with a solid thud off his coat. There was something peculiar about the insect, he thought, but it had already disappeared back into the night. Trent continued his walk.

A new person was behind the cash register at the Git-n-Git-Out Mart. She was an attractive, tanned young woman in a tight blouse. She looked up at him, arched her brows, and smiled wickedly. Trent self-consciously grinned back, feeling flustered by the suggestive look. At thirty-three years of age, he wasn't used to twenty year olds giving him the eye. He bumped into a freezer before stopping in front of the cigarette display and gazing at the brightly colored packs. He had smoked Marlboro Lights and reached for a pack but stopped his hand halfway to the display. Did he really want to go back to smoking?

Trent sighed and pulled away from the rack. The cigarettes seemed to be crying out to him. He could just imagine placing a cigarette in his mouth, flicking the lighter, and pulling in that first, sweet drag of smoke. Shaking his head, Trent turned to the magazine rack for a momentary diversion. There was nothing on the magazine shelves but coloring books. He moved some to the side only to reveal more coloring books. There were no Newsweeks, Times, or even TV Guides. He opened one of the coloring books to a picture of Dorga, the Fish-Headed God of Death. Large printing under it read, "Beware the Red Man."

Trent eyed the coloring book in bewilderment and rubbed his eyes. When he looked again, it showed an elephant holding an umbrella while balancing on a large ball. He put it back on the shelf.

"Where are all the magazines?"

"What did you say, sir?" The voice dripped honey.

"Where are all the magazines? There are only coloring books here."

"I'm so sorry, we must have sold them all," she replied.

Trent turned back to the cigarettes. He decided fate was against him as he picked up a pack. There was something funny about the cigarette package, but he couldn't put his finger on it. Trent shifted it around under the exceedingly bright lights of the store, watching the reflections move about on the plastic wrapper. Then he froze.

Trent jerked the pack closer to his face. On the side of the pack was the health warning by the U.S. Surgeon General. The lettering danced and rippled every time he tried reading it. Trent spun and picked up a pack of Hostess Cupcakes. Though the main logo was easy to read, the smaller print listing the ingredients was unintelligible. Trent took a deep breath and slowly let it escape through clenched teeth. He could only think of one obvious answer—he had fallen asleep and he was now dreaming!

Would smoking in a dream count when he made a bet with Rich that he could quit? Trent placed the cigarettes in his jacket pocket and decided he would have to contemplate the ethical implications.

"Is there anything I can help you with?" the woman's voice purred.

She was now gazing at him with naked lust and her top blouse buttons were undone, revealing the white swell of two attractive breasts and a frilly black bra. He laughed. And to think he was worried about the ethical implications of smoking a cigarette in a dream when there were more interesting moral dilemmas to try his soul.

"Hi," Trent said shyly as he approached the cash register.

Even though this was his dream and the young woman just a figment of his imagination, he couldn't help feeling awkward. Trent stopped to gaze around him and felt a touch of pride that his imagination was capable of creating such an elaborate dreamscape. It included everything from a couple cigarette butts on a slightly dirty concrete floor to numerous sale items filling the shelves. There were colorful cans of brake fluid and gas additives, windshield ice scrapers, and flashlights. Up the other aisle were aspirins, candy, chips, and maps.

The crowning glory of his creations was Peggy, whose name he could read on her tag. Peggy was beautiful, though he noticed when he tried concentrating on specific features, her face blurred and danced like the small print on the cupcake package. He did know that her eyes sparkled and she wore an interesting bra.

If he was going to become a man of power, Trent remembered, he would have to take control of this dream. Though the Yaqui wise men may have had a more spiritual intent in mind, Trent decided a novice was allowed some leeway.

"It's too nice of a night for you to be working," Trent said. "Let's go downtown and see what's happening."

It wasn't the most interesting or original pickup line, but it appeared to be adequate. Her smile showed more teeth than seemed possible without it being in a tiger cage. He walked around the counter to escort Peggy from her station and noticed the cash register drawer was open.

"We're going to need a little cash while we're at it," he added, and scooped out a pile of twenties. Peggy just giggled.

Trent took her arm and led his new date out of the convenience store. Peggy followed compliantly, even resting her head on his shoulder. The commercial area turned out to be larger than that of the waking Bear River. Dark red neon lights flashed everywhere. The streets were almost empty with only hunched-over figures occasionally crossing intersections in the distance. Cars were even more rare, with most of them being black limos that strangely seemed to exude static electricity when they silently glided by.

He stopped in front of a towering hotel, complete with a gaudily uniformed door attendant who looked more like a high school band member.

Trent leaned back to take in the numerous floors of the building. It had a busy, neo-gothic upper level.

"Thank you, Mr. Rowen," the doorkeeper said after accepting a twenty dollar bill.

The hotel lobby was a cross between the Czar's winter palace, the Vatican, Citizen Kane's Xanadu, and Grand Central Station. It was a baroque airliner hangar with sweeping arches almost disappearing high above. Trent craned his neck to observe massive, crystal chandeliers floating like radiant ice clouds. The lobby was very quiet. Two men dressed in identical charcoal gray suits looked up from their chairs as he and Peggy passed. The men had pinched, pale faces, making Trent wondered why his subconscious was populated with such dreary people.

Trent and Peggy wove their way through overly ornate Victorian furniture until reaching the front desk, an elaborate oak cave set back in a wall of 16th Century Flemish frescoes. Trent rang the desk bell and waited for the clerk.

"I'd like the penthouse," Trent ordered regally when the clerk appeared. "And send up your best champagne and caviar."

The clerk bowed and rang for a bellhop. A young man eagerly approached, garbed in a uniform similar to that worn by an organ grinder's monkey He led the way to an elevator where they waited as numbers above the door slowly counted down from sixty-four.

Peggy pulled Trent's hand to her mouth and nibbled suggestively on a finger. He laughed nervously and looked around. The bellhop was staring intently at the floor numbers.

"Al was right, I do have to get out more," he said to Peggy. "Though I don't think he had this in mind."

The young woman just smiled and began licking the underside of his finger.

"I bet you do this to all the dreamers you meet. I must be getting old, but I feel myself embarrassed at this open display of lust in public, even knowing it's just a dream." He knew he was babbling, but he couldn't help himself. "In my younger days, I'd have probably taken you on one of those velvet sofas."

Peggy glanced to the side and a brief look of surprise crossed her face. Trent turned to see a couple coming through the front door. The man looked out of place. He appeared to be in his early thirties and was dressed casually in jeans, a leather biker jacket, engineer boots, very dark sunglasses and leather, steel-studded gloves. He also had a neatly trimmed beard and shoulder length hair pulled back in a ponytail. The woman seemed strangely familiar. When the man spotted the two, he raised his hand and shouted something that Trent couldn't make out.

A bell rang and the sound of the elevator doors opening drowned out a second shout. The man left the woman and began running hurriedly across the lobby. Peggy jerked Trent toward the elevator and he stumbled through the door.

"Melissa!" The cry involuntarily escaped his lips. The woman standing far across the lobby looked like Melissa. He started forward but was stopped short by Peggy's hand firmly grasping his arm. The door closed before he could jerk free, and the elevator gave a gentle jerk as it began its upward journey. He looked around wildly for the control panel. There were no visible buttons.

Trent bit his lip and took a deep breath. This was crazy, getting upset about seeing Melissa in a dream. It wasn't as if it were an uncommon occurrence, Trent told himself, only this time he knew he was dreaming. He realized it was probably a good thing he was on the elevator. Getting involved with a dream Melissa sounded unhealthy. Al was right when he advised Trent to get on with life.

The elevator was the size of Trent's bedroom. Led Zeppelin's "The Song Remains the Same" played over the speakers.

The elevator opened to the door of the penthouse apartment, which apparently took up half the sixty-fourth floor. Trent tossed the bellhop a twenty and strode across the center of the apartment's spacious living room to a massive picture window.

Bear River, population 6,000, was only a tiny clump of winking lights clustered about the base of the hotel. The rest of the view was mostly black velvet, dotted with a few faint auto headlights traveling distant highways.

He again marveled at the complexity of the dream and knelt to run his fingers through the plush pile of the carpet. His sense of touch was as vivid as his sight.

"And to think I was considering giving up those nicotine patches," he laughed and turned to Peggy.

Another button was undone, revealing more of her bra. Trent shoved aside any question of propriety. After all, it was just a dream.

Peggy slipped into his arms. She smelled of pressed flowers. Trent shoved the wad of bills into his jacket pocket and untucked her blouse, running his hands up the soft skin of her back. He stopped at the clasp of the bra. Like real life, he had trouble unhooking it.

He pulled, twisted and yanked, but the bra would not unhook. A look of impatience was beginning to cross Peggy's face. Be master of the dream, Trent said to himself, and pulled with all his might. The clasp broke.

"I'll buy you a dozen new ones," he whispered into her ear, the faint scent of perfume seductively swirling about her hair and skin.

Trent leaned his head back and smiled dreamily as Peggy began kissing and nibbling at his neck.

"Ouch."

The nips were becoming almost bites. He pushed her gently away and felt his neck. There was a slight tenderness in one spot. He looked down into Peggy's smiling face and for the first time noticed that she seemed to have unusually well developed canine teeth.

As quickly as a match flaring, Peggy's face shimmered and the smile became a feral snarl displaying even longer and sharper fangs. She blinked and her eyes flashed a stop-light red, blazing like hot coals.

Caught off guard by her sudden lunge at his throat, Trent stumbled backwards against the window. He stiff-armed her away.

"What the hell is going on?" he sputtered.

"You are mine, little man," she laughed in the same seductive voice.

The now panther-like woman crouched low to the floor and then sprang with the suddenness of a Jack-in-the-box. Trent barely had time to dodge the attack, throwing himself to the side.

Peggy slammed into the window. It exploded into a thousand twinkling shards that seemed to twist and spin lazily out into the night, following the cat woman's falling body like the sparkling tail of a comet.

Trent rose unsteadily to his feet and stumbled away from the window. He crossed the room and sat on one of the many overstuffed chairs. Fighting off a wave of nausea, he lowered his head between his knees. Trent absent-mindedly picked up the wad of bills that had fallen from his pocket.

A loud crashing snapped Trent to attention. The door shuddered again under the impact of something exceeding large.

"I know you're in there," roared a hideous, deep, slurred voice—like that of a record album slowed by a heavy finger.

Trent jumped to his feet and looked about the apartment in a panic. There was only one other exit. He ran to it after another crash made it apparent that the front door was about to be breached. The doorknob was icy cold and he hesitated before turning it. The sound of splintering wood prodded Trent into action and he didn't look back as he flung himself into the next room and slammed the door behind him.

It was another large, lavishly decorated and furnished suite—only this one had an air of age and neglect. Dust coated everything, yellowed wallpaper peeled, and only a few of the chandelier bulbs dimly burned. Trent didn't stop to admire the faded elegance. He sprinted across the room and pushed his way through another door that led into a hall.

Trent was sure whatever had been slamming into the door was still hot on his heels. The hall twisted and turned at odd angles. Though it was a dream, Trent found himself winded within minutes. He stopped and gasped for breath while leaning against a doorway. Sounding far away, the thing wailed and its cry raced ahead like the baying of a coon dog echoing through a wooded valley. Trent took one last deep breath and began jogging at a steadier pace.

The hallway went on and on, never branching into or intersecting other passageways. The doors he tried were locked. Gradually the howls of the creature grew louder while Trent became more exhausted. A weakness flowed through his body and his legs felt like lead weights. It was all he could do to drag one foot in front of the other.

Trent's pace might have slowed, but his heart was racing. His head throbbed in time to his pounding pulse. He stumbled against a door and it swung inwards, sending him stumbling to the floor. He wanted to stay down, but the howls prodded him to his knees then trembling to his feet. He shut the door and slid a dead bolt.

Musty and dank, the dreary bedroom smelled like a damp basement. Mildew blossomed on the walls in overlapping blotches. The curtains crumbled as he brushed them to the side. A small, dirty window looked out into an inky blackness. He pressed his face to the glass and observed a small ledge just below the sill.

Trent froze when he heard muffled sniffing outside the door. He steeled himself, but still the violent crashing made him jerk. He fumbled with the window latch and heaved upwards. It refused to budge.

I am the master of this dream, Trent said silently to steady himself, and again pushed upwards on the window. It refused to slide. He grabbed a small chair and sent it crashing through the pane.

Several spikes of glass remained in the frame like crystal fangs and they had to be kicked loose. He was halfway through the window when he heard the door explode behind him. Gripping the outside window frame, he pulled himself up and pressed his back against the bricks. A fog had moved in and there was only gray darkness wherever he gazed.

Trent refused to look when the creature noisily came out the window. He began a clumsy shuffle until he came to a corner and had to work carefully around it. Knowing that an almost endless fall waited for him chewed at his courage, adding to the trembling fatigue of his legs.

The pursuit grew louder. Trent finally came to another window and he gingerly turned around, planning to kick in the glass. He didn't have time. Something, maybe a calloused hand or beast's paw, grabbed at his arm. He lurched and tumbled from the narrow walkway. Trent screamed and wildly kicked as he tumbled deeper and deeper into the darkness.

Chapter Three

Trent woke with his back arched, arms tangled in the blankets, hands clenched, and mouth locked open in a silent scream. It took several minutes for the shudders to completely stop and his ragged breathing to return to normal. The sheets were wet from his cold sweat.

Trent raised his hand to rub his forehead and found himself grasping something. He held it up to the window. There was enough light to reveal a fist full of twenty dollar bills. He pressed the bills to his face and took a deep breath. There had to be almost one thousand dollars in cash. Let Al try laughing that off as he had the brick.

~ * ~

Trent finished a replay of the dream and threw one of the twenties on the bar for another round of drinks.

"Your Peggy sounds like an incubus; evil spirits that look like beautiful women. They supposedly kill men in their sleep," volunteered Lorenzo.

"I'd say you're going bonkers," Rich said with a shake of his head as he looked at the twenty-dollar bill, "but keep it up, we can use the eggs."

"All right, say you really did bring back a fist full of money. How do you explain it?" asked Al. He was sounding progressively more worried about his friend's mental health.

"I have no idea," Trent answered defensively. "I just know what happened. I dreamed about the money and woke up with it in my hand."

"And a few assorted nicks and abrasions," observed Lorenzo. "It looks like you were cut while shaving...your forehead."

Trent self-consciously traced the outline of one of the small bandages on his face.

"Maybe you're knocking over convenience stores in your sleep," Rich joked, "like some people sleep walk."

Al gave his friend a dirty look as if it struck too close to what he had been thinking.

"An adobe brick is one thing," Al said to the others, "but Trent's dreaming is becoming more serious when he starts bringing back cash."

"Native Americans believed that a dream was the soul's sojourn into another realm or reality, a place independent of the dreamer," Lorenzo said. "I don't remember claims of them bringing back souvenirs. I do recall reading something similar to your experience in references to ancient Assyrian and Mesopotamian cults. They believed members of an advanced, god-like race brought them secrets in the arts and sciences. Some scholars theorize that those beliefs shared the same origins as those regarding mythical Atlantis. There was mention of these beings traveling by way of dreams. They could transport believers to other worlds and return with sacred objects. I'll have to do some research."

~ * ~

It looked like he hadn't pulled the patch off in time, Trent decided when he found himself standing in the middle of the Bear River of his previous dream. Like before, there were few people on the street. The memory of that monstrous voice probably had something to do with his quick pace to the brighter section of town several blocks away. He nervously glanced down each alley and into every shadowed doorway.

He stopped under the street light by a small park. Trent remembered flying in other dreams and decided to try it again. It hadn't really been flying, more like gliding or floating. He would lift his arms to the front and slowly step out like a wader getting ready to swim into deeper water. Then he'd drift up like a balloon caught in a breeze. But it was a flying that took continuous concentration. A flinch or loss of confidence would send him crashing.

Taking a deep breath, Trent raised his arms and kicked off—and fell. He pulled in his hands at the last second to keep from smashing his face on the sidewalk. Maybe he needed a little momentum.

This time Trent jogged across the grass before diving into the air. The results were the same. The landing knocked the wind out of him and jarred every bone.

This has got to stop, Trent thought as he lay on the ground. He was becoming one mass of bruises and scrapes. Even by streetlight he could make out the individual blades of grass inches from his nose. They seemed so real. Maybe that was the problem; this dream city was too real for flying. He needed more of a hazy, vague dream for flying.

Trent climbed wearily to his feet and dusted himself off. There were grass stains on the knees of his jeans and sweatshirt elbows.

Out-of-sight crickets were chirping and Trent wondered if he could bring back a live insect to his waking world. He again thought how astounding the nicotine dreams were. The little details were amazing—from the cracks in the sidewalk to the feel of the damp evening air. He did detect a subtle difference in the lighting, a trace of red that made the shadows seem even darker. Was it his nervous imagination or did the shadows stretch out farther than normal? There was a tenseness in this dream world he didn't like.

Trent was entering the downtown area. The stores were like the streets—empty. It was a ghost town. The sound of his footfalls seemed to grow louder and Trent purposely tried stepping lighter. He stopped in front of a pawnshop. In the window was a revolver with a card displaying in large print, "Double Action Anaconda Colt .45."

Guns weren't in Trent's usual range of interests. He had shot a few rifles when he was younger, but he didn't hunt. Bear River was a peaceful town and guns weren't considered a needed survival tool. A bell rang above the door as he entered. Several minutes passed with no one coming through a draped entryway behind the counter. He didn't feel like looking for the proprietor.

Stereos, vacuum cleaners, electric razors, flat screen TVs, e-book readers, DVDs, knives, and jewelry were all there in abundance. They were obviously pre-owned with small nicks and scratches adorning each one. Oh, the details, he marveled once again.

A variety of bullets were on a back shelf, and he carefully loaded the gun from the window; spinning its chamber when he had finished. Its solid weight made Trent feel more at ease as he left the pawnshop. He didn't know if the creature that pursued him through the hotel was still around, but he believed a half dozen .45 slugs would slow it down.

Across the street was a movie theater and the marquee announced that "The Birds" was playing. He wasn't surprised that there were no ticket takers or that the lobby was empty. Trent was disappointed that it was a familiar movie. It would have been interesting to see what his imagination could come up with for a new movie. Then he could have written it down upon waking, Trent thought, like Coleridge and his poem.

Around the corner was a restaurant. "Crossroads Cafe" was written across its large window in red and gold art deco letters. What caught his attention was the fact that there were actually people in it. Not many, but it looked like a crowd compared to the rest of the city. Two waiters wiped small round tables or briefly spoke to the seven or eight people scattered through the narrow room that almost disappeared into darkness before he saw a back wall. Torpid ceiling fans sluggishly drew up the isolated plumes of cigarette smoke.

No one looked up as he entered. A tall gaunt woman in black sat at one table shaded by a potted palm. She was wearing a fox pelt. Its head dangled across her left breast. Glass-bead eyes glared at Trent as he passed by the table. Her dress was vaguely in the style of a 1920s flapper.

"Sir, I am afraid guns aren't allowed in here," advised a waiter.

A startled Trent almost pulled the trigger. That wouldn't have been good since it was pointed at his feet.

Trent turned and inspected the waiter. It was difficult to tell under the red-hued lighting if the waiter's complexion was really yellowish. The man was two inches shorter than Trent, about five foot, seven inches tall. A thin mustache and greased-back hair were his only distinguishable features. The waiter had a face Trent knew he would forget within seconds of looking away.

"Uh, I really would like to keep it. I promise I won't cause a disturbance."

"I'm sorry, sir, that is quite impossible. What would our other guests think? We have a reputation to maintain."

Trent really didn't want to get in an argument with the waiter, especially knowing he was susceptible to bumps on his head after waking.

"You see," he leaned closer to the man and whispered, "the last time I was in your fair city, something huge with a very deep voice chased me all the way around the sixty-fourth floor of the hotel. I feel more safe carrying it."

"That's quite all right, sir. We are protected here. Followers of the Red Man are not allowed."

"The Red Man?"

Where had Trent heard that before? Then he remembered a page of that coloring book.

"What, or who, is the Red Man?"

"I'm afraid I am not allowed to become involved in religious disputes. Please, the gun."

"Religious disputes?"

"The gun?"

Trent handed the revolver over by the barrel. Some dream master—he couldn't even successfully argue with a waiter. He was led to a table under a velvet Elvis painting—only instead of wearing a Las Vegas show jump suit, the King was a cross between an Aztec priest and Elton John. The figure wore a gaudy cape made from thousands of colorful feathers.

"Nice decor."

The waiter remained stone faced. "Would you like time to look at the menu or would you care to order now?"

"I've been having trouble reading fine print lately so..."

"As you are well aware, you will be able to read ours."

There was something in the tone that left no room for argument. Trent doubtfully picked up the menu and opened it. The items were plainly written and easy to see. He gazed about suspiciously. There was no way he was awake.

"The writing is extra large and brief," explained the waiter as if speaking for the tenth time to an exceedingly stupid child.

"I guess I'll just have a bottle of your best wine—for now."

The waiter stepped briskly away and disappeared through a back door.

There was no rhyme or reason to his dreams, Trent decided. What this all meant was beyond him. He looked around at the few other inhabitants. They looked like refugees from different times and different worlds, all sulking silently at their tables and ignoring each other. One woman looked remarkably like Amelia Earhart. She glanced up and frowned when she noticed Trent staring at her. He gave an embarrassed smile and looked away.

Trent was playing with the ashtray and a book of matches when four musicians stepped through an archway onto a small stage in a softly-lit alcove—a drummer, pianist, bass guitarist, and saxophone player. The opening number was a cross between big band, reggae, and jazz. He found the odd mixture strangely haunting.

His contemplation of the music was abruptly shattered when he glanced to the front of the restaurant. Walking past the window was the Melissa look-alike he'd seen at the hotel. He couldn't see her face clearly, but the hair and figure were painfully familiar. Trent had always described her as looking like Donna Reed. He hadn't been able to watch any of the actress's old films since Melissa's disappearance.

The figure glanced in the restaurant and seemed as equally startled as Trent. The woman came to an abrupt halt and then made a visible effort to shake off the surprise. She shrugged her shoulders and after a brief hesitation, aimed for the restaurant door.

Melancholy, thought Trent, that's a good word for how I feel—a soft ache, a hazy pain that lingers after a fever. It was only a dream and yet he couldn't stop the tightening of his throat or shaking of his hands.

He smiled sadly at the dream figure entering the restaurant and noted that his subconscious had even aged Melissa. She was no longer the twenty-four-year-old woman he'd last seen eight years ago, but an attractive woman in her early thirties. Instead of the young Donna Reed of "It's a Wonderful Life," she was now looking the part of her later TV roles.

The soft keening of the saxophone added to his despondency. He stood and pulled a chair out for the specter. Instead of sitting, Melissa's image strode up to Trent and peered closely into his face, reaching out to flick a stray lock of his hair.

"No gray, but I see I've added some faint crow's feet," she said. "I can't believe I'm still dressing you in old jeans and a work shirt."

She circled like a prospective shopper checking out Christmas-sale merchandise. Trent was taken aback by the unexpected behavior of his dream Melissa. With the low lights and romantic music, he'd been lulled into imagining a more wistful scenario. He pulled away when she tried pinching his cheeks.

"I'm good, though. You do look how Trent would have appeared by now. Even with that thinning in front."

"I'm not thinning," he snapped back then felt silly about answering a mirage.

"And you are even a bit vain like Trent," she added in a surly tone.

"Hell, I even get insulted when I'm asleep," he said, looking at the ceiling and shaking his head. "Maybe this is how my subconscious is weaning me of Melissa—by making her obnoxious."

He sat back down and looked around for a waiter. They seemed to be hiding. Melissa sat in the chair he'd pulled out for her. She continued staring intently at him, her frown growing into a black cloud. It made Trent feel extremely uncomfortable.

"Even a hallucination should know that it is impolite to stare," he finally said.

The woman startled Trent by abruptly slamming her hand on the table and angrily shouting, "I'm sick of this. Get out of here and leave me alone. I'm tired of this dream and I want to wake up."

Just as suddenly, the frown crumbled and she buried her face in her hands and began gently sobbing. Trent was flustered. He was finding he had no way of predicting what his subconscious was going to cook up next. The image of Melissa crying was forcing Trent to feel emotions he was trying to forget. Trent decided he better walk away rather than continue torturing himself. He pushed back his chair and stood. Melissa looked up and the sight of her red eyes and tears wrenched at Trent's heart.

"Stop it," he yelled, feeling his own eyes watering. "Why am I doing this? You're dead. You've been dead for eight years. I refuse to wallow in this self pity any longer."

Trent kicked at the table in frustration and only succeeded in smashing his big toe. He yelped and collapsed back into his seat. Melissa gave a half laugh and wiped her eyes with one hand. They looked ruefully at each other.

"I guess I don't care if you are a mirage," she said after a few minutes of silence. "It can't hurt to visit with a dream any more than to look at old photos."

She reached over and took his hand.

"If only this was real," she said then looked puzzled. "I wonder why I'm having you say I'm the one who is dead. What does that mean?"

She seemed to forget Trent while she pondered the question.

He didn't know why he felt so nervous. Maybe it was because he was afraid she'd suddenly grow fangs like Peggy and attack him. It was more likely, Trent admitted, that he was afraid he'd fall in love with this older dream Melissa—what kind of pathetic person would he then be?

Looking at this Melissa so deep in thought made Trent think about her question.

"Yeah, I wonder why I'm having you act like I'm the one that died?' he asked aloud.

She looked up at him and smiled again. "Now don't go echoing me. That would drive me crazy."

"How did I die?" he asked, deciding to play along with the dream.

"You were drinking and inner tubing with your buddies down Bear River and went over the dam," Melissa answered as she continued her inspection. "There were always questions since your friends claimed you were right behind them when they headed to shore. Then you were gone and they found your body the next day several miles downstream."

"Hah," Trent snorted. "I remember when I almost did that. It was when you disappeared. We didn't realize we were that close to the dam until we were right up on it. I had to paddle like hell. When I got home there was a message from your mother asking if I'd heard from you. I never saw you again."

"So, I disappeared from your dream world when you died in mine," she said softly. "What funny thoughts I have in dreams."

"How did I disappear?" she wanted to know.

"You were visiting your brother in Chicago, only you never made it there. They found your car abandoned near Galena. The police think you were murdered by a serial killer who was known to be hitchhiking in the area. They never found your body, and he was executed about two years ago for the deaths of four other women."

It was a very surreal conversation. He wanted to reach out and touch her hand or run his fingertips across her cheek. It was almost a physical ache.

Trent forced himself to keep his hands on the table. He knew one light caress would only lead to more.

"Wouldn't it be strange if your dream world were just as real as mine," she mused.

"It's too tempting a thought. It's a path leading to madness and despair," Trent murmured in a melodramatic voice.

Melissa laughed loudly and clapped her hands. "That's just what you would have done. I can't believe how real you seem."

Trent shook his head. His eyes were almost watering again. "I haven't heard that laugh in a long time. If only we were of two worlds and this a point where they touched, like that Chou guy said."

"Chou?"

"A Chinese professor who said that since dreaming and being awake both exist in a person, there must be a point where they touch. He's not to be confused with another Chou from China who wondered if he was dreaming about being a butterfly or if he were a butterfly dreaming about being a man."

This time it was the dream Melissa who shook her head. "My, I get philosophical when I sleep. Those nicotine patches sure do a job on me. I bet if..."

Melissa and the restaurant began to waiver. He tried concentrating on the surroundings and the woman, but they slowly dissipated like cigarette smoke.

~ * ~

Trent opened his eyes and stared at his bedroom ceiling. He could make out the blurred images of several dead flies behind the frosted glass of the ceiling light fixture.

Damn these dreams, he cursed. Instead of getting over Melissa, they were bringing back all the pain and memories. Trent didn't know what hurt worse: his bruised and protesting muscles as he sat up or the memory of Melissa's voice. He was going to have to stop using the patches.

Chapter Four

"I don't believe it," scoffed Al.

Lorenzo was attempting to relate how Catherine the Great, the German-born empress of Russia, had died.

"I'm afraid so. Then the straps broke on the horse and she was crushed," Lorenzo repeated.

"Where do you hear these things? Is there some cosmic latrine wall where all the sordid facts of history are scribbled?" Al wanted to know.

"But I can say the rumor that Benjamin Franklin died from syphilis is untrue."

Trent was only half listening to the usual bizarre conversations in which his friends regularly became entwined. He was fingering a pack of matches he found next to the bed that morning. On a green background was familiar gold and red art deco lettering declaring, "Crossroads Cafe."

Trent decided he could have picked up the matches weeks ago when he was still smoking. He was always bringing home matches bearing the logos of insurance companies and taverns, or even bargains on postal stamps from around the world. The name could have stuck in his mind and reemerged in his dream.

"Ever see these matches before?" he asked, holding the book up for his friends' inspection.

They passed them around, each examining the cover.

"Crossroads Cafe, where is that?" asked Rich.

"Never heard of it," said Al.

Lorenzo continued staring at the book and then opened it. He frowned. "I wonder what this means."

Trent took the matches and saw something was written in small, black print. "Beware of the Red Man," it read. He had forgotten to mention the message in the coloring book when relating the dreams. He didn't want to explain it now after the fact and the matches were slipped back in his shirt pocket.

"I think Sam is going to become a vegan," Rich said in his usual abruptness when changing a subject."

"A Vegan?" Lorenzo asked skeptically. "Your wife is thinking about becoming an alien being?"

"You know what I mean; a vegetarian."

"Is she nuts? Do you know the unmitigated misery and tragedy that would occur to farm animals should humans quit eating meat?"

"What are you talking about?" interrupted Al. "If humans quit eating meat, all those animals wouldn't be slaughtered."

"There is an island in the Great Lakes where all the wolves were shot to protect a herd of deer," Lorenzo began in a familiar droll tone. "The deer population skyrocketed and the island was stripped bare of vegetation. The deer were soon dropping like flies from starvation and diseases.

"Try to imagine feedlots and confinement operations overflowing with pigs and cattle. Farmers, forced to work from sunup to sunset just to feed their overpopulating livestock, would start having mental breakdowns due to the stress. Farm families would be torn apart by the strife. Herds of starving cows, after nibbling the pastures down to the dirt, would wander into towns to devastate golf courses and yards like locust.

"And I'm afraid it would be an even uglier picture with the pigs," Spasm said as he turned to Trent and looked him in the eye with mock seriousness. "Hogs are omnivorous, which means they'd be just as happy snacking on the pet poodle as they would the peony bush. Right now there are millions of hogs in the United States. A sow can have a litter of ten every four months. Try to imagine how many hogs there would be after a couple years if we weren't consuming bacon and sausage.

"Simply put, if we don't eat them, they're going to eat us. Try to imagine being a captive in your own home, afraid to go outside for fear that some rogue Hampshire might pull you down."

"Don't you think you're exaggerating?" Trent asked, knowing the conversation was being carried on for his sake. His friends were trying to cheer him up with their banter.

"I haven't even begun. Did I mention chickens? You wouldn't be able to go anywhere outside without stepping or sitting in chicken shit, not to mention all the eggs they'd be laying around the place."

"Why couldn't we just stop them from breeding?" Rich asked.

Lorenzo looked at his short, stocky friend as if in shock. "What, you're ready to throw thousands in the timber industry out of work to save the spotted owl, but you're willing to condemn Herefords and Durocs to extinction? Doesn't a domestic chicken species have just as much right to life as the California condor? Maybe we should prevent gazelles from reproducing so they won't get eaten by lions?

"What would you do," Lorenzo asked as he looked Rich straight in the eye, "if your great-granddaughter came to you someday and asked why there were no longer any Rhode Island Red chickens like she'd seen in a book, and you had to tell her they are extinct because people stopped eating them?"

"Gee, I don't know...slap the little bugger, I guess."

"That's right, you don't know. Now I want you to get that crazy idea out of her head. If you love animals, eat them. Think of it as a kind of tough love."

"I like cats and dogs, but I don't eat them." Al tried one last argument.

"Fine," Lorenzo shot back as he waved an empty mug at the bartender. "Are you ready to litter-train an Angus and take it in as a house pet? Are you ready to leash-break a five hundred pound boar? Will you let a chicken sleep every night at the foot of your bed?"

"Well, er, no..."

"And yet Rich's wife, Theresa, is willing to see either the Earth overrun with starving animals or prevent the births of billions of creatures?"

"That pretty well sums it up," agreed Rich, "though she might eat fish."

"Oh, sure, the only thing she'll eat is a creature that is still part of the natural food chain. Isn't that nice? When was the last time you heard of salmon overpopulating?"

"I'll consider all this," Rich promised his friend, "but I have one worry."

"What's that?"

"Eating more meat means eating less veggies. Do you know how many seeds an uneaten broccoli or cucumber can produce...?"

Trent shook his head as he rose from his stool. He knew the banter was meant to distract him from what his friends believed were dark and murky thoughts.

"Going already?" asked Al. He continued acting worried about his pal, even though Trent assured them that there had been no more strange dreams. Trent knew Al would have worried all the more after hearing about his vision of an older Melissa.

It always seemed like a different world to Trent when first stepping into bright sunlight after a stint in the dark New Yorker. Trent's pickup was parked around the corner and he nodded hello to several familiar faces as he walked down the street.

One belonged to Lowell Simons. As always, Simons refused to acknowledge Trent's greeting. The strange little man had been infatuated with Melissa. Trent remembered Melissa saying that Simons almost scared her with his brooding, intense stares. If anything, he'd turned more brooding through the years. Simons seemed to have a special dislike of Trent and his scowl would deepen when they met.

Trent stopped at the sight of another familiar face across the street. The person was coming out of a drug store with several magazines under his arm. He was as familiar a figure as the book of matches bearing the

Crossroads Cafe logo—the last time Trent had seen this person was in his hotel dream. It was the man who had accompanied Melissa into the lobby. He was still wearing the same beard, old jeans, jacket, sunglasses, leather gloves, and hair pulled back into a ponytail.

It was getting too weird for Trent. Had he seen the man before and incorporated him into the dream like the book of matches? Trent glanced to both sides and set off across the street.

I'm going to sound like a fool or a madman, Trent thought, but I still have to talk to this mystery man.

The man was sorting through the magazines as he walked and momentarily looked up to check his course. He saw Trent, paused in mid stride, whirled, and took off running down the sidewalk. The unexpected response so surprised Trent that he stopped in the middle of the road and was almost hit by a car. The driver honked angrily as she swerved around Trent.

Lorenzo, Rich, and Al were already out of sight. Trent jumped to avoid being hit by another car. Once in motion, he found himself chasing the stranger. Embarrassment as much as anything kept Trent from catching the man. Thirty-two year olds don't run through downtown Bear River unless they are in jogging clothes. Heads turned as the stranger wove in and out among the scattered pedestrians. Trent followed at a slower pace.

He turned the corner in time to see his quarry disappear into a dead end alley. Trent followed and wasn't surprised to find the stranger had vanished, even though it appeared there was no escape route. He walked the perimeter of the dead end alley, yanking at several locked doors and inspecting two dumpsters.

A discarded newspaper caught his eye. As an afterthought, he read a few sentences dealing with international trade negotiations. Trent was pretty sure he was awake but wasn't taking anything for granted.

All the way back to the pickup, he puzzled over the odd behavior of the man.

It wasn't as if I was screaming or acting strange when I spotted him, Trent puzzled to himself. I wasn't running or doing anything that would scare a complete stranger. Why would he run like that?

Trent felt like he was in an Alfred Hitchcock movie and that made him feel watched. Trent scanned the yards and streets out of the corner of his eyes. Everything seemed normal. A teenage girl walked up to the porch of a white, wood-framed house and threw a newspaper on the porch swing. An old woman was kneeling along the side of the same house pulling weeds from a border of yellow and red flowers. A lawn mower growled unseen from someone's backyard.

~ * ~

That night Trent rented "It's a Wonderful Life." He wondered if Donna had blue eyes like Melissa. He used to kid Melissa that her eyes were so blue that when she stood against the sky, it looked like she had holes in her head. He clicked the DVD off when Al walked by the den doorway. Al was well aware of Trent's feelings about the actress.

When it was finally time to go to bed, Trent opened the bathroom cabinet and stared at the small box of nicotine patches. He pulled one of the aluminum foil packets out and tapped it against his open palm while looking in the mirror. Twice he began to return the patch to the box and stopped each time. His image looked back at him in concern. Trent jerked his head to the side and the reflection mimicked the move perfectly. When Trent was very young, he would try to catch his image off guard. He never did. Trent decided not to try it anymore just in case this was the night he succeeded. His nerves would not be able handle an independent reflection.

"Well, what are we going to do?" he asked his reflection. "Should we try another patch? All right, you first. No? Big baby."

Trent opened the cabinet and replaced the box of patches on the shelf next to a bottle of generic aspirins. He carried the single packet back to his

47

bedroom, chewing at a corner until he'd made a tear big enough to open it with his fingers.

~ * ~

Trent opened his eyes and stared at his bedroom ceiling. He could make out the blurred images of several dead flies behind the frosted glass of the ceiling light left on when he fell asleep reading.

He examined the comic books clutched tightly against his chest and grinned. Wait until he showed this to Al, Trent mused, the complete first two years of Spiderman comics. They were worth a small fortune. It had been a strange dream, but he'd made it out of the Vegan spacecraft unharmed and with the comic books. What more could he ask?

Though it was still dark outside, Trent decided to get up and make a breakfast other than cold cereal and toast. The house was chilly. He turned on the closet light and rummaged around until he found an old sweatshirt reading, "I Brake For All Hallucinations."

He felt oddly let down. The dream had been fun, but he had to admit that he would have preferred another chat with his dream Melissa.

Trent walked to a living room window and stared outside. The house was on a corner and he looked over his hedge and down the sidewalk of the next block. Little islands of light puddled under each lamppost, growing consecutively smaller until they disappeared. As old glass does, it rippled and turned the ordinary neighborhood view into a dream-like landscape.

Maybe that's because it is a dreamscape, decided Trent. Peeking over a neighbor's tree was a sixty-four story hotel.

A dream within a dream, he mused and wondered about the comics. So much for sudden wealth. The dream house was basically the same as his awake home, only the real one didn't have a wall of fog behind the doors leading upstairs or to the basement. He thrust his hand into the thick haze and hastily pulled it back, his fingers tingling from an Arctic cold.

If anything should surprise him about this latest happening, Trent decided, it should be how calmly he was taking it.

"Just call me the Dream Master. Have snore will travel," he spoke to a picture of his great-grandmother hanging over the stereo.

Trent decided to take his pickup rather than walk downtown. Though he found himself actually anxious to get to the Crossroads Cafe, the memory of the hotel chase caused him to pause at the front door. He pressed his nose to the glass and tried to see as far as he could to both sides of the front porch. What if it were waiting for him behind the lilac bush?

He remembered feeling this way as a kid after staying up late and watching monster movies. A local TV station had Dr. Boris arising from his coffin every Friday night and introducing black and white movies about bloodsucking aliens or giant grasshoppers eating soldiers at polar radar stations.

To keep the thing under the bed from grabbing his legs, Trent would line up several chairs in advance. After the movie, he'd hop from chair to chair and scramble safely under the covers. Summer was the worst time because he'd nearly smother under a hot blanket. Body parts outside the covers were fair game for monsters. He'd been forced to stick his mouth up to the blanket edge like a fish sucking air at the water's surface. Was the Red Man under the porch ready to grab his legs when he went down the steps?

This is ridiculous, Trent decided. Didn't I successfully steal the gem of Dorga and defeat his fiendish priests? Didn't I thwart an attempt by aliens to make off with some of Earth's most important cultural treasurers, including comic books? Maybe, maybe not, he answered himself.

He opened the door and stepped forcefully onto the porch, looked both ways, and then made a mad dash to the pickup. Trent locked both doors as soon as he slid behind the wheel. The dream 1953 Dodge pickup looked like his waking truck. He only hoped there wasn't a fog under the hood. If there was, it still sounded just like an engine when he turned the key and pressed down on the floor starter.

Trent stayed under the legal speed limit and came to a complete stop at all the stop signs. He was in no hurry to see if the cops were as strange as their city. Trent slowed down when he spotted one lone figure walking a dog. It looked like his neighbor, Howard Welton, dressed in a black corset and fishnet stockings. The man looked into the truck and appeared surprised when he saw the driver. Trent shook his head and wondered why his dreams had to be so obtuse.

There were no markings on the street or curb to designate parking spaces, so Trent stopped directly in front of the restaurant. He tried looking nonchalant as he walked to the door and opened it without once looking over his shoulder. Several patrons were watching him. They appeared startled to see someone arrive by auto.

At one table were three young men in khaki uniforms with Army Air Corps patches on their shoulders. They appeared lost and confused, looking about them and then almost bumping heads to whisper in frantic, hushed voices. Trent was about to talk to the men when the same waiter magically appeared at his elbow.

"The lady is waiting," he informed Trent and pointed to a small table almost hidden under one of the many potted palms.

It was Melissa. She appeared deep in thought studying her menu, but he detected a quick glance up and then back to the menu.

"Thank you," Trent said automatically, already walking to the table.

"Hello. May I join you or are you expecting someone?"

The dream Melissa looked up and stared as intently at him as the last time they met.

"I looked up your 'Chou' guy. He was Li Yuan Chou and lived in the twelfth century. The butterfly Chou was Chuang Chou. I didn't know anything about them until you told me. How do you explain that?" she asked in an accusative voice.

Trent gave up waiting for her to motion him to sit so he went ahead and pulled a chair out.

"I'd explain it the same way I'd explain anything you told me that I didn't know," Trent answered belatedly. "I must have heard it and forgotten, except my subconscious didn't.'

"Hmmm," was all she said and continued staring at Trent.

"Are you ready to order?"

It was the waiter again.

"Not yet," Trent answered distractedly and returned Melissa's intense gaze.

"You better order or you may find yourself in the same position as the drinker in Feng Ming's book," advised Melissa.

"What?"

"He was a seventeenth century Chinese novelist and wrote about a great drinker who dreamed that he had some good wine but wanted it heated before he drank. He suddenly awoke and declared sadly that he should have taken it cold."

"You looked that up too?" he asked.

"Yes, I've been doing quite a bit of reading since I was here last. If and when you wake, you might look that up yourself."

"It would only mean that Lorenzo must have mentioned it at one time over a beer."

"Lorenzo Spasm, your older brother Bill's friend?" She seemed surprised. "Yes, I guess you'd probably be hanging around him if you were alive. He is back in town, but I don't see much of him. They say he was involved in some failed rebellion in Tibet. Now that would be strange, seeing Lorenzo and you discussing philosophy and dreams at a bar."

Trent noticed the waiter was still standing at the table. "Bring us a bottle of the best house wine."

"How would you suggest we settle this puzzle about whether one of us is dreaming the other?" she asked.

"We would tell something the other could not possibly know," he answered.

"That's what I already decided," the dream Melissa said quickly. "And I know one, do you?"

"Well, er, I would have to think."

"My picture."

"What?"

"My picture," she repeated. "The framed one I gave you. It was of me on vacation with my dorm roommates when we went to Florida. I'm wearing that green bikini. Remember?"

"Uh, yes, of course I do. Why?"

I wrote a message on the back of it before I decided to have it framed. Do you still have it?"

Trent chewed on his upper lip and looked at his imaginary Melissa. He didn't want to play this game because it would hurt all the more in the end. He kept that picture in the buffet, still occasionally pulling it out to look at when he was digging in the drawer for other things.

"Yes."

"Take the back off. I wrote, 'To Trent, with all my love. Your own beach bunny.' It's corny, but I was only twenty-one. Now you tell me one."

Trent took a breath and opened his mouth then closed it again and swallowed. He looked down at the checkered tablecloth.

"OK, what's a selamlik?"

"A what?"

"S-e-l-a-m-l-i-k. I play a lot of Fictionary with Lorenzo."

"I don't know, but couldn't I have heard that somewhere before?"

Trent didn't answer.

"Please," she said and he felt a warm hand cover his.

"We were to meet at the park about a couple days before you disappeared, but it rained and you were late," Trent forced himself to speak. "I stayed under a tree by the water fountain and while I was waiting, I carved our initials into the back of a half-grown oak. I didn't want anyone else to see it so I cut into the side that was covered by the bushes. About a year ago I walked by it and remembered the carving. It was still there, though pretty hard to decipher."

"I'll look," the dream Melissa spoke, her voice sounding as shaky as Trent's. "Janice said I shouldn't do this; that these dreams are bad for me and I should quit wearing nicotine patches. But I knew I had to see you again after that last time, especially when I opened that library book and there were the Chous. It was such a shock, I almost dropped the book."

"Janice?"

"A friend. She worries about me since my parents died, keeps trying to set me up with dates."

"I know how that is," Trent laughed and then turned serious. "Your parents died? What do you mean?"

Melissa's eyes widened and she tightly gripped his hand. "Yes, they were killed in a car accident two years ago."

Trent didn't know what to say under such an intense stare.

"What about in your world?"

"They're still alive. I saw them last week. We always chat when we run into each other at the supermarket."

Melissa relaxed her grip and brushed a stray wisp of hair from her face. She looked about the restaurant as if seeing it for the first time.

The band was back and playing "Istanbul-Not Constantinople" after having finished a reggae version of "Jeepers, Creepers, Where'd You Get Those Peepers?" A violin and clarinet had joined it.

"I've got to say one thing for these nicotine dreams, they are vivid— down to the smallest detail," Trent said as he gazed to the next table.

On it was a Coca Cola can. He leaned out and grabbed it, almost falling out of his chair.

"See, you even have to be able to balance while dreaming," Trent snorted as he examined the can. "It looks like a typical Coke can, though I'm not able to read the ingredients."

Melissa didn't join the conversation. She put her chin in the palm of her hand and continued soberly examining Trent as he spoke.

"It doesn't matter that I can't read the ingredients," Trent continued, "they're secret. Even East German chemists were unable to duplicate the exact formula when they wanted to keep up with the Schmidts after Coca Cola opened plants in West Germany.

"Of course when Coke first came out, they used cocaine to give it that special zing. After 'the real thing' became illegal, company officials went on a mad rush to find a substitute. Whatever they found is still a secret."

"And what do you think it is?" Trent asked as he waved the can in front of Melissa. "Something so gross they do not dare reveal it? Maybe the sweat of a poisonous Amazon toad or jellied turkey lips?"

Melissa smiled sadly and took the can from his hand. "I can't believe how real you seem. It is just the kind of stupid thing you'd say."

Trent sighed and shook his head as he looked back at the band. The lead singer looked exactly like Jim Morrison of "The Doors."

"Say, do you remember seeing me at the hotel?" Trent finally said to revive the conversation.

"What?"

"The hotel here in this dream city—who knows how long ago. I was entering an elevator and you came in the lobby with some biker dude."

"Biker? That was my first dream after starting on the patches. I was just walking down the street and he pulled me into the hotel. I was still so shocked about being here that I let him pull me along. Then he just ran off. What about him?"

"I saw him when I was awake today. I don't remember ever seeing him before, but I must have."

"If you don't believe I am real," the dream Melissa changed the topic, "why do you talk with me and ask these questions?"

"I think you must be the voice of my subconscious," Trent answered. "I keep hoping my id or whatever will explain these crazy dreams."

"And," Trent admitted as he leaned back in his chair and looked at the woman, "it gives me an excuse to pander to my mental illness, which is the only rational way to explain your presence."

The conversation was interrupted by the waiter with a dusty bottle of wine. He poured a sip for each to try. It was delicious and Trent waved for him to leave it.

"I have an idea," the ghost woman said. "Let's not think about what is real or not or talk about things in the past. Let's pretend we're meeting for the first time and enjoy this bottle of wine. A deal?"

Trent laughed. "I've never won an argument with myself, why start now?"

The bottle went fast so they ordered another, then another.

Chapter Five

The same dead flies nestled in the ceiling light now looked like they were riding a merry-go-round as the entire ceiling spun. A bunch of trolls had obviously tied him to a tree and beaten him with two-by-fours before pouring goat pee in his mouth. Trent vaguely remembered Melissa slowly fading away at the table and himself staggering out to his dream truck. He believed there was now a dream tree belonging to his dream neighbor that had a dream gash from his crumpled dream fender. The last image he had was lying in his dream bed and waiting to either fall into another dream sleep or wake into the real world.

Trent tried standing but was forced to plop back into the bed when the floor bucked. There was no doubt about it, he had a horrible hangover. He crawled back under the covers and wouldn't come out even when Al yelled through the door.

"I've got the flu," he feebly cried. "Tell them at work. I can't even get to phone."

His friend stuck a worried face through the door.

"You need anything, some flu medicine, water?"

"No, just some rest," he mumbled through the blanket.

The worried expression wavered to doubt then outright suspicion. Al walked over to the bed and sniffed.

"More like the bottle flu," he declared. "There are enough wine fumes in the air to almost tell the year."

Trent refused to answer, burying himself deeper in the bed.

"Trent," Al said as he sat on the edge of the bed. "Drinking alone is a very bad sign, especially this much. I'm your friend and we need to talk. If you don't think you can talk to me, I know some others trained to help people get through rough spots. I had a couple myself after the divorce."

Trent mumbled.

"What?"

"I wasn't drinking alone."

"I know you didn't go any place last night, Trent, and I didn't hear anyone come or go."

"Who are you, my mom?"

"I'm your friend and I'm worried about you. '

Trent yanked the blanket down and grimaced at the light.

"Jesus!" Al exclaimed when he saw Trent's eyes. "You better close your eyelids before you bleed to death."

"Ha-ha. I'm fine. I'm happy. I didn't drink alone. I just did a stupid thing and drank too much on a work night. Thank you for being there when I needed you, now go and let me recuperate before my brains ooze out of my ears."

"Who'd you drink with?"

Hangovers tended to roughen Trent's temper and shorten his patience.

"I was drinking with Melissa."

Al looked stunned.

"It's all right; I don't believe she is real. It's just another of those nicotine dreams."

"And that's supposed to make me feel better?" asked Al. "Trent, listen to yourself. You're telling me you have a hangover and you smell like a winery from drinking in a dream. Now think a moment. Are those the comments of a rational man?"

"They are the comments of a person in a great deal of pain; one who at any moment could strike out blindly at those around him."

"All right, I'll go, but we're going to have a serious talk when I get back."

"Here, take these with you," Trent snapped after rolling on a stack of comic books. "I picked them up for you while dreaming."

It wasn't until after Trent tossed the comic books to the foot of the bed that he realized what he'd done. The treasure from his dream-within-a-dream was actually in front of him. Al's face took on an extreme look of disbelief.

"Shit," Al whispered softly as if uttering a sacred prayer and sank to the bed. He picked up the top issue that sported the web slinger duking it out with the Sandman and flipped the pages then fanned the rest out like a large deck of cards.

"Trent, where the hell did you get these?"

"I'm a little hazy on it now, but I think it had something to do with hijacking a starship belonging to Vegan looters."

"I'm serious."

"Hey, would I joke about something like this?" Trent replied as loudly as he could without sending fireworks off behind his eyeballs. "I didn't even know I had them until just now. I thought I left them in my dream house."

"Trent," said Al in the low, calm voice one uses when about to talk seriously with a four year old. "Where did you get these? They're worth a lot of money. Somebody will miss them."

"Not in our world," Trent promised.

"Hey, I've got to get going or I'll be late for work. Don't go anywhere until I get back," said Al uneasily as he closely scanned Trent's face. "I'll first take a couple of these down to the book store after work, all right?"

"Sure, sure, just let me sleep."

Trent remained sprawled across his bed for several hours before mustering the strength to stagger to the bathroom.

"Those trolls got you, too, huh?" Trent asked the equally disheveled reflection. He downed three aspirin and then headed back to the bedroom with the gait of a ninety-year-old man just out of hip surgery. He glanced at the buffet as he traveled through the dining room and remembered the dream

Melissa's story. Trent shuffled over and opened the top drawer. The edge of the picture frame was sticking out from under some cloth napkins.

He brushed the napkins out of the way to reveal Melissa sitting on a colorful beach towel. Whoever took the photo had shot into the sun, casting a shadow across most of her face and washing out the background. There was still enough detail to reveal her smile. The face was a slightly fuller version of the one he had been gazing at last night.

Trent wanted to put the photo back in the drawer and shut it. He was surprised at how he felt, as if there was a chance Melissa could be alive on the other side of a dream. He knew if he didn't tear away the brown paper sealing the back of the frame, he'd do it tomorrow, or the day after. He ran his thumbnail around the edge and peeled the paper off to reveal a square of cardboard.

Like an emcee drawing out the tension by pausing before revealing the award winner's name, Trent held the edge of the backing. He knew he was going to be in for a rough time no matter what was there. A blank sheet would verify his reasoning but not his hope. A message would turn his world upside down.

Trent pulled the cardboard away with the same jerk he'd pulled painful bandages off small cuts. He dropped the frame and it crashed to the floor, shattering the glass and sending small pieces spinning across the wood floor. He quickly kneeled by the picture of the pretty young woman and turned it over with shaky hands. There he read, "To my darling, with all my love. Your very own beach bunny."

"No, no." Trent swallowed and pushed himself to his feet while leaning against the edge of the buffet. He tightly gripped the photo as he walked back to the bedroom. For the next half hour, he flipped the photo front to back, back to front—first peering closely at the eyes, the lips, the nose and then at the message.

It wasn't exactly as his dream Melissa quoted, but it was close enough, he thought. Now what? Spend the rest of my life waiting for night so I can visit a woman who'd died in my world almost a decade ago but who now inhabits a dream city? Wait until Al hears this. That should relieve his worried mind.

The hangover had eased its crippling grip by early afternoon. Trent wrapped himself in a blanket and watched soap operas, wondering if the bizarre happenings he was observing on TV weren't also the product of some twisted nicotine dream. If Laura hadn't wanted Phil to know he was the father of Mary, why would she tell Jennifer, Phil's second wife, who was now engaged to Ted, the amnesiac with the face change? Was it because Phil had been hitting on Mary, even though she was going steady with whom he mistakenly thought was his son, James?

Trent felt like he was a kid again, playing sick for a day off from school. All he needed was his mother to safety pin a handkerchief to the inside of his pajama top and apply a thick coating of Vick's Vapor Rub to his chest.

And don't forget the 7-Up, Trent reminded himself. For some reason, his mother considered the soda pop to have a magical, medicinal property. He called up work and left a message for Al to bring him home a twelve-pack of the soda.

Trent kept the photo of Melissa on the arm of the sofa and would reread the inscription about every ten minutes. He became restless when it was time for the talk shows. One program featured vegetarian men who cooked naked and the women who loved them.

He channel surfed to several pet-owner survivors of turtle deaths. According to one of the recovering victims, hundreds of thousands of small turtles were sold across the United States. Unbeknownst to the children and their parents, the pet food sold was completely devoid of any nutritional value. Therefore, the turtles all died within several months. This created a huge reservoir of emotionally crippled Americans who were only now realizing it after intense years of therapy. Support groups were being formed across the country, said one of the guests wearing a Jerry Garcia tie, for people suffering from Dead Terrapin Trauma (DTT).

Trent remembered his pet turtle. He'd bought it at a dollar store along with a kidney-shaped plastic dish. In the middle was a small green plastic island and palm tree. He'd fed the tiny turtle what looked like fly skins—dry, hollow bug shells. Only his turtle hadn't had a chance to starve. It escaped one night and months later his father found its mummified remains in a heating duct, a common urban turtle graveyard.

Al arrived home accompanied by Lorenzo and Rich. Trent was pacing about the house feeling like a trapped animal. Daytime television had done more to make him doubt his sanity than a week's worth of bad dreams.

Trent decided not to tell his friends about the latest wrinkle. He stood at the door trying to appear extra calm and rational. Al passed right on by Trent, headed straight to the refrigerator and pulled out a beer. Lorenzo shrugged when Trent looked at him for an explanation.

"We a bit thirsty?" he asked when Al walked back into the living room.

"I took those comic books down to the used record and book store," Al went straight to the point, "and looked them up in the catalog. Four of the five titles listed pretty hefty prices."

Al paused to take a healthy swig of beer. He stared at the can as if suddenly distracted by the ingredients.

"So...?" Trent prompted him.

"So the fifth one wasn't listed. Spiderman never meets a villain called Skelatoid," he snapped. "But there it was—beautiful artwork, great story line, and excellent printing. Now who'd go to the trouble of counterfeiting a more than forty-five-year-old comic that never existed?"

"Ah, you got me. You're the comic expert."

"No one. No one would do it."

"You wouldn't think so, would you?" was all Trent could think to say under Al's glare. "And yet there it is."

"That's not all."

"Somehow I didn't think so."

61

"Look at this," Al demanded as he shoved an open comic book under Trent's nose.

Trent looked, but all he saw were two pages of panels showing Spiderman slipping out of his costume into nerdy looking clothes and glasses.

Al stuck his finger in front of his friend's face and pointed to a caption block. Trent remained stumped.

"Look, here. 'Peter Prender.' Prender, for God's sake, Prender. Everyone knows it's Parker. Why would someone spend the time and money to print excellent forgeries of Spiderman and make such an obvious screw up?"

"Alternate universe," Lorenzo spoke.

Trent had almost forgotten his other friends were there.

"What?" Al asked as if sure he couldn't have correctly heard Lorenzo's comment.

"Maybe they're from an alternate universe," he repeated, ignoring Al's look—that of someone being stabbed in the back from an unexpected quarter.

"You too?"

"Me what?"

"You also going nuts?"

"I'm just saying what Sherlock Holmes always said, or something like, 'When all the possible explanations have been discarded, then one must consider the impossible.' Not that some mathematicians at Berkeley consider it impossible."

"All right, all right," Al said in an attempt to calm himself. He motioned the others into the kitchen. "Trent, why don't we just start from the beginning and you tell me all about these dreams of yours."

Al opened another beer as the four pulled chairs out from the table and sat as they did when playing euchre or poker.

"Did you bring me 7-Up?"

"What?"

"Did you remember my 7-Up?"

Al didn't answer, selecting instead to stare at his friend as if Trent had a beetle trying to squeeze out of his nose.

"Ah, I guess a Coke will do."

Trent went to the refrigerator and searched through an endless jungle of bowls and recycled margarine tubs full of old and often moldy food. Neither Al nor Trent liked leftovers, yet they could not throw away that remaining piece of tuna fish or dab of potato unless it had first been interred for a couple weeks in the refrigerator. Trent couldn't find a Coke and finally settled for a generic black cherry when it became apparent Al was getting restless.

"Well," he finally began after returning to the table, "It started out..."

Trent took his time, hoping the wealth of details might make the dreams seem more real to his friends. Lorenzo would occasionally interrupt with a question or comment.

"A double action Anaconda Colt .45, huh?" Lorenzo interrupted. "Good gun, stainless steel with a six-inch barrel. It's made to look like the original Colt .44. Used to have one after I got out of the Merchant Marines."

Rich and Al stared at their friend until he shut up.

"So I tore off the back and there was the writing," Trent finally finished. "Not exactly as she said, but close enough."

The epic took almost an hour to recite and his throat was dry.

"Close, but not quite," Lorenzo spoke. "Just like the comic books."

"Or like song lyrics," interjected Rich, who hadn't said much so far.

The rest looked at him questioningly.

"Sam says I'm from an alternate universe and was switched with the Rich from this one," he quoted his wife, STheresa. "I can never get the words right when I sing along with old songs. She says I remember the right words...for a similar song in the other universe. And in the other universe there's a Rich singing these lyrics."

"That's fine, Rich," replied Al with remarkable constraint. "But until you start waking up clutching CDs with these different lyrics, it can only be conjecture."

"There is the possibility that Melissa mentioned writing the note and you forgot," Al said turning to Trent.

"I don't think so. I'm sure I would have remembered that."

"Let me see one of those twenty dollar bills," said Lorenzo.

Trent retrieved his billfold and pulled out five or six of the bills. Lorenzo laid them on the table next to a bill he'd pulled from his pocket. Head bent low, Lorenzo closely scrutinized the bills for several minutes.

"I don't think you better spend any more of these," he advised as he straightened. "Close, but not quite."

"Let me see," Trent said and pulled over the bills. Rich and Al peered over his shoulder. Someone watching their eyes might have surmised they were watching an ant tennis tournament. Their gazes darted back and forth between the bills until Rich thrust his hand over Trent's shoulder and pointed to Andrew Jackson.

"There, on Lorenzo's bill he's looking to the right. On yours he's looking to the left."

Al reached for an odd twenty and held it between himself and the light.

"You're right, it's a phony. But it's so good. It feels real. The printing is perfect. They even have the embedded fibers and watermarks. Why would somebody do something that stupid?"

"Why would somebody call Spiderman, Peter Prender?" asked Lorenzo.

Trent wasn't getting involved. He was the one in direct contact with from where the bills and comics came, but he didn't know what was going on any more than his friends. All he knew was that some Apaches threw a brick at him and he woke with a lump and a chip of adobe. He dreamed he was drinking wine with Melissa and woke with a hangover. It was all impossible and yet it had happened. He felt numb, like his friends were discussing things that were occurring to someone else.

Their discussion went late into the night. Why was Trent the only one they knew of to be having these experiences? Was it really the nicotine patches that did it?

Tomorrow was Saturday and no one had to work. At one point, Rich went for pizza and more beer, with Trent specifically requesting 7-Up. He still felt a bit shaky.

"So who is the Red Man," asked Rich, "and what did you do to piss him off?"

"And who is this person in the motorcycle jacket?" Lorenzo added. "If we were to accept the premise that somehow you are traveling to real, alternate universes, then that means it is possible inhabitants of those worlds can travel here. Why was he looking for you in the hotel but ran when he saw you here?"

Al had been quiet for the past hour, leaning against the wall with a boot resting on an empty chair.

"And are you..." began Al.

Trent was surprised his doubting friend ways joining the "what if?" game.

"... going to try to bring this alternate Melissa back?"

The question was bound to come up, yet Trent had been steering clear of it in his own mind. He had wrestled with Melissa's absence for eight years, and suddenly she was being dangled in front of him like yarn before a cat.

There would be enough difficult questions to answer with her just walking in through the door. Where had she been? Why hadn't she written or called? Did she still love him? Did he still love her? Had they grown too far apart? But to be offered glimpses of Melissa with no solid proof that she was real or that they could get back together, even if they wanted, was more than Trent could handle at the moment. He was afraid to believe. A dream was too slim a thread on which to hang his hopes.

"But if Melissa were dreaming when Trent pulled her back to this world, would that mean she would pop back into her universe when she woke?" wondered Rich.

"I'm beat," Trent interrupted. It was a half-truth. He didn't want to hear his friends discussing Melissa or his dreams like some puzzling car engine problem. "I'm headed to bed."

Normally such a comment would be met with half nods from his friends as they continued their discussion. This time they all stopped to watch Trent stand.

"Sure. See you tomorrow," Rich said.

"Yeah, ah, sleep tight," added Al.

Their eyes followed him as he left the kitchen, staring at him as they might have watched someone boarding a space shuttle or climbing into a deep-sea diving rig. Trent was almost afraid they would follow him into the bedroom and stand around watching as he tried to fall asleep.

He flopped across the bed, suddenly too beat to even undress. Watched pots never boil and anxious dreamers never sleep, he thought. Trent clamped his eyes shut and tried relaxing. He was having the same success falling asleep as he did at seven years of age waiting for Santa. He knew the sooner he fell asleep, the quicker he'd get his presents. Yet he had laid awake all night in a fidgeting fetal position.

After a while, he heard Rich and Lorenzo walk out the door and the steps squeak as Al went upstairs. Still he lay awake. Occasionally, the headlights of cars turning at the corner would flitter through the window and across the walls like lost souls.

Trent didn't know if he'd been asleep a minute or an hour when he was jerked awake by a creaking floorboard. He lay flat on his back, eyes wide open, as alert as if he'd just climbed into bed from witnessing an auto accident. Another board protested under the foot of the intruder. He knew it was an intruder because Al never pussyfooted around. His friend roamed the house, no matter what the hour, like a division of goose-stepping Romanian soldiers.

He knew he was dreaming when the shadow strode into his room and stretched at a toppled angle across his wall that recently hosted the auto beams. Trent was impressed by the graphic design it created, looking like the cover of some fifties pulp mystery. He was also terrified by the horns growing from the shadow figure's head.

Quickly exiting a waterbed is not easy, but Trent did the best he could. Whether the creature was goaded by Trent's scrambling or it was carrying out original intentions, it leaped through the door and dove for the bed. The impact sent a tidal wave racing across the mattress that catapulted Trent the remaining way out and against a dresser.

Batterings were becoming the norm for Trent, and he rolled to his hands and knees by reflex. Water flew everywhere as the creature gored the mattress and bellowed with rage at missing its prey. Trent scrambled across the floor and out the door.

Once in the hallway, Trent leaped to his feet and slammed the door closed. He grabbed a stout captain's chair and slid it under the doorknob. Trent had hardly stepped back when the door shuddered under the creature's attack.

The dream was following an all too familiar script, Trent decided, but at least he wasn't sixty-four floors up. This time he wanted it to end differently. He ran down the hall, into the living room and through the double doors of the den. On the wall was his grandfather's slide-action Winchester Model 12. Lorenzo had told him the shotgun was a collector's item, having been issued as a "trench gun" to American doughboys during WWI.

The bedroom door gave way with a splintering crash. Trent twice dropped the shells he had retrieved from his grandfather's roll top desk. The shells had to be at least twenty years old. He hoped they were still good as he loaded them with trembling fingers.

A locomotive was crossing the first floor of the house, causing the windows to rattle. A small vase danced across an end table and crashed to the floor. It was followed by an old print that had hung on the wall near the gun. The picture depicted a lone wolf on a hill. Down in a snowy valley was a small cabin with smoke drifting from its chimney.

Trent finished loading the shotgun and looked down at the pieces of broken glass vibrating with each pounding footstep. He spun from the desk as the juggernaut roared into the room.

The recoil took him by surprise. Trent hadn't been holding the butt firmly against his shoulder and he felt as if he had been kicked by a horse. The blast caught the creature higher than Trent intended. The creature spun and flipped over a chair before crashing to the floor. The shot took the thing square in the throat.

Ears ringing and shoulder throbbing, Trent stood in a daze over the body. It was too dark to get a good look at it. He walked to a lamp and switched it on before slowly turning. He considered not looking—just walking out of the room without a backward glance. He couldn't. It was like nose blowing; you had to look before throwing the tissue away.

There could be no mistaking what the creature was—a Minotaur. Sprawled on the floor was an extremely large man with a bull's head. There was blood, lots of blood. It drained from the body much like the water from Trent's bed. It also smelled hot and pungent. He felt sick.

"What the hell..."

Trent jumped. He hadn't heard Al running in response to the commotion. His friend had stopped in the doorway with mouth and eyes fighting to see which could open the widest.

"Al, what are you doing in my dream?" Trent yelled in surprise.

His friend didn't answer but leaned weakly against the doorframe in his ratty bathrobe.

"How did you get here?"

Al blinked a couple times and looked up. "What?"

"How did you get in my dream?"

"Your dream? What are you talking about?"

"My dream. You're here in my dream."

He looked at the body and then to Trent. "Are you sure? This doesn't feel like a dream, except for that thing."

"Yes, look out the window. See the hotel?"

Al turned. "No."

"What?" Trent whirled and peered through a window of the den. The hotel should have been towering above the trees—it wasn't.

"I-I don't understand," was all he could think to say.

"Maybe I am dreaming," Al suddenly said, "and you and that thing aren't real."

Al nervously ran his fingers through his hair and stepped gingerly around the body. Trent's eyes fell on a magazine lying next to his reading chair. He picked it up and opened it to a random page featuring an article on solar-powered cars.

"No, look at this," Trent tried speaking without his voice shaking. "I can read this."

Al seemed confused on what to do with the magazine.

"You can't read small type in a dream," Trent reminded him.

"Oh, yeah," Al replied and looked down at the page. "I can read it."

"Which means this thing is in our world," Trent spoke. "And it's made a hell of a mess here and in my bedroom. What do we do with it?"

"What do you mean? We call the police," Al answered. He looked up at his friend and back to the creature's head. "Well—maybe we don't."

Trent walked over to a small Persian rug in front of his reading chair and scooted it back with his foot, out of the way of a rivulet of blood advancing across the maple floor.

They looked at each other and said "Lorenzo" in unison. Al reached into his pocket for his phone to call their friend and Trent sank wearily into the chair. The strain was too much for him. He felt lightheaded. He shut his eyes, leaned back, and slowly brought his breathing under control.

Trent jerked upright when he felt his head start to drop. This was no time to be falling asleep, he thought.

"Al," he yelled. "Where are you?"

There wasn't an answer. Trent stood and was headed to the door when he abruptly stopped. The Minotaur's body was gone without a trace of blood. He dropped to his knees and ran his fingers across the floor. They came away with just dust. Returning to his feet, he walked slowly to the window. Rising above the trees was the hotel. He'd fallen asleep.

Time suddenly seemed important. This was the latest he'd ever fallen asleep and he had no idea if this dream city kept pace with his waking world.

The truck was parked outside with a slight dent from the night before. The motor turned over and immediately fired to life. And if it hadn't, Trent wondered, who would take it to a dream garage? He noticed one yellow light on in the dark silhouette of the Welton house as he backed out of his drive.

The city was as empty as before, lit by street lamps that lent a dim, wine-red cast to the storefronts and shadowed doorways. Trent forced himself not to run after parking the truck. The same waiter was there to greet him and led him to a corner table where Melissa sat.

"I found the note," he blurted immediately, forgetting to say hello or anything else when he looked into her face.

"Great, I'm happy for you," she answered in a cool voice. "I quit using the patch; I'm surprised I'm dreaming this. It's probably the last time."

Her frigid reception and short speech devastated Trent.

"What are you talking about?" Trent asked, bewildered. "I found your message. Even my friends now believe you're real."

"I am," she continued in the colorless voice, "only you're not. I didn't find any carving at the park. I couldn't have. This is all just a dream that I wish I could wake up from. I've been here for hours. Even when I'm sleeping I get stood up."

"Listen, Melissa, I am real. Lorenzo thinks you're from an alternate reality and our worlds, many worlds, touch here. They're almost alike, but not quite. I brought back comic books and money that look real, but they were all slightly different. Close, but not quite. I'm not the Trent you knew, but I'm close. Maybe in your world the carving didn't get completed or maybe it's somewhere else. But you and I are both real and we need to find a way we can work this out."

Trent could barely perceive the slight sideways nod of Melissa's head as she looked down at the table. Her eyes were moist when she looked back up.

"I've got to hand it to myself, I can come up with some pretty good excuses."

"Melissa, how did you feel when you woke up?"

A look of doubt disturbed her composure. "I felt as if I had a hangover."

"You did have a hangover. You know it. And you believe I'm real or you wouldn't be arguing with me."

"I-I don't know."

"Tell me you'll keep wearing the patch until we work this out, please," pleaded Trent. He was gripping her hand tightly. She seemed to find the contact confusing.

"I can't," she cried and pulled her hand away. "This is crazy."

Melissa stood so quickly she knocked her chair over. She turned and ran for the door as several restaurant patrons looked in surprise at the clatter. Trent jumped up and rushed after her. She was beginning to flicker and he made a mad lunge for her arm, grabbing it as she faded from the Crossroads Cafe.

Trent was thrust into a glaring light. He found himself rolling and then falling several feet to the floor. He landed with a thud on an oval throw rug. A ceiling fan lazily spun overhead and Trent watched it move as he got his breath back.

Hearing muffled sobs coming from the bed, Trent propped himself up on his elbows to see Melissa lying face down. He looked about in amazement. It appeared to be daylight in someone's neatly arranged bedroom.

"Where the hell are we?" he gasped.

Melissa's body went taut at Trent's outburst. She slowly turned her head and looked incredulously at her unexpected guest.

"Hi, don't scream. I have a dream and I know how to use it."

"What-t-t, what are you doing here?" she fought to ask.

71

"I believe you brought me along when you woke. I've done it with inanimate objects, but nothing ever living—if you can call this living," he said, rubbing a new bump on his head.

Trent was watching Melissa closely and wearing an inane grin, though he was very nervous. Did she want anything to do with him now that he could prove he was actual flesh and blood?

She continued staring at him, reaching out slowly in a tentative fashion. Her fingertips lightly swept across Trent's cheek.

"I'm awake and I can see and feel you."

"Here, try this," Trent said and made a bold move. He rose to his knees and faced Melissa with only inches between them, then leaned over and pressed his lips against hers. Melissa didn't respond, but as Trent started to make a disappointed retreat, she grabbed him by the shoulder and pulled him into a real kiss.

He heard her door open and turned in time to see a vaguely familiar woman standing with her hands covering her mouth. The hands didn't hold in the scream that pierced the bedroom before the door was slammed shut.

"That was my roommate," said Melissa as she sat up and swung her feet over the side of the bed. "I think she recognized you."

Melissa was on her feet and to the door before Trent could even crawl to his knees. The assorted aches and pains were starting to reach critical mass; almost to the point where Trent believed he didn't have a muscle spared some insult or injury.

Janice was still standing with her hands clamped over her mouth. The woman was in her early thirties with very short hair framing an oval face. She was wearing a sweatshirt and looked as if she had been jogging or to a gym.

"It's all right, Janice. It's not Trent, it's someone who just looks like him."

Melissa gripped her roommate's shoulders and gently shook her until she slowly relaxed and began breathing again.

"Oh, I'm so...I can't believe how much he looks like ..." Janice said between gasps. "I feel so stupid, but he looks so much like Trent. And you've been talking about him lately. I'm sorry for bursting in and...boy, do I feel dumb."

"It's okay, Janice, it's okay. When I first met him I was pretty shocked, myself."

Janice continued looking over Melissa's shoulder at Trent then whispered into her ear, "Just because he looks like Trent doesn't mean he's like him. He's probably way different. Where did you meet him?"

"In a restaurant."

"Well, at least it wasn't a bar."

Janice stepped away from her roommate's embrace and brushed a few stray wisps of hair from her face. She was slowly regaining her color.

"I've got to get going, I, ah, I'm really sorry about this. I'm not really that flaky," Janice said as she backed for the door. "Oh, I'm sorry, my name is Janice."

Trent was fighting to appear calm. The sudden exit from the Crossroads Cafe to Melissa's bedroom was almost as disorienting as any of his other recent experiences. He felt as flustered as Janice looked.

"That's all right, I understand," was all he could think to say.

It appeared to be enough. Janice smiled and made a quick gesture of shaking his hand then turned to the door.

"I'll see you later," she told Melissa and was gone.

Trent let a pent-up breath of air escape and collapsed to the edge of the bed, feeling like a quickly deflating balloon. He didn't have time to draw in the next breath before Melissa spun and confronted him with a scowl.

"Who are you? What is going on?"

He looked at her in puzzlement.

"Who am I? Who do you think I am? Haven't we already cleared this up?"

Melissa crossed her arms and gave him a cold stare.

"I'm not dreaming. This is the real world and in this world, Trent Rowen is dead. I know, I was one of the people to identify the body. I don't know who you are or how you've been able to fuck with my mind, but I want you out of here right now or I'll call the police."

"Melissa, I..."

"I said get out of here."

She walked over to her cell phone on an end table and unplugged it from the charger.

"OK, I'll go, but on one condition."

She began dialing.

"Wait. Just listen a second."

She paused.

"I'll find my friends—Rich, Lorenzo, Al. If I can convince them who I am, will you at least listen to me?"

Melissa's face remained impassive, but he could sense a struggle going on behind her blue eyes.

"If you leave now, I'll talk to them later. I won't promise anything more than that."

"All right. I'll be with them at the New Yorker when you get off work. Please be there. And if for some reason I'm not there—please, Melissa, wear your nicotine patch."

She didn't answer. Trent could see the whole situation was overwhelming her. What she could believe in the Crossroads Cafe wasn't holding up to the light of day. He walked to the door and opened it.

Trent turned to her one last time and said, "This is real. It is happening. I can't explain it. All I know is that we are being offered a second chance most people don't get."

Chapter Six

It took only a few seconds for Trent to orientate himself. Melissa's world appeared to be an exact duplicate of his own. He recognized the apartment building and knew he was about eight blocks from downtown. He didn't have his cell phone and it took him fifteen minutes to find a telephone booth. It was next to the Bear River State Bank. A message flowed across the Bank's electronic sign wishing a high school homecoming victory to the Cardinals, as well as the temperature and time. It was 8:15 a.m.

The telephone number of Midwestern Industries was the same as it was in his own world. Trent drummed his fingers on the metal binder of the telephone book. He decided not to call Al at work and instead turned the pages until he spotted Lorenzo Spasm's name. It was the same number for Lorenzo's land line as in his own world.

Lorenzo was the only one he could think of to contact. Though he hadn't been a high school buddy, being more than ten years older than Trent, Lorenzo had become a close friend. No one was ever quite sure how Lorenzo made a living, but Trent had come to trust the odd assortment of connections and knowledge of his strange friend. Lorenzo would be the one most likely to accept the current situation.

Trent could tell he'd caught his friend's duplicate still sleeping.

"Hello, Lorenzo?"

"Yes?"

"My name is Trent. We have some mutual friends, and they said I should stop by and see you. I was wondering if you were going to be free later this morning."

Trent didn't want to dive right in with the full story until they actually met. His appearance would speak the loudest.

"Is this a joke?"

"Excuse me?"

"You have the same voice as a Trent Rowen who is dead, and you tell me your name is Trent?"

Trent didn't know what to say. It had been eight years. He hadn't expected this Lorenzo to identify his voice after that length of time.

"It's not a joke, but it is a long story. I'd like to meet you at the New Yorker."

Trent wondered if Lorenzo was going to answer after a growing pause of silence.

"Sure, why not," he finally replied. "It's been kind of boring lately. I'll be there at ten."

Lorenzo hung up without saying goodbye, and Trent was left holding a buzzing receiver. That was easy, Trent thought as he pushed open the telephone booth door. Now to kill some time.

He set off to window shop and strolled through the town, trying to detect the differences. There didn't seem to be many. Not that he was all that observant most of the time. There could have been a myriad of small details he wasn't catching, but the big picture looked the same. There was the Pastime Theatre with an afternoon matinee featuring a Disney movie. Across the street was the Green Mill Café, and around the corner was Bane's, a small tavern like the New Yorker.

Trent finally stumbled upon a store that wasn't in his world, at least not any more. He was standing outside Reel's Cigar Store. It had closed when he was seven or eight. In his world, it was now a children's clothing store, but here it still bore the same old, turn-of-the-century style of sign. It had been converted into a curio shop.

In the window was a wooden and stained glass Wurlitzer jukebox and a tray of assorted campaign buttons. One red and white pin read, "Students for Kennedy."

A small placard under the jukebox showed Trent that he was able to read in Melissa's world. The card explained: "WURLITZER MODEL 616A—This model came out in late 1937. This was to become the 'Golden Age' of the jukebox. From then on, the key to art would be a combination of color, light and form. The jukebox was transformed from a mechanical music machine into visual entertainment. Paul Fuller, its designer, decided 'eye appeal' means greater 'play appeal' which spells greater 'profits.'"

The store smelled of incense, old books, and leather. He wandered around looking at the odd assortment of items. He stopped in front of a stuffed mongoose holding a cobra in its teeth. The pair appeared to be real and had been converted into a lamp.

One wall was covered with pictures of young women in long, loose gowns. They leaned against marble banisters overlooking immense, ornate gardens or fairy mountains and seas. The artist was an Atkinson Fox. There were dream-like qualities to the paintings and he silently contemplated them for several minutes.

"Can I help you?"

"No thanks, I'm just looking."

Trent turned around and there was his great aunt Fern. She opened her mouth and covered it with her hand—what was becoming a universal greeting to Trent in this world. Only Fern didn't yell, she just gasped.

"My goodness, you look just like someone I knew. My great nephew, Trent."

"Ah, people always seem to think I look like someone. I must have that kind of face."

"You sound like him too. I can't get over it. Are you any relation to the Rowens? That's the side he took after."

"Not that I know of. I'm not from around here, just visiting."

Fern must have considered it bad manners to explain that his look-alike was dead. She didn't mention the drowning as they chatted about some of the stranger items in the store. He knew his great aunt traveled widely as a young woman. Family members never spoke about it, but as a child, he'd picked up hints and glimpses of raised eyebrows that implied some kind of scandalous behavior occurred in her early years. Of course, Trent thought, his stuffy family of sixty years ago would have been traumatized by a woman smoking or saying "damn."

If the store was any clue, she must have spent those early years in tramp steamers visiting every outpost on the far borders of civilization. He picked up a heavy gold scarab.

"The Egyptians considered it a symbol of resurrection and immortality," she said, still eying Trent with more than mild curiosity. "In real life, they're dung beetles."

He walked on, stroking the webbing of an old snowshoe and then holding up what looked like a marching bandleader's hat.

"That's a shako," Fern volunteered like a tour guide in a museum. "I believe it is from the Franco-Prussian War. It resembles the British busby worn by hussars and artillerymen.

"And that," she said of a wooden carving Trent held, "is a Dahoman fetish believed to aid in curing diseases."

"It's an ugly little creature," said Trent, stroking its beak-like nose.

There was much more to see. He hefted a large, wide blade and looked to Fern for its history.

"Barong," she obliged, "made by the Moros. And this other sword is also by the Moros. They were Muslim Filipinos and expert metal workers. It took Gatling guns and howitzers for Black Jack Henry Pershing and the U.S. Army to subdue them. They were fierce warriors. Many an American soldier was slashed to death after emptying his .38 pistol into a Moro with no apparent effect. That's why the U.S. Army switched to the .45."

The second sword was wavy and had an ivory hilt made to resemble a parrot.

"The waves of the kris represent a snake in motion and the cockatoo symbolizes the ability to fly to realms where danger and death cannot reach," she continued. "The Moros used traditional Malay methods to forge the blades that are just as good as any Toledo swords."

Trent was wondering if Fern had collected these exotic objects for the store or if they were mementos of her earlier wanderings and had been stored in the attic and unused rooms of her sprawling old home.

A row of bottles and jars lined one shelf. Floating in what must have been formaldehyde were bleached frogs, snakes, spiders and even a tapeworm. They appeared to be from some old high school biology classroom. The labels were yellowed with age and the writing faded to where it could barely be read.

He stopped to admire a section of stained glass window when something out of the corner of his eyes caught his attention. He turned and stepped closer to a shelf of small statues, ranging from elephants and past presidents to fat Buddhas. Trent didn't see those figures; his eyes were riveted to a brass sculpture sitting to the back. It was about a foot high and gleamed from under a slight coating of dust.

"Dorga, the Fish-Headed God of Death," Trent exclaimed without thinking.

He reached out and gripped it with both hands. It was as heavy as it looked. Fern watched the familiar stranger lift the idol and run his fingers down its right arm to its opened hand. Embedded in the palm was a small piece of red glass.

"How strange," Fern said softly. "You are the second person this week to recognize that nasty little fellow."

"What?" Trent was almost as startled by Fern's comment as he was at first spying the statue.

"Some man; he was dressed like a motorcyclist. He also seemed surprised to see the idol."

"Black leather jacket, gloves?"

"Yes. This has got me quite curious. Can you tell me where this idol is from? I always thought it was Asian, but a friend of mine who deals in such items doesn't recognize it or the style. It could be Egyptian; they had so many minor deities that it's impossible to know them all. I'd like to know a little of the idol's history. The other man was very tight lipped and left abruptly when I questioned him."

"I, ah, I'm not sure. A friend of mine used to have one as an incense burner in college. It was a surprise seeing one again."

Fern might be over eighty, but she was still sharper than most people half her age. She didn't look like she believed Trent. He felt nervous under her intense scrutiny.

"Well, it's been very interesting visiting your shop," Trent said, "and very educational. But I better get moving; I'm supposed to meet someone in several minutes. Thank you."

He smiled weakly and turned to pick his way through the chaotically placed wares to the front door. Trent relaxed some when he was back in the bright sunshine. Walking through Reel's Cigar store had almost been like entering a dream. Seeing the statue reminded him again how crazy his life had become. The only thing keeping him from losing it was Melissa. He was ready to brave almost anything if it meant winning the Melissa of this world.

Trent was deep in these thoughts when he turned the corner and bumped into someone coming from the other direction. He was left with his mouth half opened for an apology. The other person was Lowell Simons—now back pedaling away with a look of sheer terror on his face.

"No, get away. You're dead. I'm sorry. No, please. I'm sorry."

Trent stood dumbfounded, trying to think of something to say that would calm Simons. He didn't have time. The man turned and bolted back around the corner. Trent remained standing with his mouth opened. He'd been startled by the run-in, but Simons' resulting behavior left Trent feeling confused.

There were just too many people walking around who still remembered the Trent of this world, he thought, not wanting to cause any heart attacks or having to answer involved questions. Though Lorenzo wouldn't show for over an hour, Trent sought sanctuary in a dark corner of the New Yorker.

Trent sipped his morning beer and observed the other patrons. He recognized some of them, though only from meeting them in recent years. They probably never knew the Trent of this world. He did keep his head low when Ken Cheelley stopped briefly for a pack of cigarettes. They'd been in several high school classes together. Ken glanced at the lone figure without interest and left.

Lorenzo arrived at ten a.m. sharp. He gazed quickly around the tavern before ordering a drink and then headed immediately to Trent's table. He paused to examine Trent from head to foot before sitting.

"You bear a remarkable resemblance to Trent Rowen," Lorenzo said before sitting.

"Yeah, so I've been told."

"You also dress like him."

Trent looked down at his clothes in surprise. They appeared to be no different from what everyone else in the bar was wearing.

"I didn't know him that well," Lorenzo continued, "but I remember he also wore a Mickey Mouse wristwatch. You have on the type of steel-toed boots they wear at the Lunar plant. You even have flecks of the fiber on the edge of your cuffs that are used to make the gaskets."

Lorenzo liked to think he was another Sherlock Holmes, Trent thought, so he must be having a ball with this puzzle.

"I talked to Melissa," he said when Trent didn't respond to his observations. "She wouldn't say much, but I could tell she was upset. Confused is more like it. She knew you were going to contact me, but wouldn't tell me why. She is a nice person who shouldn't be jerked around."

Lorenzo spoke calmly, almost soothingly, as if he were trying to put a baby to sleep. It didn't have that effect on Trent, who remembered the last time Lorenzo used that tone. He'd taken a cue stick away from a mean drunk twice his weight and damn near gave the thug a concussion.

"I'm not jerking her around," Trent tried to sound as earnest as he could. "It's a long story and I'm not sure you'd believe me. Remember Chou and the butterfly?"

Lorenzo raised an eyebrow, "Who was dreaming who?"

"Right, it's been kind of like that for me since I began wearing nicotine patches. I started out the first night dreaming about driving down a gravel road and there was this farm sale. A guy was selling ducklings dressed as other kinds of birds..."

It felt odd retelling the story a second time to a second Lorenzo.

"And yes, I know you think the Colt is a good revolver," he said when telling about the dream pawnshop.

"Why do you say that?" asked Lorenzo.

"You mentioned it when I was telling you this part last night. You said 'A double action Anaconda Colt .45, huh? Good gun, stainless steel with a six -inch barrel. It's made to look like the original Colt .44. I used to have one after I got out of the Merchant Marines.'"

Lorenzo raised the eyebrow a second time. "I don't remember ever telling that to anyone. Go on with your story."

Two beers later Trent wrapped up the story with his most recent experience—visiting his Great Aunt Fern's curio shop. Lorenzo leaned back and eyed the teller of this strange tale.

"Let me see your billfold."

"What?"

"Let me see your billfold," Lorenzo repeated.

Trent leaned to the side and pulled out his wallet. Lorenzo laid it down in front of him and one-by-one began pulling out items. He closely examined the several bills of different denominations as well as Trent's driver's license and assorted credit cards. He paused over a recent photo of Trent with his parents, as well as a picture of Trent, Lorenzo, Al, and Rich holding up a half dozen trout.

"That was last year near Decorah," volunteered Trent.

Lorenzo pulled his own wallet out and flipped through the plastic leaves until coming to a similar photo, minus Trent.

"This is certainly hard to believe," admitted Lorenzo, "but I can't imagine why anyone would go to all this trouble to fool Melissa. These appear to be real bills, yet there are subtle differences."

Trent watched Lorenzo drumming his fingers and studying the billfold contents.

"Your tattoo!" exclaimed Trent.

"What?" Lorenzo asked, looking up.

"Your tattoo, it isn't there."

"What are you talking about?"

"The Lorenzo in my world has a tarantula tattooed on the top of his head. He said he got it one night when he was drunk and on shore leave in Hong Kong."

Lorenzo stopped tapping his fingers and squinted at Trent.

"I was on shore leave in Hong Kong once. Even went to a tattoo parlor, but I passed out before the deed was done. And I had been thinking of getting a tarantula. It was my nickname. I didn't even tell my drinking buddies what I planned to have tattooed.

"OK," Lorenzo said as he slid the billfold and contents back over to Trent, "say I believe you. Now what?"

"I need you to help me convince Melissa I am real."

"You want to carry on with this Melissa where you left off with the other?"

"I would at least like the chance to see how we would get along. She obviously loved me—I mean the Trent of this world—very much.'

"Then what? You're dead here. How would you get a job, pay taxes, get married?"

Trent looked down as he finished replacing the contents of his billfold. He spoke slowly.

"I don't know how I know, but I do know that I am here only temporarily."

"What good is that? Melissa lives here."

"There has to be a reason for this all to happen. We were meant to find each other. I've never heard of this happening to anyone else, so it must be extremely rare—"

"Or people are closed mouthed about it," interrupted Lorenzo.

"Yes, that's possible. There are those people at the Crossroads Cafe. They had to come from somewhere. Maybe that's what happens to a lot of missing people. They become lost in these different realities. I'm not doing it naturally by using nicotine patches, so I'm always drawn back when I wake.

"But what I'm trying to say is that maybe it was a coincidence that we both started wearing the patches at the same time, but from there I think we pulled at each other, through our dreams. I feel we are supposed to be together."

"In your world?"

"Yes, it's never been proven Melissa is dead. She could make up some story. Her parents are alive in my world. I think she'd be much happier there.

"Something Rich said last night has been making me think. Since I was dragged along here while I was still asleep, I'm sure I'm going to be waking up in my real world soon. But Melissa is awake right now, which means if I could carry her to my world, she'd stay there."

"I guess it could happen," Lorenzo spoke after drawing a few circles on the wet tabletop. "I'll go with you to talk with Melissa, though I don't know what I—"

"No," shouted Trent, but it was only a muffled echo as he faded and disappeared.

Chapter Seven

Trent sat up in the old stuffed chair, still clutching the glass of beer. His first thought was that he was in his dream house because there was no sign of the Minotaur or its blood. Then the Lorenzo of his own world walked into the room.

"You're back. I guessed you'd fallen asleep when you disappeared. I was surprised. I wouldn't have guessed you actually physically traveled to these dream worlds."

"Damn," Trent almost cried. He hadn't had time to convince Melissa to come with him. His only hope was now she'd continue wearing her nicotine patches and they'd meet again.

"What happened to the Minotaur?" Trent wanted to know as he stiffly stood and rubbed his eyes. He felt like he'd been through a blender.

"I took care of our cowboy while you were off in dream world. He's now going to contribute to some rather vigorous rose bushes. I expect really big blooms next summer."

"What are you doing here? Where's Al?"

"He called me in a minor state of panic. It was the strangest phone call I've ever gotten and that's no small feat. He is now collapsed in a state of near nervous exhaustion."

"Thanks, Lorenzo. I owe you one."

"Any time. It's not often that I'm called to dispose of the body of a mythical creature. I did freeze a tissue sample for a friend of mine who is into genetics. I'm sure he'll find the material amusing.

"It does make me wonder if there are any more of these things around. It might be wise to stay at my house for a while. The next time you might not make it to that old blunderbuss soon enough. We would have Greta and Gertrude to warn us of such unwanted guests."

Greta and Gertrude were Lorenzo's two German shepherd/wolf hybrids. Trent always found them a bit hyper, but he had never considered them intimidating. They were always acting too goofy to seem mean. But then, thought Trent, he'd never seen them around a Minotaur.

"I can't think now," he answered. "Let me soak in a hot bath for a while. I feel pretty grungy. I've got some weird things to tell you."

"Sure thing," said Lorenzo. "I'm going to catch a few extra winks on your sofa. It's been a long night."

Trent lay in the tub feeling totally exhausted. At least he'd felt like he'd gotten some rest when returning from the dream city and Crossroads Cafe. The visit to Melissa's world left him feeling bone weary. He fought off a wave of drowsiness and climbed from the tub. It would do him no good going back to sleep and showing up at the restaurant this time of day. Melissa would still be awake in her own world. He once again prayed she would continue using the patches.

The Trent in the mirror appeared just as trashed.

"Looks like you're having a rough time too," he muttered at the reflection.

He flipped the medicine cabinet door open and reached for the box containing the nicotine patches. What if there had been some accidental contamination introduced to these patches when they were being made, Trent wondered, and that's causing the strange dreams. I could show up at the Crossroads Cafe tonight and it could be packed. How many patches are made with each batch? How large an area are they distributed in? Does every city have its own ghost twin in that dream world?

Maybe the restaurants are franchised like the Hard Rock Cafe, he continued the idle flow of thought as he shaved. I could get a T-shirt reading "Crossroads Cafe—Paris." It would be written in the same art deco lettering as the sign. Now that one would be a party dream restaurant.

Trent decided he looked a little better now that he'd shaved. He noticed the faint circles of previous patch applications scattered about his chest and arms. He rubbed at one and could still feel small amounts of adhesive.

The view outside his bathroom window was soothing in its plainness. There was something about daylight that made the recent occurrences seem remote and unreal. He knew he should feel a little more alarm about being attacked by a man with a bull's head, but he couldn't quite seem to get the energy up.

He sat on the edge of the tub and tried placing his latest experiences in some kind of context. Who was the motorcycle dude? If it is the same person, Trent concluded, he's been to the dream city, my world, and to Melissa s. He knows about Dorga, which means he could have even been there—or from there, Trent realized with a start.

What if he were a pissed-off priest? Picturing the man in his mind, Trent realized the gloves would cover the fish scale tattoos. And when he thought back, the beard looked kind of fake.

Trent found Lorenzo rummaging through the refrigerator.

"Thought you were going to take a nap."

"Couldn't. Too much going on. Where's your garlic?"

"In the butter compartment."

"I should have known."

"Lorenzo, when did you come back to Bear River—10, 11 years ago?"

"About then. It was a couple years before Melissa disappeared. Why?"

"I think I've convinced the Lorenzo of the other world that I'm real."

"You've been to Melissa's world? You met me?"

"Yes, and you're just the same there—pulled a Sherlock Holmes on me. I was just trying to imagine how well he knew the other me before I drowned."

"I've known you since you were a little kid. I hung around with your brother, Bill, though it's been only the last five or six years that I've been hanging out with you and the others."

"It's kind of weird talking to someone you know pretty well and they hardly know you," said Trent. "Though I wasn't aware your nickname used to be Tarantula."

"How'd you know that?" Lorenzo asked in surprise.

"Your alter ego."

"There's something else," Trent continued in a more serious tone of voice. "I'm guessing the dude in the motorcycle jacket is one of Dorga's priests seeking vengeance. It would explain the gloves—to cover the tattoos. They must have traced me here. The Minotaur was sent by them as an assassin."

"Could be," admitted Lorenzo.

"That's not all; I think there is something fishy about my death."

"You do?" Lorenzo was laying the groundwork for an omelet. The ingredients were spread across the table. He looked over his shoulder at Trent. "I'm still listening. Why do you think that?"

"I ran into Lowell Simons when I was there..."

Trent started from the beginning and told of his latest dream journey then backtracked to his encounter.

"It wasn't just surprise. He acted guilty, kept saying how sorry he was, as if he had something to do with my death."

"Not 'your death,'" corrected Lorenzo.

"You know what I mean," continued Trent, refusing to be sidetracked. "I don't know why, but I'm sure he had something to do with it. Why did I make it to the river bank in this world and not there?"

"A few seconds longer in reaction time, a slightly different current," Lorenzo answered. "Why are the Spiderman comics different? They just are."

"You'd know what I mean if you'd have been there. He was really freaked out. How would you react if you ran into someone on the street in broad daylight, a slight acquaintance, who you thought were dead? I'd think I must be mistaken about the death or it was someone who looked like that person. I wouldn't assume it was a ghost and break down blubbering, unless I'd personally killed that person."

"Hmmm."

"Is that all you have to say?"

Lorenzo had paused in his slicing of mushrooms and was staring at the wall in front of him. "Maybe you have a point. If I remember right, Simons seemed quite enamored with Melissa. It wouldn't be the first time someone attempted to get rid of a competing suitor. That leads to other interesting thoughts. I think I'll see where the Simons of our world was when these incidents took place.

"But," Lorenzo pulled himself from his reverie, "there are more immediate matters to consider."

"And those are?"

"Who is the motorcycle dude, who is the Red Man, and who sent your early morning visitor? I'm led to believe that your life depends upon finding these answers. I think the answer lies in this dream city of yours. Tonight I'm going with you."

"With me! How are you going to do that?"

"Simple, darling, you're going to go to sleep with me in your arms," said Lorenzo as he began chopping a green pepper. He looked up at Trent and smiled. "Hey, if you can't sleep with your friends, whom can you sleep with?"

~ * ~

Trent couldn't remember feeling more weary and yet further from sleep. He lay fully clothed in the middle of his den floor. So was Lorenzo—who was also armed.

"Just a little insurance," Lorenzo had said with a grin as he crawled into bed lugging what was once a semi-automatic Colt M-15 rifle and now an automatic M-16. "It's light, easy to buy, and even easier to convert to an automatic."

Lorenzo had disappeared earlier in the day and returned with the rifle as Al was getting up. From there, they met Rich at the New Yorker and Trent related the most recent adventure. Both Al and Rich shook their heads when they heard what Lorenzo proposed to do.

"Do you think you'll actually travel with Trent?" Rich asked.

"I would think so," Lorenzo replied. He was being uncharacteristically brief in his answers.

Al wasn't saying much more. The sight of the Minotaur had obviously unnerved him and he was still in a mild shock from the experience.

"Why don't we all go?" asked Rich. "Yeah, let's all go. I'll tell Theresa we're going hunting."

"Yeah, right," interrupted Trent. "Four men in bed with guns. We might as well invite over my neighbor, Welton, and see what stuff he's recently gotten from the Whip of the Month Club."

"It doesn't seem fair that only Lorenzo gets to go," protested Rich.

Al eyed his friend sourly. "This isn't a game. They're not going camping for the weekend."

"Where are your cigarettes?" Al asked, looking at Rich's empty shirt pocket. "I just noticed you haven't lit one up since we've been here."

"I quit."

"And you're on those patches, aren't you?"

Rich's silence was answer enough.

"You're all crazy," snapped Al as he set down his glass and stood. "This is all crazy."

They watched their friend stomp out of the bar.

"He'll be all right," promised Trent. "You must admit he is right. This is crazy. And if you had seen that Minotaur you might not be in as great of a hurry to go night tripping. Al isn't over the shock yet. Give him time and he'll be back to normal."

"But thanks for wanting to help," Trent said to soften his comments. "Tomorrow is our Sunday afternoon card game. I'll see you then and hopefully Al will be out of his funk."

They left Rich still feeling odd man out as they went to their cars. Trent drove his pickup back to the house and parked it across the street. He noticed Al's car wasn't home yet. His neighbor was raking leaves and Trent waved while walking up the front sidewalk. He was surprised when Welton looked away as if embarrassed.

An hour later, Lorenzo and Trent were on the hard floor, Trent wishing he'd gotten around to repairing the torn waterbed mattress.

"Do you think you're going to need that?" Trent asked of the rifle.

"You never know. I probably should have taken my Ruger Super Redhawk .44 Magnum revolver instead," Lorenzo answered as if discussing what club he was going to use next in golf. "It's only good up to a one hundred yards with the 2X Pentax scope, but it's more likely any problems we face will be at close quarters. Then again, as a carbine, the M-16 is a pretty versatile rifle."

Lorenzo looked over at his friend. "What are you thinking?"

"I'm thinking that if you keep that babbling up, I'll have no trouble going to sleep."

"Good, let me tell you about these nifty new bullets I've found for my .38. During Strasbourg tests on live goats..."

"Wait a minute," said Trent as he rolled to his side and propped himself up on an elbow. "They use live goats to test bullets?"

"Sometimes, or pigs."

"That's disgusting, let's change the subject."

"The Army has used dogs..."

"Live dogs?" Trent couldn't help himself.

"Not for long."

Trent eyed his friend, who innocently returned the critical gaze.

"That's sick. It should be against the law. But we'll discuss the ethical considerations behind my opinion some other time. Right now I want to get back to the Crossroads Cafe and this subject is not conducive to sleep."

"You eat meat, don't you?"

"I said I don't want to discuss it."

"Fine."

"Fine."

"Did you know that in India they eat the brains of live monkeys?"

"Lorenzo, I..." he turned again to his friend, only to see him grinning widely.

"Kind of reminds you of having friends over night during junior high, doesn't it?" laughed Lorenzo.

"Yes, it does," Trent admitted then hit his friend with a pillow.

"Hey, I'm only trying to get you to relax a little. You're never going to get to sleep as tense as you are."

"Thank you, I'm not tense any more. I'm ready to go to sleep now."

Trent shut his eyes and realized that he hadn't been lying; he was feeling more relaxed. Maybe it was just the absurdity of the image of the two of them on the floor with an automatic rifle. Maybe he should have let Rich join them—the more, the merrier.

And what about his neighbor? Trent's thoughts were drifting. Why did he look so sheepish? Was that really Welton in the corset and fishnet stockings walking the dog? Had he also quit smoking lately? There were just too many questions anymore, Trent decided.

Trent was jerked back to alertness when he felt Lorenzo lifting his arm. He opened his eyes to see his friend with a roll of duct tape. He was wrapping it around their wrists.

"I couldn't find my handcuffs," Lorenzo apologized. "Besides, they wouldn't offer skin contact, which might be important."

Several minutes later, Trent was silently cursing Lorenzo. He was wide awake again while his friend softly snored. Trent considered punching

Lorenzo in the side. He hesitated when he realized the benefit of his friend being asleep.

If Lorenzo tagged along while awake, Trent wondered, would that mean he'd stay wherever we wound up unless he was in contact with me when I woke? And by being asleep, did that mean he could return by himself? He thought of his plan to meet Melissa at the Crossroads Cafe, go with her to her world when she woke, and then drag her back awake to this world where she would theoretically stay because she'd been awake when she had crossed over. His thoughts began to muddle.

The transition was so smooth that Trent wasn't aware of the shift until he felt a light breeze tickling his face. He opened his eyes. It was unnaturally dark. Even in the dead of night, there is always some faint light. If there wasn't a street lamp, the stars and moon cast just enough light to see faint images. That wasn't true for wherever he was now. He reached out with his hand and was stopped only a foot above his face by a rough surface that felt like sandstone. Trent was reminded of his connection to Lorenzo when he tried to roll to his side. The movement woke his friend.

"Where are we?" Lorenzo immediately asked.

"I don't know, but there is a very low ceiling,"

Reaching out with his left hand, Trent came in contact with a wall about two feet away.

"Reach out with your right hand and see if you touch anything," he told Lorenzo. "There's a wall on my left."

"Yes, there's a wall over here, too."

Trent's hand was lifted and he could feel his friend peeling off the tape.

"Another fine mess you've gotten us into," Lorenzo said. "At least we won't smother before we wake. I feel a draft."

Trent could hear his traveling companion roll to his stomach and he followed suit.

"Let's crawl a ways and see what happens," Lorenzo spoke, already scooting off down the shaft.

As Trent followed, he wondered what the rough stone floor would do to the tips of his boots and knees of his jeans. He was about to stop for a break when Lorenzo shouted that he could see something. Trent squinted and could just make out what might be a far off pinhole of light. They quickened their pace and the spot steadily grew.

"Damn," Trent swore when he reached the opening.

They found themselves looking across the interior of a massive building. They were about forty feet above the floor.

"I think we're in a ventilation duct," said Lorenzo as he gazed across a scene of barbaric and opulent splendor.

Giant gold and blue columns rose from the marble floor to soar above their heads like the trunks of ancient redwoods. On the ceiling was a huge scarlet cross with flared ends. On one far wall was a fantastic mural of a giant eagle soaring above a city with a beautiful woman clutched tightly in its talons. Another wall depicted an elaborate battle scene between almost naked human warriors and savage, four-armed white apes bearing swords and spears. The human warriors also rode on what looked like giant flying surfboards. The wall to their right showed a gold casket being opened and bright ray of light bursting forth. In the background was a pyramid with a giant eye at its top.

"There is something very familiar about that one mural with the white apes," Lorenzo said with puzzlement in his voice.

Trent wasn't gazing at the murals or watching the tiny figures moving below. His eyes were locked far across the immense temple. Gazing back at them from atop his altar was Dorga, the Fish-Headed God of Death.

"I don't believe this," groaned Trent. "Why are we here?"

Trent's whining drew Lorenzo's attention to the brass statue. He recognized it from Trent's description. Pulling up his rifle, he used the sight as a telescope to examine the idol.

"Hmmm. Interesting," Lorenzo said as he scanned Dorga.

"What's so interesting?" asked Trent sourly. "We're in this crummy temple while Melissa is probably waiting for me at the Crossroads Cafe."

"Relax. We still might wind up there. You snagged those comic books in one world and woke in your dream city. It might happen this time," Lorenzo tried placating his friend. "I was noticing, though, that the gem you described is still missing from the idol's hand. I wonder what became of it."

"It's probably in Dorga's belly where I was before I woke. Or that nasty priest kept it for himself. Who cares? Dorga is not the sort of divine entity I can feel any sympathy for."

"This is a very peculiar structure," Lorenzo changed the subject.

Trent glanced around at the cavernous temple. "What? You don't like the color scheme or is it the naked, fat mutant with the carp head?"

"It's the mishmash of styles. That massive cabinet over there is French Romanesque from the late 1100s. Those pillars are Russian Ornament, after the Byzantine style was modified by the Tartar influence. Then we have Celtic trim along the ceiling and that bronze Sphinx is not Egyptian as you might suspect but Pompeian Ornament. I must admit I am puzzled by the winged steer with the human head. I'll guess Babylonian-Assyrian."

"Great. I'll recommend you as an interior decorator the next time the Shriners are looking to build a club house."

"You might be on to something," Lorenzo answered enigmatically as he stared intently at the mural of the golden casket and bright ray of light.

"And can you tell me what style those white, four-armed apes are from?" Trent asked sarcastically.

"I'd say Barsoomian."

"What?"

Frowning, Trent tore his gaze away from the murals and glanced to the floor below. A clump of ornate furniture covered with colorful silks and furs was centered in the chamber. Several priests reclined on couches and a number of slaves were scrubbing the floors. One slave immediately caught his eye, and Trent leaned forward so suddenly that Lorenzo instinctively grabbed him by the shirt.

"Look down there." Trent was pointing at one female slave chained to a massive wooden post she was forced to drag behind her.

The other slaves were dressed in simple, but clean clothing. The woman Trent pointed out was clothed in rags that barely covered a bruised and dirty body. Even under the grime, Trent recognized the sacrificial slave he'd saved.

"That's the slave woman I told you was about to be sacrificed," Trent explained. "They let her live, but they sure aren't making her life easy."

"These priests appear to be a nasty bunch of leeches," opined Lorenzo. "It's too bad I didn't bring some plastic explosives. We could have taken out Dorga and his evil brood. This is one nest of vipers that shouldn't be allowed to live."

Trent turned and looked at his friend. "You're starting to sound like some 1930s pulp magazine."

"Why not?" smiled Lorenzo. "How often does someone get thrust into a scene like this? We might as well enjoy it."

"Just remember that this may be a dream, but a dream where we can still profusely bleed very easily."

Trent was getting restless, and he began examining their immediate environs. A small ledge several feet below their opening appeared to run the entire way around the temple. It would have even been possible to reach Dorga by it, Trent guessed, if it weren't so visible from the floor. Anyone trying it would be spotted immediately.

He looked over to see Lorenzo playing with a rope ladder that hung over the edge.

"Hey, watch it. We don't want to bring attention to ourselves."

"This is probably for maintenance or cleaning crews," Lorenzo conjectured. "I wonder how long it would take to climb down and back up it?"

"Probably just long enough to get a spear up your butt," Trent answered. "Don't be getting any ideas. Let's just wait this one out."

Trent glanced again at his friend and then in the direction Lorenzo was staring. A priest had stopped near the slave girl and was slapping her. He grabbed her hair and began forcing her face into a bucket of scrub water.

Trent clenched his fists and despite his just-spoken recommendation of non-involvement, wished he had another spear to throw. When several seconds passed and the priest did not pull the woman's head from the water, Trent rose to his knees and rocked back and forth in helplessness. He was considering screaming at the priest to draw his attention from the slave when a bang went off only inches from his ear. The priest let go of the girl and fell to the floor, gripping one leg as he collapsed. Another pop followed and Trent pushed the heels of his hands into his ringing ears.

Lorenzo had fired his M-16 and its blasts, despite what Trent guessed was a noise suppressor at the end of the rifle, were echoing through the temple. Slaves and priests alike stopped what they were doing and looked excitedly about the temple. The screams of the wounded priest soon drew their attention, and half a dozen figures from about the huge room ran to the fallen figure.

"Let's keep low," advised Lorenzo as he dropped to his stomach, though still watching the scene below.

A crowd gathered about the priest and examined his wound. The slave woman took advantage of the distraction and slowly crawled away from the excitement until she was beneath Trent and Lorenzo. It was only then that Trent noticed she was no longer dragging the post.

"Not bad shots, eh?" whispered Lorenzo. "I was certain it would take more than one bullet to break the chain, but it must be pretty soft iron."

"What good is that going to do?" hissed Trent. "They'll just lock her up again."

"Maybe not," he replied and began wiggling the rope ladder.

"What are you doing?" Trent was aghast and looked with worry at the clump of priests.

"We know the priests have it out for the slave woman since she lived and their head man bit the big one. They'll keep their punishment up until she dies from the abuse. You don't want your heroic effort to be in vain, do you?"

Trent peeked over the edge. The woman had just noticed the moving ladder and followed it up with her eyes. Lorenzo leaned over the edge and motioned for her to climb it. She looked suspiciously at her would-be savior then turned when she heard shouts. The wounded priest was relating what led up to the mysterious injury. He had reached the slave's part. When he turned to point her out, he saw only a foot of chain and the wooden post. They looked about and saw her beneath the airshaft—an airshaft with a stranger's head looking over the edge.

Screams of rage broke from the group and several howling priests charged the girl. This sacrilege so soon after the despoiling of Dorga was just too much for them.

That was all it took for the woman to decide the unknown couldn't be worse than the known. She scrambled up the ladder. Another shot rang out and the lead priest tumbled head over heels. This slowed the rest for only a moment.

The woman was almost to the top when the priests reached the wall. An exceptionally large follower of Dorga grabbed the ladder and began wildly swinging it. The woman stopped her climbing and clung desperately to a rung. Lorenzo leaned over and snapped off a shot. The priest released the ladder to grab a bleeding foot. He shrieked and hopped about until he bowled several of his companions to the floor.

Trent reached over the edge to help the woman. She halted, surprised by the appearance of a second person. Her eyes grew large and she gasped, "You! You are the one who did slay Dayd, the high priest."

An arrow clinking against the wall prompted the slave to quickly finish her climb. Lorenzo and Trent pulled her away from the lip of the tunnel as several more arrows clattered about them. After pulling the woman to safety, Lorenzo grabbed the rope ladder and attempted to reel it in. It wouldn't come. Trent stuck his head nervously over the edge and saw several priests holding the ladder while a line of warriors began their climb. They were dressed like the mural's battle scene, in loin clothes and light leather harnesses from which their swords hung.

"Do something, will you?" demanded Trent.

Lorenzo had joined him at the edge. "I hate shooting into a crowd like that, I might kill someone. But I can do something better."

He reached behind his neck and slid a wicked looking knife out from under his jacket collar. It was bent in the middle and looked to be almost a foot and a half long.

"What the hell is that?"

"A Kukri fighting knife," answered Lorenzo as he took his first hack at the ladder. "I got it in Nepal. It might not be as practical as your basic survival knife, but I've found it makes people a lot more nervous."

The lead warrior stopped climbing when he felt the vibrations and looked up. He was about twenty feet off the floor. He looked with worry back at the warriors beneath him and grunted something. One of the priests could clearly be heard ordering him to continue. The warrior looked up again to see Lorenzo's devilish, grinning face peering over the edge. It didn't seem to make the warrior feel any better. He began climbing again, but only half-heartedly.

Lorenzo had to duck several times to avoid arrows, but he didn't stop sawing until the last strand parted and one side of the ladder collapsed. Two warriors shouted, lost their holds, and fell. The lead warrior was again verbally goaded to continue climbing the single knotted rope. Knowing that the other rope was about to go, he instead started scrambling back down. That set off howls of protests. One exceptionally shrill voice was abruptly silenced when the last rope was severed and the warrior dropped—onto the priest.

Lorenzo and Trent retreated from the opening and crawled back to the young woman. She made a tentative move to touch Trent's arm.

"I knew you would come back to save me," she whispered, looking at the object of her salvation with awe.

"Ah, well, it really wasn't me who did the saving this time. My friend, Lorenzo, was the one who shot that priest who had you down in the water."

"Shot?" she said sounding confused. "I saw no arrow."

Lorenzo smiled at Trent's discomfort. The girl was clinging to Trent's arm.

"Not arrows," Trent tried to explain. "Little slugs of iron. My friend's weapon hurls them at very high speeds, enough to go clear through a man on the opposite side of the temple."

She looked with respect at Lorenzo's rifle and then turned back to Trent. "But it was you who killed Dayd, the high priest, and came back to save me once again."

"Yes, I did do that. But it wasn't that much, really. Just a toss of the spear."

Trent was becoming more flustered as he noticed the woman's garb definitely did not do a very good job of covering certain strategic areas. Though her hair was in oily tangles and she was desperately in need of a bath, what showed through still looked good. He had a hard time not following the length of her long legs up to firm hips, tiny waist, and swelling breasts. One nipple peeked through a tear in her wrap.

"We better see if this vent leads somewhere," Lorenzo interrupted Trent's momentary lapse into reverie. "Our boys have reinforcements, and it looks like they're planning to turn us into pin cushions."

More warriors were pouring into the temple and flowing across the floor to below their hideout. They all carried bows. They were also hauling wooden ladders. The woman offered no arguments against crawling into the dark tunnel.

"Do you know where these go?" asked Lorenzo as they began their retreat.

"No," she answered. "I am new to the Temple of Dorga. I was taken prisoner two seasons ago from my village. Since then I have either been kept in the slave pit or released only to do cleaning on the temple floor or in the kitchens and priest quarters.

"My name is Varva," she added.

"I'm sorry," Trent spoke up, embarrassed at his forgetfulness. "I am Trent Rowen and this is Lorenzo Spasm."

They continued in silence for several minutes. They passed the spot where they initially woke, Trent decided, when they came to a T in the tunnel. They stopped to rest.

"I think our friends have joined us," Lorenzo spoke up.

Holding his breath, Trent strained to detect the sounds of pursuit. He could hear the breathing of his companions. Besides that there were the faint echoes of voices.

"We better keep moving," Trent said. "Which way should we go?"

"Let's follow the source of the draft. That's to the right," said Lorenzo.

They ran into two more intersections, each time pausing to feel which way the breeze was blowing. They abruptly came to another opening after taking a third turn. Ten feet below them was what looked like a large bathhouse. Several young women were bathing nude in a marble pool.

"This is where the priests keep their women," whispered Varva. "There is a hallway that leads to the priest's quarters and in turn to an outside garden. If we can reach that, we may be able to escape over the wall."

"I say we wait it out here," advised Trent. "We'll just be asking for trouble if we leave this tunnel. Those women will start screaming and set the guards after us."

"You mean we should wait for dark?" asked the woman.

"Whatever he means," interrupted Lorenzo, "it isn't going to work. Listen."

Trent cocked his head. He could again hear the faint sound of pursuit.

"Here, take this," Lorenzo said as he handed the girl his knife. He reached into another pocket and brought out a tiny handgun.

"And for you, buddy," he said, "take this."

"What is it, a toy?" Trent asked.

Lorenzo passed it to Trent.

"No, it's a Heckler and Kock P7K3 .38. It has a barrel length of only three point eight inches and weighs twenty-six ounces, but it will stop somebody if you can hit them."

Trent looked doubtfully down at the pistol. He didn't want to shoot anyone, and he had just started thinking about the priest. As they crawled through the inky blackness of the vent, Trent had realized he had tossed a spear into a real person. He didn't have time to dwell on it now, but he knew it would come back to haunt him some night in bed. Asshole or not, the priest hadn't been just some dream figure. He had been a real man and Trent had killed him.

"What?" Trent asked when he realized Lorenzo was speaking to him.

"We better get going before they show up," repeated Lorenzo, who was already lowering himself over the edge.

One of the bathers looked up and spotted the three strangers. She screamed and pointed to them, setting off the rest of the women. They splashed wildly to the opposite end of the pool and turned to continue shrieking as they watched the intruders.

Trent almost slipped halfway across on the wet floor. He caught himself on a pillar before running to catch up with his companions. Varva led them down a narrow hallway past dozens of doors. They turned into another hall and finally exited into the garden. They all paused to catch their breath and look about. Stately old trees lorded over the garden and its numerous small pools. Giant black and gold fish flashed in the clear waters. Borders of hedge followed the stone walkways through eruptions of aromatic blooms of every hue.

Trent had a hard time believing that the creators of this beautiful garden were the same ones disemboweling young women. His thoughts were interrupted by the shouts of two soldiers taking a shortcut across the grounds, holding their spears above their heads, and wading in waist-deep flowers as if they were fording a stream.

A cry of anger escaped from Varva, and she launched herself at the first soldier to reach the walkway, going in low and bringing the knife up under his breastplate. By the way the man dropped immediately, Trent guessed she must have reached his heart with that one lethal thrust. The other soldier stopped to lower his spear before stepping onto the path. Varva circled him like a hunting dog keeping just out of the reach of a bear's claws.

Lorenzo was raising his rifle when Varva caught the soldier by surprise. She shifted out of her crouching attack posture and hurled the knife with a powerful underhand throw that began from behind her hip. The knife caught the man in the throat, and he dropped just as quickly as the first soldier.

Lorenzo let out a long, low whistle. "I'd say she has been repressing some built-up hostility."

Trent watched stunned as Varva kneeled to retrieve the knife and wiped it on the dead soldier's clothing. She stood and proudly turned to face her companions.

"That was for what they did to my village. The next I kill will be for myself."

"Yeah, s-s-sure," stuttered Trent. He didn't feel like arguing with Varva after that demonstration.

The three continued across the garden until they reached the foot of the wall. It was over twenty feet high. Lorenzo ran his hands across the stones.

"There's no way to climb this wall," he said. "We'll need to look for a ladder..."

The shouts of more soldiers cut him off. They swarmed into the garden like a nest of angry ants. Trent looked frantically around for another exit. There were none in sight. They instinctively grouped closer together. Varva was once again holding the knife in front of her, and an exceptionally wicked smile played over her clenched teeth.

"This doesn't look good," said Lorenzo as he raised the rifle to his shoulder.

"No shit," snapped Trent.

Varva turned to face her would-be rescuers. "Thank you for letting me die with honor."

Trent didn't have a chance to answer her. He felt the odd and familiar buzzing fill his body. The surrounding landscape began flickering and he impulsively grabbed his companions.

Where the temple gardens had been was now the front room of his dream house. It was as dark as always, only the dim light from the outside streetlights entering by way of the tall, narrow windows. Varva gave a gasp of surprise and backed into Trent.

He maintained a grip on her arm and tried to comfort her. "It's all right. We have traveled to another world."

"This is how-w-w you managed to sneak-k-k into the temple," she fought to speak despite her fright. "You are a wizard who can jump from world to world."

"Do you know of people who can do that?" asked Trent, thinking of the mysterious stranger dressed in leather.

"No," Varva replied as she looked about her in wonder, "but our legends tell us that is how we first arrived on our world—through the doors of our dreams."

He would have liked to question her more on the subject, but was anxious to see if Melissa was at the restaurant.

"Listen, Varva," Trent said as he turned and took both her hands. "I am not a wizard. I have no control over this travel. It happens when I sleep. Right now I am in a hurry to meet someone and I would like your help."

"I would do anything for the one who saved me from the blade of Dorga and has given me my freedom," she replied eagerly.

"I will explain it as we walk there," he promised. "But first we need to find you some better clothing."

Trent led her into his bedroom and rummaged through a closet that seemed to replicate the one in his real house. He handed her a pair of jeans and a flannel shirt. None of his shoes would fit her, so he dug around until he found sandals. It was then that he noticed the condition of her knees. They were badly scraped from crawling in the ventilation shafts.

She followed him out of the bedroom and down the hall to the bathroom. He started the shower and instructed her in the operations of the faucets. He tried not to look as he was exiting the bathroom and she was stepping out of the rags.

Trent found Lorenzo making an inspection of the dream house.

"It's amazing," Lorenzo admitted. "This place is very much like your own home—only there is no upstairs or basement. If I was to hazard a guess, I'd say this whole city is not part of any real world such as the ones your Melissa or Varva inhabit, but an odd microcosm that touches them all. I think this really is a dream city. It's partially the creation of your mind and of others who have tapped into it. It exists everywhere and nowhere. I'd even bet that H.P. Lovecraft and Edgar Allen Poe visited here."

Trent's thoughts had also wandered down such strange paths, but he had retreated in the face of such outlandish ideas. Hearing them voiced by Lorenzo didn't make them sound any saner. They both walked to a window and gazed at the hotel rising from above the trees, examining the scene for several minutes in silence.

"I am ready," Varva said from behind them.

Trent turned and was surprised even though he expected to no longer see a ragged barbarian woman. Instead there stood an ordinary looking, though beautiful, young woman dressed casually in jeans and a flannel shirt. Her hair was washed and Trent was left wondering how she managed to untangle it in such a short time. He saw that she had slipped the knife into the front of her jeans. She smiled when she noticed both men staring at her.

"It is funny," Varva laughed. "I am more used to men looking at me like that when I am less clothed."

Trent smiled back, still amazed at the transformation. She looked like a college student taking the weekend off for camping.

"Well, shall we be off?" called Lorenzo over his shoulder as he walked out the front door. The other two followed and they entered the dream city's night.

They went on foot. Trent guessed his truck was still parked outside the Crossroads Cafe. He tried outlining his past adventures to Varva. She took it very well when he explained Melissa. Trent had worried the woman was developing a crush on him, and she would become upset at the mention of another woman. He didn't want to anger someone so handy with a blade.

Varva acted a bit disappointed but also touched at Trent's lengthy mourning. She walked a little more warily when he described the mysterious creature that had chased him through the hotel. Lorenzo had never let down his guard. He scanned every shadow and doorway.

Varva was the first to hear the faint sound of claws clicking down a side street. She whirled into a crouch to face the creature with her blade drawn. Trent turned to see what looked like a wolf madly dashing down the middle of the street. He whipped out his pistol only to have Lorenzo touch his arm.

"Don't shoot wildly," Lorenzo snapped, though he held his rifle ready to fire.

Trent was about to panic. The creature was eating up the distance between them. Lorenzo unexpectedly lowered his rifle and stepped in front of a surprised Varva.

"It's just a dog," Lorenzo said as the creature lunged at his face and began wildly licking him.

"Whoa, boy. Yeah, that's a good dog. Settle down," he laughed as the dog danced around him making frantic yelps. "You look like you're certainly glad to see us. I could tell by the way you were running that you were happy to see us."

Trent could now see that it was a large German shepherd. Its tail was wildly beating against Trent's and Varva's legs. It turned its attentions briefly from Lorenzo and tried licking the other two in the face. Varva pushed it away, still gripping the knife nervously. He could tell it was taking all of her self- control not to stick it.

"He won't hurt you," Lorenzo told her. "He is just excited to see us. I wonder how he got here."

Trent pulled the dog away when it tried to jump on Varva again.

"Haven't you ever seen a dog?" he asked.

"Yes," she replied with just a trace of a quiver in her voice, "but never one so large."

Lorenzo was finally getting the animal calmed down. He was on his knees scratching the dog behind its ears and whispering to it.

"Come here," Lorenzo said to the woman. "Make friends."

He reached out and took her hand and placed it on the dog's head. The German shepherd looked up and licked Varva's wrist. Varva braced herself and began hesitantly petting it. She slowly relaxed and even smiled.

"Now what's a dog doing here?" Lorenzo repeated.

"Dogs dream," offered Trent. "Maybe it got here like the rest of us."

"Or maybe it was in bed with someone who slipped over," added Lorenzo.

"I guess it can come with us," Trent said to his friend, knowing he was saying the obvious. A dog lover like Lorenzo was not going to leave a German shepherd lost in this world. He was afraid it was going to be a crowded floor when they returned.

Trent was anxious to get to the restaurant and set off at a faster pace. The others followed. Varva caught up and walked on his left side. She hadn't returned the knife to her jeans.

"This is certainly a strange world," she said to Trent. "The lights are very strange and no one is about."

"There are a few people around," he answered. "Now and then you'll see people several blocks away. Around six or eight customers are always in the restaurant."

They continued talking as they crossed the town. Varva was overflowing with questions. He tried answering them as best he could or had Lorenzo fill in details.

He was getting more nervous as they neared the Crossroads Cafe. Had Melissa continued wearing the nicotine patches? Would she be there? Had she spoken to the Lorenzo of her world? Did she now believe he was real? Would she want to return with him?

Trent stopped outside the window and looked between the letters into the cafe. In a dark far corner was somebody who might be Melissa. He took a deep breath and was preparing to enter when Lorenzo called for him to stop.

"Hide the weapons if you don't want them confiscated." he advised. "Mine is too big so I'm sure I'll have to check it in."

The band was playing "Tuxedo Junction" when they entered. The same waiter magically appeared and motioned for Lorenzo's M-16.

"Thank you sir, I'll put it with the other rifle."

Lorenzo looked puzzled at the comment and continued following Trent and Varva across the room. Amazingly enough, the waiter hadn't said a word about the dog quietly trailing them.

Trent stopped. There were two people at the table. The woman's back was to Trent and the man was hidden in the shadows. Still, the woman had Melissa's hair.

"What are you waiting for?" Varva whispered in his ear. "Is that your woman?"

"I'm not sure"

"You will not find out standing here," she whispered again and gave Trent a shove that sent him stumbling forward.

The noise caught the woman's attention and she slowly turned. It was Melissa. She stood and waited for Trent to reach her table. He felt as if the room's temperature had dropped ten degrees. He nervously licked his lips and wondered what to say. He didn't have to say anything. She stepped forward and embraced Trent in a firm hug.

"I was afraid you wouldn't come," she whispered. "I was afraid the patches didn't work anymore or I'd scared you away."

"Not on your life," Trent answered in a strained voice. He found his throat had tightened. When Melissa stepped back, he saw that her eyes were also watering.

Lorenzo and Varva remained a few steps back and a confused look passed over Melissa's face when she noticed Lorenzo. She turned to the man in the corner. He stood and stepped from the shadows. It was another Lorenzo.

"You brought him too,' laughed Trent.

"It wasn't my idea," Melissa replied. "He wouldn't take no for an answer. He duct taped himself to me and brought along a big gun."

The waiter's comment now made sense to Trent. He saw Melissa inspecting Varva and quickly introduced the two. Varva looked back and forth in wonder at the two Lorenzos. Trent had explained recent events as best he could to Varva in the short amount of time they had while walking. She still looked confused.

"I guess we don't need an introduction," said Melissa's Lorenzo to his twin. He turned to Trent. "I knew you were telling the truth when you vanished at the bar. It took a while to convince Melissa. Then she dragged me down to the park and had me inspecting tree trunks."

"I found a small heart carved into the stump of an elm tree that had been cut down," Melissa interrupted as she squeezed Trent's hand. "It was hard to read, but I could make out your name. That was enough for me.'

A couple had taken the stage, with the attractive woman immediately launching into a solo. She had the appearance of someone who had been plucked from the 1930s, but the slinky silk dress was sexy in any age. The man wore the bright red of a Canadian Mounted Police. The woman's bright and soaring voice glided eerily through the shadowy cafe like a radiant butterfly, accompanied by the additional sound of violins.

Lorenzo shook his head. "I love that song."

Trent, distracted by Melissa, halfheartedly asked, "What?"

"'The Breeze and I,'" replied Lorenzo.

"Do you think they'll sing 'Indian Love Song?'" the other Lorenzo asked.

Both Melissa and Trent tore their glances away from each other to look at their respective Lorenzos in puzzlement.

"What?" Trent asked again.

"They look like Jeanette MacDonald and Nelson Eddy clones," one of the Lorenzos explained. "And she even sounds like McDonald. Don't you watch those old musicals on cable?"

The waiter returned and was preparing to pull two of the small tables together for the group when a Lorenzo spoke up, "That's all right. Myself and I thought we'd do a little exploring. It's not often we have a chance to visit a dream world, as well as getting to know ourselves better."

The other Lorenzo looked to Varva. "You are welcome to join us."

She flashed a thankful smile and nodded her head, appearing to understand why they were wanting to leave the two alone for a while. The three humans and the dog retraced their steps to the front door where the waiter returned the two rifles.

Neither Trent nor Melissa spoke. They sat on opposite sides of the table and stared at each other. The waiter dropped off an unordered bottle of wine. The singers were performing "Beyond the Blue Horizon."

"Do you think we should drink that?" Melissa finally spoke.

"Why not? It was the wine that finally started me believing you might be real."

"It's still hard to believe. Not that I don't," she quickly added. "But this restaurant, two Lorenzos, and you—it's crazy. Janice would lock me up if I told her about this."

Trent didn't answer. He was content enough watching Melissa's face and listening to her speak. She smiled at his total concentration.

"What are we going to do?" she asked.

"Do?"

"Yes, do? Do we keeping using nicotine patches for the rest of our lives and meet only at night?"

"Ah, I was thinking you might want to come back with me," he answered.

"To your world?"

"Yes, wouldn't that work?"

"Why not my world?"

"Well …" Trent began, "I'm dead in your world. It would be hard for me to come back when there's a body. In my world, you're only missing. Your parents are also still alive in my world."

"And how would I explain my eight-year absence?"

Trent tried reading Melissa's face. Was she having cold feet? His world seemed the logical choice.

"We could say you were in an accident and had amnesia and that you finally regained your memory," Trent offered.

"Does that sound plausible?"

"Well, all I know is that it happens all the time on daytime TV."

Melissa wrinkled her nose and Trent caught his breath at the familiar expression he hadn't seen for eight years.

"Since when have you been watching soap operas? My Trent couldn't stand them."

"They get a bum rap," Trent retorted. "Daytime TV drama presents an existential view of modern life, detailing the subtleties and vulgarities of the American cultural fabric which we—?

"Cut the crap."

They both grinned. They had fallen into their old pattern of banter.

"Since I stayed home a couple days ago because of a hangover," he explained. "Jim, or was it Robert, was a C.I.A. agent who received a head injury resulting in amnesia. He came back under an assumed identity and for years was not aware that his neighbor was really his wife."

"Why didn't she tell him?"

"She didn't know."

"Didn't she get out much?"

"He had plastic surgery so she didn't recognize him," Trent explained.

"Oh, that makes sense. It happens all the time."

"So, what about my world?"

"I'll have to think about it. I would be leaving friends behind. What about Janice? What would I tell her?"

"Tell her you're going on a long trip."

Trent slowly opened the bottle of wine to give himself more time to think. He cautiously filled two glasses and handed one to Melissa.

"Why don't you come for a visit and see how you like it?"

"For a visit?"

"Yeah, a visit. Don't ask how I know; it's like a dream where you just know certain things. If I carry you back when you've been sleeping, you'll be drawn back to your own world when you awaken. We could do that now.

"And if you liked it there, I'd have to be taken to your world after falling asleep—just like that last time. Then you'd be awake when I brought you back to my world and would stay there—I hope."

Melissa looked confused.

"I know I'm not explaining it very well but trust me," Trent pleaded.

"OK."

"OK?"

"Yes, all right. I'd like to visit and maybe see my parents. Not up close, I wouldn't want them to know about me unless I decided to stay."

Trent felt relieved. At least she was going to consider it. To have found Melissa after all this time and then face the possibility that it might not work was almost more than he could stand. The whole crazy week would have driven him mad if it weren't for Melissa.

"It's funny how we seem to be taking all this for granted," said Trent after sampling the wine.

Melissa took a sip and said, "Humans are versatile. Expose a member of an isolated, primitive culture to modern technology and they'll soon be using iPads, motorboats, and chain saws.

"There's one problem. I have to take Lorenzo back to my world," Melissa pointed out.

"Was he asleep when you jumped here?"

"He was snoring like you wouldn't believe," replied Melissa.

"Then don't worry about him. He'll pop back by himself."

"Are you sure? He hasn't been using a nicotine patch."

Trent frowned and stared at his wine glass. He was pretty sure Lorenzo could get back on his own, but he had found during the last week that there were no certainties. He hated waiting another night to bring Melissa back to his world. Hell, he thought, he hated to let her out of his sight for five minutes.

"If that's the case, he should be here right now," Trent said. "He needs to stay close in case you start flickering. There are only a couple second's warning."

Melissa nodded in agreement. "Maybe we should look for them."

Trent couldn't help himself when they stood and she walked around the table. He took her into his arms and for a second she fiercely returned his kiss.

He was amazed at how right it felt—the smell of her perfume, the way his arms fit around her, how they kissed. There were always little differences that didn't fit with the women that came after Melissa. They were like pieces from the wrong puzzle.

She gave a flustered laugh and pulled away.

"That's not fair," she said. "Keep that up and you'll have me talked into anything."

He pulled her back.

"No, you big lug. There will be time for that later when we have time alone."

The waiter approached them as they reached the door.

"Sir, your handgun."

He held out the .45 Trent had taken from the pawnshop. Trent accepted it as Melissa watched on with a questioning look.

I'll explain later," he said then turned back to the waiter. "Do I ever have to pay?"

"I have been putting it on your tab, sir."

"My tab?"

"That is correct."

"I didn't even know I had a tab."

"You've had one for quite some time."

Trent shrugged and pulled out his billfold. He handed over three of the strange twenty dollar bills. "Keep the change."

The two paused outside the restaurant. Trent was suddenly wondering if this was a good idea.

"Maybe we should wait here for them," he told Melissa. "I have no idea where they are."

"Why don't we try the hotel? I've been dying for a visit ever since I first spotted it."

Trent looked nervously up and down the empty street. He shoved his hands into his pocket and realized he had two pistols—Lorenzo's small gun and the .45.

"I don't know if that would be a good idea," he said. "I had a bad experience there a couple nights ago."

"What kind of bad experience?" she wanted to know.

"Somebody or something tried killing me. I think the Crossroads Cafe is like a sanctuary and the rest of the city is inhabited by very strange people."

Melissa stared intently into Trent's face then uneasily glanced about. Trent was about to suggest they return to the cafe when the city's unnatural silence was shattered by the sound of gunfire. Melissa grabbed Trent's arm and they both stepped back against the door. The shots were coming from at least two blocks away.

"Sounds like someone is in trouble," he said.

Trent nervously rubbed the handle of the .45 then made up his mind.

"Go back into the restaurant and stay there until I return. I'm going to see what's wrong."

"What?" she said and tightened her grip on his arm. "You're not going anywhere without me."

"Please, Melissa. You haven't seen some of the strange things I have. It's dangerous out there."

114

"OK, I'll live in your world. Just don't leave me," she pleaded. "I just realized that I don't want to let you out of my sight again. Let me go with you, and I'll go to your world."

"Melissa, your promise won't do me any good if you're dead."

"I don't care. I'm going with you."

Trent had seen that determined look before and knew there was no arguing. He looked down the street in the direction of the gunfire then turned back to Melissa.

"All right, but take this." He passed her the small handgun given to him by Lorenzo. "Here's the safety."

He grabbed her arm and began running down the street before she could protest.

They paused at the end of the block, trying to decide if they should go straight or turn. Another round of gunfire made Trent decide to continue one more block before turning. Trent stopped at the next corner and listened for further sounds of combat.

The dark, red shadows had taken on a more sinister quality. A squalid brick building looming over them had a flickering yellow neon sign in a window that read, "COLD BE R." A stained curtain behind the sign hid the interior.

It was the dog's barking that led Trent ahead.

Halfway down the block was an alley. Trent stepped into its entrance and fanned the .45 in a one hundred eighty degree arch. The alley was empty, but the barking echoed from the opposite end. He noticed Melissa was holding her arms bent, gun pointed straight up, just like on TV.

"I took a self-defense course," she replied when she observed his expression.

"And the proper way to hold a pistol is like this," Melissa corrected his grip.

Their discussion on the finer points of gunmanship were interrupted by more gunfire. They set off jogging down the alley. The deeper shadows made Trent even more nervous. Trent dropped to his knees near the end of the alley behind a pile of rubbish. He motioned for Melissa to do the same.

Across the street was a large vacant lot. It was strewn with junk cars and trucks. He searched the gloom for any sign of life and detected motion near an ancient dump truck. He peered more intently and was rewarded with the sudden flash of metal.

Varva leaped from the battered shell of a bus and swung her blade, cutting through a moving shadow Trent couldn't quite discern. She followed the wicked slash with a victory cry that sent a cold shiver up his spine.

"Thank God she's on our side," whispered Trent.

The sound of Melissa's shoe soles spinning on the gritty street caused Trent to look over his shoulder. He was in time to see Melissa swing up her gun and flames spit from the barrel. She fired three times into the deep shadows, and the explosions were followed by the sound of a heavy body collapsing into a pile of rubbish.

"What the hell was that?" he asked hoarsely. The unexpected gunfire sent his heart racing.

"I-I-I don't know for sure. But it was getting ready to throw a knife."

Trent could hear the trembling in Melissa's voice, and he put his arm protectively around her.

"Good shooting," Trent said as he sought to make out the fallen form half hidden in a jumble of cardboard boxes. "Cover me."

Trent scooted across the alley, trying to keep a low profile and kept his gun pointed at the body. He decided that he must be getting hardened by the recent experiences. He didn't flinch when he saw that the body was clothed in a Pepsi T-shirt and jogging pants and had the head of a dog. Blood was seeping from its nose and the eyes showed only white.

"Trent, is that you?" yelled a voice from the junk autos.

"Yes. Melissa's with me," he shouted back when he returned to her side.

"I thought so," a Lorenzo replied. "I recognized the sound of a Heckler and Kock. Stay where you are, we're coming your way."

Out from the autos came four human figures and a dog—one too many!

Trent cursed and raised his gun. There wasn't enough light to clearly identify any of them. He aimed at the figure to the far right that was just catching up with the main group.

It was happening too fast. Trent knew if he waited too long, a friend could be dead in seconds from a knife in the back. One would be just as dead if he chose wrong. He took a breath and fired at the figure in the middle and to the rear. It was a miss. A trickle of sweat rolled down his forehead despite the chill of the night. He aimed the gun lower and fired again. Another miss. He took another deep breath, tried to relax and slowly squeezed the trigger. The thing stumbled and fell.

"What are you doing?' cried Melissa as she grabbed his arm. The remaining three runners crouched and spread out.

Trent let the hand holding the gun drop to his side. He felt weak and leaned against the brick wall. The dog reached them first and danced around the pair. Trent put a trembling hand on its head.

"For a second I thought you were shooting at us," gasped one of the Lorenzos. They were all breathing heavily from the run. "When I heard something fall, I turned and saw you'd nailed one of those creatures. Good shooting."

"I didn't even notice," Melissa said. "It was too dark to make out anything. How did you know which one to shoot?"

"I've seen Lorenzo run before. He runs like he has a cob up his butt," Trent explained. "There were two running like that. Another was running as if they had on too big of sandals—that would be Varva. That left an odd 'It' out."

"That's not a lot to go on when it comes to shooting someone," said a Lorenzo.

"Tell me about it," Trent agreed. He pushed himself away from the wall. "What the hell are those things?"

"I'm wondering if they're from the same place our Minotaur came from," said one who might be Trent's Lorenzo. "They looked like they stepped out of the Egyptian Book of The Dead. This one here could easily be Anubis, the jackal-headed guide of the dead."

"That would mean the one Varva took out could be Shebui, Lion-Headed God of the South Wind," the other Lorenzo said.

"Or Nefer Tem or the lion god, Aker. There were a lot of lion-headed gods and goddesses. Each district in Egypt had its own pack of gods, and they were always being confused with similar gods of other districts. There was even Bast, the cat-headed goddess."

Trent decided the last speaker was his Lorenzo and noted the blue shirt he wore. The other Lorenzo was wearing black.

"They are dream weavers," spoke up Varva. "Our legends tell us they inhabit the dream worlds and net lost souls. Dorga was a dream weaver who escaped to our world."

"They sound like cockroaches under a refrigerator," Trent decided. He turned to Melissa's Lorenzo. "Do you mind if I call you Spasm and my frien Lorenzo? It would lessen the confusion."

"No trouble," he answered.

Varva walked over to the fallen creature shot by Melissa and kneeled to wipe her blade across its shirt.

"This one is a brother to Dorga," she said before spiting on the corpse.

Melissa watched in fascination.

"It's a long story," Trent said when she glanced at him, "but needless to say, she isn't chummy with whatever these things are."

"I think we should head back to the restaurant," Trent said to the rest of the crew. "I'd feel safer there."

"Me too," agreed Melissa.

"All right. How about me taking point and you covering the rear?" Lorenzo asked Spasm.

"No trouble."

They retraced their steps as quietly as they could. Trent expected the silence to be ended any time by gunfire or a shout. He wished he had a rifle instead of the handgun. The pistol was too difficult to aim. He knew it was just luck that he had managed to hit the creature and not one of the others by mistake.

They reached the street and turned to the Crossroads Cafe. Trent could see a faint light three blocks away coming from its window. He also saw several figures scatter into the shadows at the appearance of the humans.

"I think we are going to have a welcoming party," Lorenzo spoke over his shoulder. "If I'm not mistaken, I just spotted the ibis-headed Thoth, and Ra, the Hawk-Headed God of the Sun."

"Well, you know what they say, gods of a feather..." Spasm said from the back. "And by the way, I think the ram-headed god Khnemu and crocodile-headed god Sebek are coming from behind with several of their friends."

The group closed its ranks in front of a bar bearing a yellow neon beer sign.

"We can probably make it," Spasm said, "but..."

"... we're going to have to take out a lot of these beasties," continued Lorenzo, "and it would be best if we didn't leave a blood bath the first time we visited. For all we know...'

"... they might not be that bad. We could have just gotten off on the wrong foot with them," concluded Spasm.

Both of the Lorenzos looked at the nearby bar and then to each other.

"Right, I'll go first this time," said Spasm.

Varva closed the distance between herself and Melissa and Trent.

"They have been speaking this way since we left the inn," she whispered. "It is very annoying."

"I hope not too annoying," Trent whispered back, thinking of the creature and two soldiers she'd disemboweled.

Varva laughed and swung the blade up. "No, not that annoying."

Spasm began pulling the door open while Lorenzo continued watching the street. Trent forced himself to relax his trigger finger before he fired the pistol by mistake. Spasm took two steps back and held the door wide open. Trent looked over Spasm's shoulder into a smoke-filled tavern lit only by a number of beer signs scattered on the walls and candles on the tables.

"Hold the door," he told Trent and stepped in to scan the room.

There were several figures sitting at the bar and another half dozen scattered among the tables. None of them appeared to have animal heads. A short, fat bartender looked at the open door with only mild curiosity before going back to wiping the counter.

"Defecate or get off the pot," Lorenzo yelled in to his twin. "The natives are getting restless out here."

"Follow me," Spasm answered simply.

Trent led them to a corner table as the patrons and bartender continued to ignore the new party. He was surprised no one questioned their weapons until he noticed several others in the bar packing heat in one form or another.

Two men in a booth wore roughly cut leather and had two spears leaning against the wall next to cue sticks. The spearheads looked to be made of copper or bronze. A lone figure at the bar, dressed in a soiled white suit, carried an old Thompson machine gun.

"Nice place," Melissa whispered to Trent, "Come here often?"

"It grows on you," he replied. "I think we have to order at the bar. Anyone thirsty?"

"I would like some ale," Varva answered quickly.

He raised his eyebrows at the Lorenzos.

"We'll have a pitcher," Spasm spoke for the two.

Melissa looked at the others in surprise then shook her head as if to clear it. She laid the pistol on the table and leaned back.

"Sure, I'll share a pitcher of beer. What else is there to do in a nightmare? See if they have a light."

Trent walked up to counter. He felt like he had wandered into a biker bar while wearing a Honda T-shirt.

"Hi," he greeted the bartender who returned Trent's gaze without answering.

"Ah, what do you have on tap?"

"No tap, just bottles."

"Okay, what do you have in bottles?"

"Bud, Bud Light, PBR, Old Milwaukee, Hamm's, Kalona Classic and Dubuque Star."

"All right, Dubuque Star. Didn't think they brewed it anymore."

The bartender continued his refrain from idle chatter.

"Let's see, I'll have four Dubuque Stars and a Bud Light."

Trent looked about the tavern while he waited for the bartender to retrieve the drinks. Everyone at Trent's table appeared to be watching him with trepidation. He smiled and waved. Only Varva returned it.

"That'll be twenty-two dollars," the bartender spoke.

Trent pulled a twenty and a ten out of his wallet. The bartender held the twenty up to better lighting, snapped it once, and seemed satisfied. He brought back the change and Trent stuffed it in his jacket pocket, wondering what kind of silly money he'd received this time.

"Sorry, no pitchers," Trent apologized as he set the bottles down.

"So, what's up?" quizzed Spasm.

"Don't ask me. The bartender is about as talkative as a Dorga with a dead priest in his belly."

"'A woman drove me to drink, and I never even had the courtesy to thank her,'" saluted Lorenzo as he hoisted his beer. "Or so said W. C. Fields."

"He also said," added Spasm, "'I always keep a supply of stimulant handy in case I see a snake—which I also keep handy.'"

"Or as G. K. Chesterton said..." continued Lorenzo.

"'... no animal ever invented anything so bad as drunkenness—or so good as drink,'" Spasm completed the quote.

"Ah-h-h-h," Trent groaned. "Enough, enough, or I'll be forced to seek companionship with those dog-faced boys."

Trent glanced at Varva and found she had already drained her bottle. She returned his look and smiled.

"Good ale, though weak. I would like more. Killing loathsome creatures is thirsty work," Varva said.

"I'll get the next round," volunteered Spasm.

Melissa opened her mouth to protest, having only taken several swallows from her own bottle. Spasm was gone before she could speak.

"Varva," Trent spoke softly, wanting to get one problem out of the way. "I don't know when or if I can get you back to your world. I told you I am no wizard and have no control of this dream traveling."

"Is your own world like this?" she motioned with her hand, taking in the whole of the bar.

"No, we have normal days and nights. I call this a dream world. I don't think it is quite real."

"Though we have a few bars that might fit in this dream city," Lorenzo interjected.

"If I were to come to your world, would I be a slave there?"

"No," Trent laughed, "we don't have slaves where I live."

"But you can still expect to make only three-fourths pay of what a man does for doing the same thing," Melissa interjected.

Varva looked perplexed.

"Never mind, you'll find out if you go there," she added and then asked, "Just where do you come from, Varva, and where did you learn to use a knife like that?"

Spasm returned and distributed more drinks. "I guess this is as good of place as any to wait for the return trip. I think we ought to decide where we are going so we know who to sit by. Are you going with Trent or to our own world, Melissa?"

"I told Trent I'd visit his world. Since I was asleep when I came here, Trent thinks I will ultimately return home like he did. He thinks you will automatically return since you were also sleeping."

"I think I'd like to see the whole thing through and tag along, if that's all right," Spasm said.

"Of course," said Trent, "it really depends upon who wakes first. If Lorenzo or I go first, we can all circle hands and see if we make it to my world. But if Spasm or Melissa start flickering first, we'd all travel to her world."

"Let's go with whoever flickers first," offered Lorenzo. "No matter what, everyone but Varva will theoretically return to their real world sooner or later."

"That's fine with me," Spasm said. He was followed by the rest agreeing. "That means when anyone starts feeling they are going, yell, and we'll all link hands."

"But what about you?" Melissa returned her attention to Varva. "What do you want to do?"

Varva looked hesitantly at Melissa and Trent, then spoke, "I know you two are promised, so I am not trying to take your man. But I would feel safer going to the world of Trent."

Melissa smiled and said, "That is all right with me, but I am interested where you are from and how you got here."

"It started when I woke in my village to the sounds of screaming and fighting..." Varva began. The group listened entranced to her story. Lorenzo got up part way through the tale for another round of drinks.

Trent ran his fingers across the pitted table top, feeling the graffiti that had been carved into the thick planks of wood. The ashtray was an empty tuna fish can. Most of the butts in it appeared to be hand rolled. He picked up one especially suspicious looking butt and sniffed—it was definitely marijuana.

Varva finished her story by relating the most recent rescue and how she took vengeance on two of Dorga's guards. She spit when she mentioned the priests of Dorga.

"They're paralytic sycophants, effete betrayers of humanity, carrion-eating servile imitators, arch-cowards and collaborators, gang of women-murderers, degenerate rabble, parasitic traditionalists, play-boy soldiers and conceited dandies," Lorenzo decreed as he lifted his bottle high.

"Don't tell me, W.C. Fields?" asked Trent dryly.

"No," said Spasm, "those were approved terms of abuse for East Germans when describing Britain in the early 1950s."

Trent turned to Melissa. "I believe this will turn out to be quite an educational night."

"I think I am beginning to see a pattern in some of this," Lorenzo stated. "What threw me was Dorga. I've never heard of him before. And the creature with the bull's head also sidetracked me. I only thought of the Cretan Minotaur not the Egyptian myths. There's a strange thread running through here and I think it even runs a stitch or two through the Knights of Templar."

"Oh, no," groaned Trent. "Here we go again. Lorenzo's pet topic is the Illuminati, some mystical, secret society formed when the Templars were forced to go underground."

"What about Thoth?" Spasm asked Lorenzo.

"The god who brought knowledge to the Egyptians?"

"Yes. And The Ark of the Covenant and the Ethiopian connection..."

"Very interesting. It is something I'll have to look into when I get back," replied Lorenzo.

Trent sighed and decided he needed more to drink.

"None for me," Melissa yelled as Trent headed back to the bar.

"Another round, Herr Obber, minus the light," he told the bartender then asked, "How long have you worked here? Are you from around here?"

"I thought you would have learned by now," the bartender replied in a gravelly voice. "You don't ask questions in this drinking establishment."

"Learned by now...?"

"Don't ask me again."

"Boy, these guys are a sour lot," Trent said when he returned to the table.

"Don't bother the natives," Lorenzo cautioned him. "I've seen you get into trouble before in strange bars."

"Me?" asked Trent in mock surprise and shock. "I always exhibit only the highest standards of proper tavern etiquette and bar behavior. It is the occasional other patron with no sense of humor who causes trouble."

"Crap, he's starting to get silly and I gave him a gun," Lorenzo moaned. "Get it away from him. Break his thumbs if you have to."

Melissa looked at Spasm and shook her head. "I may have wondered if this Trent was like the one from my world, but I no longer have to worry."

Trent picked up his bottle and weaved through the mostly empty tables to a jukebox. It was situated beneath a giant skull and antlers of some kind of elk. He was pretty sure nothing that big lived today on his world and guessed it was some extinct ice age stag. A spider was making its web in one of the eye sockets.

The jukebox was covered in dust. He could read well enough to make out "Rockola Super Rocket." It looked like what someone in the 1950s would have considered futuristic. The music machine's lights were barely bright enough to illuminate the record titles. He dropped in a handful of quarters, punched the buttons and returned to his seat.

Varva jumped when the first song came on and looked about in surprise. She was calmed down by Lorenzo, who explained another mystery to her. Lee Marvin's coarse voice erupted from the jukebox, singing "I Was Born Under a Wandering Star."

"He sang that in 'Paint Your Wagons,'" Trent explained.

"What made you play that?" Melissa asked.

"There isn't anything else on the thing but WWII German military tunes," answered Trent. "You don't want to hear 'March Into Paris,' do you?"

"What else did you play?" Spasm wanted to know.

"Nothing."

"This will be a short musical experience," said Spasm.

"Not really, I played it ten times."

Everyone at the table groaned and continued their conversations. Melissa answered questions from Varva while the two Lorenzos conversed in only half sentences.

Trent stood and looked around for the restrooms. He spotted a door marked "Men's" and chose the most direct route through the tables. The room was small and dimly lit. Cigarette butts floated in the two urinals and there was no toilet paper. A prophylactic dispenser was to the side of the sink next to a cracked mirror. Trent unzipped and played "sink the battleship" with one of the butts as he emptied his bladder.

The wall was covered with graffiti. Above his urinal was "Save Russian Jews, Win Valuable Prizes." There were also dozens of names, dates and cities scribbled in different styles and inks.

Some read: Dave, Dubuque, 1963; Frank, Des Moines, 1884; Karl, Heidelberg, 1923; Mickey, Jamestown, 1917; Bill, Rock Island, 1972; Nikita, Cherkassy, Ukraine, 1993.

He didn't know if one was a joke—Stephen, New Rome, Luna, 2068.

Trent returned to hear the Lorenzos discoursing in their unique style of conversation.

"Yes, this city could be a local projection of Jung's collective unconscious..."

"... evolving as each generation changes."

"Do you think this city is connected...?"

"... to other localized...?"

"Yes. Maybe they could be reached..."

"... two ways."

"Exactly. If Trent went to sleep..."

"... in another city?"

"Yes, would he wake..."

"... in a different dream city?"

"Or, could we right now..."

"... travel to another city if we had Trent's truck?"

"I wonder what the countryside looks like?"

"Maybe isolated farm houses, but..."

"... is one farm family enough to create a locus in this world, or..."

"... does it take a greater number of dreamers?"

"I wonder if every world has its dream image?"

"If so, why are there people here that do not appear to be from our worlds?"

"It's obvious that similar worlds share the same dream city..."

"... because Melissa and Trent both arrived here."

"Maybe it's only in the perception and..."

"... someone from another world, such as Varva, sees it in her own terms. This tavern might look like one from her world."

"No." Varva took time out from her discussion with Melissa to comment on the conjecture. "This city is very strange. I have never seen its like before."

She turned back to Melissa and continued their conversation. Trent sat back, sipped his beer, petted the dog, and partially listened to both groups.

Marvin was on his fourth time around on the jukebox and Trent believed he was finally seeing the other patrons reacting. They had been morosely staring at their drinks, concentrating on ignoring each other and their surroundings. But Lee's flat voice and monotonous chorus of "I was born under a wandering star" appeared to be cracking their studied indifference.

A graying individual in a pea coat and stocking hat was actually fidgeting and once looked up to give Trent a brief, murderous glare. Several others seemed to be scowling more than usual and Trent believed he even heard a couple villainous mutterings. Trent had wanted to breach the silent shell of the bar patrons, but he wasn't sure this was a good reaction.

Lorenzo leaned over and said, "Another fine mess you've gotten us into."

A giant of a man had risen from his table at the opposite end of the bar. He stood about six and a half feet and probably tipped the scales at four hundred pounds. He was staring pointedly at Trent.

"Maybe he just wants to talk," Trent whispered back to Lorenzo.

"Right."

The other patrons were shrinking away from the human mountain as he began crossing the floor. The dog stopped wagging its tail and warily eyed the man as he neared.

"Shit," he heard someone mutter under their breath.

The guy reminded Trent of Bluto in the Popeye cartoons. He had a shock of very black hair and needed a shave. It was hard telling what color the wrinkled, collarless shirt was under the beer sign lights, but the giant's baggy pants were khaki and his suspenders black.

"Your idea of a joke?" rumbled a voice to match its source.

"Ah, no. I, ah, had already put my money in when I noticed it was the only song I liked."

"You got a lot of nerve coming in here again after your last trick. Maybe you need a reminder..."

The giant halted in mid-sentence. He had grabbed Trent by the shirt collar and was about to hoist him out of his chair. He stopped talking when Trent began flickering.

"He's going," shouted one of the Lorenzos. "Quick, link hands."

Trent felt more hands grabbing him and saw the tavern blink bright and dim before he felt the floor drop from beneath him. He was suddenly horizontal and hit the floor from what felt like a drop of several feet.

Trent's den was chaos. There was shouting and barking. A pile of arms and legs wildly kicked and waved. An elbow smacked Trent below his right eye.

Trent managed to crawl clear. Both Lorenzos were already standing and Melissa was pushing herself up off the floor. Varva had landed on the giant's shoulders and slid to the floor as he stood.

The stranger looked about in confusion. The morning light shone welcoming through the windows and birds could be heard chirping.

"My God," he roared. "I don't believe it. I'm out of that nightmare."

"What the hell is going on...?" Al was opening the den door. He carried a shotgun and looked as if he had just woken up. He froze when his gaze met the crazy scene.

The giant bellowed again and with a fist almost as big as a ham, punched the den door further open, knocking Al to the side. He barely escaped being trampled as the mountainous stranger rushed out the door. He could be heard tromping down the hallway into the living room, followed by the sound of the front door being hurled open.

Chapter Eight

"I have a feeling the Chamber of Commerce isn't going to thank you for bringing that visitor to town," one of the Lorenzos said of the now disappeared giant.

Al stood as a man dazed by a sucker punch. He looked back and forth between the two Lorenzos, then at Melissa. Varva stood in a corner, on guard with her evil blade drawn. The dog seemed as excited by the daylight as the giant had and stood with its paws on the windowsill.

"Hi, Al, what's new?"

Trent's friend remained frozen, not even blinking when the dog rushed passed him and out the door.

"Trying to catch flies?" Lorenzo asked as he patted the opened-mouth Al on the shoulder and headed into the hallway. "Anyone else hungry? How about..."

"... some omelets, pancakes, and sausage," finished Spasm, close on his twin's heels.

"You better sit down before you fall down," Trent said, taking his friend firmly by the arm and sitting him in a chair. "Now you know I'm not crazy. Here is Melissa."

She leaned over and softly said, "Hello, Al. I'm glad to meet you, though we know each other in my world."

"And this is Varva, recent slave of the priests of Dorga, the Fish-Headed God of Death."

Varva approached Al and smiled. "Greetings, I am honored to meet a friend of Trent."

She eyed Trent when Al didn't respond, obviously puzzled. "Is there something wrong with your friend?"

"He's always this way before his morning coffee," Trent explained. "Come on, buddy, let's get some breakfast."

Trent took Melissa's hand. "Varva, would you drag Al along?"

He didn't wait for an answer but pulled Melissa down the hall toward the kitchen.

"I'm almost scared to see the kitchen of two bachelors," she said.

"Don't worry," Trent reassured her, "Al's a neat freak. Every plate in its place and cup in its cranny."

They entered the kitchen to see the Lorenzos already bustling about, cracking eggs, chopping onions, and stirring batter. Trent turned and looked back down the hall. Al appeared to have finally come out of his stupor and was talking to Varva.

"Things seem to be well in hand. Why don't you and I go for a walk so we can talk about things alone?" suggested Trent. He desperately needed to be in the sunshine after the horrid night in the dream world. He hoped the fresh air would help clear a brain still slightly fogged by the Dubuque Star.

"And now for something entirely different," he said as they stepped onto the front porch.

A beautiful morning greeted them. They both paused at the steps as if the extreme shift from the night world was too much for their senses. Trent felt like a scuba diver ascending too fast after a deep dive.

It had rained during the night and the sidewalks were still wet. Someone had recently mowed and the fragrance of cut grass scented the air. It made the neighborhood seem all the more bright and clean after the dream city.

Trent stopped to rescue a night crawler from a curbside puddle.

"I feel numb," admitted Melissa as she paused to watch him fling the worm into the grass. "So much has happened that nothing seems real any more. Antennas could sprout from your head right now and I'd probably not even flinch—well, maybe a little.

"I must admit," she said, looking about the neighborhood, "there doesn't seem to be any difference in your world. I recognize all these houses. The flowers and birds all look the same."

Trent gazed about and said, "The same with your world. I only detected slight differences, such as my Aunt Fern's curio shop. Here, she is still active in a half dozen clubs, but so far has steered clear of commerce.

"You know," Trent said as he stopped and shoved both hands in his pockets. "I'm not going to hold you to your promise to move to this world. I know it was under pressure. But I do hope you decide to come here."

Melissa reached out and touched Trent's cheek. "Thank you. I appreciate that. It reminds me how thoughtful you always were. Goofy, but thoughtful."

She took his hand and they returned to their walking.

"I can't wait for another couple weeks until the oaks bloom," Trent said as he paused to admire an exceptionally large tree. "They're so pretty with those giant, red flowers."

Melissa tilted her head and looked at Trent in surprise then up at the thick, green foliage.

"Blooms?" she blurted out.

Melissa saw the wicked smile when her gaze returned to Trent.

"Don't make me hurt you," she laughed and punched him in the arm.

Melissa pulled back for another swing and Trent grabbed her hand. They were laughing and wrestling in the middle of the sidewalk when a loud cry disrupted their play. They turned and saw Lowell Simons. His complexion was that of bleached flour, and he was uncontrollably opening and clenching his fists.

"No, no. Get away from me. Keep her away from me," he began in a whisper. It quickly turned to screams. "You're dead. You can't be here. What kind of joke is this?"

By now, all of Simons' body was trembling.

"Lowell, she's not dead. She was just missing..."

"No, I said get away from me," he was now shrieking. He stumbled backwards several steps then turned and fled.

For a second time Trent was left dumbfounded by Simons' reaction, this time by the one of his own world.

"There's one who might be a hard sell in explaining your return," admitted Trent as he took Melissa's hand. "But don't feel bad, I bumped into him in your world and he reacted just the same. They seem more than a little surprised to see us."

The run-in with Simons dampened their spirits and cast a pall on the morning that clouds couldn't have done.

"Lowell has always been an odd duck," Trent said to break the silence as they walked back. "He's been even more gloom and doom since your disappearance, if that's possible."

"He visited me the first few months after your death," Melissa said then covered her mouth with her right hand. "God, that sounds ghoulish. We're going to have to quit talking this way.

"Anyway, I think he finally got the idea that I wasn't interested," she continued. "It was as if he expected me to fall into his arms once you were gone."

They entered the house to find the Lorenzos dishing out breakfast. They had seated Al and Varva at the table and were feeding them first.

"You're just in time for a gourmet's delight, though I believe my partner uses just a little more cayenne powder than I care for. Being a traditionalist, I'm still a black pepper man."

Al looked up from his meal at Trent and Melissa. He seemed on the road to recovery, and it appeared navigational services were being provided by Varva.

"This is weird," said Al. "Real weird. But I'm adapting."

"Nothing like a nubile young woman to make a man malleable," muttered Spasm under his breath to Lorenzo.

"Ditto," he answered.

They pulled out the table and brought in extra chairs. Soon the group was crowded in a circle and chowing down. Trent dug out leftovers almost finished with their refrigerator wake and due for a landfill interment. They still smelled okay so he gave them to the dog.

"What are you going to call the pup?" Trent asked Lorenzo. "You can't just keep calling it 'the dog.' You'll give it a complex."

"What do you mean my dog?" answered Lorenzo. "He's yours. I already have two."

"My dog! What am I going to do with a dog?"

"What everyone else does with a dog," interjected Spasm. "I wouldn't argue. With the types of uninvited guests you're prone to, I'd be happy to have her. You should have seen her jump one of those creatures."

Varva reached out and petted it.

"Yes, this dog is a very brave warrior. I would be proud to have her with me in any fight."

"Her? I guess that means I'll have to spay it," Trent said, giving in without much of a fight.

The part about uninvited guests made the dog seem like a good idea. He looked at her for several minutes trying to picture the dog with a variety of names. Bloodletter? Creepkiller? Princess? Poochie? Duchess? Bonemasher?

"I'll have to ponder for a while," Trent finally said. "Nothing I can think of seems to fit at the moment."

He was about to ask Melissa if she wanted seconds when she began flickering. Spasm quickly leaned over the table and grabbed her arm, apparently not wishing to test the theory that he could return by himself. They both disappeared and a whoosh of air rushed in to fill the vacuum. Trent was left with his mouth open and arm halfway extended to grab her.

The kitchen was silent. The rest could see the look of loss on Trent's face. Her sudden disappearance caught Trent off guard, even though he knew it had to happen. Lorenzo patted his friend on the shoulder.

"Hey, what's going on?" came a shout from the living room. Rich stomped into the kitchen. "Anything happen last night while..."

The 17-inch blade held to Rich's throat had stopped him in mid-sentence. His sudden entrance had startled Varva.

"Yes, Rich," sighed Trent, "Something happened last night."

Varva released her hold on Rich when she realized he was not an enemy. He quickly stepped away and gingerly rubbed his throat. He looked at the others, as if expecting them to deliver some punch line.

"Rich, this is Varva. Varva, this is another friend of mine, Rich Stuart."

Varva moved forward and offered her hand. He smiled nervously and took it, still eying the blade in her other hand.

"I am honored to meet another friend of Trent."

"Same here," Rich replied, though his tone of voice was not totally convincing. "I, ah, was just stopping by to see if our Sunday afternoon card game was still on."

"Sure, why not?" Lorenzo replied before Trent could answer. "Trent needs something to keep his mind off other things."

"We're going to need some more beer and snacks," Al said. "We went through all we had Friday night."

"I'll get some," Trent quickly volunteered. He wanted to get out into the sunlight again.

"I would like to go with you," added Varva. "I want to see more of this world and its markets."

Al looked as if he were about to say something but instead felt in his pocket and pulled out a pack of smokes. He fumbled with the matches and lit a cigarette. Varva looked at his actions in surprise.

"What are you doing?"

"Ah, just smoking a cigarette."

She approached Al and thrust her nose up to the cigarette and sniffed several times.

Rich watched in continued amazement. He eyed the blade again and whispered to Trent, "She isn't one of those militant non-smokers, is she?"

"It does not smell good," she proclaimed. "Why do you do it? Is it good for you?"

"I don't know. Just a habit, I guess. And no, they're not good for me."

"Then you should stop," Varva declared as she wrinkled her nose in distaste.

"Come on, Varva, we'll go shopping," Trent called as he headed out the kitchen door. "And you can leave the blade here. We won't need it."

Varva reluctantly handed the knife to Rich, who held the weapon as if it were a large leach. He quickly placed it on the table. Al watched the pair leave and then held the cigarette in front of him and looked sadly at the wisps of smoke.

Trent grabbed a pair of sunglasses as they passed a bookcase. Varva looked at him in puzzlement.

"What are those?"

"Sunglasses. They make it easier to see in bright light. Here, try them on," Trent said as he backed to the bookcase and grabbed another pair. Both were black and thick framed. "Hey, they're you."

Varva walked down the sidewalk looking through and then over the glasses for several minutes before finally deciding to wear them.

"They make things look like the dream city," she said.

"You'll get used to them," Trent told her.

He decided to walk to the store because it was such a gorgeous day and to give Varva a chance to see more of the town. She surprised him. He thought she would act like a child visiting the zoo for the first time. Though he could tell by small body movements that she was continually being surprised, her outward appearance remained calm.

Not that she probably didn't want to gape or run on several occasions, he thought, but hadn't she traveled all the way to the capital of the mighty Ostiv Empire and to the Temple of Dorga?

A young kid in a souped up '65 Mustang zoomed by and she missed just one step. Trent guessed he was her key. She watched him out of the corner of her eye. If he showed indifference to roaring iron chariots that

136

moved by themselves, she did, too. It did take a great deal of will power, he thought, for her not to stop and watch a giant, iron bird fly high above them.

She eyed him skeptically. "No wizards?"

"No. I can't expect you to believe it at first, but those vehicles and aircraft do not use magic. I'll ask Al to explain them to you. I'm sure he won't mind."

Trent could tell Varva wished she had brought the knife. He hoped she noticed that none of the people they passed were carrying weapons. He didn't want her to go into a cultural shock, so he tried distracting her. He stopped and kneeled by a puddle full of earthworms.

"I shouldn't get started on this," Trent said as he threw the worms into the grass. "I decided to walk to work one morning after a rain and there were these night crawlers in puddles. I rescued the first couple and then realized the magnitude of the tragedy I was witnessing. Thousands of these suicidal worms had thrown themselves into these tiny pools.

"It made me stop and wonder. Just what kind of sordid and sleazy lives do these worms live that they're trying to drown themselves on such a mass scale? After all, they are hermaphrodites, so who knows what kind of twisted and sick relationships they become involved in. Thank goodness they don't have fingers, I thought, so they can't use revolvers. Then not only would we have to put up with all those damn chirping crickets, we'd have to listen to hundreds of tiny pops through the hot summer nights as they tried blowing out their tiny brains.

"But a bullet to the head wouldn't work either," Trent continued as he held a worm up for Varva's observation. "You see, they have such a distributed nervous system that if you cut a worm in half, both parts grow. So drowning is about the only way, other than throwing themselves in front of robins, for them to commit suicide."

He noticed she was looking at him strangely. "So anyway, I got trapped into saving all the worms I saw along the route to work. I had to. I'd have been playing God if I'd of only picked a few here and there to save. I was three hours late by the time I got to work and completely covered with slime."

She looked at the worm he was holding and back to his face. "I have no notion of what you are talking about."

Trent shrugged and tossed the worm into a yard. "Oh, well, it isn't that important."

They continued their stroll. He struggled not to think about Melissa. Patience was all that was needed, he continually told himself. It wouldn't be long and they'd be permanently together again. What were a few days compared to the last eight years?

The two walked by a church just before a service. Trent noted Varva carefully examining the women's clothing.

"What do you think?"

"About what?"

"The clothing."

"I like some of it, especially the different materials. Here the men do not dress as colorful as the women. In my village the men like to dress with many silks, jewelry, and feathers." She turned to him. "And you have no tattoos, so I cannot tell if you are a priest, warrior, trader, farmer, or slave. I can tell that your friend, Lorenzo, is a warrior. Though hiding his totem under his hair is very strange."

"I work at a factory, and it's hard to tell what Lorenzo does."

"Factory?"

"That's another thing I'll have to have Al explain."

They were approaching the supermarket and Trent pointed it out to Varva. She clenched her jaw and tried not to flinch as they walked through the parking lot traffic and the automatic door. Trent grabbed a cart and they slowly made their way down the aisles. He named and described what many of the boxes and cans were.

"We won't buy a lot now since we have to carry it," he said as they turned a corner. "You can help me shop for more tomorrow. We'll go looking for clothes, too.

"Grocery shopping is an art. Take this bacon," he said, holding up a pack. "This little tab in back lets you see how much fat the meat has. It doesn't look too bad, does it? Yet if we were to take it home and open the package, the bacon would still be all fat. It's one of those unexplainable mysteries, like just what exactly is 'Brown Gravy?' Why don't they have other colors of gravy—yellow or green? And who eats those necks they leave in frozen turkeys? Take a look at this hair conditioner—there's more proteins and fruit juice in this than many food products. Whereas this supposed soup appears to have more chemicals in it than the conditioner. Does that make sense?"

Varva admitted that it didn't. They turned another corner and almost bumped carts with the mystery stranger. He appeared just as surprised to see them as they were to meet him.

Trent guessed the Lorenzos had briefly discussed the stranger while walking in the dream city with Varva. From that and Trent's surprise, Varva apparently guessed the man in front of them must be a priest of Dorga. Having no knife, she grabbed what was at hand—a can of pumpkin pie filling. She flung it before the stranger could raise an arm in defense and the can caught him squarely between the eyes. He folded like a leaky accordion.

"What the hell!" gasped Trent, who frantically looked up and down the empty aisle. "What did you do that for?"

Varva didn't reply. She leaped around the carts and grabbed the fallen can in one hand and the man's ponytail in the other. She raised the pie filling to finish the job but was stopped by a panicking Trent who tore the can from her hand.

"Varva," he fiercely whispered. "You can't attack people like that in this world. At least not in public."

Trent kneeled by the stranger and after checking the aisle, pulled off one of the gloves. There was no tattoo.

"Shit," he cursed. "This is not a priest of Dorga."

By now Varva had calmed down and was looking back and forth between the unconscious figure and Trent. He couldn't see Varva's eyes behind the sunglasses, but he could tell she was seriously puzzled.

"Do you recognize him?" he asked.

Varva reached out and lifted the stranger's sunglasses from his face. The face looked vaguely familiar to Trent.

"It is you."

Taking a second look, Trent realized the stranger on the floor was the person he looked at every morning in the mirror—plus a beard.

"My God, you've killed me," was all Trent could think to say.

"No, he is just stunned," Varva assured him after feeling for a pulse below the second Trent's ear.

They were lucky so far. The store wasn't very busy this time of morning, and no one had yet come down the aisle.

"Quick, help me get him in the cart," Trent ordered.

He tossed out several bags of chips and dip and then bent to grab his look-alike under the armpits. Varva grabbed him by the knees and they swung the limp body up and into the cart. It didn't look like a comfortable ride, Trent had to admit to himself. His twin's head flopped to one side and his legs hung out the front of the cart.

They ran the cart to the front of the store and peeked around the corner. A woman had her back to them, examining frozen fish sticks. A young boy was sitting in her cart and his eyes went wide when Trent pushed the cart across the main aisle and into a closed checkout lane. There was only one line open, and it was three counters down. The cart was hidden from view on both sides, though someone walking into the store and passing in front would see the cart. Trent knew they had to work fast.

"I'll get the attention of the checkout person. When you see she's not about to look this way, unhook the chain and wheel him out the door as fast as you can."

He tried not to look as frayed as he felt when he placed a box of doughnuts in front of the woman. The recent fast pace of his life must have been telling. She stared at him oddly from the corner of her eyes. He knew he hadn't shaved lately, and his clothes were very wrinkled.

"Mommy, there's a real big baby over there," the little boy was calling to his mother.

"Yes, dear, that's nice," she replied without looking up from her shopping.

Trent swallowed and tried to smile at the woman as he watched Varva pushing the cart into view and towards the exit.

"That'll be $4.87," the clerk told Trent.

He reached into his pocket and almost threw down five one-dollar bills before he caught himself. He scrutinized them before handing them over. They appeared all right. Trent could tell the woman thought she had a nut case in front of her.

He scooped up the change and hurried out the door. Varva was waiting for him between two parked cars. Trent threw the doughnuts on the unconscious Trent's chest and grabbed the cart's handle.

"Let's get out of here," he hissed and gave the cart a shove.

It made a great deal of noise as it rattled across the parking lot. His twin's head flopped with each bump. Trent could feel sweat trickling out of his armpit. A minivan pulled in and parked at the end of a lot. Trent sped up in hopes of passing the vehicle before the driver got out. A front wheel locked up and Trent almost dumped his load. He kicked the wheel free and was passing the van when a woman opened the door and stepped out.

"I hate it when he drinks this early in the morning," Trent huffed as he rushed by.

The woman snorted in disgust and headed into the supermarket.

Trent took the least traveled streets, yet cars continued to pass by them. He feared an accusing or questioning voice each time he heard a car approach. But they all passed with only an occasional odd look. Violent crimes in Bear River were almost unheard of—Trent guessed the motorists thought of the sight as some weird prank.

"I believed the Trent of Melissa's world was dead," Varva said as the cart rattled and shook down a rough alley.

"Must be from a third world," Trent answered. He had been chewing on the same question. "But what he is doing here is another matter. Just because he looks like me doesn't mean he has to be a good guy."

"I think he is not bad," Varva said as she studied the face in the cart. She was holding his head in an attempt to lessen the bouncing. "The wrinkles around his eyes and mouth are from smiling."

"What wrinkles? All I see are faint lines." Trent protested.

They stopped the cart at the foot of the porch steps. Trent ran up them and threw the front door open to yell, "Hey, I need some help out here with the groceries."

He walked back to the edge of the porch and leaned against a wooden pillar. His legs were shaking and he slid down to sit on the top step. Things were happening way too fast, with no periods of rest between them. He stared at the body in amazement, seeing an angle of his face he'd never viewed before.

The door opened behind Trent and Lorenzo complained, "That doesn't look like beer to me."

The voices of Al and Rich joined in.

"What the hell is going on?"

"Is he dead?"

"Who killed him?"

Lorenzo skipped down the steps and felt for a pulse. He peeled an eyelid back and then looked closely at a rising bump and faint bruise appearing in the middle of the doppelganger's forehead. Trent was surprised to see Lorenzo unbuttoning the unconscious figure's shirt.

"Hum-m-m, no nicotine patches. He's alive, though he's going to have one hell of a headache and stiff neck when he comes to. We should take him to the hospital to make sure he doesn't have a concussion after we've talked to him," Lorenzo concluded. "Let's get him into the house before the neighbors get the right idea."

They crowded around the body and hoisted it up and out of the cart and then up the stairs and into the living room.

"On the couch," Trent said.

They stepped back and viewed the Trent in amazement.

"I suppose there is an explanation for this?" Lorenzo asked.

Trent looked at his twin and then to Lorenzo. "Yes, the beer wouldn't fit."

Varva knelt by the couch when the figure began stirring.

"I am terrible sorry," Varva said as she brushed a stray strand of hair from the bruised face. "I thought he was a priest of Dorga, and I attacked him."

"Hit him with a canned good," Trent explained further. "I believe it was pie filling."

The Trent on the couch blinked several times and raised a hand to his forehead. He hissed when he touched the darkening spot.

"Christ, what hit me?" he groaned.

"Pie filling. Pumpkin, I think," Trent answered.

Trent was surprised to find himself suddenly nervous. He didn't know what to say to another Trent. He licked his lips and looked to Lorenzo. His friend noticed Trent's discomfort and kneeled next to Varva to question the twin.

"Who are you and why have you been shadowing Trent? Are you from another world?"

The Trent look-alike tried sitting up. Varva gave him a helping hand. He grimaced as he massaged his neck.

"What did you do, throw me down a flight of stairs?" he moaned and looked at Trent. "You'd think you'd be more careful with yourself."

"What are you doing here?" Lorenzo continued to press now that one part of the question was answered.

"Could you at least get me a couple aspirins?" he asked. He bent over to cradle his face in his hands. "I think my head is going to explode. And how about some ice for this goose egg?"

Remembering his own recent injury that started the whole mess, Trent left for the kitchen to get the first aid items. He was returning when he met his twin and the rest of the gang coming the other way. Varva was holding the not-so-strange stranger's arm and helping him walk.

"He has to go to the bathroom," explained Rich, who then turned to the twin of his friend and asked, "Do you play cards?"

Trent Two didn't answer. He was very shaky as he stepped into the bathroom and shut the door.

They leaned against the hall walls.

"This is something I better not tell Theresa," Rich said to Al. "I don't think she'd believe any of it. Boy, I wish I could have gone with you guys last night."

He turned to Trent and asked, "How about tonight?"

Trent rubbed his eyes and sighed. "Sure. Why not? Maybe we could bring along some jugglers, a clown, and a couple dwarves."

"This Trent opens a new line of questions," Lorenzo spoke. "Why did he try to contact you at the dream hotel but has been avoiding contact here?"

"We will just have to ask him," Trent said. "I wish he would hurry up."

"You don't think he'd try and get away, do you?" Al asked.

"There are no windows, how could he?" answered Trent, who then slapped his head and spun around.

He flung the door open. The bathroom was unoccupied.

"Well, we now know some people can travel without nicotine patches," noted Lorenzo. "It also appears your twin can travel at will."

"Damn," Trent swore. "Why'd he leave? You'd think he'd want to help me. I would have aided him."

"At least he didn't knock you out and haul you across town in a grocery cart," Lorenzo reminded him. "He was probably not feeling in a helpful mood."

"This just makes one more crazy thing that doesn't make sense," continued Trent. "I find that the mysterious stranger who has been watching

144

me is myself, but I won't tell me why. It does explain why I have a tab at the Crossroads Cafe and why the oaf in that bar said I had a lot of nerve coming back after my last trick."

"He probably drank too much and played some stupid song too many times," offered Lorenzo, who received a dark scowl in return.

"I tell you," Trent raised his voice as he began pacing in the hall, "I am throwing those stupid patches away once I manage to get Melissa to this world. I never want to see another person with a bull or fox head again. I never want to visit another phantom bar or crawl up the brass belly of a fish-headed god of death. And I certainly never want to see two of the same person again, even if they are real twins."

"It's too nice of day to fret indoors," Lorenzo said as he took his pal by the arm. "Let's all go outside and sit around the fish pond."

The group filed into the large back yard shaded by several old oaks and maples. The picnic table was near the fishpond, a kidney-shaped pool of water lined with blocks of carved limestone. Several goldfish surfaced in hopes of being fed as the people neared. Al brought the box of doughnuts out and offered one to Varva. She cautiously took a nibble, smiled, and made a quick end of it in several bites.

The backyard was completely enclosed by a nine-foot tall hedge. Trent's home was in an old neighborhood with large lots, which meant the houses were far enough apart that Trent could hold backyard parties well into the night with no complaints from his neighbors.

"How about a barbecue?" Rich suggested. "Only this time I'll get the food."

"Sure, but what about Theresa?" said Trent.

"She's shopping with her sister this afternoon. Won't be home until seven or eight."

"I'll go with you," volunteered Lorenzo. "I need to get a few things."

Trent lay on the picnic table after the two left. He watched the clouds float by and could hear the faint voices of Al and Varva as they toured the yard and discussed the flowers. They disappeared around the side of the house.

With things settled down, Trent slipped into a mild funk. He missed Melissa and wished it were night so he could rush to the Crossroads Cafe. He closed his eyes and imagined her face. She smiled and her one dimple appeared.

He tried imaging what life would be like when this was all over. They'd fall into a routine. One night they'd do laundry; the next evening they'd visit a friend's. On Sunday afternoons they would go for walks in the park. They'd have a kid and let the grandparents take turns babysitting on Friday evenings. It would be nice and predictable.

Trent's thoughts were too calming. He fell asleep.

Chapter Nine

"Crap" was the first word that came to mind when he realized he was no longer laying on a picnic table. He could still feel the warm sun on his face, but there was grass tickling his neck. Trent decided that he wouldn't open his eyes and maybe he'd fall asleep again and travel home.

He might have traveled on if he hadn't heard the rustling sounds of something large rushing through leaves. His eyes snapped open just in time to see a large open maw and very sharp teeth inches from his nose. His scream was abruptly silenced by a very wet tongue slurping across his face. It appeared to be the German shepherd they'd rescued in the dream city.

Trent grabbed its fur and pushed the head away so he could sit up. The dog happily threw out a few barks before trying to again lick his face. He looked around to find himself on what looked like a sloping Alpine meadow. Vibrant green grass and an assortment of red, blue, and yellow flowers a foot tall were bowing in a gentle breeze. Circling the clearing was a thick, dark wall of trees. They weren't evergreens but appeared to be oaks and maples. It looked like a park.

Trent shook his head in resignation. He was becoming very disenchanted with dream traveling. Several crows flew from the nearest wall of trees when Trent climbed to his feet. He brushed off the back of his pants and slowly turned to view his new surroundings.

Looking up the slope, Trent observed distant, white-capped mountains. He was on one of the foothills. Small outcroppings of wind-smoothed stone were scattered among the sea of grass like small islands. They were covered with green, purple, and gray lichens.

Was there any method behind this madness, Trent wondered? Were his jumps purely random? His train of thought was being derailed by the dog that insisted on making noise. She would bark a few times then spin and run ahead a few feet only to stop and look over her shoulder at Trent. After waiting a few moments, she would return to bark and begin the process over again.

"No, no, no," groaned Trent. "I don't care if Timmy is down a mine shaft and can't get out. I'm not leaving this spot. It appears a pleasant place to wait until it's time to go home."

The dog stopped its whining and lowered her head to begin growling.

"Are you now trying intimidation?" Trent asked. "If so, it isn't going to work."

It was the dog that was now ignoring Trent. She appeared to be looking over his right shoulder.

"Oh, sure. I've seen that one before. I look behind me and then you pull some trick."

Trent decided the dog might not be joking and suddenly his back felt very vulnerable. He slowly turned. On the edge of the meadow were what could only be three mastodons—a bull, cow, and a calf the size of a buffalo. They first appeared artificial, like some well-made museum exhibit—until the bull mastodon swung its head to examine the dog and man with one bloodshot eye the size of a softball. The movement stirred up a cloud of flies that swarmed around its head. The hairy elephants looked very shabby, as if shedding their winter coats.

The dog began barking.

"Shut up, dummy, shut up," hissed Trent out of the corner of his mouth, afraid to move a muscle.

The barking only grew louder and suddenly the dog darted up the hill toward the trio.

"Oh, hell," Trent said to anything that would listen.

The parents angrily trumpeted at the dog as they moved between it and their calf. They nervously shuffled around as if fearing more members of a pack hidden in the trees or grass. The bull shot out and almost caught the dog by surprise. It was a mountain of tusk, hair, and muscle, but the mastodon was able to move pretty fast for short runs. It stopped after a one hundred foot charge, shook its head, thundered again and then angrily ripped up clumps of sod with its tusks. The calf peered at the two strangers from behind its mother's back legs.

The dog circled and carted in at the mother. It was clearly enjoying this new game. The bull turned and charged again. This time the bull continued its chase even after the dog pulled away from the mother and calf. Trent decided this was not a good thing since the dog was now happily leaping through the tall grass straight back to him.

That was enough to convince Trent it was time to move. He found it easy to ignore the stiff joints and aching muscles with a bellicose ice age giant hot on his heels. Trent was running from a rampaging locomotive with no way to jump off the tracks. For several seconds, he could hear the monster seemingly breathing down his neck, its laboring lungs sounding like giant bellows.

The mastodon wasn't the only one gasping for breath. Trent's lungs were on fire, and the trees didn't seem to be getting any closer. Time had slowed down and any moment Trent expected a tip of the creature's yellowed and scratched tusks to erupt from the middle of his chest.

The trees were looking larger and the sound of the mastodon charge ceased, but Trent wasn't stopping to see if the bull had ended its chase. He dodged a low limb and hurled himself into the dark shadows of the forest. He allowed himself to begin slowing after jumping several giant, fallen trunks and zig-zagging a number of monster trees still standing. Trent staggered to a halt beneath a hickory tree and turned to lean against its rough bark, only to have his knees give out.

He should have given up smoking sooner, Trent decided as he sat gulping for air. His temples were throbbing and he felt like vomiting. He reached out to steady himself and his fingers sank several inches into the leaves.

The carpeting under the ancient tree growth was a thick layer of half decayed leaves covering rich, black soil. A purplish incandescent beetle scuttled across his hand before disappearing back into the leaves. Between two fingers was a small tree seedling only three inches tall. He almost unthinkingly uprooted it. How much of a change would he leave behind by plucking the sapling? Would it have grown to join its towering cousins?

The dog was sitting about fifteen feet away, barely panting. She was watching Trent as if trying to will the human to do her bidding.

"Are you nuts?" he yelled at the dog, though it came out more of a croak.

He picked up a cracked and wormy hickory nut and tossed it at the dog. It fell several feet short. Trent didn't feel well enough to stand for another ten minutes. The dog began the same Lassie routine once Trent was back on his feet.

"Okay, okay," he surrendered. "Let's go find Timmy."

The dog danced around him several times before shooting off deeper into the forest.

"You're going to have to slow down if you want me to follow," he yelled after the quickly disappearing animal.

Trent would have normally worried about getting lost, but one spot was as good as another for this long, strange trip. He did wonder about other animals. Did giant cave bears and saber-toothed tigers also inhabit this forest? Trent wished he had Lorenzo's M-16. The dog returned to prod him on with more barks before spinning and again fading into the shadows.

This continued for at least ten minutes. Several times Trent decided to stop, but each time the dog convinced him to continue. He halted again when an unexpected creaking in the treetops sent him ducking into heavy brush. He looked between his upraised arms to see wooden ribs showing through a long gash in yellow fabric. It took several seconds for Trent to orientate himself.

He spun around to get a different angle and almost fell when a wave of dizziness hit. He grabbed a tree and waited for it to pass.

The object had bold, black lettering across it and Trent suddenly recognized it as a small airplane wing. Sheered cables dangled from one end. He followed the direction in which the tree limbs were snapped to discover another wing then another.

Trent picked his way through the trees to finally find the twisted fuselage half buried in the soft soil of the forest. It appeared as small as the wings. He decided it had been a bi-wing aircraft. Only torn metal and twisted braces showed where the engine had been mounted. He made up his mind not to look into the cockpit. No one could have lived through the crash.

The dog continued its barking. He scanned the forest and spotted her still acting like she wanted him to follow. This time he didn't argue. The forest floor was bare in many places under the dark canopy. Small trees, grass and brush erupted wherever an elder tree had crashed to the ground and opened a hole for the sunlight.

He came upon such a downed giant. Large ferns bordered it as they would have a Victorian front porch. Sunlight streamed down like a spotlight and turned it into a postcard-perfect scene. The edges of the circle of sunlight pulsated as the above limbs gently moved in the wind. A shadow swung back and forth across the ferns like a clock pendulum. Trent squinted into the patch of bright blue sky. A man was swinging from the end of parachute lines about fifteen feet above the forest floor.

Trent shook his head and followed the lines up to the parachute caught in a distant limb. He had no idea how to get the man down safely. He walked to the trunk of the tree that held the unconscious figure. The bark was coarse enough that he could almost climb the tree. But then what? Even if he could shinny out on the limb to the parachute, he couldn't pull up the pilot's weight. The drop could seriously hurt or even kill the unconscious man if he cut the cords. The dog walked over and sat next to Trent as if waiting for him to do the obvious.

Trent was getting a kink in his neck looking up at the unlucky plane passenger. He sat, and then laid back for a more comfortable observation position directly beneath the parachutist. No matter where he gazed in the forest ceiling or what kind of creative problem-solving skills he brought to bear, Trent still kept returning to the starting point—zero.

The dog's ears perked up and she cocked her head. Trent put a hand to his eyes for shade and squinted. Was the guy moving? He was. His head rolled a few times before straightening up.

"Hey," hollered Trent, "are you all right?"

The man rubbed his head and gazed slowly about.

"Hey, I'm down here. Are you all right?"

The guy was definitely groggy. He looked like he still wasn't aware of where he was.

"Hey, don't do that," Trent yelled even louder. "No, don't do that, I said..."

Looking up through the man's boots, Trent could see him fumbling around with his harness buckles. He jerked several times and the clasps opened, sending the man hurtling straight down.

Trent rolled frantically to the side and hit the dog.

"Move, damn it," he screamed while wildly kicking and waving his arms.

The dog didn't move and the man landed with a sickening thump just feet away. Like the interior of the demolished airplane cockpit, the man was also something Trent didn't want to see. He clenched his jaw and forced himself to roll over for a look. The man, barely more than a boy, was laid spread eagle on the ground, face up.

He had died with a frown on his face. No, now more a pained grimace, now a frown again. The man wasn't dead, just apparently in a great deal of pain. Trent rolled to his knees and bent over the fallen figure. He didn't know what to do. He knew moving a man with a broken back or neck could kill him. Still, no ambulance was going to be coming this way soon.

Trent guessed him to be the pilot. He wore a leather flying helmet like the comic strip dog, Snoopy. Goggles were pulled up over his forehead. Trent could see why the pilot appeared to be fumbling so with the buckles. He was wearing bulky leather mittens that appeared to be wool lined. They had spots for the thumb and index finger, with the remaining three fingers in the third, larger section.

Trent bent over to shade the young man's eyes. The kid was nineteen or twenty with dark brown hair, a thin face and a narrow, large nose. He appeared to be about six-feet tall. Trent let out a long rush of air he didn't know he had been holding when the pilot finally opened his eyes. He blinked a couple times and smiled/winced.

"Shit, there goes the summer," he said and tried getting to his elbows,

"Hold on a second," Trent warned. "You might be hurt. Just lay there until your head clears."

The pilot took Trent's advice and tried to relax. He gazed at his would-be rescuer and then the parachute with its empty harness swinging in the wind.

"No wonder I have a hell of a headache. That was kind of a bum move to make," he noted. "Today is just not my day."

"You're still alive, aren't you? Can you wiggle your toes? Do you have any sharp pains anywhere?"

"Yes, yes, and all over," the downed pilot replied. "Help me up, will you?"

Though it was against Trent's better judgment, he took an arm and guided the young man to his feet. Color had been returning to the pilot's face, but the effort to stand was quickly draining it away again.

"Whoa, talk about the walls spinning," the young man said as he clutched Trent's arm for support. "I feel like I'm going into a corkscrew dive without a plane."

Trent led him to a log and unceremoniously forced him to sit.

"My name is Trent Rowen," Trent introduced himself as he sat next to his new acquaintance. "In a way, I'm glad you made that stupid move. I was having a hell of a time trying to figure how to get you down."

The pilot let out a shaky laugh and unsteadily offered his hand. "My name is Henry Fredericks. I appreciate your help. I was flying to Duluth when I must have dozed off. The next thing I knew I was smacking into a bunch of trees. Am I on your farm?"

Trent looked at the stranger's seemingly innocent blue eyes and boyish smile and then gazed about the forest. He chewed on his lip and wondered how best to describe the current situation.

"Ah, how old was your plane?"

Henry sighed and looked over at one of the wings twisted around the trunk of a chestnut. "She was old and slow, but she was paid for."

"Old, huh." That made Trent feel a little better. He'd been worried the kid was going to say the antique plane was brand new.

"Yup. She's about fifteen years old. Bought the Jenny last year in St. Louis for fifty dollars."

"A Jenny?"

Trent had that sinking feeling in his stomach again. He didn't know much about airplanes, but even he recognized the nickname for a WWI trainer. Henry noticed the odd expression.

"Are you feeling okay?" he asked Trent. "You're starting to look a bit pale."

"Oh, I'm all right. I just haven't been getting enough rest lately. Can you walk?"

Trent helped him back to his feet and they walked to the remains of the fuselage. The dog followed closely behind. Henry limped but seemed remarkably intact considering his recent experiences. They rolled the plane's fuselage so Henry could get into the front cockpit where he'd stored his gear. It consisted of a battered leather suitcase, umbrella, fedora, brown leather jacket and a rifle.

"When you fly over the rough country I do," Henry explained as he pulled out the gun, "it doesn't hurt to carry one for bears."

"Or mammoths," Trent added.

Trent took the suitcase and rifle and led the way back to the meadow where he had first found himself. Henry assumed he was being led to a farmhouse.

"I didn't know there was this much hardwood around here," Henry said as he ducked under a low limb. "I could have sworn this was all pine."

"There's something I have to tell you, Henry. You're going to find this hard to believe."

"Yes?" he replied when Trent didn't continue.

"You think you're in Minnesota, don't you?"

"What? I strayed into Wisconsin?"

"No."

"Come on, I couldn't have been off course enough to be in Canada."

"No, you're not in Canada."

"So, we're in Minnesota. We can't be over thirty miles from Duluth."

They came to the clearing. Setting the suitcase and rifle on the ground, Trent took out his belt and made a leash. He then reached down to grab the dog.

"I think seeing is believing in this case," he answered Henry as they stepped out into the sun.

Henry gave his new friend a puzzled look then glanced about. He stepped back and almost tripped over his suitcase.

"W-w-what the hell is that?" he forced out the question. "They're elephants. God damn hairy elephants."

He turned to Trent. "You in the circus?"

"Those are not elephants. They're either mastodons or mammoths."

"Mammoths? You're kidding. Those are prehistoric animals, aren't they? Didn't they die with the dinosaurs?"

"In our world, yes," Trent answered. "Though technically, dinosaurs became extinct a great deal earlier."

"What do you mean, in our world?" Henry asked as he ran his fingers nervously through his greased-back hair and looked again at the hairy elephants.

"Maybe I should say 'our worlds.' I'm not even sure we're from the same one. It's a long story," said Trent. He sighed as he watched Henry staring back in disbelief.

"I know it sounds strange but look at those mammoths. They don't live near Duluth. I still don't know what's going on myself, but it appears there are alternative universes and now and then people pop from one to another. I only arrived here about an hour ago."

"I've hit my head harder than I thought," Henry groaned and leaned against a small walnut tree. "This has got to be a dream."

"If it's a dream, it's one that you can get bruised in just as easy as when you're awake. That is one thing I am certain about."

Trent yanked on the belt to keep the dog from dragging him into the meadow. Several times the bull looked over at the dog and humans but seemed satisfied to let bygones-be-bygones as long as they stayed on their side of the meadow.

"Come on, let's head down hill," said Trent. "Maybe there's a creek with fresh water. I'm dying of thirst."

They walked in silence for several minutes before Henry asked, "You said you've only been here for an hour? How did you get here?"

"That's a long story," Trent replied, "but since it looks like we have nothing but time on our hands..."

It sounded crazy no matter how many times Trent told the story. He wondered how it must sound to Henry.

They came upon a creek and Trent paused in his story long enough to take a few sips of icy water. They decided the spot looked as good as any for a break and sat on the bank while the dog splashed below.

"So there I was, scrambling up the brass belly of Dorga, Fish-Headed God of Death," he continued the story while Henry looked even more confused and stressed.

"Wait a minute," Henry interrupted as the story progressed, "what year do you think it is?"

"Ah, I was going to bring that up. In my world it's 2016. What year were you in?"

Henry rubbed his temples and let out a deep breath. "It was August 8, 1935."

Trent let that bit of information sink in for a moment before resuming.

"Let's walk back to the clearing," said Henry. "I'd like to look at those elephants some more."

Trent continued his story as they retraced their steps. He finished just as they arrived at the meadow.

"I used to think that if you had a problem, you'd find an answer sooner or later," Trent concluded, "but it keeps getting murkier. Who is the Red Man? What's with my biker twin? What is the dream city and who are these animal-headed creatures?

"You don't believe a word I'm saying, do you?" Trent commented as he looked at Henry. "You think I'm nuts."

"I'm not saying I don't believe you. Those hairy elephants are definitely something else," Henry replied cautiously, as one would humor a madman. "But you must admit, partner, it is a lot to swallow in one sitting."

"Tell me about it."

Trent was trying to think of something else that might lend weight to his story when the dog began a soft, deep growl. Both men quickly looked to the mastodons. They were peacefully ripping up tufts of grass and stuffing it in their cavernous mouths.

Following the dog's intense stare off to the left, Trent spotted four creatures cautiously entering the glade. They were crawling on their stomachs as they worked to keep a low profile. They were wolves, but no wolves Trent was familiar with. They made the German shepherd look like a toy poodle. He guessed they would stand at least five foot at the shoulders if they quit their slinking.

Henry also saw the wolves. His mouth was hanging open and the coloring was once more making a hasty retreat from his face.

"I believe those are called direwolves. They became extinct at the end of the last ice age," Trent whispered. "Do you have those around Duluth?"

Henry didn't answer. He was totally engrossed with the primordial drama about to unfold. Whether the four wolves could have separated the calf from its parents would always remain a mystery for the two men. Trent forgot that he still had the dog on the end of the belt and relaxed his grip.

The German shepherd leaped without warning and almost yanked Trent to his knees. The belt slipped through his fingers and the dog shot across the meadow towards the wolf pack. For one second Trent swore time came to a halt. The birds flying across the sky, the grass bent in the breeze, the bull mastodon with his head thrown back in alarm—all looking as if they had been overtaken by some magical glacier and were now frozen within crystal-clear ice.

The magic flowed away, the ice melted, and the hunters were extremely upset. The dog's noisy arrival warned the beasts and they grouped into a defensive posture. The wolves rose to their full heights and turned to meet this crazy intruder only half their size.

"I've been here before," Trent yelled as he grabbed the rifle. "I think it's time to climb."

Trent turned to a low oak limb only five feet off the ground. It was a beginner's tree, the limbs arranged like rungs for a missing spiral stairway. Once the first branch was attained, the rest were a matter of stepping from limb to limb while using higher branches as hand supports.

The two climbed a good twenty feet before stopping. The glade was now a scene of chaos. The dog was leading the howling wolves on a merry chase that included a route hazardously close to the mammoths. The bull and cow were in a rage, snorting and stomping and waving their long, curved tusks back and forth. The noise alone was enough to give anyone the cold sweats—which it appeared to be doing to Henry.

Trent reached out a reassuring hand to Henry, who looked like he needed a little steadying.

"Don't worry," he told the young pilot, "we won't be here over a couple hours. I'll take you back with me and we can figure out where to go from there. As for now, we might as well just enjoy the show. We're safe up here and it isn't every day you get to see extinct prehistoric mammals running around."

The dog appeared to be a veteran of such antics. She masterfully wove in and out among the mammoths and wolves, just barely missing snapping fangs and lashing tusks by inches. Her luck ran out when one of the wolves dropped from the pack and waited for her to return around the glade to where it crouched. The dog found itself trapped between the pack, mammoths, and lone giant wolf. Both Trent and Henry tensed and held their breaths as the pack closed in. As the jaws of the lead animal closed on the dog's throat, the German shepherd disappeared.

The wolf was thrown of balance after hurling itself on a vanishing prey. It looked around in disbelief and swerved to miss getting its back broken by a massive mammoth leg. The winded pack stopped in a corner of the glade. The members hung their heads and panted heavily. They looked several times at the still grumbling mastodons before slinking back into the woods.

"The dog; what happened?" Henry finally asked. "It just disappeared."

"If dogs could talk, I think that one could explain a lot to me. It seems humans aren't the only ones who can travel voluntarily from world to world," said Trent.

Henry shook his head. "I liked it better when I thought you were crazy. I think I'm actually beginning to believe you now—or else we're both nuts."

The young pilot looked beneath the tree. "Too bad the suitcase isn't up here. I have a couple boxes of Crackerjacks in it. My stomach's growling."

"Sh-h-h-h," warned Trent, "I think I hear something."

Henry joined Trent in listening. They could hear the light rustling of leaves in the breezes, the continued feeding of the mammoths and the scattered bird cries. Trent was just about to relax and admit to an overwrought imagination when he heard it again. So did Henry, who looked about nervously before taking the rifle from Trent.

"I hope I remembered to load it," Henry said as he checked the gun. "Well, we at least have three shots. What do you think that was, a big cat?"

"I thought it sounded like a scream," Trent replied. "There, it's coming from that direction."

Neither of them had time to say anything further. Bursting out of the far wall of trees, not far from the mammoths, came two running figures. One appeared to be an old man and the other a young woman. Both were wearing only wraps around their hips. Three more figures came running into the glade in obvious pursuit.

Trent shrugged his shoulders. "If it isn't one damned thing after another."

The mastodons must have felt the same way. The bull snorted and turned to lead his family back into the timber in search of a less trafficked pasture.

Though the first two seemed to be normal looking humans; the pursuers were definitely a step or two down the evolutionary ladder. A receding hairline to them would have meant their foreheads were bare. Though the three had upright postures, they seemed wider in the shoulders, longer in the arms, and shorter in the legs than the two they were chasing.

As the newcomers crossed the meadow toward the two men, Trent could see the pursuers were naked with both receding brows and chins. They also carried heavy sticks and paused just long enough to give several lethal whacks to the old man's skull after he stumbled and fell. The young woman ran only paces further before she too fell, more from exhaustion than tripping. The three subhumans grunted in glee as they circled her and raised their clubs.

It was difficult to tell whether they first heard Trent's yell or the echoing fire of Henry's rifle. At the most, the yell would have distracted them—the gunshot dropped the biggest of the three. The other two looked about in confusion and then in dismay when they saw their buddy sprawled on the ground. The young woman moaned and they raised their clubs again. Trent scrunched down, his right ear already ringing from the last shot. Henry fired and a second hominid flopped over backwards.

"Good thing I had three bullets," Henry said as he aimed one more time and slowly squeezed the trigger. The rifle jumped and grass and dirt kicked up several feet behind the last hominid. "Shit."

By now the hominid had traced the origin of the loud noises. He stood in a crouch, lips pulled back to display large, yellow teeth. He threw his head back and began making baboon-like screams then jumped up and down while beating the club on the ground.

"I think he's pissed," observed Trent.

Henry appeared to be on an adrenaline high. The sight of the savage-looking trio about to bash in the brains of a semi-naked girl had the young man riled.

"Come on, before he finishes the job," Henry shouted as he threw himself down the branches and to the earth.

Trent followed as fast as he could. They rushed out into the glade and stopped. The two men and the hominid eyed each other across the fallen woman. Though there were two of them and only one of the ape men, Trent still didn't feel like making any rash moves. The creature might be only five foot tall, but he was very muscular and thick boned, as well as brandishing very sharp canines. And he swung the club around like he knew how to use it.

"Now what?" asked Trent, wishing he had the .45.

Henry was now gripping the rifle by the barrel and holding it like a baseball bat.

"There's two of us and just one of the runts," he answered. "We should be able to take him."

The woman was now half sitting up, still taking deep breaths and looking very weak. She looked at the two approaching men in amazement before snarling at the ape man. She tightly gripped a flint knife. Henry reached down and offered a hand when she started to rise.

The hominid was now facing three opponents. His two partners were dead at his feet. Deciding the odds weren't looking good, the subhuman screeched insults before turning and running back into the forest.

"Well, wasn't that something?' was all Trent could think to say.

"Do you speak English?" Henry was asking the young woman.

She was very attractive, with long black hair and high cheekbones. The top of her head came to Henry's chin. He was trying not to look at her naked breasts, but it wasn't easy for the blushing pilot. He appeared more flustered by the woman's presence than when facing off the ape man. She continued to look at both men in surprise then answered Henry in a language obviously not English.

Henry couldn't quit fidgeting and finally turned and walked to his suitcase. He kneeled and opened it as the woman watched in puzzlement. He pulled out a flannel shirt and closed the lid.

"Here, wear this," he said as he offered her the shirt.

She reached out, ran her fingers across the soft fabric and smiled. The wrap she was wearing looked like coarse burlap. Henry had to help when she looked in puzzlement at the buttons. He fumbled in embarrassment while showing her how to button it.

"We should try and take her back to her own people," suggested Trent. "We could go any moment and she'd be left by herself."

Henry agreed and they set off in the direction she had exited from the wall of trees. The three tried communicating as they walked. Her name was Tarra. That was about all the information that passed between them, despite Henry's persistent questioning.

"Maybe we should take her with us," he suggested to Trent.

"What?"

"I mean it's not safe here for her."

"This is her world."

"I know, but it doesn't appear to be a very safe place."

"She is not some stray puppy you can just take home," argued Trent. "She's a human. And she probably wouldn't be happy in a modern world. She might even have a husband."

"I don't think so," Henry said and coughed.

Trent looked over to see that Tarra had taken a possessive looking grip on Henry's arm. He shook his head but had to admit he could see why the young pilot wanted to take her along. Tarra was now wearing Henry's fedora and looked very cute in it.

What made Trent nervous was how quickly the girl rebounded from her recent ordeal and the resolute manner in which the girl was now acting toward Henry. He had a feeling that the snub nose, rosebud mouth, and inviting dimples concealed a very strong personality. A world like this was bound to toughen all its inhabitants.

They stopped to rest and snack on the Crackerjacks. Tarra smiled at the sweet caramel taste and hogged one of the boxes for herself. The prize was a small whistle that Henry showed her how to use. She blew it for several minutes until Trent almost grabbed it away from her.

The three stopped in one wide valley to watch a herd of elk fording a small river. They were magnificent, huge animals. They made Trent think of the skull and antlers above the jukebox in the dream city bar. The land was swampy around the river, with shallow lakes filled with cattails and water lilies. The wetland was also filled with numerous kinds of ducks and geese that thundered into the air in huge flocks when the humans approached.

They came to the top of a hill where Tarra pointed across the valley. On the other side was a rough stockade built into a natural indentation of the hill. Tree trunks three to four inches in diameter formed a wall standing at least eight-feet high. On the hillside were a dozen small plots of land under cultivation. Several women and a handful of children were working in the gardens.

"Well, this is it," said Trent. "I think the safest thing to do is just send her across by herself. They might not prove friendly to strangers."

Henry was obviously of a different mind, but he sadly took Tarra's hand from his arm and pointed for her to go to her village. Tarra realized that he didn't intend to go with her. She shook her head and spoke loudly in her unfamiliar tongue.

"No," said Henry. "You must go back by yourself."

She gazed into the young man's eyes with a look heavy with heartbreak. Trent turned away, shook his head and looked at the sky. He had already given up. Who was he to say what anyone else should do? The only way to survive these crazy leaps from world to world, Trent was finding, was to go with the flow. Besides, he knew it would only be a matter of seconds before Henry capitulated to those dimples.

"Ah, Trent. I can't just shove her away like this."

Trent turned back to the two.

"Do what you want," he said in resignation. "But I still don't think it is a good idea to go to her village."

Tarra could tell from the tone of the conversation that she wasn't going to be abandoned. She laughed and again began tugging Henry in the direction of the primitive fortification.

The decision was taken out of the two men's hands. Emerging from a grove of trees behind them came a dozen screaming hominids, led by the survivor of the trio Henry had decimated. The noise alerted the women in the gardens, who looked up to see the three and their pursuing mob. They turned and yelled to the stockade as they rounded up the youngsters and herded them through a small opening in the fence.

Trent tripped and almost fell, but caught himself and continued running. Knowing how the ape men treated prisoners was all the motivation he needed. The terrain was rugged with outcroppings of rocks. Trent could only admire Tarra's stamina as she leaped barefoot over the rough stones. Heads appeared above the wall and yelled encouragement to the three, as well as screaming insults at the ape men. The pursuers began shrieking even more lustily.

Henry wasn't completely recovered from the crash and he started dropping back, his limp growing more pronounced.

"Henry," Trent huffed, "we're almost there. Keep running, you can make it."

"I'm trying," was all the gasping young pilot could answer.

Trent slowed as Henry dropped further back. They had crossed the small valley and were headed uphill toward the village. Tarra also slowed and fell back to Henry's side. The lead hominid was bent on vengeance and led the pack. He screamed in glee when he saw his prey faltering and surged ahead. Henry stumbled and Trent grabbed his arm to keep him from falling. The ape man raised his club and ran in for the kill.

Tarra slid to an abrupt halt and spun with her knees bent. The hominid tried braking while whipping his club at the girl. She straightened her legs and shot up inside the arc of the swing and drove the flint knife deep into the creature's stomach. The two were sent cartwheeling, but only Tarra leaped back to her feet after they rolled to a stop.

The pursuing ape men screamed in rage and cheers erupted from the stockade. Hands were waiting to pull them through the small opening. Tarra shoved Henry in first before following. Trent expected a club up his butt as he squirmed in last, but he fell safely to the ground on the other side. He lay gulping in air as he watched the villagers slide a gate across the hole and prop it shut with heavy logs. Men and women shot primitive arrows at the attackers from a flimsy scaffold along the wall. A few others just threw rocks.

The ape men realized they weren't going to get anywhere with their enemies now secure and they beat a hasty retreat. The defenders hurled taunts and insults to their backs.

Tarra still grasped the bloody knife in one hand as she kneeled protectively over Henry. She fired off rapid responses to questions from the villagers who were circling the trio. An old lady with no teeth bent to finger the flannel shirt Tarra was wearing and gasped in surprise at its texture. She turned to the rest and gibbered loudly.

They backed away as Henry and Trent stiffly stood. None of the villagers looked much taller than five and a half feet. The crowd divided at the approach of a lone woman. She wore the same rough skirt as the others, but her long hair was decorated with colorful bird feathers and shells. Purple circles were tattooed around her nipples and eyes. Dabs of blue paint marked her cheeks and she wore a necklace made of ceramic beads.

The woman looked in puzzlement at the strangers then turned to question Tarra.

"I believe the big cheese is here," whispered Trent to Henry. "And if I'm not mistaken, this is also Tarra's mother."

Side by side, the resemblance was striking. Though older, the woman had the same strong chin and high cheekbones of her daughter, as well as the blue eyes and straight nose.

The conversation did not seem to be going well. Mother was definitely not happy when Tarra took Henry's arm and held it tight to her chest. She snapped at her daughter and pointed to an older man who stepped out from the crowd. He was balding and was missing several front teeth.

"I've seen this before," Trent whispered again to Henry. "Melissa's mother looked at me like that the first time I showed up to take her daughter on a date."

Henry looked at Tarra's intended and then down into Tarra's pleading eyes. He took her hand and turned to look defiantly at the mother. Mother's eyes flared and a determined twist found its way to her lips. She shouted orders to several men with spears. They pushed their way to the front of the crowd.

"I think the honeymoon is over," warned Trent. He stepped closer to Henry's side and scanned the suddenly unfriendly sea of faces. "Maybe you should try buttering Mom up—"

His suggestions were cut short. The scene began flickering and Trent was so surprised that he almost forgot to grab Henry's other arm. His last glimpse of the world was the shocked face of Tarra's mother.

Chapter Ten

Trent found the picnic table a much harder surface to appear on—and roll off of—than his waterbed. He grabbed at the top of the table as he hit the seat, missed, and tumbled to the ground. The landing knocked the wind from him.

The other two fared better. They didn't roll off the top, but Henry had his hands full as Tarra screamed in surprise and waved her flint blade in the air.

"What the hell?" Rich was standing opened-mouth next to the barbecue grill. A bunch of burgers were sizzling noisily over the coals.

"I hope you have enough for guests," Trent managed to draw in enough air to speak. Al and Varva came running out the back door.

"Trent, are you all right?" asked Varva anxiously. She took his hand and helped him to his feet then brushed his hair from his face and looked with worry into his eyes as if she could detect any injuries by his gaze.

Trent squeezed Varva's arm and smiled, feeling warmed by her obvious concern.

"Yes, I'm okay. Nothing six months of rest wouldn't cure."

"You better sit down, buddy. You still look a little shaky," Al advised and almost forced him to sit at the table.

Lorenzo came out the back door as Trent turned to introduce his new companions.

"Henry and Tarra, this is Rich, Al, Varva and Lorenzo."

Henry was also looking a bit battered. Tarra clung even tighter to his arm as she looked about the strange landscape. Henry placed his arm protectively around her and nodded at the others.

"Rich, why don't you put on some more hamburgers," Lorenzo said. "It looks like we'll have to set a few more plates."

Trent gratefully took a beer Rich handed him and motioned for Henry to help himself from the cooler.

"Go ahead, Prohibition is over," said Trent.

"I know," replied Henry, picking out a can and staring at the top. Trent walked over and showed him how to work the flip.

"Maybe we ought to give Tarra a soft drink," Trent said and handed her a Cherry Coke. She gave it an experimental sip, seemed to like it, and took a few more gulps.

"Well, are you going to keep us in suspense all afternoon?" Rich finally burst out. "You've been gone since this morning. What happened?"

Al brought additional lawn chairs from the garage and they gathered in a semicircle around Trent.

"Well, I awoke to find myself in a beautiful glade surrounded by a very old forest of hardwoods," began Trent. "Some of the oaks had to be seven feet in diameter. I was going to wait it out there when our German shepherd showed up..."

Trent continued his story as the hamburgers were passed around, pausing to fix his bun and load up with potato salad. Tarra took a ravenous bite out of her sandwich. She looked like she was planning to stuff the entire burger into her mouth when she noticed how everyone else was eating. She forced herself to chew and swallow the first bite before taking another, though she decided forks were just too much. Tarra picked up her plate and scooped up the potato salad with her fingers.

Henry looked embarrassed for her as the others watched the young woman out of the corner of their eyes. She looked up and caught Henry's gaze then looked with worry at the others. Trent smiled, picked up his plate, and scooted a clump of salad across the plate with his fingers and into his own mouth. She looked relieved and shoveled down her pork and beans.

"There's plenty of time to learn how to use a fork," Trent said after swallowing. "She's going to run into enough cultural shock the way it is."

"Though maybe we should wait a while before taking her to a McDonald's," he added.

The story began again after Trent washed down the last of his sandwich. Once he noticed Henry staring wide-eyed at the jet trails of an airliner across the sky. Trent's throat was sore by the time he finished.

"So you were flying a Jenny?" asked Lorenzo. "There are only a couple still flying today."

"And this is really 2016?" Henry asked. "I feel almost as out of place as Tarra. Do you think there is any way I can get back?"

"I have no idea," said Trent. "Maybe if we could get a hold of my other self. He seems to be able to travel at will."

Trent stood and stretched then looked at Henry. "Maybe you should take Tarra in and introduce her to the miracles of modern plumbing."

"Me?" the young man replied helplessly as he turned red.

"I will show her," said a laughing Varva, coming around the table and taking the young woman's hand.

Henry nodded and smiled when Tarra looked questioningly at him then hesitantly followed Varva into the house.

"We'll try and find a way to get you back," Trent told Henry. "But until then, I have a big house, and there is plenty of room for you and Tarra until things get settled."

"That's swell of you," Henry replied gratefully. "Though when I saw that rocket going across the sky, I almost felt like I wanted to stay here. Are we in outer space yet?'

"Barely. We've been on the moon several times, but things came to a standstill until we put up a station. I have some history books inside that you might want to see."

169

"I'd like that, but I think I need to visit the john first and then I could use a nap."

Henry was looking beat. Trent led him into the house and after showing him the bathroom, checked the upstairs guest room to see if it were fit for company. Though the old furniture of his grandparents' was a little dusty, the room seemed habitable. Trent turned down the blankets and went back downstairs.

Henry blushed again as Tarra followed him into the bedroom.

"Don't worry," said Trent as he closed the door. "You outweigh Tarra by enough that I doubt she'll be able to take advantage of you."

"Lorenzo said I could go with you tonight," Rich said as Trent entered the living room.

"What?"

"Hey, it's only fair," the friend said defensively. "Everyone else has been jumping from world to world and I just get to hear about it. Anyway, it sounds like you will need help when you go back to the dream city tonight."

"I'm beginning to feel like an elevator," protested Trent. "And what is Theresa going to say about you being gone?"

"That's the beauty of it," Rich replied with a smile. "Theresa and her sister are going to be on an overnight visit to an aunt in Illinois. It's either now or never."

"God, I don't know..."

"Quit you're whining, Trent. It's so unbecoming," Lorenzo said from the hall door.

"The next thing you're going to tell me is that Al also wants to come along."

"He does."

"What? What's going on? How do you expect me to drag along everyone? What if you are all too many? What if I short out?" Trent asked as he began pacing the room. "I just want to get in there, get Melissa, and head back. This is way too complicated."

Lorenzo grabbed his friend by the arm and shoved him down on the sofa.

"Listen, Trent, that would be great for you to just pop in and pop back with Melissa, but you're going to have to make it to the Crossroads Cafe first and that might not be easy," Lorenzo spoke solemnly. "Things are coming to a boil in that dream city of yours. The animal-headed bunch seems awfully anxious to personally make your acquaintance. I doubt you'd be able to travel from the house to the restaurant without help."

"So, what are we going to do, start taping one of you to my wrist, another to my elbow, another to my ankle, another to—?"

"We'll think of something. Remember our exit from the bar, we were only linking hands and we all made the transfer."

~ * ~

The evening seemed to drag on and on for Trent. He could only think of Melissa. Henry and Tarra came back down stairs and Lorenzo gave him several books dealing with recent history and a couple coffee table books containing mostly photos. The den appeared to be the preferred meeting place and Trent started the fireplace. Henry and Tarra picked a spot on the floor in front of the fire and he sat entranced at the unfolding of sixty plus years of progress. Tarra remained quietly at his side stared into the flames, the only familiar thing she'd seen in this new world.

Varva and Al had returned just minutes before from shopping. She had picked a simple wardrobe of jeans and a black, hooded sweatshirt, along with sturdy hiking boots. Varva had a practical streak running in her, Trent decided as he watched her enter the room and model the new look.

"I chose similar garb for Tarra. We should be dressed to face unkind landscapes," Varva told the room.

"Wait a minute," Trent protested for the hundredth time that day. "We shouldn't drag her into this. She can't even speak English. We can't tell her what's going on or where we're going. It would scare the hell out of her."

"We can't leave her alone," Henry said as he looked up from his book.

"You can stay with her," replied Trent, "and guard the place while we're away."

"Oh, no." Henry closed his book and looked from Tarra to Trent. "I need to find the answers to all this as much as anyone. I'm not going to get back to my world sitting around doing nothing."

Trent shook his head and walked to a far window. It was a clear night and he could see the moon coming over the trees in the same spot the hotel was in the dream city. Lorenzo came and stood by him.

"None of this makes sense," Trent complained. "I don't know what's going on."

"Maybe there is no sense."

"What do you mean?"

"Just that. I've tried placing all the recent events in a logical context," Lorenzo said. "But they refuse to fit. Take Varva. She speaks very good English, minus our idioms and colloquialisms, and with only a slight accent. Yet English is a fairly modern language. Look how our speech has changed since Shakespeare, and the English spoken just one hundred years before him would sound almost unintelligible to us. Was there some kind of mass language conversion in her world within the last one hundred years? Or is her world just an illusion? If so, how do we explain the flesh and blood Varva?

"Tarra makes a little more sense. It appears she speaks a language close to the original Indo-European stock that most of our Western tongues evolved from. I tried talking to her earlier. She rubbed her shirt and said 'mel,' which meant soft in Indo-European and has come down as 'melt' in English."

"You understand what she is saying?"

"Not much, I just recognize a few words. Indo-European is probably at least 7,000 years old. The region where it evolved is still debated. But from that ancient tongue has evolved the Germanic, Celtic, Balto-Slavic, Ibdo-Iranian, Hellenic, and Italic, to mention a few. Languages as different as Punjabi, Greek, Spanish, Dutch, Czech, Latvian, Welsh, and Sanskrit have their origins in Indo-European.

"She mentioned 'wlp,' which is wolf. She also said 'nekwr'—that has evolved into 'night.' She was talking about the mammoths and said 'kerdh,' which changed to 'heord' in Old English and entered into modern English as 'herd.' She spoke of the attack by the proto-humans and mentioned 'rendh' and 'sketh.' Those have come down to us as 'rend,' which means 'tear,' and 'scath,' which means 'harm.' You must have been traveling by a fen, which means a marsh, because she spoke of a 'pen.' Some linguists even believe we still retain some words from an Ice Age language 15,000 years old.

"Those animal-headed creatures also don't make sense," Lorenzo continued with his original topic. "If they are artificial, who made them, why did they make them? I went home and dug around in my library while you were gone this morning. I'm falling into some pretty odd lines of thought. I've always been a decidedly heathenish individual, but these last few days almost have me believing in a supreme being, a supreme being with one twisted sense of humor.

"Then again, maybe it's best to look at these dreams like a scientist views quantum physics. The Newtonian view of the universe works for macroscopic events—throwing a baseball or a planet revolving around the sun. But it doesn't work for the microscopic, the subatomic realm. Here all bets are off and nothing can ever be predicted with certainty, only probabilities. You can see Newtonian events and easily picture them in your head. Subatomic actions cannot be seen or even conceptualized. Our common sense and ordinary intuitive concepts don't work.

"Our belief that we cannot understand something until we can picture it in our heads, like a game of pool, is part of our Newtonian heritage. When thinking about quantum physics, we have to be open and forget about visualizing it.

"Werner Heisenberg, one of the founders of quantum physics, said, 'The mathematically formulated laws (Trent smiled, thinking that in a crazy world of maddening dreams and insane creatures, he could always count on Lorenzo to lecture) of quantum theory shows clearly that our ordinary intuitive concepts cannot be unambiguously applied to the smallest particles.

All the words or concepts we use to describe ordinary physics, such as position, velocity, color, size, and so on, become indefinite and problematic, if we try to use them on elementary particles."

"No," sighed Lorenzo, "don't drive yourself crazy looking for answers. And even if we do find the answers, they may prove too outlandish. Just go with the flow and we'll try and get Melissa back. Then you can throw those patches away and hope your dreams will remain just that, simple dreams. Until then, let your friends help you."

"I don't want to endanger any of you guys," said Trent as he looked out at the others sitting around the room, their profiles lit by the dancing flames of the fireplace. The peacefulness of the scene was in direct contrast to the tension most of them felt.

"Don't worry about it," laughed Lorenzo. "I'm looking forward to it. I'd never speak to you again if I were left out of this. Talk about adventure, it doesn't get any better than this. Rich has been bitten by the bug. He went back home to get his shotgun. Even Al wants to go now, though I think it is more to impress Varva. I believe he is quite smitten with the young woman."

Trent decided his friend was right—as always. If all Lorenzo's esoteric knowledge hadn't allowed him to bring order from this chaos, then maybe there was no order. He watched Lorenzo sit next to Tarra and continue his linguistic investigation.

A cloud was slowly gliding across the moon. It wasn't thick enough to completely hide the glowing orb and he watched the faint glow move through the cloud like a deep sea fish.

Everyone seemed deeply engrossed in books or conversation, so Trent prepared for his expected night-tripping. He checked the pistol Lorenzo gave him, loaded his grandfather's shotgun, and placed a couple dozen shells in his jacket pockets. Trent knew his grandfather once owned a number of hunting knives and he went to the basement to check through old hunting and camping gear.

A large, musty smelling canvas tent had to be dragged away from the wall to expose an assortment of cooking equipment. Trent smiled at the childhood memory of his grandfather frying eggs over a green Coleman stove. He held up a tin cup and ran a finger over the familiar dents and scratches.

He opened a box to find poles and spikes for the tent. Another held what he was looking for—along with a fishing tackle box and reels were a half dozen knives. Trent picked out his grandfather's favorite pocketknife. It was a Scout-type knife with a jigged bone handle. With it, his grandfather had cleaned fish, opened soda pop bottles, and made wiener-roasting sticks. Also in the box were his grandfather's favorite hunting knife and its leather holder. Trent had admired the handle as a boy with its scrimshaw scene of a towering Kodiak bear.

Trent stood and slipped the jackknife in his pocket and belted on the hunting blade. He tried to imagine what his grandfather would have thought of all this craziness. Not much, he decided, and returned the rest of the gear as he found it.

No one appeared to have missed him while he was gone. Al was in a deep conversation with Varva. Henry looked dazed by what he was reading. Lorenzo seemed to be making progress with Tarra. She was definitely excited to find someone who spoke even a little of her language. Lorenzo was continually forced to slow her down when she spoke.

Trent walked back to the window. The moon still floated serenely over the trees. It looked so peaceful perched above everything. Trent finally found himself starting to relax, which was why the gunshot caught him so by surprise. He spun to see everyone else in the room reacting with shock. Lorenzo leaped to his feet and ran to a pack he'd brought from his house. He pulled out a revolver and flashlight.

"Everyone stay right here," Lorenzo ordered. "Trent and I will check it out."

"It came from the front yard," Lorenzo said as he ran past Trent who turned and followed.

Lorenzo turned off the lights on his way through the living room and they both stopped at the bay window looking onto the front yard. Rich's small pickup was in the drive. Lorenzo cautiously opened the door and slid silently onto the porch, again closely followed by Trent. They could hear a retching noise by the hedge.

"Hold it right there," Trent ordered as he turned on the light and shined it on a doubled-over figure.

"Hey, it's me," Rich protested weakly, straightening and shielding his eyes from the glare. "I think I killed something."

Rich's voice sounded very strained.

"I didn't mean to shoot it. Well, I mean I did. It tried jumping me when I came over to check on a noise. I thought I heard somebody screaming, not real loud. But I didn't mean to kill it. I mean I would have if I had to, but I—"

"Calm down," Lorenzo told Rich as he arrived at his side and shined the light on the body. "It's all right, I believe you have shot Ament, the hippo-headed monster hated by most of the other Egyptian gods."

Rich was beginning to shake and Trent led him up to the porch. Despite Lorenzo's order, the others had come to the front door and were asking what happened.

"Rich just shot one of those creatures," Trent told Al. "Take him into the den and try to calm him down. Lorenzo and I will take care of things out here."

"That's not all," Rich said as he was taken in tow by Varva. "There's somebody else there. I think he's dead."

Trent returned to Lorenzo's side and they searched the area around the fallen monster.

"Oh God," Trent gasped when the light exposed the second corpse. "It's Lowell Simons!"

Lorenzo kneeled and examined Simons' battered and bloodied body.

"It looks like Ament trampled and chewed the hell out of poor ol' Lowell," Lorenzo said as he ran the flashlight up and down the corpse. "I wonder what he was doing in your yard at this time of evening, and with a gun."

"With a gun?" Trent asked in surprise.

"A revolver," remarked Lorenzo, who was shining his light several feet from the body. "It's an old, single-action Colt .45. He even had the hammer pulled back. It must have caught him by surprise."

"Hell, why would he be in my yard with a gun? It's crazy."

"Have you seen him lately?"

"Early this morning, when I was with Melissa. He really lost it when he saw her. I thought he was going to have a coronary."

"That explains it."

"What do you mean, that explains it?" he snapped back. Trent had been trying to go with the flow, but Simons' death in his own yard was pushing him back to the edge.

"What would you do if you ran into someone you'd murdered eight years before?" Lorenzo asked as he walked back to the hippo-headed creature.

Trent followed close behind him. "What are you trying to say?"

"I'm saying a Simons murdered your double in Melissa's world to get rid of the competition. In this world, he murdered the object of his love when she wouldn't return his affection."

"What? Lowell killed Melissa?"

"Yes. And he probably did almost have a coronary today when he saw a Melissa with you. Imagine seeing the ghost of someone you murdered. Lowell never was that stable. He came here tonight to put his victim back in the grave for a second time."

Trent looked back to the shadow where Simons lay. He felt lightheaded, dropped to his knees and sat on his heels.

"The bastard," was all Trent could choke out.

"If it's any consolation," Lorenzo relayed as he examined Ament, "Lowell didn't have a pleasant death."

"It's not," said Trent bitterly, fighting back a rush of tears.

"It appears Rich is shooting deer slugs," Lorenzo continued as if not noticing his friend's discomfort. The Lorenzo Trent knew was seldom at a loss for words or action, unless it was an emotional situation like this, and now he acted as helpless as if he were tied and gagged.

Trent looked over at the creature. It had very wide shoulders and the thick neck needed to support such a large head.

"They are ugly," Lorenzo observed. "I wonder why they've decided to visit our world after all these thousands of years."

"You don't think it's a coincidence that they look like figures from Egyptian myths?" Trent asked, trying to pull himself together.

"I did at first. But that ibis, the jackal, lion, and this hippopotamus are all North African animals. We haven't seen any that weren't native to Egypt. I'd say they are connected. The question is, what are they after? Whatever the connection," Lorenzo concluded, "We best get this thing out of sight. We don't want to upset the neighbors with the corpses of Simons and an Egyptian deity."

"Wait a minute, Lorenzo," protested Trent. "It's one thing to fertilize a rose bush with some mutant, but we can't just bury Simons in my backyard."

"Why not?"

"Why not? Because, number one, I don't want that asshole in my backyard. And second, what if a water line had to go through the yard ten years from now right where he was planted?"

"Okay, Okay," Lorenzo surrendered. "We'll take them both with us and leave them in the dream city."

"Ah-h-h," Trent started sputtering. "You, you plan to tape a couple bloody, maggoty corpses to me and then expect me to fall asleep?"

"Any better ideas? Hey, quit giving me such a hard time. I didn't off the little creep, did I? Besides, blowflies are the first to lay eggs on a corpse and their maggots won't hatch for twelve to seventy-two hours, depending upon the temperature and species of blowfly."

Trent stood up and rubbed his eyes. "That really comforts me."

"We should at least drag the bodies around the corner and cover them with a tarp," Lorenzo argued.

"All right. Which one first?"

"We'll take the beastie boy first," said Lorenzo. He grabbed one foot with his left hand and kept his right free for the pistol. "Pick up that .45. You never know when you might need it."

They returned to the den ten minutes later to find Rich on the sofa looking a little fitter.

"You did good, buddy." Lorenzo said to Rich as he slapped him on the shoulder. "Nailed him right in the chest. I think you tore the aorta. Looks like he drowned in his own blood."

Rich looked like he was going into a relapse.

"Thanks, good going," snorted Al, who sat next to Rich and put a comforting hand on his arm.

"What? What did I say?" asked Lorenzo in puzzlement.

"We've got somebody at the door," yelled Henry from the hall. "It looks like coppers."

"Oh no," groaned Trent. "I don't think I can take any more of this."

Lorenzo tried to be supportive. "Steady, Trent. I'll go with you. Somebody just probably parked on the wrong side of the street."

"Or it could be because we have a backyard full of corpses and house full of armed men and knife-wielding barbarian women," Trent said.

"That too," admitted Lorenzo. "Let's all put our guns away, shall we?"

Trent took out the small pistol and Simons' revolver. They were shoved under the sofa with the shotguns and Lorenzo's M-16.

Trent tried to relax and forced himself to smile as he went onto the porch.

"Can we help you, officers?" he asked two young patrolmen, neither one much over twenty-one.

"And you are?" asked the shorter of the two, who also had a bad case of acne.

"I'm Trent Rowen. I live here."

"And you?"

"I'm just a friend. Lorenzo Spasm."

"What?"

"Lorenzo Spasm."

"That's your real name?" asked the cop suspiciously.

"Listen, sonny," Lorenzo said testily, "if you're trying to violate my civil rights by mocking my nationality and surname, I'll be glad to sit down with the chief tomorrow with my attorney."

"Hey, just asking," the cop said, taken aback by Lorenzo's outburst. He turned to Trent. "We had a report of a gun being fired around here. Know anything about it?"

"Gunfire? Around here?" Trent asked innocently. "Did you hear anything, Lorenzo?"

"Hmm. I think I might have heard a car backfiring a while ago. But nothing like gunfire."

"Hey, what's this?" the other officer asked, pushing to the front and motioning to the hunting knife Trent had belted on.

"Ah, just a hunting knife. I was getting out camping gear for a trip I'm planning and I belted it on to see how it felt," Trent answered.

"Oh, yeah," the cop replied, his tone stating that he thought something was fishy.

"Do you think my friend somehow managed to fire his knife?" asked Lorenzo.

"Are you trying to be funny?" the cop asked then squinted into the light of the doorway. "Who is that?"

Trent turned around to find Varva watching the proceedings. She didn't look happy.

"Ah, that's just a guest."

"Would you mind stepping out here, ma'am?" asked the second officer.

Varva pushed her way through the screen door and stopped next to Trent. She eyed both police officers from head to toe. Her expression left no doubt that she was not impressed. Officer number one huffed up under her cold stare.

"You have a problem, ma'am?"

"No, I do not. Do you, little man?"

Trent could feel the cold sweat spring to his forehead.

"Ah, Varva is from Eastern Europe. She associates uniforms with the secret police. They took her mother away in the middle of the night when she was four."

Lorenzo was eyeing his friend with new respect. The young officer seemed only partially mollified.

"Do you mind if we come in?" asked the second cop.

"Yes, we do," cut in Lorenzo, "unless you have a search warrant. I'm tired of this harassment. You get a report of some noise and you start acting like the Gestapo. I'm afraid I'll have to talk to the chief tomorrow morning, as well as the editor of the Bear River Sentinel."

"Oh, yeah, well listen to this—"

"Hey, Bob, calm down," said the second cop to his partner. He turned to Trent. "Sorry to have bothered you. Please let us know if you hear any gun fire."

"I'm getting a headache," Trent complained as the squad car drove away.

Varva uncrossed her arms and turned to the door. "They remind me of Dorga's guards. They believe they are fierce warriors, but I could take them even with Trent's puny knife."

"I'm sure you could," Trent said to Varva, worried about that glare in her eyes, "but please don't. They frown on that kind of behavior around here."

"It appears it might be unsafe to walk outside tonight," Lorenzo spoke to the group once everyone was back in the den. "I suggest we remain together for the rest of the evening."

Lorenzo turned to Trent. "I believe the best spot for tonight's gala event is right here on the den floor. We'll just spread a bunch of blankets on the floor and it will be just like..."

"... a big slumber party," Trent completed his friend's sentence. "Yes, what fun, a half dozen heavily armed people duct taped to each other. I haven't done that since the third grade. What is poor Tarra going to make of that?"

"I think I've managed to get the gist of it across to her," said Lorenzo. "She knows we plan to cross into another world for your woman. Like Varva, she seems to find that very romantic. I get the idea that the males of her tribe are not very gallant."

The rest of the evening dragged slowly on for Trent. Lorenzo continued his attempts at communicating with Tarra, to such an extent that Henry was distracted long enough from the books to appear a bit jealous.

At nine o'clock, Trent checked the doors and windows to make sure they were locked. He threw several more logs on the fire and brought out an armful of blankets. Rich helped him spread them across the floor while Lorenzo handed out the weapons. Rich and Trent had their shotguns, Al took the small pistol, and Lorenzo retrieved his M-16. Henry took the .45 Trent had borrowed from the dream pawnshop. Varva was again armed with the Kukri fighting knife.

Tarra showed her proficiency with the flint blade when battling the ape man, but Trent decided she needed something more efficient. He finally dug up a machete. Though it was old and rusting, she excitedly danced around the room and waved the blade about as if it were the finest Damascus sword.

Lorenzo had everyone lay in a circle, feet touching in the center.

"This way our hands will be free," explained Lorenzo as he duct taped everyone together by their ankles.

To spare everyone the distasteful experience of being bound to the bodies, Lorenzo placed them above his head. They were wrapped with blankets in such a way that Lorenzo could slip his hand under the covers to grasp a hand.

This is impossible, thought Trent as he looked at the flickering fireplace shadows on the ceiling. All the lights were turned off and it was finally quiet, but Trent was about as close to falling asleep as he was to understanding Indo-European. The corpses were especially disquieting.

"I have to go to the bathroom."

"What?" Trent snapped.

"I have to go to the bathroom," repeated Rich.

"Why didn't you do that before we got taped up?"

"I didn't have to go then."

"Can't you hold it?"

"No."

Lorenzo sat up and cut the silver tape around Rich's feet.

"Does anyone else have to go?" Trent peevishly asked. "This is your last chance."

Rich returned and was taped back into the human circuit.

"It would help if I had a bigger pillow," Al said. He was using a cushion from the coach.

"You can use Lowell," Lorenzo graciously offered. Al didn't mention it again.

A grandmother clock ticked away the minutes and the logs crackled and popped, occasionally shifting as they burned down. Trent tried to relax using a breathing exercise taught to him by Lorenzo. He could feel his heart slowing down. Now and then someone in the group would cough. Trent felt an irrational surge of ill temper when he detected Lorenzo lightly snoring.

The firelight began dimming and the clock ticked on. The floors and wooden joints of the old house occasionally creaked and moaned as the night turned cooler. Trent's thoughts drifted until he noticed the fire was out. He propped himself up on his elbows and looked at the others. They appeared to be sleeping. He bitterly shook his head at the injustice of it all.

The room was cool and Trent was tempted to rise and throw a few more logs in the fireplace, only he didn't want the hassle of cutting and re-taping his feet. Lorenzo stirred and sat up.

"So, we're here," he said casually.

Trent eyed his friend. "Here?"

Lorenzo smiled and nodded to the window. Trent turned and was surprised to see the slender hive of lights climbing above the trees.

"The hotel!" he exclaimed. "We are here."

Trent's shout woke the rest and one by one they sat up to look about.

"What's the matter," muttered Rich sleepily. "Didn't it work?"

"We're there, dummy," said Al as he fumbled in his pocket for a cigarette. He was also looking out the window at the hotel.

"We are? Wow, let me see." Rich eagerly pulled and tugged at the tape until Trent leaned down and sliced through the binding. He noticed that the two corpses had also arrived.

Standing and stretching, they crowded around the window. Lorenzo checked the clip in his rifle and walked to the door to peer cautiously up and down the hallway. Varva hefted her blade. Trent noticed the way she stood on the balls of her feet when she looked tense, ready to jump or spin at the slightest sound or movement. Their vigilance made Trent grip his shotgun tighter.

"Well, what are we waiting for?" he wanted to know.

Lorenzo smiled at his friend's impatience. "Let's get one thing straight; don't shoot at noises or things you can't see well. Fire only if you're being attacked. The most danger could come from the person next to you. Shoot at anything that moves and you might wind up putting a hole through a friend, so let's be careful. Keep your guns pointed straight up unless you're actually going to fire."

They filed down the hall and into the front room where they paused at the front door. Trent opened the door and continued into the yard.

Trent was once again struck by how similar the dream city could be to his real world, and yet possess numerous, subtle differences. He walked to a maple and rubbed his thumb across a dry, brittle leaf on a low branch.

"The sun must come up sometime or these trees wouldn't be here," he said over his shoulder to Lorenzo.

"Should we walk or drive?" asked Lorenzo.

"What?" Trent spun around. His truck was back in his driveway. "How'd that get here?"

184

Both men walked to the old pickup. Trent opened the front door. Everything looked in order. He slid behind the wheel and leaned over to open the glove compartment. In it was an Iowa map and his registration.

He held the registration slip up to the dome light that cast a slightly ruby glow.

As far as Trent could detect, because he couldn't read the print, the registration appeared to be just like his real one. He unfolded the map and could immediately tell it was very different. The number of highways crisscrossing the state was dramatically lower, as well as showing fewer cities and towns.

"Think we can all fit?' Rich asked through the window.

Trent looked at the group and did a fast body count.

"If some of you don't mind riding in the back, we can fit three in the front and four in the back," he answered.

"I suggest the men ride in back," Lorenzo said, "and not because of some misguided sense of chivalry. The women are carrying knives. We're carrying guns. I believe firearms are more effective from a moving vehicle."

"Relax, Lorenzo," laughed Rich. "I don't think these women have ever heard of sexual discrimination."

Varva walked nervously around the pickup. "Are we going to ride this?"

"You bet," Trent answered, hanging his arm out the window and slapping the door. "This old girl is as dependable as any new pickup."

"Girl?" Varva raised her eyebrows and stepped back to examine the vehicle.

"It's just a figure of speech," Lorenzo explained. "Let's get hopping. Everyone in."

Al opened the passenger door for the two women and Tarra looked cautiously inside. Lorenzo spoke a few words to her. It didn't seem to allay her fears. Varva climbed in, took the other woman's hand and pulled Tarra in after her.

The pickup started immediately. Varva patted her companion on the leg and murmured words of encouragement. Tarra looked with frightened eyes at Trent, who smiled in reply and said in as soothing of voice as he could, "It is all right. Don't be frightened."

Trent backed out the drive and headed downtown. Tarra tightly gripped the door handle and for the first minute stared stiffly ahead. She slowly relaxed to where she began gazing at the swiftly passing scenery.

Trent turned and glanced through the back window. Lorenzo and the others were sitting facing outwards, their hair whipping in the wind.

It took only ten minutes to arrive at the Crossroads Cafe. The trip was amazingly free of incidents. The ease in which they traveled from the house to the restaurant made Trent nervous. He picked up his shotgun as he slid out of the truck. Lorenzo was standing in the back and spun slowly as he scouted out the surroundings.

"We'll have to hand in the rifle and shotguns at the door," Lorenzo reminded the group. "Those with hand guns should keep them out of sight."

Trent wasn't waiting for the others. He impatiently headed for the door and walked in, automatically holding out the shotgun as he passed the ever-present waiter.

Melissa didn't appear to be at any of the tables. He squinted and looked into the shadows partially enveloping several of the tables then headed toward the back. Several of the restaurant patrons looked up as Trent passed and quickly averted their eyes as he met their gazes.

"She isn't here yet," Lorenzo said as he caught up with his friend. "Let's sit at the large table by the palm tree. We can wait for her there."

Trent was disappointed not to find Melissa already at the cafe and tried to control his impatience. He shifted uneasily in his chair as he watched the waiter crossing the room to their table.

"Would you like to see a menu?" he asked.

"Yes, we would," answered Lorenzo.

"I'll have the Fricassee de porc au romarin et a l'ail," said Lorenzo after the waiter returned with the menus. "Feel free to go all out with the hot pepper. I've always like that Basque touch."

"May I order for you two?" Lorenzo inquired when he noticed Varva frowning at the menu. He looked at Tarra and said, "Ed?"

She nodded her head in agreement.

"That's Proto-European," he explained to the others. "It comes to us in the forms of 'edible' and 'eat.' I think they will like the Cotes de chevreuil grand veneur. I'm sure Tarra will enjoy the venison. I once had this at the Auberge de l'Il in Alsace. It was served with a marvelous red wine sauce, accompanied by apples poached in a wonderful white wine, with fresh noodles, airelles, and sautéed, fresh chanterelles.

"How is your Faisan au cognac, aux ecalotes, et aux raisans?"

"Everything on our menu," the waiter explained in a chilly voice, "is excellent."

"Just checking."

"Excuse me," Lorenzo caught the waiter before he could get away. "Do you use seedless grapes?"

"No, we do not."

"Then I take it you peel and seed the grapes?"

"But of course."

"I would like to meet the chef of the Crossroads Cafe. He prepares that meal the old fashioned way," Lorenzo told Trent as the waiter went off with the orders. "Though with seedless grapes and their tender skins, such a tedious process is no longer needed. I hope the pheasant is tender."

"Pheasant? I thought it was fish."

Trent began impatiently drumming his fingers on the table to the beat of the band. Tonight's musical genre was hard to pin down. The band included a number of horns, piano, bass violin, xylophone, and drums. To Trent, it seemed like a cross between mall music, background tunes for the Pink Panther cartoons, and a Big Band sound influenced by beatniks.

"It's jazz—Henry Mancini circa 1958," Lorenzo volunteered when the next song came on, as if he were reading his friend's thoughts. "Along with the theme song, he wrote this number for a television detective show called 'Peter Gunn.'"

The music made the surroundings even more surreal. Trent expected Doris Day to walk in any minute with Rock Hudson on her arm.

"I wonder where these other people come from," Trent said to no one in particular. "Are they stranded dreamers?"

"None of them look real happy," noted Henry. "Maybe the food isn't very good."

Trent got up and strolled to the front window. The streets were as empty as usual. He was about to return to his table when he saw a lone figure running across the intersection toward the restaurant. It was Melissa. A man came hurtling around the corner and quickly gained on her. He grabbed Melissa as she reached the front of the restaurant, spinning her around and slamming her into the side of the pickup.

It was too much for Trent. He slapped the palms of his hands against the window and shoved before he overcame the initial shock, and then rushed to the front door. Lorenzo glanced up just in time to see his friend disappearing outside.

Trent didn't recognize Lowell Simons until after he had grabbed him by the shoulders and thrown him to the ground. Simons scrambled back to his feet and faced Trent with the ugly snarl of a cornered animal.

"You," Simons howled. "You think you have me. But I killed you once and I can do it again."

Trent threw up his arms to ward off a rain of erratic blows. Simons was screaming incoherently and flailing wildly. One punch managed to slip through Trent's defense and struck him in the eye. Caught off guard, Trent stepped back and tripped on the curb. Simons took advantage of his opponent's faltering and kicked him ruthlessly in the head.

Melissa cried out and tried to go to Trent's aid. Simons slugged her, opened the passenger door, and shoved her limp body into the truck. He quickly ran around to the driver's side and leaped behind the steering wheel.

Trent forced himself to his knees and steadied himself by placing one hand on the pickup's running board. Simons was cursing loudly from the cab as he vainly tried starting the truck. He wasn't aware that the starter of a 1953 Dodge pickup was located on the floor next to the gas pedal.

Lorenzo came flying out of the restaurant as Trent climbed trembling to his feet.

"It's Simons. He has Melissa."

Simons found the starter and the engine sparked to life. Trent grabbed the door handle in time to have it jerked from his grasp as the truck lurched ahead. He stumbled back and Lorenzo grabbed his arm to keep him from falling. It was too late to do anything after that. The truck was roaring down the street.

"Quick, follow me," Lorenzo ordered as he turned and began running.

Trent stood in bewilderment, watching the pickup disappearing in one direction and Lorenzo in the other.

"Come on," Lorenzo yelled again.

Trent didn't know what Lorenzo was doing, but he decided there wasn't much else he could do but follow his friend. He caught up to Lorenzo after they both turned a corner. It was then Trent realized the plan. Parked along the curb was a dark blue 1964 Dodge Dart.

Lorenzo came to a dead stop on the driver's side and peered into the interior then whipped the door open.

"Get in, it has the keys."

Trent was barely into the car and hadn't yet shut the door when the tires squealed loudly. The rubber protested again as they took the first corner. Trent's door flew open and he almost slid out before frantically grabbing onto the seat. He managed to slam the door shut as the auto again accelerated.

"Nothing like a slant six," grinned Lorenzo as he flicked on the headlights. "You can beat the hell out of these motors and they just keep running."

Just as Trent was relaxing his grip on the dashboard, Lorenzo slammed on the brakes and the car went into a slide, the scenery now passing sideways in front of the car. They came to a stop in the middle of an intersection.

"There they are," said Lorenzo as he looked through the back window. "They turned here."

He hammered the gas pedal to the floor and accelerated into a U-turn. There were taillights barely visible four or five blocks away.

"Are you sure that's them?" asked Trent.

"Don't see that many other pickups about."

Trent didn't know how Lorenzo could tell it was a truck, but he let the matter rest and concentrated on the two small, red lights. The pickup began turning on almost every other street. Simons must be aware he was being followed, thought Trent. Little by little, they gained on the truck.

The scenery changed quickly, from dark stores and offices to equally dark houses. Then they were out of the dream city. The landscape turned to barren fields and sporadic clumps of twisted, stunted trees. Trent decided the moon, at first glance appearing no different from the one in his world, now looked like a swollen tick as it floated over the blighted landscape.

"I bet the gang back at the Crossroads Cafe is wondering what the hell is going on," said Lorenzo. "I hope they stay there until we get back."

"I think all of them were asleep when we crossed, which means they ought to be able to get back by themselves," replied Trent, his attention more on the truck ahead of them than on the conversation.

They continued to draw closer. Trent leaned over and saw that they were traveling just a little over one hundred mph.

Lorenzo noticed Trent looking at the speedometer. "That old pickup shouldn't be able to do much over seventy or eighty, but she's hauling ass in this world."

"What happens when we catch it?" Trent wanted to know.

"That's a good question," Lorenzo admitted. "I suppose you wouldn't want to leap out of the window into the back of the truck?"

Trent didn't answer. Lorenzo looked over and smiled.

"I guess that means no. Well, now that you mention it, I don't know what we're going to do. I can't run Simons off the road when Melissa is with him. He might run out of gas first, but then again, so might we. Got any ideas?"

Trent chewed his lip and watched the scenery flash by as the old car's engine whined under the strain.

"Hell," he suddenly shouted and fumbled around inside his jacket then pulled out the old .45 dropped by the Simons of his world. "I forgot I picked this up."

Lorenzo glanced at the gun. "You can shoot out its rear tires, but we better wait until it slows down. We don't want to send them into a ditch at this speed. We'll wait until we hit some curves or a hill."

The waiting soon got on Trent's nerves. He couldn't see Melissa through the back window and worried she was seriously hurt. Several times they came to bends in the highway, but the speeds never slowed to where Lorenzo thought it would be safe to shoot. It was at a sudden tight bend in the road and appearance of an old overhead, iron-framed bridge where Simons was finally forced to slow down or risk crashing through the guard rails. The moon reflected across the surface of a river that appeared sluggish and oily.

Trent had the window down and the revolver aimed as they left the bridge.

"Now, before he speeds up again," yelled Lorenzo.

Trent squeezed off a shot. The gun leaped and he almost dropped it in surprise. He was wondering if he should fire again when their windshield shattered and sent flying a blizzard of broken glass. Trent raised his hands in front of his face and felt the car weaving wildly.

"Christ," snarled Lorenzo. "It looks like this Simons also carries a .45. Get his tire before he pulls away. We won't be able to keep up without a windshield."

Trent aimed the gun out the front and tried aiming as his eyes teared from the wind. This time he held the gun with a tighter grip and fired once, twice, three times. The truck was no longer pulling away.

"I think you did it, buddy," Lorenzo shouted over the wind. "Save the last two shots, we may need them."

Simons hit his brakes and Lorenzo had to whip the car into the left lane to keep from ramming the back of the pickup. They went flying past the truck. This time it was the back window of the car that exploded. Trent crouched low in his seat as Lorenzo braked and pulled the car onto the shoulder.

Both men turned and slid to their knees, keeping their heads as low as possible as two more bullets smacked into the car body. The truck's headlights came through the back window and lit up the interior of the Dodge Dart.

"Why did I stop here?" Lorenzo wondered out loud. "This is a damn awkward position to be in. We can't get out the doors or even look over the seat without making perfect targets."

He turned and sat on the floor with his knees under his chin. Arching his back, Lorenzo reached up and slapped the overhead mirror. A bullet buzzed through the back window and out the front like an angry bee. He leaned his head back onto the seat and stared into the mirror.

"He's still in the truck. Hand me the gun."

Trent leaned over and passed the revolver.

"Hey, what's going on here?" Simons screamed from the truck. "Where are we?"

"Where do you think we are?" Lorenzo yelled back.

"I don't know. This is all crazy. I-I think I'm going crazy. This can't be..."

In one fluid motion, Lorenzo twisted around and popped up over the seat, not even appearing to aim as he straightened his arm and fired twice.

"Never give a sucker an even break," muttered Lorenzo as he pushed open the door and climbed stiffly to his feet.

"Did you get him?" Trent asked incredulously. He looked up above the seat but could only see the blinding headlights.

The window of the driver's side of the windshield was a large web, with one large hole instead of a spider at the middle of the circular pattern. Trent rushed to the passenger side and flung open the door. He caught an unconscious Melissa as she began to fall and carefully eased her to the ground. Even in the poor light, he could see a dark bruise above her left eye.

Trent shifted Melissa in his arms and sat on his heels while resting her head in the crook of his left arm. He brushed stray wisps of hair out of her face.

"How is she?"

"She's breathing," replied Trent. "I think he hit her pretty hard."

Chapter Eleven

Melissa joined the conversation with a soft moan. She began struggling to free herself until she opened her eyes and saw who was holding her.

Raising one hand to lightly touch her bruise, she groaned once and said, "God, do I have a headache. Where are we?

"Where's Lowell?" she cried as her memory returned. Before either Trent or Lorenzo could answer, she gasped, "Oh, Trent, he killed you. He told me."

Trent helped Melissa sit up and hugged her as she began sobbing.

"He, he told me how he hit you with a rock as you were climbing out of the river. You were downstream from the others. That's why he was so upset to see you the other day. He came with a gun tonight and demanded to know where you were. He was crazy."

"It's okay, everything is all right," Trent said softly as he gently rocked her.

"We sat there for hours. I tried falling asleep, but I was too scared. I finally did, but when I woke here, he was with me. That made him really freak out."

"Melissa, stop just a second and take a deep breath," Trent interrupted her almost hysterical recital of the recent events.

She took in several deep breaths and then looked about her in confusion.

"Where are we?'

"We're outside of the dream city," Lorenzo said. "I'd say about four or five miles, which means we ought to start walking now if we want to get back to the others before we begin waking."

Trent helped Melissa stand. She looked at the truck's shattered window.

"This Lowell won't be bothering anyone again," Lorenzo explained simply.

"Walking?" asked Trent.

"It appears one of your shots put a hole in the truck's gas tank. We're lucky it didn't blow. One of Simpson's bullets put a hole in the Dart's radiator."

Trent looked with worry at Melissa. "Can you walk?"

"Yes. I guess I'll have to. I doubt any buses are going to stop for us."

Trent didn't look into the pickup as they walked past it. He was more than willing to take Lorenzo's word.

"We suspected Simons had something to do with the death of the Trent of your world," Lorenzo told her as they left the scene of the fight behind them. "We also believe the Simons of our world had something to do with the disappearance of your counterpart. I'm afraid he is no longer a problem, either."

Melissa shivered and Trent placed an arm around her.

"How did that happen?' she wanted to know.

"I'll let Lorenzo explain," said Trent. "I think I'm about to lose my voice from repeating the recent occurrences."

Trent looked about as they walked along the edge of the narrow road. It appeared to be asphalt. Once he stopped to examine a road kill. Lorenzo paused in his story to watch Trent kneel besides the flattened creature. The light from the full moon was surprisingly bright, but it still did a poor job of illuminating the object of Trent's curiosity.

"I think this toad has six legs," he said in surprise as he lifted it by one stiff, dried foot.

"Yuck, don't pick it up," protested Melissa.

"Here, put it in this," Lorenzo offered as he held out a re-sealable plastic bag. "I have a friend who would be interested in it."

"You always carry these around with you?" Trent wondered as he accepted the bag and deposited his treasure.

"I try and come prepared."

Lorenzo stuck the toad in his jacket pocket and they continued their march; with him continuing the story until he came to the part of the hippo-headed monster.

"Just what are your ideas about these animal-headed things?" Trent asked. "You just keep hinting."

"It's all conjecture, of course, and pretty wild at that. But after recent happenings, I guess we will have to admit that almost anything is possible," said Lorenzo, falling into his lecturer's voice. "Let's start with Egypt. What has puzzled historians is how could a Neolithic people suddenly erupt into a sophisticated culture with monumental architecture, medicine, astronomy, mathematics, writing, art, and sciences?

"Remains from the pre-dynastic period before 3600 BC showed no traces of writing then suddenly complete and complicated hieroglyphs, along with numerical symbols, were all over the place.

"The Egyptians said Thoth the Ibis-Headed God of Great Wisdom, gave writing and the sciences to them. In the Egyptian Book of the Dead, Thoth was the keeper of very secret and esoteric learning. But where did Thoth come from?"

The unearthly landscape lit only by the moon lent an eerie ambiance for Lorenzo's tale.

"Ah, maybe..."

"You don't have to answer, it was only a rhetorical question," Lorenzo interrupted Trent.

"Some respected scholars have suggested Atlantis, though they fear discussing it in public because of the sensationalistic New Age nonsense that has been bandied about. Remember, Plato, one of the founders of Western rational thought, stated Atlantis was real and not a myth. He also said one source of his information came from an Egyptian priest. This priest said the island of Atlantis had been rich in gold, jewels, grain, timber, and cattle, as well as a metal that no longer exists called orichalc.

"I believe some technologically advanced race was inundated and destroyed by floods, with survivors fleeing to Egypt where they found primitive inhabitants. There the cult of Thoth with its scholar priests was impressed upon those simple savages as the best way to preserve an ancient body of wisdom. They used these closely guarded mysteries to create an extraordinary culture and rule over surrounding countries.

"I always believed the animal heads only represented the qualities the Egyptians believed their different gods possessed. Now I'm not sure since I've been rudely shown these creatures actually exist. Ancient writings say these gods ruled Egypt until 5,500 years ago—then they disappeared just as mysteriously as they arrived.

"The builders of the pyramids supposedly used this knowledge to build the pyramids. Certain magical tools were also rumored to have been left behind. These could supposedly raise giant stones and cut through rock like it was butter."

"This sounds a little far-fetched, doesn't it?" asked Trent.

Lorenzo stopped so suddenly that Trent almost bumped into him.

"Look around," Lorenzo said to his doubting friend. "Try to imagine explaining this and all that has happened during the last week to your parents, coworkers or neighbors."

Trent had to admit Lorenzo was right. He was holding on to the arm of a woman from a parallel universe, was in a dream world, and earlier in the day had watched prehistoric wolves attack mastadons.

"Okay, Okay, I'm sorry. Go on with your story."

"I am not taking this from thin air," Lorenzo remonstrated Trent. "Copernicus stated he devised his revolutionary theories of the earth circling the sun from studying secret writings of the Egyptians, including the hidden works of Thoth. Kepler admitted he formulated his laws on the orbits of planets from information stolen from ancient Egypt. Sir Isaac Newton was quoted saying that the ancient Egyptians concealed mysteries under the veil of religious rites and hieroglyphic symbols. Though Newton is considered the father of modern science, he spent much of his time delving into hermetic and alchemical writings. He was obsessed with the belief that secret wisdom was hidden in the writings of the Old Testament. He even learned Hebrew and used information from the Bible to draw up floor plans of Solomon's Temple."

"What does that have to do with the Egyptians?"

"I'm getting to that," Lorenzo curtly answered. "The Hebrew were enslaved by the Egyptians to help build their temples and monuments. Moses was raised in an Egyptian royal family and taught 'all the wisdom of the Egyptians.' After becoming adept in this sorcery and ancient knowledge, we know Moses later performed a number of miracles. In ancient times, he was even compared to Thoth. Moses was forced to flee Egypt with his people and used a miracle to part the waters of the Red Sea.

"The Bible tells us how God gave Moses the Ten Commandments written on stone. Many religious scholars believe the stones were meteoric fragments since it is known that many ancient Semitic cultures worshiped pieces of meteors. Others have wondered if they weren't created from orichalc, that mysterious metal, possibly radioactive, from Atlantis. Had the Egyptians chased Moses because he was making off with sacred artifacts, as well as secret lore?

"The stones were carried in an 'ark,' a box with a golden lid. But ancient Jewish traditions also maintain that the Ark of the Covenant contained the root of all knowledge. The Ark is an interesting subject. Moses gave instructions on how to build it to the artificer, Bezaleel. It was a powerful instrument. According to the Bible, it could be used to slay whole armies and tear down the walls of cities. Those who came unprotected and too close to it were stricken with cancerous tumors. It could send off a blinding light.

"When Solomon built the temple to house the Ark of the Covenant, he built a special room deep in its bowels with immense walls, so it could rest in 'thick darkness.' The room was lined with nine-thousand pounds of gold and built by a master mason, Hiram of Tyre. He is also a personage of great importance to the Freemasons, who use his name in their most important rituals."

"Not the Masons," groaned Trent. "What have the Masons to do with animal-headed creatures from Atlantis?"

"Sh-h-h-h, Trent." This time it was Melissa frowning at his interruption. "Let him talk."

"Thank you, Melissa," Lorenzo replied with a smile then turned and frowned at his friend. "As I was about to say, Masonic tradition also holds that Hiram built two massive, hollow bronze pillars for the temple that held ancient and secret writings. In these writings was the secret of the magical Shamir. Old Talmudic-Midrashic sources said it was used to slice and shave the mighty stones of the temple walls. It could silently cut the toughest materials, including diamonds. Also stored in the temple were Urim and Thummim, magical objects that were part of the high priest's breastplate since the time of Moses.

"All these disappeared when Nebuchadnezzar sacked and destroyed Solomon's Temple and enslaved the Hebrews. Later, when freed, they were forced to build the second temple without the Ark."

"Wasn't the Ark supposedly buried under the second temple and is still hidden within the Temple Mount?" asked Melissa.

Trent waited for Lorenzo to chastise her, but he just smiled and said, "No. The Ark was gone long before the Babylonians trashed the place. When the second temple was constructed, it was without the Ark. A scholar named Graham Hancock has written that it occurred in the time of Manasseh and was subsequently taken to Ethiopia. Manasseh ruled the Hebrews during 687 to 542 BC and was decidedly paganistic. He installed altars for Baal in the Temple and placed a graven image of Asherah, a pagan deity, in the cell made for the Ark of the Covenant. Needless to say, many Israelites were pissed. A great blood bath in Jerusalem was recorded.

"The Levites removed the Ark from the Temple for safe keeping. Josiah, Manasseh's grandson, finally took power and removed the 'abominations' from his country. The second book of Chronicles records that he asked of the traditional Ark bearers, the Levites, 'Put the Holy Ark in the house that Solomon the son of David, king of Israel, did build; it shall not be a burden upon your shoulders.'

"It was too late. Sometime earlier, the caretakers of the Ark had spirited it out of the country to save it from falling into pagan hands. It was taken to a Jewish settlement in Egypt where a duplicate temple was constructed on an island in the Nile called Elephantine. The site of the temple is currently being excavated by archaeologists.

"The Ark stayed there until tensions broke out between the Hebrews and followers of the ram-headed god, Khnum. They had a temple next door and were upset with the Jews sacrificing lambs. A war broke out in 410 BC and the Hebrew temple was destroyed and the population dispersed. Caretakers of the Ark were then forced south to Ethiopia where there were scattered Jewish settlements. Their descendants, who mixed with the local populace, are today known as the 'black Jews' of Ethiopia, or the Falashas.

"The Falashas guarded the Ark for centuries. In the Fourth Century A.D., Christians came to Ethiopia. As time passed, the two religions clashed, often in very bloody warfare. The Christians slowly gained the upper hand and eventually captured the Ark, incorporating it into their religious ceremonies in the city of Axum.

"During the Crusades nine knights arrived in Jerusalem and founded the Knights of Templar."

Trent rolled his eyes but didn't say anything. He looked over at Melissa, who returned his glance with a warning frown.

"They established their headquarters on the Temple Mount where the two Jewish temples had stood. It is also the site of the Dome of the Rock, a sacred Moslem area. For almost seven years, they hardly ever left the site, making it off-limits for others as they tunneled beneath the rock. They were looking for the Ark, which they believed was buried on the site.

"They didn't find it, of course. But they did find other relics and manuscripts that contained the secrets of Moses and ancient Egypt. These were passed on to new initiates and the order grew and became wealthy. As these knights returned home with their newly gained knowledge of science and architecture, Europe witnessed the sudden outburst of elaborate, gothic churches. By the twelfth century, the order was fantastically powerful and wealthy, running a large banking empire.

"The knights also discovered the secret whereabouts of the Ark. Among the ornamentations of the many churches built by members of the Knights of Templar are hidden clues. Maps point out Ethiopia and the Queen of Sheba, who was from Ethiopia, is featured among sculptures.

"A royal refugee, Prince Lalibela of Ethiopia, had arrived in Jerusalem and came into contact with the Templars. It was from him that they learned of the Ark now residing in the Ethiopian city of Axum. He was exiled by his brother, Barbay, known in Europe as the mythical Prester John, king of an unknown Christian country in Africa or Asia.

"Lalibela returned home and with the help of a contingent of Templars, deposed Harbay, and seized the throne. He then created the spectacular churches carved into the sides of mountains. These were built with the secret mysteries learned from the Mount of the Rock dig and their final contact with the Ark.

"The Templars finally overstepped themselves. The King of France and the Pope, jealous of their power and wealth, outlawed the order. Across Europe, their property was confiscated and members arrested, many burned at the stake. Some escaped. The entire Templar fleet disappeared. In Scotland, the king was too busy fighting the English to bother with the Templars. They fled to that country and fought at King Robert the Bruce's side. After the battle of Bannockburn, victorious Scotts marched behind an Ark-shaped casket of the type used for displaying relics.

"The Knights of Templar went underground, taking form in Freemasonry. The oldest lodge was founded by the King of Scotland for the Templars. Many of the secrets are still passed down through the Masonic

Lodge. In the early days, the Masons regarded Thoth as their patron. Of course, they are only preserving the more mundane of these secrets. The real mysteries and powers were passed onto an even more mysterious sect, known as the Illuminati. Some believe they now secretly control many governments and world banking institutions, as well as retain the ancient secrets of Egypt and Moses."

Lorenzo paused in his narration and only the sounds of their footsteps on the asphalt pavement could be heard. When a couple minutes passed and Lorenzo didn't continue his narrative, Trent couldn't control his impatience.

"What, that's all? You went through all that to tell us there may be a secret cult today that knows the mysteries of a bird-headed god from Egypt?"

Lorenzo looked at his friend and sighed. "Trent, what was the symbol on the ceiling of Dorga's temple?"

Trent pursed his lips and tried to recall the image of that great building. "I think it was a cross."

"Yes, a stylized version of the cross called a croix patte. It was the cross used by the Knights of Templar and can be seen in the churches they built in Europe and Ethiopia. And in one of the murals was a depiction of the Ark, as well as the symbol of the Illuminati, a pyramid with an eye at the top."

"You think the temple of Dorga is connected with the Knights of Templar and the Illuminati?" asked Melissa.

"It could be some of the Knights found a way to escape the King of France's persecution by fleeing into other worlds. Maybe they found the secret of dream travel when they were digging in the Temple Mount or from the Ark itself. I don't know; maybe it was later with the Illuminati," Lorenzo answered.

"What does this have to do with me?" Trent wanted to know, still confused by his friend's elaborate story.

"There were other treasures besides the Ark at the Temple of Solomon. Remember the mysterious Shamir, Urim and Thummim? I'm guessing that giant ruby you pried out of Dorga's hand was one of those three or another of Moses' items he made off with when he fled Egypt. And I think those objects originally came from Atlantis, home of our beastie boys.

"I'm guessing that these creatures also escaped via dreams to other worlds; either as their island was sinking or after they left Egypt. Whatever the finer points of these connections, I think they believe you have this gem and they want it back."

Trent didn't know what to say. He remembered the feel of the gem in his hand, the feeling of warmth and power. He guessed it could have been more than just a jewel. How was he going to get out of this mess? He looked in the distance and saw a shaft of light on the horizon.

"There's our tower of Babel," Trent said of the hotel, feeling biblical after Lorenzo's history lesson. "It looks like we have about two miles to go."

The three marched on in silence, each to their own thoughts. Passing a farmhouse and barn, Trent wondered what made the buildings seem not quite right. Were they built with slightly odd angles? Were the proportions off? There were no lights in the house, but he thought he could detect motion through an open window. Was it a person or just a breeze teasing a lace curtain?

Trent stopped and stared at the house.

"What is it?" inquired Melissa. "Is something wrong?"

"I thought I saw someone in that house, in the bottom right window."

"Curiosity killed the cat," Lorenzo volunteered. "It's best to let sleeping apparitions remain in their homes."

The pale moonlight angling in through the window was reflecting off someone, Trent decided after he caught a glimpse of more movement. A figure moved closer to the window and stared back at Trent. A sad, bloodless face in an ivory white dress.

"It's a child, a little girl," Trent blurted out. He made several involuntary steps forward until Lorenzo placed a firm hand on his shoulder.

"Careful, Trent. Remember the incubus in the hotel," cautioned Lorenzo.

"But what if it is a lost little girl?" Melissa asked as she, too, made out the pallid figure. "She could be lost like some of those others in the city. We couldn't just leave her here."

Lorenzo sighed. "If we had our weapons, I'd say fine, let's see if it's some kid. But we're pretty vulnerable right now—too damn defenseless for my liking. It could easily be a trap."

Trent had to admit Lorenzo was probably right. But there was something about the small, haunted face looking out at him.

"Hey, who are you?" Trent yelled. "Are you okay?"

There was no answer and Trent reluctantly turned away. He looked several times over his shoulder but could no longer see the small shape. Melissa took his hand and gave it a squeeze.

He passed several more road kills. Trent stopped his examinations after stooping to look at what he first thought was a rabbit or cat. What he made out in the dim moonlight caused a wave of nausea that threatened to empty his stomach. He circled the dead creatures after that.

The colorless, gray and black landscape was beginning to get on Trent's nerves. Several times, he found himself unconsciously running his fingers over the handle of his grandfather's hunting knife that was still hooked to his belt.

"I've decided to come to your world."

"What?" Melissa's statement caught Trent by surprise. He came to a halt in the middle of the highway.

"I've decided I want to go to your world," she repeated. "I find myself going through the days just waiting for the nights, just waiting to see you. I'm not going to be happy until I can live with you."

"That's great," laughed Trent as he put her in a bear hug.

He closed his eyes and enjoyed the feel of her pressed close to him and the smell of her hair. When Trent opened his eyes, he saw a small, ghostly figure following far behind them. It was the child from the house. Melissa felt Trent's body tense and she pushed away to look at his face then turned to follow his gaze.

"It is a child," she said, startled, "and she's following us."

The girl had stopped when the trio halted.

"Come on, we won't hurt you," Melissa entreated. "Do you need help?"

Lorenzo moved next to Trent and Melissa. The girl remained silent.

"Who are you?" asked Trent.

"Who are you?" the small figure asked back. "Where do you come from?"

"We're friends," answered Melissa. "We're not from here. We come from a much nicer place."

The girl took several hesitant steps forward then continued advancing at a very slow pace until Trent could clearly see her features. She looked about ten years old.

"Who are you?" the girl asked again, stopping twenty feet from them. "Are you real?"

"Real?" Trent echoed. "Yes, we're real. At least more real than this around us."

"Am I real?"

Trent turned to Melissa, who looked as equally confused.

"What do you mean by real?" Lorenzo asked.

The girl looked down at her feet in anguish. "I know I was real...at one time. I'm scared that if you're here too long you aren't real anymore, like the Taylors down the road."

Melissa took several steps towards the girl and held out her arms. "I can tell if you're real or not. Come, take my hands."

The movement surprised the girl and she retreated several feet.

"Who are you?"

"We're just ordinary people," Melissa replied, "who were somehow transported to this place while we were sleeping."

"Then you're trapped here, too. Pretty soon you won't be real either." The girl looked nervously at Melissa's outstretched hands, but again began cautiously walking to the group.

This time she stopped just out of reach and looked into the Melissa's face. The pale figure took two more steps and slowly raised her hands to brush fingertips. Melissa didn't move. The girl stared at her hands. Melissa smiled and suddenly the young girl was in her arms.

"There, there. Everything is going to be all right," Melissa softly spoke as she hugged the girl and rubbed her back. The top of the child's head came to her chin. "My name is Melissa and this is Lorenzo and Trent."

"My name is Abby Moreland," the girl said as she turned her head and gazed at the two men. She looked back at Melissa and said, "You feel so warm, I know you must be real."

Melissa laughed. "You feel a little chilly. We should get a jacket on you."

"I'm okay. Just don't leave."

"We'll take you with us," said Melissa. "We have to get back to the city where some friends are waiting for us."

Abby's eyes grew wide. "Aren't you afraid to go there? Mrs. Taylor said there were monsters living in town."

"They won't bother us," Melissa assured the girl with more confidence than Trent felt. "How did you get here?"

"I don't know. I was staying at my grandparents' and I woke up and it was still night. Only things changed. My grandparents were gone and it looked strange outside. I waited and waited and it never did get to morning. There was food in the cupboards and refrigerator, but it didn't have much taste. I got scared and tried calling home on my mom's cell phone, but all I got was weird voices. I walked to the house down the road and there was a Mr. and Mrs. Taylor. They would hardly talk to me, said I asked too many questions. Mrs. Taylor said some people aren't real. They're like those cutout people and animals you see in yards, just there for decoration. I don't know if they were always that way or if it's because they stayed here too long. I'm ten years old. Can you get me home?"

It was like pulling a plug from a dam. The adults could hardly keep up with what Abby was madly spouting, as if she had stored up the words while having no one to speak with. They were now bursting loose.

"We will try to get you home," Melissa said. "But no matter what, we will get you back to somewhere normal. How long have you been here?"

"I don't know," Abby replied, finally relaxing her bear hug and stepping back, though she took Melissa's hand as if needing some physical contact. "There's no days here. Sometimes it almost looks like morning will come and the sky will get kind of gray. But then it just turns black again. I tried watching TV, but it had stuff on that scared me."

"Scared you? Like what?" quizzed Lorenzo.

"There were talking animals, but I couldn't understand them. They sounded bad."

"You don't have to worry anymore, Abby. We'll take care of you. You've been a very brave girl," Melissa told the girl. "Come with us."

The troupe continued its march, now plus one. Trent couldn't blame the child for wondering if she was real. With her pallid complexion, blonde hair, and white cotton dress, Abby looked more of an apparition or washed-out photo than a ten year old child.

Abby kept a firm grip on Melissa's right hand and continued chattering. Trent would follow what the girl was saying and then his thoughts wandered to the surrounding scenery or past events. Lorenzo was the first of the four to stop and turn. The others followed suit. Trent was about to ask why Lorenzo had halted when he heard the distant whine of tires.

"We better get off the road," advised Abby. "Those trucks go by here awfully fast."

"You've seen trucks on this highway?" asked Trent.

"Not a bunch, but I've seen 'em go by. They're real big and black."

"Let's get up by that tree," said Lorenzo. "I'd rather not be seen at this stage of the game."

They waded through the brittle weeds in the ditch and up the hill to what looked like an ancient willow tree. A fence ran next to the tree and Trent noticed it had extra vicious looking barbs, at least twice as long as the ones he was used to seeing.

The hum grew louder as the four watched the crest of the hill they had walked over only minutes before. Abby gasped and pointed when the first hint of headlights was an odd glow in the misty air. Seconds later, the blinding beams of the truck topped the hill, more like the laser lights of a rock show than those of a motor vehicle.

It roared by, shaking the ground and making even the air seem to tremble. Trent could feel the passing of the truck in the tree he was leaning against. He tried getting a good look at the semi, but it left only the impression of something massive and dark thundering by like a giant, black buffalo.

Trent cleared his throat and said to his friend, "Maybe you should try thumbing a ride with the next one that goes by."

"You first. I've noticed you look like your feet are getting sore," laughed Lorenzo. "It does make you wonder where it is coming from and what it is carrying. What kind of bizarre commerce goes on in this world?"

"I'd rather not know," Melissa said with a slight shudder.

They picked their way back through the ditch and weeds to the road to continuing the walk in silence. Even Abby seeming finally to have gotten enough speech out of her system, though she maintained a tight grasp on Melissa's hand.

The hotel grew larger and larger and soon they could make out separate streetlights. Lorenzo wasn't far off when he joked that Trent's feet were getting sore. He did feel like he was getting a couple blisters where his shoes were rubbing.

The string of dark houses they were now passing took Trent's mind off his feet. The dark windows looked like gaping eye sockets in a row of skulls. He stopped after they crossed the first intersection. Trent stood in a drive and examined a 1958 Cadillac; its fins looking bigger than the ones on a space shuttle. He walked to the driver's window as the others watched. The keys were in the ignition.

"We're in luck," yelled Trent as he opened the door and slipped behind the wheel. The door slammed shut with the solid thunk of an old luxury car. "We can drive the rest of the way."

Abby didn't want to let go of Melissa's hand, and she climbed in the front seat, pulling Melissa in after her. The car started immediately and idled in a low, confident rumble. Trent turned his head and looked past Lorenzo as he backed out of the drive.

"It feels like I'm driving a battleship," Trent said, "or a tank. There's almost enough room in here for a game of basketball. This would be a great car for a road trip. I wonder if I could bring this back with me?"

"It might screw up the water bed," noted Melissa.

"We left from the den floor," Trent replied, "which also probably wouldn't be a great spot for an old Cadillac."

It wasn't hard to find the Crossroads Cafe. Trent used the hotel as a giant guidepost. He parked where the pickup had been. The group climbed from the car in a collective weariness.

If Trent was expecting a huge welcome, he was disappointed. The table they had been sitting at was empty.

"Where are the people we were with?" he asked the waiter.

"They left after you went running out. They left a message that they would be back soon if you returned before they did."

"Where did they go?"

"I'm afraid I was not privy to their plans, but I believe they went looking for the three of you," the waiter said coolly.

"Crap, what do we do now?" asked Trent as he turned and looked with worry at Lorenzo.

His friend didn't appear to hear him. Lorenzo was staring intently at the corner table hidden in shadows under a palm tree. Trent couldn't tell who was at the table and turned back to Lorenzo.

"Who is it?"

"I believe it's your long lost twin."

"What?" yelped Trent. He spun around and faced the table. The figure did have on a black leather jacket.

"Melissa, would you take Abby to a table and see if she'd like to order something?" Trent said as he eyed the shadows ominously. "Lorenzo and I have to chat with someone."

Melissa looked like she wanted to ask what was going on, glanced questioningly at the shadowy figure, and then led Abby away. The two men walked to the table and pulled seats out on each side of the Trent duplicate. He looked up from a double cheeseburger and fries and smiled.

"What? My bump has gone down so you figure I need another smack?"

Trent had forgotten how disconcerting it was to face his doppelganger. It was eerier than meeting a twin—this person across the table probably had many of the exact memories that he did. He was himself.

"Who was your kindergarten teacher?" Trent asked.

Trent II raised his eyebrows then answered, "Mrs. Dartman."

"Who was your first girlfriend?"

"Helen Mueller."

"Who was the next?"

"Melissa. Now, why these questions?"

"I'm trying to figure when you and I separated," answered Trent. "How long has it been since you went with Melissa?"

"I still do."

"What?" Trent leaned forward and propped his arms on the table. "How is that?"

Trent II sighed and leaned back in his chair, popping a fry into his mouth and looking almost with pity at his counterpart.

"I think you and I separated right after Melissa was murdered..."

"I thought you said you were still going with Melissa," interrupted Trent.

"I did. We're married..."

"But..."

"Please, let me finish," Trent II said patiently. "Why don't you call your Melissa over here? She should hear this."

Trent turned and motioned for Melissa to join him. She came with Abby close on her heels.

"Melissa, this is me. Me, this is Melissa and Abby," Trent introduced them. "Abby, I'll explain it all to you later when we have time. There are duplicate worlds and this is another Trent."

Both Melissa and Abby gazed in surprise back and forth between the two Trents.

"This is going to come as a shock to both of you," Trent II continued, "but about eight years ago in my world, Lowell Simons was arrested for strangling the Melissa I was going with and burying her along the Mississippi. He had caught her alone at a rest stop on her way to Chicago. Simons might have gotten away with it if two people fishing hadn't seen him trying to dispose of the body.

"I realize you never knew what happened, but the Simons of your world tried the same thing with your Melissa," Trent II said to his twin then turned to Melissa. "And I believe the Simons of your world killed your Trent."

Abby sat quietly in her chair looking very confused.

"I've already found out that Simons killed Melissa," said Trent to Trent II. "My Simons flipped out when he saw this Melissa. He showed up at my house with a gun earlier tonight, but one of those animal-headed creatures got him."

"Well, you still haven't discovered everything, but we'll get to that," Trent II promised abstrusely. "Anyway, I was pretty broke up about it. Unlike you, I didn't have to wait around in case Melissa showed up. She was very dead in my world. I took a leave of absence and bought an old Harley. I planned to ride around just for the summer, only I ran into some Native Americans in Mexico who turned me onto peyote.

"It was a crazy summer. I rode a lot of miles in the Southwest before crossing the border. I wasn't living real careful, but then I really didn't care.

Trying the peyote followed a hard night of tequila. I woke in my boarding house room but not the one I'd crashed in. I didn't know it at the time, but it was a Mexican dream city.

"Now that was a rush," Trent II said as he shook his head. "I got up to take a wizz in the bathroom down the hall and ran into a dude with a camel head. I thought I was still tripping so I just said hello as I passed.

"I couldn't sleep and I waited hours for the sun to come up. It was crazy. I decided I might as well head north, even if I was still hallucinating my brains out. It stayed outlandish. First, none of the gas stations had attendants. I chalked that up to the crazy Mexicans; maybe it was siesta time or something. It really blew my mind when there were no guards at the border crossing.

"I was running on my auxiliary tank and couldn't find a station with an employee. I finally filled up and left money on the counter. I did the same thing a couple hours later. This continued all day—or I should say all night. The sun just wouldn't come up. It was pretty freaky."

"I know. That's how it was with me," chirped in Abby. "Only I thought I was maybe dead and a ghost."

Trent II paused and smiled at the little girl. "Yeah, I wondered if I was dead too. But I kept riding. I took me five days to get back to Bear River. All the interstates were gone and I had to travel on these small back roads that had the God-awfulest looking road kills, especially these things down south that looked like mutant armadillos.

"The little towns looked like they hadn't changed since 1940. I'd stay in small motels and was always the only guest. The restaurants were empty, though occasionally there'd be a half-empty cup of lukewarm coffee at the counter. The only song I recognized on the jukebox was a song by Lee Marvin..."

"... called 'I Was Born Under a Wandering Star,'" Trent filled in.

"Right. It was weird. At least there wasn't that much traffic on the road. Occasionally I'd almost get blown off by these damn big semi-trucks.

Once, a whole string of Shriners passed me going the other way, all driving those cars you see in the parades with two fronts.

"I knew I was in big trouble when I got back home and the sun still wasn't up. My house looked too spooky for me, so I checked into the hotel. I was surprised to find a clerk behind the counter and a few people wandering around the lobby, though none of them wanted to talk much. It was pretty strange. One night I got drunk and picked a fight with some dude with the head of a horse. He picked up a chair and batted me across the room like a Whiffle ball.

"I passed out when I hit the wall and woke up in daylight. God, was I happy. Not recognizing the place didn't keep me from jumping for joy. What stopped my hopping was a brown and yellow dinosaur about two feet high. He wasn't very big, but that didn't stop him from trying to take a chunk out of my leg. I was packing a revolver, and I blasted the little bastard. Unfortunately, the noise attracted its mother. She was very big. The only thing that saved me was being next to some heavy timber. I was able to lose her in the brush but not until she'd plowed down enough trees to build a dozen houses.

"It wasn't over yet. The forest was filled with giant snakes and monster chickens with teeth. I spent the day hiding in a tree from this really crazy banty rooster. That night, I fell asleep and woke back here in the city. I think that other world got missed by the big one. You know, the meteor or comet that hit our earths and killed all the dinosaurs. I fell asleep in a tree and woke back up here.

"I hung around this town after that, occasionally venturing to nearby cities. There wasn't anything to see, so I always returned. I started drinking even heavier and one night drove the Harley into a tree. This time, I woke up in a timber full of giant wolves and ape people. Again, when I went to sleep, I woke back in the city.

"Later, I was drinking pretty heavy and suddenly felt strange, kind of like I was out of focus—or more like everything around me wasn't clear. My hotel room looked like some cable program that wouldn't quite come in. I suddenly knew I could change channels. It's hard to explain, but it was like I had invisible hands that could reach out and pull aside the curtain. I tried it and found myself back in Jurassic Park, which meant climbing another tree. After that, I got to where I could do it without getting stupidly drunk.

"I don't think I can explain how I do it. Maybe it's a form of self-hypnosis. I blank out everything—sound, sight, feelings. Not thinking is the hardest part."

"Stopping the chattering monkey," Lorenzo interjected. "That's what it is called in meditation."

"Yeah, that's what it sometimes seems like. After erasing my mind, I can feel something. It's not an actual breeze, but that's the easiest way to describe it; a draft slipping through a cracked door. I can lean into this breeze and nudge the door open.

"That's all it takes," Trent II told the others as he picked up a french fry and waved it in front of him. "Do it once and after that, it's the simplest act in the world, but until then it's the most difficult feat imaginable. It's easier jumping to worlds already visited. Unfortunately, I couldn't find my own world."

"I've had plenty of time to think about all this," Trent II said. He dipped the fry in ketchup and doodled on his plate. "I'm guessing a small number of people are born with the talent, or susceptibility, to slip into this dream world. Some pop back in the morning and must think it was an odd dream. Or maybe they can't remember it. Others never return home and are listed missing, along with the thousands of others who disappear for various reasons.

"Traveling to actual worlds must be even rarer, though it happens more often to less populated and primitive worlds. Don't ask me why, that's just been my experience. I finally gave up trying to get back to my home world. Random jumps are too dangerous. Once I found myself swimming in frigid salt water and another time I almost passed out from poisonous air before I could jump back.

"Then one day I was walking around the hotel and stumbled onto a billiard room. A woman was playing by herself. I'd already learned that most people here don't like to talk. This place seems to suck them dry.

"I was going to pass on, but something about the woman stopped me. I think it was her hair. She had her back to me and was about to make a shot. I paused in the doorway and watched her sink two balls. I don't remember what I said, something to do with it being a good shot. I thought I'd startled her when she froze over the table. I apologized and backed away before she could spin and nail me with the cue stick.

"She slowly turned and I found myself facing Melissa," Trent II said, shaking his head in wonderment at the memory's vividness.

"I've never been to the hotel's billiard room," Melissa said.

"You haven't," Trent II replied then looked uneasily at his twin. "It was the Melissa from your world."

Trent looked mildly bewildered, then the meaning of the statement abruptly hit him and the blood rushed from his face.

"What are you talking about?" he asked angrily. "She's dead, you said so."

"No, you said she was dead, killed by Simons. I answered that there was more to it than that. He thought he killed her when he hit her with a tire iron, wrapped her in a tarp and buried her in a thick woods. Melissa told me she came to as he was starting to bury her. I guess it was pretty horrible. She couldn't scream, couldn't breathe. Then Melissa woke in this world."

"And you married her?" Trent again growled.

"Yes," Trent II replied, shifting uneasily in his chair.

Trent noticed through his shock that the Melissa sitting next to him also appeared upset. He struggled to regain his composure and reached for her hand.

"This is crazy," Trent said. He took a deep breath. "Why am I reacting like this? I'm sorry. Too many things keep happening. It's wonderful news."

"That's all right," Trent II assured him, "I'm sure I would have reacted the same in your place."

Trent smiled wryly. "Yes, I'm sure you would have. Go on with your story."

"Melissa woke still wrapped in the tarp at the bottom of the hole. She said it took her quite a while to work her way free. She thought Simons must have been scared off. He was gone when she climbed out of the hole. Her car was still there so she scrambled into it, planning to stop in the closest town and call the cops. Melissa was so shaken that it took several minutes of driving before she noticed her troubles weren't over. She'd awoken from one nightmare into another.

"The bizarre landscape frightened her. Melissa tried blaming it on shock until she entered the first small town and found it deserted. She tried her phone and got only crazy gibberish. It was the same for her radio. Melissa said she would have thought she was dead if it weren't for her killer headache.

"She turned around and headed straight home, only to find Bear River also changed. Unlike you," Trent II said, looking at the Melissa next to his own double, "she didn't snap back to her own world. I don't know why you two do, unless it has something to do with those nicotine patches.

"I'm guessing she moved into the hotel a couple months before I wound up here. She looked pretty wiped out. At first I thought she was an apparition because I knew my Melissa was dead. After a while I didn't care. I discovered I could take her along on my jaunts and we'd tour other worlds for weeks at a time. We'd be drawn back to the hotel to rest in real beds and eat real food here at the Cross Roads."

"Then I spotted you arm-in-arm with that incubus," Trent II said to his double. "I was too far away to see who you were, but I could tell you were new, and I tried shouting a warning as you went into the hotel. Then I ran into a Melissa who didn't recognize me. It got crazier when I entered the lobby and saw a clean-cut version of myself entering the elevator.

"The strange Melissa disappeared and I was left wondering what the hell was going on when I felt everything roll around me like I was in the wake of some large boat. I knew I had to act fast when I realized it was you going back to your own world. I leaned into that wake and fell into your world. I hung around just long enough to be sure I could get back when I wanted to. It was that jump that let me find my way to other similar worlds, including this Melissa's."

"Why did you run those times I saw you?" Trent asked. "I would have helped myself, and you're me.'

"I would have. But my Melissa thought it would be too much for you to see her. She wanted to spare your feelings. Then later I found out that the Atlantians were after you and I didn't want to get involved. They're bad asses. I don't know what you did, but it's even got the silent bunch in this town talking. I hear some of Dorga's friends are out for blood."

"I think they believe Trent is in possession of the jewel that rested in the Dorga idol's hand," Lorenzo said.

Trent II whistled in surprise. "No wonder they're hot. That's supposedly from the original Atlantis. It has some secret power or something."

Lorenzo smiled in triumph with the validation of his theory.

"I wonder if that's also why the Rotarians are after you?"

"What?" Trent asked in disbelief. "Why the hell would the Rotary Club be after me?"

"Maybe it wasn't Rotary," Trent II admitted. "I overheard a conversation and they were talking about some group. It was confusing because they were using more than one name for the bunch. Maybe it was the Knights of Columbus or Kiwanis."

"Could it have been the Freemasons, Knights of Templar, Illuminati, or Rosicrucians?" Lorenzo suggested.

"Yeah, some of those sound familiar."

"Fine. That's just great. I have both ancient cabalists and animal-headed people looking for me."

"Where is your Melissa right now?" asked Lorenzo.

"She's in this Melissa's world."

"My world?" Melissa said in surprise.

"Yup. I followed you over a couple nights ago. When I found out you two had connected, we guessed she'd be joining you, leaving an opening for my Melissa to fit into. It would be a lot easier if one of us had a real identification rather than having to make up two complete new ones," Trent II replied.

"You're taking a lot for granted, aren't you?" Melissa asked, sounding slightly indignant.

"I didn't, my Melissa did. She said she was sure you'd do it. You are joining him, aren't you?"

Melissa opened her mouth then closed it without saying a word.

"What are you doing here then?" Lorenzo wanted to know.

"I came to see if the move was actually going to take place. That's all I needed to know. I guess I can go," he said and started to rise.

"Hold it a minute," Lorenzo said and pushed Trent II back into his seat. "No switch is going to take place with the Atlantians and Knights of Templar chasing Trent, who you also happen to be. They'll be after your tail soon. We have to solve my friend's problem first and it is to your advantage."

"As well as finding where our friends are," Trent added. "I thought they'd be back by now."

Trent stood and looked around for the waiter, who magically appeared as if called.

"May I help you, sir?"

"Did you happen to hear where my friends said they were going to search for me?"

"I believe I overheard them saying they were going to visit the hotel."

"Let's get out of here," Trent said impatiently. "I have a feeling things aren't going well with Rich and the others."

The waiter appeared, carrying their guns as they reached the front of the restaurant. Trent led the group out the door and to the Cadillac. Trent II eyed the old car inquiringly as he watched the others climb in.

Chapter Twelve

"The truck wasn't big enough," said Lorenzo as he held a back door open for Trent II and then climbed in behind him.

They scanned the sidewalks as the car lumbered down the street. It was deserted. Trent stopped directly in front of the hotel.

"Let them give me a ticket," he said, pulling the key from the ignition and opening the door.

The lobby of the hotel was just as he remembered it—a vast cavern dwarfing the furniture and few people lounging in the scattered pools of light thrown off from art deco floor lamps. Some of the potted palms were as tall as twenty feet, but looked much smaller in the immense chamber. Trent paused at a fountain on his way to the desk. Atop a black marble column was the sculpture of a young woman, naked from the waist up and kneeling with a vase. Water poured from the vase and fell to a deep, dark pool. Gold and black fish, most at least four feet long, swam lazily in circles. The artist had captured the beautiful young woman so well that Trent couldn't help but stare closely at the figure to see if it moved.

"It is amazing how they've managed to intertwine so many different styles. And yet it works," mused Lorenzo as they stood gazing about the lobby in awe. "I am especially impressed by the blending of Byzantine, Mahomet and American Colonial."

Trent was forced to move on by Abby's restless shufflings.

"Yes, how may I help you?" The clerk looked like the guard of the Emerald City in the "Wizard of Oz;" plump and with a large, curled mustache.

"Did you happen to notice two women and three men in here earlier?" Trent asked. "I'd guess about three hours ago."

"Yes sir. They went with a group of Atlantians. One of them left a message for you."

Trent looked with dismay at Lorenzo then turned back to the counter to accept a folded sheet of paper. He quickly unfolded it to see, "COME TO DREAM MEMPHIS, BRING THE SACRED JEWEL."

"What the hell is this?" he asked, holding it up to Lorenzo.

"Hmmm, how strange."

"What? Can you read this stuff? What language is it?"

"It's English," Lorenzo answered.

"English?" Trent examined the writing again. "Are you nuts?"

"They must be trying to be cute. It's a font based called Egyptian Hieroglyphics. I have it on my Mac. It says, 'Come to dream Memphis. Bring the sacred jewel.' Another puzzling occurrence."

"Memphis? They're telling us to go to Memphis? What do they want to do, give us a recording contract? Am I going to meet Elvis?"

"I'm afraid they're not talking about Tennessee. I believe they want us to go to Egypt."

"You are correct," interrupted the clerk, "and they gave me these to deliver to you."

In his hand were a half dozen copper bracelets.

Trent was still in shock from the note. He looked at the bracelets in bewilderment.

"What are those?"

"It appears they are to keep you and your friends from returning to your own world until you have completed your task," the clerk replied. "You will remain in this world as long as you wear these."

"And did they tell you how we are supposed to get to Egypt?"

The clerk was holding out another envelope. Trent wearily tore the envelope open and pulled out a red and blue card. On it was the stylized picture of a hawk.

"It will get you and your friends a flight to Memphis."

"You're kidding," Trent said in disbelief. "This is a joke, right?"

The clerk didn't reply but maintained his slightly sneering smile that was beginning to drive Trent nuts.

"And where do we catch this flight?" asked Lorenzo.

"Moline."

"There is also an airport there in the real world," offered Trent II. "It will take us about an hour and a half to get there."

"There's no reason for us all to go," Trent said as he looked at Melissa. "Why don't you take care of Abby here while we see about getting the others?"

"No," Melissa replied simply, her tone of voice speaking volumes.

"I'm going then," said Abby as she tightened her grip on Melissa's hand.

"Why not?" Trent asked as he looked to the ceiling. "Why should any of us act sensibly when nothing makes sense?"

A rose centered on a crucifix at the ceiling's apex caught his attention. It was the symbol of the Knights of Templar.

Trent smacked his forehead and looked to Lorenzo. "Well, what are we waiting for? It looks like one hell of a road trip."

With the way things were going, Trent almost expected the Cadillac to have been towed away. But it sat where they'd left it, and Trent climbed wearily behind the wheel.

"We're going to have to fill up before we leave," he told the rest after noticing the gauge reading almost empty.

"There's a station on the edge of town. Just go three more blocks ahead and hang a right. It will take you right out of town on Highway 61," Trent II spoke.

The station was where the dream city abruptly ended and the night-filled country began. Trent pumped gas while the rest used the bathrooms. Melissa returned first with an arm full of soft drinks.

"Here, I got this for the car," she said after putting down the cans. Melissa was holding a cardboard air freshener featuring an almost plump blonde perched on a wood rail fence. She was only wearing a cowboy hat and bikini. Her hairstyle was from the early 1950s.

"It looked like it went with the car," Melissa laughed.

Trent smiled and held it to his nose, immediately getting a strong whiff of pine.

"Doesn't it make you wonder where all this comes from?" Trent asked, nodding towards the gas station as he continued pumping. "Who delivers this gas or the food to the Crossroads Cafe?"

"I have no idea, and I don't think I want to get to know this place well enough to find out," Melissa answered. Her smile returned, it having briefly fled as she gazed about her. She reached out and softly touched Trent on the cheek. "After we find the others and settle your problems with the Atlantians, I never want to see this place again."

The others returned before he could release the nozzle and embrace Melissa.

Trent found himself driving out of town on the same highway he'd pursued Simons on just hours before. Abby was sitting between him and Melissa. He looked over to see the young girl craning her neck to get a glimpse of the house where they found her. If it were possible, he thought, the house looked even more barren and lifeless than before.

It took only a few miles for Trent to realize the road was the Highway 61 of at least fifty years in the past—when it was only two lanes, much narrower and still had curbs. Dozens of the houses they now passed were gone and forgotten in his own world. As Iowa farms expanded from a couple hundred acres to a thousand or more, most of the houses were abandoned and torn down.

If it weren't for being hunted by Egyptian gods and members of some secret cabal or worrying about his friends, thought Trent, this dream world could almost be fun. Habit made him slow down through one small town. Everyone in the car peered with curiosity as they passed a grocery store advertising Gold Bond trading stamps in the window.

Trent tried the radio a couple times in vain. He could only find a couple stations that featured droning, flat voices speaking nonsense, like random computer-generated speech.

Abby was sleeping by the time they reached the airport. They would have been there at least a half hour sooner if Trent twice hadn't taken wrong turns. Again he flaunted parking rules and pulled up to the main entrance. The terminal had a weary air about it, and for the first time there was a noticeable wind that was rhythmically banging an out-of-sight door.

The small group warily entered the lobby. The airport was different from how Trent remembered it. To the right was a row of ticket windows and on the left was an atrium featuring a giant, slowly spinning globe at least 15 feet high. Trent circled the base and noticed a second floor balcony that enabled visitors to view the Northern Hemisphere. He watched as Africa slowly came into view and pinpointed a dot of light at the mouth of the Nile that must be Cairo. There were several other nearby lights, but he had no idea if any of them were Memphis.

Melissa and Abby were standing next to him gazing up at the globe. Lorenzo and Trent II circled it once then walked back to the ticket windows. Trent looked over to see the two men talking with a lone clerk. He smiled down at Abby and took her free hand, the three of them heading to join Trent II and Lorenzo.

"And your luggage?" the clerk was asking Lorenzo.

"No, we're traveling light," Lorenzo answered casually, though he was gripping an M-16 automatic rifle. "We can always pick up something when we land."

"Your plane leaves in ten minutes from gate three."

"What?" a startled Trent exclaimed. "Ten minutes?"

"Yes, and you better hurry. There are no delays."

They followed arrows until they arrived at their departure point. It was level with the outside pavement and passengers had to walk across the tarmac to a ramp that was already in place. No one was at the gate so they exited the terminal and stopped in amazement when they saw their transportation. It was white and big with a three-forked tail. Four giant propellers created a backwash that blew grit in their faces. Across the side was written TWA.

"It's an early Lockheed Constellation from the 1940s," shouted an enthusiastic Lorenzo over the rumbling of the idling engines. "I think there's only one still in flying condition in the United States, and it's an updated, larger version called the Superconstellation. The newer ones carried ninety-nine passengers, this only carries fifty-four. What a treat."

Trent looked sourly at his friend and then glanced up the ramp at the ominous open door. "Yeah, a real treat. I can hardly wait."

Trent was surprised to see Abby with a big smile on her face. She looked excited about the prospect of boarding the ghost plane. He hesitated at the bottom of the stairs and Abby pushed passed him. He reluctantly started the climb when Melissa followed the girl.

There was no airline attendant waiting for them in the cabin, nor were there other passengers. Though the aircraft looked large from the outside, the interior seemed cramped compared to modern jets. The door to the cockpit was locked. Trent rattled the handle several times and listened in vain for a response from the other side of the door.

"Do you think there is anyone in there?" he asked Lorenzo.

"I guess we'll find out if the plane takes off."

"Doesn't this make you nervous, flying in a plane that you don't even know for sure has pilots?"

"This plane has been around for a while. Obviously, it has completed a number of successful flights," answered his friend. "You're not scared of flying, are you?"

"No. Not much, anyway," Trent grudgingly admitted. "I just don't like placing my life in the hands of some zombie flight crew. I feel like I'm in an episode of the 'Twilight Zone'."

Abby had already picked a window seat in front of the wings and Melissa joined her. Trent II took a seat across the aisle from the two.

"This is your captain speaking," a voice unexpectedly boomed from the intercom. "Please be seated. This flight will stop in New York, from where you will be able to catch another flight to London. For those traveling farther, other flights will leave London for Frankfurt, Paris, Rome and Cairo, with a final destination of Memphis. Please extinguish any cigarettes and fasten your safety belts."

Lorenzo was surveying the cabin as he walked down the aisle.

"You know, the wings for this grew out of the design for the P-38 Lightning, a World War II fighter with a double fuselage," Lorenzo gushed. "Its contoured profile cut drag by two to three percent, as well as allowing the tail surfaces to ride above the plane's slipstream, making it easier to control. Unfortunately, the straight-line fuselages of the competing Douglas planes were cheaper to maintain and repair. Storage costs were higher for the odd shaped parts of the Constellation. Even the three tails tripled the number of spare parts needed, though this baby has so much power with the Wright 3350 engines that it needed the extra tail surface.

"I wonder what we'll be flying from New York to London? I'm betting we stay with props. This Connie could do it, or a DC-6 or 7. I'm hoping for a Boeing 377 Stratocruiser. It'd take about twelve hours to cross the Atlantic. They were made in the late 1940s and seated sixty passengers, had spacious sleeping quarters that included a honeymoon suite in the tail, and a cocktail lounge in the belly of the plane that passengers could get to by way of a circular staircase. It was a giant, flying whale; luxurious as hell, but slightly unwieldy. I think there were six fatal Stratocruiser crashes."

Trent stopped and eyed his buddy with less than total belief. "You're making this up, right?"

Lorenzo sniffed and looked as if he was about to offer a sharp retort when he was interrupted by the pitch of the engines shifting to a higher speed. Trent seated himself across the aisle from Trent II and next to Melissa. He was pushed slightly back into his seat as the plane began moving forward. Lorenzo was sitting next behind Trent II and he looked across to smile at his nervous buddy. The plane taxied down a narrow asphalt strip and onto the runway. Trent decided there wasn't anything to see as he looked past Melissa and Abby and out the porthole into the dark.

It was a smooth takeoff, which at least made Trent a little more relaxed. Melissa smiled and gave him a reassuring pat on the hand. There was a similar expression on Abby's face. Trent was getting tired of the patronizing looks. He wasn't that big of a baby just because he was nervous about going aboard some phantasmic airliner.

Abby was in a talking mood and Melissa began quizzing the girl on events leading up to her shift into the dream world. Abby had been living with an older sister after her parents were killed in an auto accident. She first stayed with an aunt, but the arrangement proved unsatisfactory due to a surly, alcoholic uncle who was seldom employed. Bear River was too small for Trent not to have heard of a missing child, which meant she came from a parallel universe.

He pulled an airline magazine from a seat pocket and found he could only look at the color photos. Most of the print was impossible to read. Some of the headlines read, "Vermont, Maple Sugar Capital of the World," and, "Ted Nugent, That Motor City Madman, Still Into Bow Hunting." He looked over to see Trent II with his seat back and eyes closed. Lorenzo was cleaning his M-16.

Not being able to do anything meant having to think; something Trent didn't want to do. There were no answers for most of the questions and he felt guilty when he thought about the others as captives of the Atlantians. He couldn't help thinking that he must have screwed up royally for this mess to have developed.

Chapter Thirteen

"Do you know Botticelli?"

"What?" Trent asked, not quite believing the question.

"Do you know Botticelli?" Lorenzo repeated himself.

"Not personally."

"You know what I mean."

"Listen, I know you're just trying to start a conversation because you think I'm about to freak out. I'm not, so cut the small talk."

Lorenzo rolled his eyes and returned to cleaning his rifle. Several minutes of silence followed.

"OK, what about Botticelli? He was an Italian Middle Ages artist, wasn't he?" Trent couldn't contain his curiosity any longer.

"He was born in 1445 and there was no Italy at that time. He was a native of Florence."

"And...?" Trent had to prod.

"His name wasn't really Botticelli, it was Alessandro di Mariano Filipepi. Botticelli means little barrel."

"Are you trying to drive me nuts?" Trent asked as calmly as he could. "Okay, why was he called Little Barrel?"

"His father died when he was little and his older brother took over as head of the household. Little Barrel was his big brother's nickname and younger males of households often took the name of the family head, in this case Botticelli."

"Boy, I'm sure glad you told me that. How did I ever live until now not knowing how Botticelli got his name?"

"You know, I wish we were going to Pakistan instead," Lorenzo continued, unfazed by his friend's ill temper. "Camel wrestling season is beginning."

Trent refused to respond.

"The best ones are at the tomb of the Muslim saint Mohammed Musa. About one hundred randy camels duke it out deep in the Thal desert about two hundred fifty miles south of Islamabad. It's quite a sight. Up to 10,000 spectators often attend."

"Now how in the hell do camels wrestle?" Trent snapped.

"They dress them up in beads, bells, and garlands of flowers. Each camel only wrestles once. They start by locking necks, go in for leg bites, tripping, butting heads, and kicking. A bunch of refs with sticks keep the animals from biting each other's genitals. The winner has to take his opponent down or send him running."

Trent was about to lean across the aisle and strangle Lorenzo when the entire group was startled by the appearance of an airline attendant. The woman was in her late twenties or early thirties and wore a wool, knee-length, dark-blue uniform. Silver wings were pinned on her right chest. She had a thin, attractive face with high cheekbones and dark eyes. Her hair was pulled back into a bun. The whole effect was that of the early 1950s. She pushed a stainless steel cart filled with Coca Cola bottles and cans of Hamm's Beer.

"Beer or soda?" she asked in a muted voice that mirrored an expressionless face.

"I'll have a beer, please," Trent answered and grabbed a can, not able to wait until it was handed to him. He stared in puzzlement. It wasn't a flip top.

The attendant reached out and retrieved the can, picked up a can opener, and made two triangular punctures in the lid.

"I'll have a Coke," shouted Abby. "Do you have any peanuts?"

The woman silently passed over a bottle of Coke along with a small bag of peanuts.

Lorenzo stared intently at the woman, so much that the aloof object of his attention faltered for a second as she handed Trent II his drink.

"You are a very luscious lady," Lorenzo unexpectedly said. Even Trent was astonished by such an untypical outburst.

It took the woman by surprise. She blinked and appeared to see the five passengers for the first time. She examined each of them then turned back to Lorenzo.

"What did you say?"

"I said, 'Can you tell us when lunch is ready?'"

"No, you didn't. You told me I was a luscious lady."

"Did I?"

"Yes."

"Then why did you ask?"

She paused and again examined her small group of passengers, this time noticing the similarities of the two Trents despite their different hair styles and the beard. Her eyes widened briefly when she observed the shotgun and rifle. "Who are you people?"

"Who are you?" he asked in return. Lorenzo appeared to be purposely aggravating the attendant. It was working—she was scowling.

"I'm your flight attendant, Jolene Adams," the woman answered slowly as if not used to saying her name.

The conversation seemed to distress her. She placed the fingers of her right hand to her temple and rubbed her head lightly.

"Here, sit down," Lorenzo spoke, standing and gripping the woman by the elbow. "You're looking pale."

Melissa caught Trent's eye and raised her eyebrows in a questioning look. Trent shrugged his shoulders and turned to watch Lorenzo help the attendant sit in the seat behind his own.

Once sitting, a clouded look returned to the woman's face and a trance-like composure settled over her.

"There are lice on your collar," Lorenzo spoke softly.

The attendant's lips twitched slightly and her eyes refocused from a distance beyond the cabin walls to Lorenzo's face.

"What?"

"Do you have ice for my cola?"

She looked down at her uniform and tried pulling the collar out far enough to examine. "You said I have lice on my collar."

"Just a figure of speech, I assure you," Lorenzo replied as he kneeled in the aisle beside her. "Tell me, what's a nice girl like you doing in a plane like this?"

"I, ah, I..." The woman paused and shook her head. "I..."

Melissa leaned around Trent. "Quit harassing the poor woman, Lorenzo."

"I'm just trying to get her attention. It seemed sadly lacking."

He turned back to the woman. "My name is Lorenzo Spasm and these are my friends. We're here only temporarily. You do know this is not a real world?"

A slight shudder ran through the attendant and she covered her face with her hands.

"This is a nightmare that I can't wake up from," she sobbed through her fingers then looked up with her eyes watering.

The slap took everyone by surprise and almost knocked Lorenzo on his butt. He grabbed her wrists before she give him another stinging blow. Her eyes were now filled with rage.

"Why did you wake me? I had almost forgotten where I am, who I am. Now I can go crazy all over again."

"You'll never get out of here if you give up," Lorenzo shouted inches from her face as she struggled to free her hands. "Jolene, we can help you."

"How? There is no help. I've seen it. You get more numb, less connected, until you actually do fade away. Or become like those others, the ones who usually are on this flight."

"We aren't fading away. We're real."

She stopped and again looked closely at each of the five passengers. "You're not like the rest. Who are you? Where did you come from?"

"We're from the real world," piped up Abby. "I know how you feel. I woke up in my sister's farmhouse, only she wasn't there and the sun wouldn't come up. The lady down the road said most of the other people weren't real. I didn't think you were real at first."

Jolene stared at the girl for several seconds. "I think they once were all real."

She turned to Melissa and Trent. "And you, are you as real as your friend?"

"That's the second time I've been asked that," Trent replied. "And yes, I'm real, or at least as real as Lorenzo. So is Melissa."

The struggle was evident as she turned away, facing the back of the cabin. She was fighting against the hope seemingly offered by the strangers.

"Who are you?" she asked again and faced Lorenzo. "You're new here. You don't know what it is like. You'll become just like all the rest."

"We can go back when we want to," Lorenzo told her. "We can take you with us."

Jolene looked around the cabin. "Leave here?"

"When we land, I can jump you to a real New York," Trent II spoke for the first time. "It might not be the exact world you left, but it will be close."

"How?" she demanded fiercely, disbelief still in her voice.

"I'm not sure I can explain it, I just have the talent. There are a lot of worlds touching this dream one, many of them very similar. Like I said, I can take you to one, but I'm not sure it will be the exact world you're from."

"Anywhere, anywhere but this place. I hate it."

"Tell me, ah, Jolene," Trent said hesitantly.

His strained voice switched her back into an attendant mode. "Yes?"

"Ah, is there anyone flying this thing?"

Jolene's eyes flew wide open for a second as she looked to the cockpit door. "I've never thought about it before. I don't ever remember seeing the pilots when I come on board."

"How did you wind up here?" Melissa asked.

"I was on a flight to Honolulu. We were still over the water and making the approach when something happened, I don't know what—just that there was an explosion and a lot of smoke. We hit the water and I was slammed sideways into the wall. I think it knocked me out. The next thing I knew I was lying on the beach and choking on water. It was dark and the ocean was cold. I crawled up a hill to a small road, but there was no traffic.

"It was so eerie. I knew something was wrong. There were no stars, only the moon. I walked and walked until I came to the edge of the city. I-I-I, I couldn't find anyone. The stores were empty. No one was walking on the sidewalks. It was horrible. I thought I was dead and this was hell.

"I found a hotel with a clerk, but she wouldn't say much. She gave me a key to a room and I fell asleep as soon as I hit the bed. Nothing had changed when I woke. I discovered several nightclubs and other hotels that had people. Some were very unfriendly, others like zombies. I borrowed cars and wandered around the entire island. It was all the same. Finally, I stumbled upon the airport. There was a uniform hanging in the locker room with my nametag on it. Putting it on seemed like the thing to do."

She sighed and leaned back in her chair. "Outside was this plane or one like it. The next thing I knew, I was flying on an antique airliner with no passengers. I landed at an unfamiliar terminal, though a sign said I was at the Los Angeles International Airport. I found another hotel, and after a while came back to the airport and caught another flight. This time there were passengers, two of them with animal heads. By now I was too out of it to be surprised. Since then, I don't know for how long, I've been flying. I don't even know where this flight is headed."

"We're ultimately arriving at Memphis," Trent said.

"Memphis? I thought you said we were going to land at New York."

"We are, but we're traveling to Memphis, Egypt," Lorenzo explained.

"Egypt? That's where a lot of those things with the animal heads go and come from. Why do you want to go there?"

"It's a long story," he answered and stood to uncramp his legs. Jolene slid over to make room and Lorenzo sat next to her. "It started..."

Trent couldn't stand to hear another repeat of the tale and he unbuckled his seat belt.

"Gotta hit the can," Trent said to Melissa as he stood and looked about for a sign directing him to the bathroom.

Jolene turned from listening to Lorenzo long enough to point the way. The bathroom was cramped but adequate. He paused to look into the mirror.

"Still there, huh?" he asked his reflection.

He was about to head back to his seat, but the cockpit door seemed to beckon him. He tried the knob again and found it still locked.

Trent pounded on the door and yelled, "Hey, who is in there? Open up."

Nothing happened. The door stayed locked and the cockpit remained silent. He gave up and returned to his seat. Abby and Melissa were sleeping, dark circles under both of their eyes. He mentally kicked himself when he gazed down at the little girl. Why hadn't he thought of having his double take the girl back to Melissa's world where her counterpart could have watched after Abby?

He looked at Lorenzo and Jolene. It might have been his imagination, but he believed some color was already returning to the attendant's pallid face. She smiled several times as she watched Lorenzo rehashing their recent adventures. Trent frowned when he saw the other Trent sound asleep.

If we're basically the same person, he wondered, how come this other Trent seems so much calmer? He guessed that it had to be the last eight years Trent II spent in this dream world.

Sitting quietly with nothing to do was forcing Trent to start thinking about a number of things, things he'd pushed aside because of the mad pace they'd been forced to keep. Did it bother him that the Melissa of his world was still alive and married to the other Trent? Did it change his feelings toward the woman next to him? He looked at her and felt an overwhelming sense of protectiveness when he saw how vulnerable she looked sleeping. Was he so shallow that he could interchange Melissas like switching light bulbs? Trent didn't think he was that superficial; he'd grieved for his Melissa for almost eight years.

And what the hell was he going to do when he got to Memphis? He didn't have their jewel. Would they believe him? Lorenzo didn't seem worried about the encounter, which made Trent feel a little better. He still felt guilty about dragging everyone along.

Looking back over at his sleeping twin, he wondered for the first time why Trent II hadn't already jumped back to his Melissa. There was no way they could force him to do anything. Of course, he could escape anytime he wanted. Would he stay in one of the other worlds when he took Jolene over? He decided to make more of an effort to be nicer to his counterpart. It was as if since Trent could be hard on himself, it was all right to be hard on the other Trent.

He sighed and rubbed his eyes. The flash of the copper bracelet caught his eye and he pulled the sleeve back to get a better look.

It looked Egyptian, but it was crudely done—as if made in a craft class offered by the YMCA. He now noticed that it wasn't copper but extremely tarnished silver. The band was about an inch and a half wide, with silhouettes of pyramids, the Sphinx, pharaohs, slaves, and palm trees cut out. A roughly done scarab was enthroned in the middle, painted green to resemble jade.

All in all, thought Trent, it was a very strange piece.

The flight droned on and Trent drifted into a light sleep. He came alert when the intercom crackled and a voice spoke, "This is your captain speaking. Please extinguish any cigarettes, return to your seats, and buckle your safety restraints."

Jolene jumped with a guilty start, as if caught in a dereliction of duty. Lorenzo took her hand and pulled her back into her seat.

"Relax," Lorenzo smiled at the attendant. "What are they going to do, fire you?"

This was another unexpected development, thought Trent. There seemed to be some kind of electricity between the two. He wondered if this attraction was as obvious to the others as it was to Trent. Lorenzo had been a loner for so long, Trent had a hard time imagining his friend willingly becoming enmeshed at this stage of the game.

Pilots or no pilots, the airliner made a smooth landing and Trent was relieved to see the lights along the taxi strip leading to the terminal. This airport was much bigger and a dozen large propeller-driven airliners were parked in the area where their own plane was stopping.

"Those are DC-7s," Lorenzo pointed out a couple four-engine planes, "and that smaller one is a DC-3."

Trent watched as two men in dark coveralls pushed a ramp to the aircraft. Jolene was up and at the door. She nervously looked at the group as if scarcely believing that she might be finally leaving this nightmare world. There was a muffled thud as the ramp connected with the airliner and Lorenzo helped Jolene open the door. Melissa led Abby down the aisle. The little girl was rubbing the sleep from her eyes and asking where they were.

They filed down the stairs and across the tarmac to a row of large double doors. To the left were massive picture windows. The doors opened to a large room filled with rows of seats, a few which had slumped, dark figures in them. Like every other building in this dream world, Trent found its lighting far too dim.

"Your next flight doesn't leave for an hour," Jolene told Lorenzo after looking at their pass. "It will be pulling up outside within twenty minutes. I could show you around the airport until then."

"Ah, would anyone else like to come?" Lorenzo said as an afterthought.

"Sure, I'd like to see...ah, no thanks," Trent said after getting an elbow in the side from Melissa.

"I want some hot chocolate," Abby said and pointed to a row of vending machines, one of which pictured a steaming cup.

The drinks were only a dime, and the small group sat at one of the tables next to the machines. Trent still felt awkward carrying the shotgun and laid it on the floor next to his chair. He also set his coffee down, it being far too hot to drink. The end of his tongue was scorched from trying a sip.

Melissa shifted suddenly in her seat and placed her hand on Trent's arm. He looked up to see about a dozen Atlantians crossing the room to the vending machines.

"Looks like we're going to have company," muttered Trent II.

Trent slowly reached under the table and picked up the shotgun. He laid it on his lap, hoping it was out of sight under the table. He had to force himself not to stare as the crowd neared. Two of the Atlantians were hawk-headed, their shiny eyes blinking slowly from the bottom. One turned his head sideways to the humans at the table, staring with one eye like a bird of prey. The rest were mammals; several with cat heads and the others included jackals, hippos, lions and a camel.

Melissa's hand tightened on Trent's arm.

"Don't worry," he said softly to Melissa, "they won't bother us since we're traveling to their headquarters."

The Atlantians all wore what looked like uniforms—khaki shirts and pants tucked into the tops of brown boots. Strapped to their sides were brown leather holsters. The hawk Atlantian showing interest in the humans maintained a watch as the others worked the vending machines. He suddenly raised his beak and gave off a sharp, loud keening. The rest spun around, one dropping his coffee.

Melissa gasped and Trent II pushed his chair away from the table. But the Atlantians weren't interested in them. They looked instead across the terminal at the approach of a dozen humans. It was easy to see they meant business. The men were spreading out as they approached. The way they held their hands suggested weapons under the long dark robes they wore.

"I think we should be prepared to hit the floor," Trent II whispered. "It looks like these guys aren't real chums."

Trent's stomach did a flip-flop when saw what the approaching men were wearing at the end of gold chains around their necks—the croix patte of the Knights of Templar. The lead figure, a broad-shouldered man with gray hair down to his shoulders, glanced away from the Atlantians long enough to pierce Trent with his steel gray eyes. The two parties squared off not thirty feet from Trent and his party.

"I think those guys are connected with that other bunch you said were after me," he said softly to Trent II. His counterpart didn't answer, too absorbed in what was going on to do more than nod.

The jackal barked out a few words. It was scarcely intelligible to Trent. It sounded like a warning. The lead human threw back his cape to expose a short broad sword on his left hip and a pistol on the right. The hawk-headed Atlantian hissed and placed his hand on his own weapon.

The lead human haughtily raised his hand and turned to point at Trent.

"This man belongs to us," the man's voice boomed. Two of the shadow people sitting in chairs across the room stood and hurriedly fled the lounge. "He is ours and you shall not have him."

The second hawk-headed Atlantian jerked his head sideways and eyed the man as a chicken would examine a tasty worm.

"Day are on deir vay do our eaders. Ou shall nod sop dem," hissed the Atlantian.

"They come with us," the man repeated.

Trent didn't like the looks of any of this. Though he didn't mind the two parties shooting it out, he worried about Melissa and Abby getting hurt in the crossfire. What to do? He wished Lorenzo was here.

He leaned over and whispered to Trent II, "Can you jump with us all and bring me back?"

"Yes, but you'll have to take off those bracelets," he whispered back. Melissa and Trent slipped the bands off their wrists, hiding their actions under the table. Abby wasn't wearing one.

Trent II leaned over as if to speak to his companions, reaching out to take both Abby's and Trent's hands. They in turn were holding hands with Melissa, the four now forming a circle. Trent nodded his head and the room wavered. A searing flash of agony made Trent grunt and jerk his hands free. Two extra bracelets in his jacket pocket were jolting him with shocks.

Both the Atlantians and Templars grabbed for their weapons at the action erupting near them. A whoosh of air rushed in to fill the vacuum left behind when Trent II, Melissa, and Abby vanished. Trent jumped to his feet in pain and sent his table crashing over. One of the men panicked in the confusion and fired his revolver. The slug missed the Atlantians and ricocheted off the concrete wall and crashed through a plate glass window.

All hell broke loose. Screams and bullets filled the air. Trent dropped behind the table and held his fire since none of the participants seemed interested in using him as a target. He peeked around the table long enough to see that the surviving Atlantians had thrown down several of the vending machines for cover. The humans had fallen back, hiding behind pillars and overturned furniture. A half dozen humans and Atlantians lay on the floor.

Trent was surprised any were left alive after the hail of gunfire each side had unleashed. He felt extremely insecure behind the table. It was not thick enough to stop a bullet. He wanted to get as far as he could from the ongoing battle but couldn't without exposing himself even more. Trent broke open the shotgun to make sure it was loaded and felt in his jacket pockets to assure himself that he still had extra shells.

He involuntarily threw himself to the floor at another wave of gunfire. More glass shattered and an automatic rifle cut above the sound of handguns. Trent guessed Lorenzo had entered the fray, but he wasn't about to stick his head above the table to find out. Sporadic gunfire followed for several minutes and then silence filled the room, except for the occasional groan or cry of the wounded.

The temptation to stick his head around the table and see what was occurring was growing. Trent pushed himself up to his hands and knees and was about to spy around the edge of the table when the lights went out. Gun fire erupted only halfheartedly with no visible targets available.

Not stopping to consider the advisability of his actions, Trent jumped to his feet and ran as silently as he could towards the doors leading to the aircraft. He moved in a half crouch and expected a bullet to slam into his back any second. Each gunshot sent his stomach lurching.

Trent headed towards the doors he had earlier entered. He didn't see a floor ashtray and slammed into it, sending it rolling noisily across the floor while he took a tumble. Trent felt like puking as he lay on the floor clutching his bruised shin. The combination of the pain and fright momentarily incapacitated him. He fought to climb to his feet and suddenly felt a pair of strong hands help him stand. Trent found himself being shoved in the direction of the exit. A bullet screamed by in the dark and sent splinters of shattered concrete tap dancing across the floor.

Trent's over-enthusiastic rescuer shoved him ahead before he could raise his free hand to push the doors open. His forehead slammed against the glass and he fell through the swinging doors, stumbling across the pavement before catching himself against an empty luggage cart.

He angrily shrugged off the helping arm and turned to find himself nose to nose with the leader of the humans. The man appeared to be in his sixties, though he was still wide of chest and his grip was firm when he grabbed the end of Trent's shotgun and forced it to the side.

"Where is the Heart of Thoth?" he demanded.

Trent stepped back and jerked the barrel free.

"What the hell are you talking about?" Trent shouted, his nerves frayed by the battle.

"Do not play with me. I know you are the one who took the jewel from the temple."

"If you are talking about that ruby from the hand of Dorga, I don't have it. The last time I saw it I was in the statue's belly. Try looking there or ask the priest who attacked me in the idol."

"The priest is dead as you well know," the old man spit back, "and the Heart of Thoth is gone. Do you think we would not have found it if it were still there, no matter how well hidden?"

Trent found himself glancing nervously back and forth between the ranting man and the doors. He expected a rush of humans or Atlantians to pour out any second.

"Why do you think you own it? Doesn't that jewel belong to the Atlantians? Isn't that what Thoth was? And what about the worshipers of Dorga," Trent asked, "don't they have first claim?"

"The Heart of Thoth belongs to the Knights of the Templar. We are the legitimate heirs of King Solomon and Moses. It was stolen from us by that bastard Atlantian, Dorga, over two hundred years ago. He fantasized himself another Thoth and sought to create a city state like his kinsman did along the Nile thousands of years ago. With the Heart of Thoth, he usurped a colony of Templars and repopulated it with kidnapped humans. The jewel is a very powerful tool and must not fall back into the hands of the Atlantians, or no human world is safe.

"Both the Atlantians and Templars have other inheritances from the Golden Age, each enough that our powers are roughly equal. That balance would be seriously jeopardized should they acquire the Heart of Thoth."

"So why didn't you just take it back from Dorga? You and your buddies didn't seem too shy a couple minutes ago."

"Dorga, having performed years of inquisition into the use of the Heart of Thoth, knew how to instruct the jewel to repel those who would possess it. Many Freemasons and even other Atlantians died trying."

"So why was it so easy for me to pry it lose?"

"Dorga was caught unaware and hacked to pieces several years ago. I can only guess that his spells grew impotent after his death. But now it shall again be ours that we may finally wipe the vermin from Shadowland, the hub to all human worlds."

Something felt wrong. The Templar is stalling, Trent thought, trying to keep me distracted while he waited for help. Trent looked about but saw only parked airliners and the open, dark door of a giant hangar.

"Don't the Atlantians have as much right here as anyone?' Trent asked.

That seemed to enrage the old man. "Look about you. Does this seem like a world created by those devils? It was created by the dreams of humans. The Atlantians infest it like rats in a grain shed and have turned it into a nightmare world."

"But aren't they the ones who gave knowledge to mankird? I mean, you know, in Egypt thousands of years ago."

"They gave nothing," he hissed. "They used it to rule over humans as if we were ignorant children. What we learned was stolen a crumb at a time until they were driven out."

The conversation was dramatically brought to an end. A plane sitting in the shadows of a hangar suddenly roared to life. Both men spun in surprise to see a behemoth slowly exiting into the dim lights of the parking area. Across its side was written Pan American World Airways. Whatever the old man was waiting for, which was probably reinforcements, it had failed to show up in time. A look of frustration swept across his face and he turned angrily to Trent.

"You must not be a traitor to your own kind. Give me the Heart of Thoth."

"I don't have it and I don't know where it is."

The Templar closely scrutinized the younger man's face as if he could read souls. Slowly a look of defeat replaced the rage. "You don't have it?"

"No."

"Then why are you going to their nest?"

"They have my friends. What else can I do?" Trent replied.

"This does not make sense," the Knight of the Templar shook his head. "If you do not have it, where could it be? We would have sensed its presence if it were still in that devil's likeness."

They were forced to retreat as the giant plane ambled into the loading area. Its massive propellers were kicking up dust and the engines swallowed their voices.

"Aren't you worried about those Atlantians inside?" Trent screamed above the roar.

"They are dead," the old man answered simply.

"How do you know? It was dark."

"We have our ways."

The Templar no longer seemed interested in talking now that he believed Trent did not have the jewel.

"What about my two friends?" Trent continued his questions. "One was an airline attendant and the other was the man with the automatic rifle. Did you see them?"

"The woman fled and the man followed. I must find the others of my order," he said and began to walk away, only to turn and pause for a moment. "I would say you are a fool to walk into that viper's nest, but I understand duty to one's comrades. I wish you luck."

Trent watched the old man walk back into the pitch-black interior. Two featureless men appeared from nowhere and pushed the ramp to the airliner. He guessed this must be the Stratocruiser of which Lorenzo had been waxing poetic.

Chapter Fourteen

After ten minutes of fidgeting at the foot of the stairs and anxiously peering into every shadow, Trent decided to wait in the plane. He paused at the door and gave one last look about before entering. Inside was a fairly broad cabin for an old prop-driven airliner, with a spacious aisle dividing rows of two seats on one side and three on the other. He picked a window seat from where he could watch the terminal for Lorenzo and Jolene.

His patience or temper didn't improve after fifteen minutes of torturous silence. He impulsively stood and walked to the cockpit door. It was locked. This time he didn't just timidly rap, but stood back and kicked the door as hard as he could. It shuddered but didn't give. He was preparing for another blow when the door exploded open and sent him stumbling back. A .45 was stuck under his nose and Trent found himself looking at a very irate man in a white captain's shirt and cap.

"What kind of fetal droppings are you? What do you want?" the pilot snarled.

"I, ah, just wanted to make sure there was somebody flying this thing," Trent sputtered.

The pilot looked incredulously at his lone passenger. "Are you insane? Look out the damn window. Does it look like we're flying? God, are you lame or what?"

"Ah, I think I, ah, could speak better without that gun in my face."

"I certainly hope so, because you're doing a piss-poor job of it right now." The pilot lowered the gun while still maintaining a close watch on Trent. "Who the hell are you, anyway? You certainly don't look like the usual geeks I get on this flight."

"My name is Trent Rowen," he answered, holding out his right hand.

"I'm the captain," the pilot introduced himself by tapping on his nametag with the tip of his gun barrel. It read William Arick. He didn't make a move to extend his own hand for the shake.

"So, when do we depart?" Trent asked after a stretch of uncomfortable silence.

William looked at his wristwatch, frowned, and shook it a few times. "Sometime soon, sometime soon. Relax, grab a beer from the back. I never know if we're going to have an attendant or not. Hope we get a woman this trip; the last guy was as silly as Mother Goose. While you're at it, get me a beer."

It was Trent's turn to inspect the pilot. The guy needed a shave and his eyes were very bloodshot. If he wasn't mistaken, the smell of burning marijuana was drifting out from the cockpit.

"You're allowed to drink?"

"Am I allowed to drink? Who the hell do you think is going to care? The Federal Aviation Administration? The Department of Transportation? One of those dog heads?" The pilot waved the gun wildly around as he spoke. "Have you ever flown one of these monsters? They never did design the power plants right. There are twenty-eight cylinders in each cursed engine with one hundred twelve spark plugs. Cylinders fly off at the drop of a hat. And those damn propellers can snap and come hurtling through the wall, decompressing the cabin and sucking the air right out of your lungs, not to mention any luggage or luckless passengers next to the hole. You can't fly this bitch unless you drink. Now get me a beer, damn it, before I throw you off this flight for insubordination."

Trent hurried to get the beer. He slowed long enough as he passed his seat to kick the shotgun further out of sight. He didn't want to find out what the captain thought of passengers and weapons.

It took him several minutes to locate the ice box and remove a six-pack of Black Label beer. The pilot was sitting in the front row and smoking a vile smelling cigar. He took the beer without voicing thanks and opened it with a pocketknife. Trent hesitantly asked to use the opener and William handed it over with a snort of disgust.

"Don't ever go anywhere without a pack of rubbers and a pocketknife," the pilot advised after taking a long draw.

"I'll remember that," Trent promised and walked to the door. There was still no sign of Lorenzo.

"Looking for someone?"

"A friend, Captain. We became separated in the terminal."

"I bet you did," he laughed. "I heard the uproar. You can call me William; I never stand on formalities once I've drunk with someone. What was going on in there? You having trouble with the dog heads?"

"No. There was a slight disagreement between some of the Atlantians and Knights of Templar."

"Hah! They're at it again. They do that now and then. Let me warn you, those Templars are arrogant bastards with sticks up their butts, but those dog heads are worse. Stay away from both bunches and you'll be better off."

"Thanks for the warning," Trent said.

"Then take it," William snapped. "Get off this damn flight. Last stop is right in the middle of their headquarters where you can't spit without hitting one."

"I can't. I have some friends there."

"Friends there? They might as well be in hell. That's one place where I don't even get off the plane."

The pilot looked down at his wristwatch and shook it several more times.

"I'll wait ten more minutes then we'll have to leave. Usually there are a few dog heads on this flight and occasionally some Templars. The Templars, though, go only as far as London. They know where they're not wanted."

Trent's curiosity was killing him. "Who are you? What are you doing here? You don't seem like the others I've met in this world."

"We call it Shadowland. I woke up one night stuck in a hellhole that looked only vaguely like the Cape Town where I had gone to sleep. It was full of zombies and smartass waiters. I flew cargo planes in Afghanistan and stumbled upon an old DC-3 at some backwater airport. Flew it to what should have been Nigeria then to Algeria and on to France. I began hopping around, working my way up to this, Connies, and DC-7s.

"One day, I started the flight check for a Vickers Viscount and a bunch of dog heads came on board and started making a big stink about the plane going to Berlin. After we arrived, one of them let me know in no uncertain terms that I wasn't to screw around with the bigger planes. Pipers or Cessnas, yes, but leave the big boys alone unless I played the game. By now that was the only thing I could find to do of any interest—so instead of fighting 'em, I joined 'em."

"You haven't tried to return to your own world?" wondered Trent.

"I could go back. I did a few hush-hush favors for some Templar lads. They've offered to jump me back a number of times. I probably will someday, but right now I have the free run of an entire world, be it ever so humble. Those people that bitch and moan when they find themselves here are a bunch of spineless wimps."

William paused between sips and looked at Trent. "You're not one of those crybabies, are you?"

Trent tried to sound indignant. "I'm not a crybaby, but I don't find much in this world that is very pleasing."

"How about freedom from petty bureaucracy, free beer, and no stupid narcs? You people don't know when you have it good," he snapped. "Well, I better get back to the front. I'll have to be taking off in a couple minutes. Until then, remember, it isn't too late to jump ship."

Trent returned to the door after the captain disappeared back into the cockpit. The same two men were crossing the pavement to pull away the ramp when Lorenzo and Jolene came running from around the corner of the terminal. A vast weight evaporated at the sight of his friend. Trent realized again how much he had come to depend upon Lorenzo.

"God, I was worried something had happened to both of you," he said while stepping aside to let them in. "You cut it pretty close."

"We had trouble finding another route from the building after I shorted the lights," Lorenzo breathed heavily. Jolene was closing and locking the plane's door.

"You got your wish,' Trent said as they sat in the front row and buckled their seat belts. "We're in one of those Stratocruisers."

"It sure is and what a beauty," Lorenzo replied. He took a deep breath and slapped his palms against his legs. "I'm going to enjoy the long ride. I need a rest."

"Humph-h-h. Who can rest knowing that there are twenty-eight cylinders in each cursed engine with one hundred twelve spark plugs and that its cylinders fly off at the drop of a hat?" Trent growled. "Or that those damn propellers can snap and come hurtling through the wall, decompressing the cabin and sucking the air right out of your lungs not to mention any luggage or luckless passengers next to the hole. I don't think I could fly in this bitch unless I was drinking very heavily."

Both Lorenzo and Jolene stared at Trent in surprise.

"What the—"

Lorenzo was cut off by the intercom. "This is the captain speaking. Shut up, buckle up. We're going up. Don't drink all the beer or you'll throw up."

Lorenzo looked even more bewildered.

"Go ahead, sit back and relax. I think it is going to be a long flight," Trent smiled as he opened another beer.

The second beer didn't help Trent's nerves as the airliner lumbered down the runway. It picked up speed but didn't seem to be leaving the concrete as it ate up more and more of the runway's length. The engines were straining, and he could feel their vibrations through the floor of the cabin. At what seemed the last possible second, the old airliner lurched away from the earth. Even then it seemed to force its entry into the air.

"I need another drink," gasped Trent, now as white as the attendant. He stood on unsteady legs and staggered down the aisle to the back of the plane, returning shortly with a half dozen cans of beer.

"Help yourself," he said while opening a beer with the captain's knife. Trent held it up and quoted, "Never go anywhere without rubbers or a pocketknife."

It wasn't until his third sip that Trent realized Jolene hadn't been able to escape from the dream world with Trent II.

"I can wait a little longer," she replied to Trent commenting on her being left behind. "It's not so bad now that I know I'm not crazy and that it is possible to leave this world. I feel safe with Lorenzo."

"Yes, he is such a comfort," Trent acknowledged only half in jest. "Have him tell you about camel wrestling sometime."

The intercom crackled and the captain's voice blared, "Hey, Trent, bring me up a couple brewskies."

"As you have heard," Trent said as he rose from his seat, "we actually have a pilot on this flight. He may not remain conscious for the whole trip, but he is up there."

He knocked on the cockpit door with two unopened beers.

"It's unlocked."

William motioned for Trent to sit in the copilot's seat. The cockpit was an amazing jungle of levers and dials and smelled of old leather and oil. He opened one of the cans and handed it and the pocketknife to the captain.

Riding in the cockpit was mesmerizing. It was lit only by the many small dials gleaming in the dark as if making up for the lack of stars out the windshield. The moon was off to the right like an instrument that had floated away. Trent found himself relaxing and shifted into a more comfortable position.

The two sat for at least twenty minutes without speaking until William said, "See why I stay?"

Trent nodded in agreement. "Say, my friend Lorenzo Spasm would love to see the cockpit. He's a real airplane nut and was raving earlier about this very plane. Is that all right?"

"Sure, send him up." William had miraculously mellowed now that he was off the ground.

Lorenzo eagerly went forward and left Jolene to show Trent to the lower lounge. The two descended a narrow spiral stairs into a lounge. He was amazed at the luxuriousness of the real wood and leather. They sat by a window below and to the rear of the giant engines. He could see the moonlight reflecting off the spinning blades. Trent had to admit that it was a splendid way to travel.

Trent watched the attendant while she gazed out the window. Though she was a very attractive woman, he wondered what else there was about her that attracted Lorenzo. He'd never known his friend to display such attention to a member of the opposite sex. On occasions, Lorenzo had hinted about some woman in his past, someone that still had a hold over him. No one had ever been able to get more than that out of him.

"If only there were stars," she said with a sigh, "then I could almost believe this was a real night."

She looked at Trent thoughtfully for a second and asked, "Have you known Lorenzo long?"

"Since I was a kid. He was a friend of my older brother. We've become pretty close the last half dozen years. A bunch of us guys get together a lot. He's probably already told you about Al and Rich and where they are."

Jolene replied that Lorenzo had filled her in on most of the last week's happenings. She then began plying Trent with more questions about Lorenzo. He answered most of them but admitted to the woman that his friend was a man of mystery in many ways, with holes in his past that even his best friends didn't know about.

Jolene was nearly sprayed with beer as Trent choked in the middle of a swallow. Climbing down the spiraling stairs was William.

"What are you doing here?" he managed to wheeze after a fit of coughing. "Who in the hell is flying the plane?"

"You're a nervous little guy, aren't you?" the pilot laughed as he walked behind the bar and rummaged through the cupboards. He pulled out a bottle of Henry Daniels. "Holy shit, the date on this is 1942. I bet it is real smooth."

William seemed to enjoy Trent's discomfort and waited until he had tossed down two shots of the whiskey before answering. "Your buddy Spasm took over for a while."

"Lorenzo!" Trent almost went into another coughing fit. "What does he know about flying one of these?"

"Hey, if he was flying B-17s during his year with the Confederate Air Force, he can fly anything. I told him I know where a honey of a Ford Tri-Motor is that he should give a try."

Trent looked over at Jolene. "See what I mean?"

He soon began feeling sleepy and excused himself. Trent climbed to the main cabin, walked to the back of the plane, kicked off his boots, and climbed into a sleeping berth. He knew he'd have no trouble sleeping despite his initial apprehension. He wondered what Melissa was doing at that exact moment. Though he missed her, Trent was relieved that she and Abby were safely out of the way. If only the rest of the group had stayed home.

Trent couldn't tell if he'd been asleep for ten minutes or ten hours when he woke, but he felt more refreshed than he had in over a week. He found Lorenzo alone in the main cabin.

"Good morning," Lorenzo cheerfully greeted him.

"Don't you ever sleep?"

"Sure, I caught about five hours and I feel great. Jolene is still sleeping."

"You two seem to be hitting it off very well," Trent noted.

"She's a very nice person. I've talked her into coming back with us to Bear River when this is all over."

The mention of "this" reminded Trent of their final destination and his spirits took a tumble. "Just what are we going to do when we get there? What if the Atlantians don't believe me? How are we going to get the others out of there?"

Lorenzo smiled and waved his hand languidly in the air as if chasing the troubles away. "I have a plan."

That didn't make Trent feel much better. Lorenzo was notorious for his plans and their convoluted turnings. That they always seemed to work was little consolation for Trent, thinking of how he was flying through an eternal night in a sixty-five year old airliner on his way to meet animal-headed Atlantians.

"Good morning."

The two turned to see Jolene pushing a cart down the aisle.

"Ah, the perfect hostess," said Lorenzo.

"Attendant," she corrected him and handed out two orange juices. "Breakfast is in the covered tray, I'm going to take a plate to William."

Trent was pleasantly surprised to find sausage, toast, biscuits and gravy, pancakes, and bacon. He was wiping up real maple syrup with his last piece of pancake when Jolene returned with the untouched plate.

"Our pilot sure looks rough. I don't know if I'd want to fly with him too often."

"Wasn't he hungry?" Trent asked, nodding at the plate.

"He said he didn't eat breakfast but woke up best to a couple shots of Henry Daniels. He also said we'd be landing in a half hour."

Minutes later, Trent was brushing his teeth with a complimentary toothbrush found in the sleeping berth. The guy in the mirror didn't look as bad as he would have guessed. He might even look half civilized, Trent decided, after using the complimentary razor and shampoo. He took off his shirt and washed himself with a cloth hanging near the sink.

Trent returned to his seat just in time.

"This is the captain speaking. We are approaching our destination and should be on the ground in approximately ten minutes. Sit down and buckle up. The landing may be a bit rough due to turbulence and a hangover."

Trent wasn't nervous about the impending landing. Maybe it was just knowing there was a pilot was enough, he thought. He knew there was a face in the cockpit, no matter how bloodshot the eyes.

The landing turned out to be adequate. The plane did seem to plop to the concrete at the last moment and bounce a bit, but Trent chalked it off to the behemoth's flight characteristics. William came out to give them a sendoff.

"Maybe I'll catch you on the flight back," the pilot said as he shook their hands.

"Why don't you fly us on to Memphis?" Jolene asked.

"Can't. Even the dog heads know enough not to let me fly again after a twelve hour flight. I'm sticking around here a couple days. There are flare guns in the emergency kit by the door. Grab one and if you need me when you get back, just send a flare up. I usually don't venture too far into London. There are packs of cretins roaming the streets who get kicks out of dressing strangers up in garter belts and net stockings and then setting them on fire. Don't ask me why, I think it's some kind of British thing. The Templars and dog heads keep the airports pretty safe.

"You're lucky," William continued as he looked out the door. "Your next plane is a DC-7. It's a lot faster and smoother than this beast, though not as interesting. It leaves in an hour."

William didn't blink an eye when Trent and Lorenzo retrieved their guns from under the seats. He waved goodbye once more then disappeared down into the lounge.

A good breakfast and plenty of sleep had worked miracles on Trent's outlook. He was still apprehensive about arriving in Memphis but didn't feel as frazzled.

Lorenzo said he needed some things in the terminal before boarding the other plane. They wound up in a clothing shop where he began picking out clothing and a traveling bag.

"Can't arrive in the court of the Crimson King in sweaty clothes," he explained.

The other two followed suit and soon Jolene was leading them to the locker rooms. Trent had to admit the shower and clean clothes made him feel even better. Trent was transferring his billfold and change from one pocket to another as Lorenzo combed back his wet hair and tied it into a ponytail then slipped on a jacket that went with his new black suit. He completed the power dressing with a burgundy tie and a pair of very dark sunglasses.

"You're dressing pretty spiffy, aren't you?" queried Trent as he zipped up a plain windbreaker. "You either look like a very important pimp or a British cabinet member on drugs. I feel shabby in these jeans and sweatshirt."

"And well you should," Lorenzo rejoined. "We're meeting with representatives of a race who taught the ancient Egyptians how to build the Pyramids, who are probably responsible for much of our own culture, and you're going dressed like it was a picnic at the Bear River Caves State Park."

Trent glanced dubiously down at his clothes. He looked back at Lorenzo who was kneeling and strapping a small handgun to his left calf.

"Do you really think I should dress better?"

"No," his friend said. "It doesn't matter. They'll hate you no matter what you wear for stealing their Heart of Thoth. You could wear a clown's suit and I doubt it would make any difference."

"Thanks for cheering me up," Trent responded. "Do you think your monkey suit will make a difference?"

"This isn't for the Atlantians," his friend laughed as he stood and tightened his tie.

"It isn't?"

"No, it's to impress the babes,' Lorenzo said as he disappeared through the door.

Jolene was out of her uniform and wearing jeans and a baggy sweater. Trent smiled in approval when he noticed she had also changed from pumps to stout hiking boots.

"Lorenzo said we might be going over some pretty rough terrain," she said, noticing Trent looking at her feet.

"What do you think of our friend's attire?" he asked.

She looked over at Lorenzo and shook her head. "I think he looks very nice, but it's not how I picture desert explorers."

"Don't worry," Lorenzo said as he patted his bag, "I have some Indiana Jones apparel in here."

This time it was Trent's turn to stop at a store. It was a souvenir shop, and he walked slowly around the odd variety of merchandise. He picked up a small spoon that featured a warped image of Big Ben and slipped it into his pocket.

"I know a few months from now I won't believe any of this happened," he explained to the others. "I'll need a few of these trinkets to remind me."

"You'll have Melissa," pointed out Lorenzo.

Trent broke into a sheepish grin. "Yes, I guess she'll be more than enough to make this real."

That didn't stop him from picking up a pocketknife.

"You should never travel without one," he reminded them.

A ramp had been pulled up to their plane and its engines were idling. The cabin was longer and more modern looking than the Stratocruiser. The flight also seemed more anticlimactic. There were no attendants and Jolene had to show them where the food and beverages were kept.

Jolene also discovered there was a screen and a projector in the first class section. They snooped around until they found the reels to a number of movies, including "The Seventh Voyage of Sinbad," "Lassie, Come Home," "King Kong," and the 1950s version of "The Invasion from Mars."

The films helped pass the time, though Trent was finding himself getting tenser as the flight continued. He had a long conversation with Jolene, paced the aisles, and once knocked on the cockpit door—there was no answer.

Trent finally fell into a fitful nap and woke as the plane touched down. He groggily rose from his seat and followed Lorenzo and Jolene to the door. The flying was becoming a monotonous routine, and he was glad that they were finally at their destination. The airport didn't look much different from any of the others, though the air was drier and full of dust and unrecognizable scents.

"What now?" asked Trent as they passed through the terminal and were standing at the entrance next to a broad boulevard.

Weary palm trees lined the street, lit only by the same full moon he had seen everywhere else in the dream world. There was no one in sight. Trent was about to suggest they return to the building and look for a map when the lights of a parked car flashed on. It was a half block away and slowly rolled along the curb until it stopped in front of them. It was a 1956 Plymouth with an unlit taxi sign on the roof.

Lorenzo bent and peered at the driver. Trent looked over his friend's shoulder and saw a bearded silhouette of a man in a beret. The driver motioned for them to climb in the taxi. Lorenzo opened the back door for Jolene and slid in besides her. Trent guessed that meant he had to sit in front with the mystery taxi driver.

It was an eerie, silent ride. Neither of the three had given the driver a destination, yet he set off like a man in a hurry to get somewhere. The cab was racing along a narrow, twisting road that headed away from a dimly-lit city. They wound through a growing number of ruins, most only large mounds or small hills, others tumbled jumbles of stone blocks.

"These ruins were trucked away, stone by stone," said Lorenzo from the back seat. "They were carried for centuries to Cairo as precut building materials. We should soon be coming to the village of Saqqara where the first pyramid ever built is located. It started out with a ninety-two foot shaft chopped into the desert bedrock with a burial vault at the bottom. The king was Djoser, who probably founded the 3rd Dynasty in 2686 B.C. His chief architect was the genius Imhotep, who some believe was an initiate into the secrets of Thoth.

"The upper structure started out as a massive, square tomb. It was the first in Egypt built entirely of stone. Imhotep wasn't satisfied and since the king wasn't dead yet, decided he had time to enlarge it and build three more tombs on top for family members. It was the first pyramid. He built two more steps and then covered the soaring pyramid in white stone. Around it were built courtyards, chapels, halls, temples and a wall over a mile long to enclose it all.

"I would bet that is our destination," he concluded.

Trent shook his head and gave up fighting the grin. He wondered what Jolene thought of Lorenzo's history lecture.

Lorenzo was right. They came upon the pyramid. It dominated the skyline and beyond it was drifting gray sand. The pyramid didn't look like the postcard shot of the three Giza pyramids. Instead of the hundreds of blocks making up the steps to the top of its more famous brothers, the Saqqara pyramid had only six, gargantuan steps. The white covering stone was long gone, and the corners of the steps were smoothly rounded by centuries of blowing sand.

Not all was in ruins. The taxi remained on the small road that twisted and swerved among a number of fallen structures. Abruptly they emerged from the heaps of stone and the occupants of the car found themselves looking across a broad plain at the foot of the pyramid. The pale moonlight revealed a towering obelisk. It stood at the foot of a massive stone ramp leading to a courtyard the size of a football field. It, in turn, covered the roof of a four-story high temple. It looked more like it had been carved from a small mountain than built block by block. A legion of columns the size of redwood trunks ran the length of the two visible temple walls.

Remaining true to his silence, the driver stopped the car and patiently waited for his riders to get the hint. They were left standing in the dust as the taxi roared away. Trent followed its one tail light until the taxi disappeared behind a statue of a reclining toad.

"This must be the place," Lorenzo said.

"Yes, 'The Road to Memphis' is about to come to a grand finale," answered Trent.

Jolene took a hand of each of her companions and said, "That must make me Dorothy Lamour."

"Or some other Dorothy," Lorenzo added. "Maybe the one just about to enter the Land of Oz."

"Personally, I hope the wizard isn't home," said Trent. He threw the shotgun over his arm and led the way. "And I hope they're not offended by their guests carrying weapons."

Thousands of torches lit the temple, running along the foot of the walls, up the ramp and across the courtyard. The pillars were beautifully adorned with paintings and etchings of numerous Atlantians in classical Egyptian poses. Trent felt like an ant on a breadbox as he started up the ramp. He could see dozens of tiny figures at the top, silhouetted by a forest fire of wavering torch flames.

All three of the humans broke into a sweat halfway up the ramp. Trent was breathing heavily and his legs ached by the time he reached the top. The vision that met them was almost inconceivable. The splendor of ancient Egypt was reborn. Banners snapped in the brisker air high above the desert floor. Two lines of hundreds of richly dressed Atlantians formed a promenade across the courtyard to the foot of a leviathan figure made from a lustrous white stone. It was an Atlantian, and it wore the head of an ibis, just as Thoth was described.

"It looks like we are expected," said Trent.

"That or they think we're the caterers," Lorenzo replied.

"No," joined in Jolene. "They'd have expected us to use the servant's entrance."

Trent's question about the weapons was answered. A squad of six Atlantians approached and disarmed the two men in a silent, no-nonsense manner. They each towered over seven feet. The guards proceeded to encircle the trio and escort them across the courtyard to the statue of Thoth.

For the first time, Trent saw female Atlantians. They made up half of the retinue sitting about Thoth's feet, wearing necklaces of gold that fell between very human-looking breasts. The only garb was a thin linen wrap that wound around the hips and fell to the knees. It was if some of the most beautiful women in the world were attending a lavish Halloween party; all dressed in the same skimpy costumes and animal masks. He found the incongruity of the gleaming hawk eyes, jackal fangs, or cat grins above the supple bodies more disconcerting than the colossal architecture all about him.

"Ou are the one who has the Heart of Thoth," shouted a barrel-chested Atlantian with the head of what looked like a red Angus bull. The close-cropped fur carpeted his head like some cheap car seat cover and shimmered under the torchlights. His speech was clearer than that of the hawk-head at the airport. He and the other Atlantian males were dressed as the females, though the one talking wore an even more massive gold necklace, along with matching belt and armband. His wrap was of red silk and a large ruby adorned the bottom of the gold chain.

"I think we've discovered your Red Man," whispered Lorenzo.

"Ah..." Trent found himself speechless. He leaned closer to his friend and whispered back, "What's your plan?"

"I don't have one."

"You don't have one," Trent squeaked, barely able to keep his voice down. "You said you had a plan."

"I only said that to keep you calm. You were a nervous wreck."

"And what do you think I am now?" he hissed.

"Quiet," thundered the bull. "Stop ore monkey gibberings. Ou will give me the Heart of Thoth."

"Not so fast." Lorenzo stepped forward and looked up to return the Atlantian's unwavering gaze. "Where are our friends? We must be sure they are safe."

"It is not for ou to demand anything. Give me the jewel," the Atlantian bellowed and turned to Trent. "I have squandered too much time seeking ou already. I will have the Heart of Thoth now or ou will die very painfully."

"I don't have it," Trent sputtered. The nightmarish creature was scaring the hell out of him. He'd have yanked the fillings from his own teeth if the creature had demanded them. "I don't know where it is, I swear. The last time I saw the jewel, it was in the belly of Dorga. One of his priests must have made off with it."

The bloodshot eyes of the ox gazed deeply into Trent's. Like the Knight of Templar at the airport, the Atlantian appeared to be able to read truths and falsehoods. An ear-shattering bellow burst from the lips of the bull, and he angrily waved the honor guard to take them away.

"We will have this conversation again tomorrow and you had better remember something of importance by then."

Trent stumbled and the spear tip of a closely following hippo-head prodded him painfully in the back.

"Another fine mess you've gotten us into." Trent muttered out of the side of his mouth as they were led to a doorway in the corner of the building, which in turn opened on to a stairway.

"Me?" objected Lorenzo. "I wasn't the one fooling around with Dorga, the Fish-Headed God of Death."

Why did you have us walk into this place like lambs for the slaughter? Shouldn't we have tried sneaking in and rescuing the others?"

"Why? They know where we live. They'd have just come after us again. I wanted to finish this once and for all."

"Yeah, getting us murdered is one way to settle the matter."

"Don't worry, I have a plan," said Lorenzo.

"It won't work. I'm too tense for that to help now."

"I mean it. I only said I didn't have one in case our bull-headed high priest was listening."

"What is it then? I'd love to hear it."

Lorenzo leaned over and whispered, "You take the two on the right, and I'll take the two on the left."

"What? That's a plan?" Before Trent could protest further, Lorenzo spun and lashed out with his right foot, catching one guard in the knee. The blow sent the Atlantian stumbling back and collapsing in pain. Lorenzo followed with an upward jab to the Adam's apple of the other guard. The beast man clutched its throat and sank to its knees, there to be dispatched by a kick to the head.

Trent whirled and grabbed the spear of the closest guard and tried yanking it free. It remained locked in the giant's hands. The Atlantian raised the spear and Trent found himself staring into the muzzle of a jackal, his feet kicking a foot off the floor. Yellowed fangs were only a few inches from his nose, and the creature's breath stank of fish. The guard opened his mouth as if to bite off half of his captive's face.

Trent dropped to the floor with a grunt. He performed an extemporaneous attack as he straightened his knees, bringing his fist up to slam it into the guard's crotch. It wasn't as professional or as gentlemanly as Lorenzo's blows, but it had the same effect.

Trent jerked around to dodge a possible spear thrust from the remaining guard and saw that Lorenzo had already dispatched it.

"What the hell are you doing? Are you crazy? What do you mean telling me to take on two of those monsters?" Trent screamed.

Lorenzo grabbed him by the shoulder and started dragging the protesting Trent deeper into the temple. "We have no time to waste. We have to hurry if this is going to work."

Trent jerked his arm free but followed after the running Lorenzo and Jolene. "OK, what is this plan?"

The three settled into a fast jog, though the dash uncomfortably reminded Trent of his panicky flight in the hotel.

"We have to get into the pyramid and to the bottom of the burial shaft."

Trent was getting tired of repeating himself, but he couldn't help shouting a disbelieving, "What?"

"Hasn't any of this past week seemed fishy?" Lorenzo said between pants.

"Sure, every damn thing that's happened."

"No, if the Atlantians really thought you possessed something as important as the Heart of Thoth, they'd have gotten you right at the first. Why send Atlantians armed only with knives and swords in the dream Bear River? Why send only one-man parties into our world? They knew you patronized the Crossroads Cafe—why not ambush you at its entrance?"

Trent hadn't given up cigarettes long enough. He was starting to get short of breath and had to force out, "All right, why didn't they?"

"It is because they have either grown incredibly stupid or because they wanted you as a red herring to keep the Templars busy trying to locate you in your home world instead of snooping around here."

"They knew I didn't have it?"

"That's right. They know you couldn't possibly have it because they do. My guess is they were going to publicly torture you, where you would unfortunately die before relating the jewel's whereabouts. The rest of us would soon follow. Then they could claim they were in the dark as to its whereabouts as much as the Templars."

By now Trent was too busy breathing just to keep enough oxygen reaching his brain. He stopped and leaned against the wall by one of the endless number of torches mounted above their heads. Next to the torch was a five-foot inset that sheltered a statue of a frog-headed Atlantian. The stone carvings were spaced about every one hundred feet down the hall like silent sentinels.

"And...and..." he finally was able to gasp. "And what are...we...going to do now?"

Lorenzo stopped to wait for his friend, as well as Jolene, who appeared not to be affected by the exercise.

"We're going to bring the jewel out where everyone can see we don't have it."

"But if we bring it out, won't we have it?" asked Trent, again stumped by his friend's twisted logic.

"Not for long. It's time this thing was destroyed once and for all. It's too dangerous to fall into the hands of either the Templars or Atlantians. And from what you told me about your run-in with that Templar, he now knows you don't have the Heart of Thoth. That means he'll guess who might have it—the Atlantians. I bet a bunch of the Knights are on their way here right now to question the Atlantians, who can still bluff their way out of the mess if we don't expose their evil plot."

"That's crazy," Trent objected. "Wouldn't it be too dangerous for a bunch of Templars to show up here?"

"I meant more than a bunch, probably a whole damn army. A lot of fireworks will go off if the Atlantians can't satisfactorily answer the Templars' questions."

Lorenzo pushed himself away from the wall and took one more deep breath before motioning the two to follow him. This time he maintained a slower pace and Trent soon found himself falling into a daze as they headed down the seemingly endless hall.

But it had an end, with massive bronze doors blocking the way. Trent slumped dejectedly against the wall. He felt beat and broken.

"Run back about one hundred yards, crawl behind a statue, and cover your ears," Lorenzo instructed as he searched through his jacket pockets and pulled out a plastic bag. He opened it to display a grayish lump of clay.

"Plastic explosives," he grinned and again motioned them to retreat. Trent took Jolene's arm and retreated down the hall. He looked over his shoulder to see Lorenzo unwinding about ten feet of cord, light the fuse, and then spin around to chase after his friends.

Trent and Jolene hastily squeezed themselves into a cramped space between the small alcove and a statue. They both pressed their hands over their ears and clamped shut their eyes. Trent felt Lorenzo crawling in beside him and then the world became one big bang. The explosion roared down the hall like an invisible tidal wave and a battering ram of sound waves ferociously slammed against his eardrums. A swirling cloud of dust followed on the heels of the shock wave. Trent couldn't hear the stone shards skipping down the hall floor because of the ringing in his ears.

The three stumbled out coughing and shaking their heads. Lorenzo was yelling something, but Trent couldn't hear him. He finally grabbed Trent and Jolene by the arms and started dragging them down the hall. They could see that the doors were down as the dust thinned. They began jogging and Trent realized they must be in the actual pyramid; the walls now giant, roughly-cut blocks of stone. The torches closest to the doors were extinguished, though more could be seen burning farther down the tunnel.

Several minutes later, the ringing decreased enough that Trent could yell, "What were you doing with plastic explosives?"

"You don't think I'd come here without a number of precautions, do you?"

"A number? What else do you have?" asked Jolene.

"Professional secrets," he answered enigmatically. "But enough that I didn't have to depend upon the good luck of being escorted by only four of those thugs."

Lorenzo paused to pull a small gun from his pant leg as they neared what must be the center of the pyramid. They slowed their pace and tried walking as quietly as possible. For some unexplainable reason, the entrance to the shaft was also unguarded. Rungs were carved into the shaft's wall, and Lorenzo swung himself over the lip to feel with the tip of his shoes for the first toe holds.

"Wait here, I'll be right back," Lorenzo ordered as he traded Trent the gun for a torch he'd taken from the wall.

It was easier said than done. Trent found the waiting worse than running for his life. A dozen times he thought he heard the faraway sound of footsteps or voices. He was relieved to finally see Lorenzo's torch growing larger rather than smaller. Minutes later, a thoroughly tired Lorenzo was helped over the lip, where he collapsed unceremoniously on the floor.

He rolled over and smiled weakly. "It isn't there."

"Not there? Then where could it be?"

"They must have hidden it somewhere else. No wonder there were no guards," Lorenzo said as he rolled to his knees. Trent and Jolene helped him the rest of the way to his feet. "Then again, they might be more clever than I thought, using us as bait to draw in the Templars. Then they could wipe out the Knights with the jewel in one single battle. Why didn't I think of that?"

Lorenzo pulled his arms free and turned back to the tunnel. "We've got to return to the temple roof. That's where the others probably are."

Jolene even moaned at the thought of a return run, only it wasn't much of a run this time. The three kept to fast walks with occasional bursts of slow jogging. The dust had settled at the site of the explosion, and Trent noticed there were no footprints on the floor.

During one of their brief rest stops, Trent asked Jolene how she was able to take the recent occurrences so calmly.

She took a couple of purposeful breaths before answering. "Easy, anything is better than that half death you rescued me from. And none of this still seems real. I don't think I will be able to take anything serious until I see the sun again."

Lorenzo was right about the Templars. The Atlantians were lined along the edges of the temple roof, guarding against attack by an army of humans forming at the bottom of the ramp.

"Why aren't they using planes to attack?" Jolene asked.

"I don't know," admitted Lorenzo, "but there must be some reason for it, or I'm sure they would be dropping bombs right now. Maybe there is some kind of pact not to use too advanced of technology. I've given up trying to make sense of this world.

"Look there," Lorenzo shouted, grabbing Trent's arm and pointing past the statue. "I think that's them."

Trent squinted into the flickering shadows. He could only make out a cluster of figures almost hidden by the dark. Lorenzo was either sure of their identities or left to find out. He started off across the courtyard and Trent and Jolene ran to catch up. They had to pass in front of Thoth. Trent almost stumbled when he glanced up at the towering stone figure and felt a wave of vertigo wash over him. He steadied himself against the wall and continued running.

Lorenzo was hugging Rich when Trent finally caught up with his friend.

"Are we glad to see you!" exclaimed Henry. "Can you untie us?"

They were bound in a line like fish on a stringer. Varva was tugging impatiently at the rope as Tarra looked happily at the newcomers.

Lorenzo fumbled in his pockets and swore, "What the hell happened to my knife? I must have dropped the damn thing."

"Here," Trent said as he held out his pocketknife. "You should never go anywhere without one."

His friends eagerly held out their hands and Lorenzo sawed furiously through the cords while introducing Jolene. Trent kept lookout as they crouched in the shadows. The Atlantians were too intent upon the Knights of Templar below to notice the goings-on of their small cluster of captive humans.

"OK," Lorenzo said when they were all free. "There's no way we can escape the way we came, which means we'll have to find another way out through the pyramid."

Lorenzo ignored Trent's moan and soon they were re-crossing the courtyard in single file beneath the blind gaze of Thoth.

"If they really do have the jewel," Trent whispered to Lorenzo as they neared the passage doorway, "how come they're not zapping the Atlantians?"

"Who knows? They must be waiting for the right moment."

Trent knew an Atlantian would sooner or later notice their escape. He waited for the alarm to be sounded, but none came. They all made it through the doorway and headed safely down the stairs.

"Boy, are we glad to see you," puffed Rich. The clatter of the numerous running feet echoed loudly down the stone hall. "We went looking for you and Lorenzo and ran into a bunch of those Atlantians outside the hotel. I think they were planning to sacrifice us to that guy with the bull head."

"I only wish I could cut the throats of some of these animals," growled Varva.

"I just hope we don't run into any," said Trent. "I can't believe we made it this far without being seen."

"What's the plan? Do you have a getaway car waiting?" Al asked.

"You'll have to ask Lorenzo about the plan. He swears he has one," replied Trent.

Lorenzo gave a hurt "humph."

"Sometimes it is just best to improvise," Lorenzo continued. "That way the opposition doesn't know what our plan is."

"Nor we," added Trent.

Henry and Tarra ran silently at the rear of the group. Trent looked over his shoulder at the two and sensed they had grown closer together during the recent ordeal.

"What went on here?" Al asked when they paused to catch their breaths at the shattered doors.

"Lorenzo and his party toys," said Trent, which seemed a satisfactory answer.

They entered the tunnel into the pyramid. The mountain of stone seemed an almost physical, oppressive weight upon them. They passed through the by-now familiar shaft and continued into unexplored territory. It finally ended at another set of large metal doors that Trent guessed led to the outside on the opposite end of the pyramid. Lorenzo began another search through his pockets.

"Wait a minute," Trent said and walked closer to the obstruction. "I don't think my ears can take another blast."

He played with one of the two large brass rings and found that it turned. Trent gave the door a gentle push and it smoothly and silently swung open. He turned and smiled at Lorenzo then and led the group out into the dream night.

Trent felt like a kitten stuck on a garage roof as they walked the rim looking for a way to the ground far below them. He lay on his stomach and peered over the edge. The stones weren't eroded enough to offer safe handholds the entire way to the bottom.

The group was distracted from their predicament by a shudder of the stone under their feet. The pyramid was silhouetted by a brilliant explosion of light. It came from the vicinity of the temple on the opposite side of the pyramid. The nova was followed by a second explosion, and this time a large stone tumbled from above and bounced past them to disappear into the dark.

"The Atlantians or Templars might not have recovered the Heart of Thoth, but I believe they've both dusted off some of their other heirlooms," Lorenzo said. "I'd suggest we get out of here as quickly as possible."

There was no argument on that point and they hastily continued their way along the rim of the pyramid's first level. The flustered band came to the corner without finding a means to the ground, but they could now directly observe the battle. Fires were raging along the temple wall, shooting hundreds of feet into the air from between the immense pillars. Trent guessed that matching columns of black smoke towered high above them, invisible in the eternal night. Atlantians rushed about the rooftop courtyard like ants on a hot sidewalk.

Another explosion thundered and seconds later, a gale-force wind battered at the eight humans. A small volcano was erupting in the midst of the Templars. Through tearing eyes, the group of friends watched fleeing knights close to the conflagration burst into flames. Others, already flattened by the initial shock wave, twisted on the ground in agony. Those farther away sought protection behind tumbled stones and in deep depressions.

Trent felt a hand slap his shoulder and he turned to see Lorenzo pointing into the darkness. He followed the sweep of his friend's arm and saw a Templar crawling onto the head of a crumbling sphinx. His robe whipping from the fiery tempest's rage, the Templar stood and defiantly held a radiant globe above his head.

The crystal ball gave off a pure white light that even pierced closed eyelids. Trent shut his eyes to see the ghost image as a brilliant moon floating in a blood-red sky. The orb began pulsating, dimming and flaring.

"Everybody, get your heads down," screamed Lorenzo. "Don't look at that light."

The warning came none too soon. Even with his face pressed against the pyramid, Trent saw a flood of light surge through the blocks beneath him as if they were ice instead of stone. The ground bucked and he couldn't help but let slip a startled yelp. He heard someone moan nearby and thought it might be Henry.

Then the earth itself groaned. They all looked up to watch a quarter of the temple collapse like a castle of playing cards tumbling down in slow motion. Trent jerked his gaze away from the devastation to see the Templar still holding the globe, which was now a dark, molten mixture of burgundy and purple.

Trent had to blink his eyes several times to make sure the dust and tears weren't distorting his vision. The knight slowly dissolved and blew away like the ashes at the end of a burning cigarette. The orb hung in the air for several more seconds then winked out.

Al's voice shook everyone from their trances. "Shit. Let's get out of here."

"Where?" asked Rich. "How do we get down?"

Trent could see both of his friends' faces lit a dusky red by the fires. They looked about them in consternation.

"There must be a way down," Lorenzo said. "We're going to have to backtrack."

The shadows that once seemed ominous now felt sheltering. The holocaust slipped from sight as they retraced their steps on the leeward side of the pyramid. Ahead, they could see the far landscape, like that at their rear, dancing in the inferno's light.

Two more explosions shook the ground and sky before they arrived at the far end and looked around the corner. That side of the temple was also in flames as if some kind of oil coated the stones. Several columns slowly toppled as they watched. Though the group could feel a slight shudder through their feet, any sound of the impact was washed over by the roar of the wind and flames.

"Look over there," Varva shouted. She pointed to a huge section of pyramid that had collapsed in an avalanche of rock.

"It looks dangerous," Trent yelled back, "more stones could fall anytime."

"I will try it." Varva leaped away before anyone in the group could protest.

Al chased after her and the rest of the band quickly followed. It wasn't easy climbing down the rubble. Some of the stones were precariously balanced and needed only a nudge to send them tumbling. The ragtag group quickly spread out so no one would be above or below another person. Jolene caught her foot and Lorenzo angled over to help her pull free.

Trent's shoulder muscles knotted painfully each time the ground trembled from aftershocks. He knew another explosion could send a second wave of rock pouring down the side.

There was no slowing when they finally reached the bottom. They stumbled and crawled across the heavily littered ground until they were safe from another rock avalanche. Trent was limping painfully from a bruised shin and he noticed Tarra was also hobbling.

Lorenzo led them on a wide detour toward the road they had earlier traveled. The entire temple was now ablaze and sections continually collapsed like spoonfuls of powdered chocolate dissolving in hot milk. Other fires flickered about them—the former sites of Templar battle positions. Once Trent climbed a toppled statue to scout the area and was called down by Lorenzo.

"You make a tempting target," observed his friend.

They walked for several hours and still they could see the horizon glowing. Several more faraway rumbles revealed the battle continued.

"That's a prime example of MAD," Lorenzo said to Trent. "Mutually Assured Destruction. I'd say both factions will take a while to regain their numbers. The power structure in the dream world will be in a state of flux for a long time."

"Does this mean the London airport won't be safe, and we might wind up on fire in garter belts?" Trent wanted to know.

"I think it's one of those British things," Lorenzo answered to the puzzled stares of the others.

Trent was contemplating what a hot bath would feel like when he nearly walked into the back of a bus. He was circling when it finally surfaced to his conscious thoughts. His whooping stopped the others in their tracks and they wheeled around to see Trent dancing in the dim moonlight.

It was an old, double-decked tour bus with a line of Arabic writing flowing across the side. Rich beat him to the door and was already sitting in the driver's seat when Trent rushed up the steps.

"Hey, get out of my seat," Trent yelled. "This is my bus."

"Says who?"

"Me. I saw it first."

"Shotgun," yelled Al close on Trent's heels.

"First come, first served," Rich said as he fumbled with the ignition.

The engine groaned a few times and then started with a cough. Trent sighed in defeat and took a position behind Rich as the rest filed aboard. The bus shuddered and lurched forward.

There was surprisingly little conversation once they were on their way. Most of the party was too tired to talk and slumped in their seats in total exhaustion.

Al did lean over and whisper to Trent, "What's with Lorenzo?"

"What do you mean?"

"That suit. He looks like a hobo mortician."

Trent turned and examined his friend. The recent adventure had left its mark on the once natty suit. It was now torn and dirty.

"It's to impress the women," he replied.

"Who, bag ladies?"

Trent laughed and shook his head.

"I only have one question!" Rich yelled over his shoulder.

"What's that?" Al asked.

"Where the hell are we going?"

"Try the airport," Trent said. "Unless you're ready to ride a ghost tramp steamer back."

"Do they have them?" Rich asked.

"What?"

"Tramp freighters?"

"I don't know and I don't want to find out," admitted Trent. "And don't mention it to Lorenzo or he might get some wild hair to rejoin the Merchant Marines."

They called Lorenzo to the front of the bus to help locate the airport, which they finally found after a number of wrong turns. Trent was relieved to see the same DC-7 parked outside the terminal.

"How do we find out which plane is leaving for London?" Trent asked Jolene as they exited the bus.

"Before, I just seemed to know—now I'm not sure. I think the plane we arrived on will be returning soon, but I can't be sure."

The members of the group were hurrying to the terminal, most bent on being the first to reach the bathrooms.

"I'll go ahead and reserve the plane," Trent shouted at the others and sprinted across the concrete to the waiting airliner.

There was no way to tell if a refueling had occurred. The ramp was against the plane, either having never been moved or recently replaced. He skipped anxiously up the stairs and through the door. Nothing had changed. The cabin was dimly lit and empty. He picked a seat by the right wing and waited for the others. He began nervously pacing the aisle when they didn't show within ten minutes. Trent just knew the engines were going to start up and the plane leave before the rest arrived.

He was right about the engines. One by one they purred to life. He rushed to the door and looked out at the terminal. He was swearing under his breath when the first of the group began spilling out of the building.

"Hurry up," he yelled impatiently.

Their slow pace was driving him mad. He stood to the side as they entered the door. Tarra paused and looked nervously about, only to be shooed along by Trent.

"Are we all here?" he asked.

They looked around at each other before Varva noted Al's absence.

"Damn," Trent muttered and slapped himself on the forehead. "What's keeping him?"

"I think he was looking for a pack of cigarettes," Henry stated.

"Cigarettes," yelled Trent. "Our only way out of here is about to leave and Al is looking for cigarettes?"

Two men were walking towards the airliner, seemingly bent on retrieving the ramp. Trent leaped down the stairs.

"You can't move this yet," he told the pair. "We're still waiting on someone."

Trent didn't know if they didn't understand English or if they were just ignoring him. They began pushing the ramp away from the plane.

"Hey, I said you had to wait. The plane can't leave yet. Not all the passengers are on board."

The small wheels under the ramp squealed in protest as they rolled slowly across the tarmac. Trent glanced up to see a gap of five feet expanding to six between the stairs and the plane. Looking helplessly out the hatch were Rich, Lorenzo, and Jolene.

Trent shrugged his shoulders helplessly and yelled through cupped hands, "We'll try and catch the next flight out and meet you in London. If not, we'll meet you back in the dream Bear River."

"Be careful," Jolene shouted back before closing the door.

"Hey, where are they going?" a voice came from behind Trent.

It was Al, holding a can of Pepsi in one hand and a lit cigarette in the other.

"I'm going to kill you," answered Trent.

Chapter Fifteen

Melissa listened to a cat bird crying in neighbor's maple tree. She was sitting on a porch swing with her knees pulled up under her chin. The voices of several people talking and laughing could be heard through the screen door. Melissa knew she should go in and join them before she started crying.

It was an Indian summer, those preciously few summer-like days tucked between October frosts. The bright oranges, yellows and reds of the leaves were set off perfectly by the deep blue sky. The screen door creaked and the porch swing shifted as someone sat next to her. She looked over to see Lorenzo.

"Aren't you hungry?" he asked. "There's still plenty of pizza."

"I will in just a minute. I'm just enjoying the afternoon."

"I'm having a hard time eating knowing you're out here moping. Trent is okay. He may act like a klutz, but he always pulls through. I'm sure he and Al will show up any time."

"What if he's waiting for me in the Crossroads Cafe? I haven't been able to crossover since the other Trent brought me here."

"Then I'm sure he'll get rid of those bracelets and return home," Lorenzo tried to assure her.

"But why should it take him this long? It's been over three weeks."

"It'd take you at least three weeks, too, if you suddenly found yourself in Memphis, Egypt without a passport."

A rather ragged pair had suddenly appeared at the bottom of the steps. Lorenzo was nearly tumbled from the swing as Melissa sprang to her feet and rushed to throw herself into Trent's arms. Al continued up onto the porch and looked questioningly at Lorenzo.

"She's inside," he replied with a smile.

Lorenzo watched Al hurry through the door and then turned back to Trent and Melissa. "Thank God. I can finally get something to eat."

Melissa looked over Trent's shoulder with a grin and commanded, "Well, go then."

It was a happy reunion when the whole group gathered later in the den.

"Why did it take you so long?" demanded Rich. "Your bosses have been calling all over looking for the two of you. I told them you were called away on family emergencies. I hope they don't compare notes."

"We had to make several stops for cigarettes on the way back," Trent answered sourly as he glanced at a sheepish looking Al. "What really happened is that we waited around for eight or ten hours and no other planes showed up. We decided to look for a restaurant and drove the bus into town. We found a hotel and decided to get some sleep before returning to the airport. We picked a room with double beds and I took off my jacket. I began flickering as soon as I was separated from the bracelets in the pocket.

"I just had time enough to grab Al, and we found ourselves standing in a real world hotel. There was enough light shining through the window to show there was a couple already sleeping in the bed. I thought Al was going to wake them with his blubbering."

"I didn't blubber," he protested. "I was just startled."

"Anyway," Trent continued, "we slipped out of the room and into the street. To make a long story short, we were forced to sleep in a park fountain that no longer worked. It looked like an eight-foot high Champagne glass made of stone. The next morning, we found ourselves virtually penniless and illegally in a foreign country. I don't even want to go into detail about the next week, but we managed to sneak aboard a Japanese tourist cruise ship and were dropped off in Portugal."

"Come on," protested Al, "we had some good times."

He winced under Trent's glare.

"Hey, you were the one that didn't want to call for help." Al turned to the others. "He wanted to be macho man and get here by ourselves."

"We luckily ran into some people who operate a Lisbon advertising agency," Trent went on. "They needed Americans for a commercial for a new Kentucky Fried Chicken restaurant. The money was good, though it was rather humiliating."

"You looked cute in that chicken outfit," Al interrupted, only to immediately clamp his jaw shut under another frosty stare.

"By this time, I was getting desperate," said Trent. "We now had enough money for plane tickets, but we needed passports. We finally were reduced to rolling two drunken Mormon missionaries and taking their IDs. We were broke when we hit New York and had to hitchhike the rest of the way. But during that time, not once did I wake in any strange places. I've sworn off nicotine patches."

He looked around the crowded room. "But enough about me, what's been going on here?"

"I've been helping everyone settle in," Rich piped up, "and Lorenzo has already got IDs for Varva, Henry, Abby, and Tarra."

"It wasn't much," he shrugged modestly. "Just called in some favors from a couple of spooks who are in charge of a witness protection program."

"Abby," Trent blurted, feeling guilty that he hadn't thought of the small girl until now. "Where is she?"

"Abby is staying overnight at a new friend's house," Melissa told him. "Her new identity is that of my adopted daughter. I hope you don't mind an instant family."

"How good are these identities?" he asked Lorenzo.

"Hey, if you can't trust old Company friends, who can you trust?" Lorenzo asked.

"I've been waiting for you to return before I announce my miraculous return to life," Melissa said as she squeezed Trent's hand. "I wasn't brave enough to face my parents without you."

"I guess we can catch up on the rest tomorrow," said Trent, barely able to keep himself from yawning. "I'm going to die if I don't get some sleep."

"I replaced your stupid waterbed mattress," Lorenzo said as Trent and Melissa stood to leave the room. "I thought you might prefer that to sleeping on the floor."

Minutes later, Trent left the bathroom and walked barefoot across the chilly wood floor of the hall. He paused at the doorway when he saw Melissa's head peeking above the blanket. Suddenly, he didn't feel that sleepy.

"Do you have an alarm clock? I'd like to get up early tomorrow and visit my parents."

"It's between the bed and the wall," Trent answered as he crawled in beside her. "But don't make it too early. I could use a good, long rest."

"What's this?" she asked, pulling up a chunk of rock from under the magazines on the night stand.

Melissa handed it to Trent and he examined the stone while turning it in the light.

"It looks like a piece of adobe rock from that dream I had with those Native Americans. Years from now, when this last month seems like just a dream, I'll have this and a spoon to remember it was real."

"Don't forget me," Melissa reminded him as she blindly felt about the floor for the clock. She was still sorting through the clutter for the clock.

Trent slid his hand under the blankets until he came in contact with her warm, naked back.

"What's this?"

He wasn't paying attention, concentrating on the feel of her soft, smooth skin.

"Look, what is this?"

Trent was forced to answer when Melissa shoved her fist under his nose. He leaned back so he could focus on what she was holding—it looked like a large, lustrous ruby—the Heart of Thoth.

"Crap," was all Trent could think to say as he stared at the jewel he'd pried from the palm of Dorga, the Fish-Headed God of Death. "Don't tell me it's been here all the time."

"What do we do?" Melissa was sitting with the blankets falling around her waist. Donna Reed never looked this good.

Trent stared at the jewel and then back to Melissa. Taking the stone from her hand, he tossed it into a corner and leaned over to turn off the light.

"We'll sleep on it."

About the Author

Dan Ehl has been a journalist and editor at both weeklies and daily newspapers in Iowa. The winner of numerous journalism and photo awards, including first in humor from the National Society of Newspaper Columnists, he enjoys breaking out of dryer newspaper writing to pen fantasy novels.

He served in Germany as an Army photographer during the Vietnam War. "With a lot of Vietnamese lining pits with sharpened stakes for people just like me, I knew I wasn't wanted. Being from Iowa, we always try to be polite. Stationed in Germany during the early 1970s was interesting enough with the barracks on weekends smelling of beer, vomit and hashish."

His favorite hobbies are hitchhiking and hopping freights.

Lorenzo Spasm is also featured in these books
by Dan Ehl
available at
Rogue Phoenix Press

Jak Barley-Private Inquisitor
and the Temple of Dorga, Fish-Headed God of Death

As a private inquisitor, Jak Barley's job is fairly mundane-finding errant debtors and missing property, or proving the unfaithfulness of roving spouses. It's not a vocation that makes many friends.

Though a frequent patron of dark, wretched bars seldom visited by the more fastidious citizens of Duburoake, he still can be squeamish about some things--such as ghosts and rabid magicians.

Barley's latest cases are just that more upsetting, dragging him into contact with sinister specters, malicious mages, irate harpies, creepy death deities and royal plots.

It will take all of his backstreets cunning to stay alive, as well as the help of alchemist Olmsted Aunderthorn, his half brother, who uses the latest metaphysical laboratory techniques in solving crimes.

Jak Barley-Private Inquisitor
and the Case of the Seven Dwarves

Private Inquisitor Jak Barley wonders if his drinking cohorts at the King's Wart Inn are playing an elaborate prank on him. What else is he to think when seven dwarves want his help against a wicked witch they blame for poisoning an innocent young maiden staying with them named Frost Ivory?

Jak Barley-Private Inquisitor
and the Case of the Dark Lords Conspiracy

Private inquisitor Jak Barley is ready for some down time after battling Ghennison Viper Mages, being attacked by piss dragons, and fighting off priests of Dorga the Fished Headed God of Death. That is why Jak was not a bit amused to have a scruffy mage insist that he is to be one of a group of questers decreed in an ancient prophecy that must cross the icy Alf Mountains to foil the return of the Old Gods. To do so meant using a map all too heavily dotted with "Here Be…" warnings that read like an "Idiot's Guide to Monsters."

And why are Westian Lizard Wizards targeting young red-headed maidens and who is behind the numerous and bizarre attacks upon Jak? Once gain Jak finds himself saying, "I hate adventures."

VISIT OUR WEBSITE
FOR THE FULL INVENTORY
OF QUALITY BOOKS:

http://www.roguephoenixpress.com

Representing Excellence in Publishing

Quality trade paperbacks and downloads
in multiple formats,
in genres ranging from historical to
contemporary romance, mystery and science fiction.
Visit the website then bookmark it.
We add new titles each month!